RED GRANITE

The Grains of Truth
Beneath the Sands of Egypt

V

GIZA - ALEXANDRIA

RED GRANITE

The Grains of Truth Beneath the Sands of Egypt
V
Giza - Alexandria

Alexander Retrov

Editor: Alexander Retrov
Graphic Design: Goran Djcinovic
Publisher: Renaissance Entertainment Pty Ltd
Printer: Amazon books

This work is 90% fact and 10% fiction.
It's up to you to determine which is which.

To see the truth for yourself and join Krystal or Alex
on one of the Red Granite or Goddess Reawakening Tours
go to the website for more details on the next tour.

www.alexanderretrov.com

www.alexanderretrov.com

RED GRANITE

The Grains of Truth
Beneath the Sands of Egypt

V

Giza - Alexandria

ACKNOWLEDGEMENTS

My deep gratitude goes to Krystal,
without whose support and patience
this book would never have been written.

I also want to acknowledge Source
for choosing me as the conduit for this work

To my brother in Egypt, Abdou Ashour

This book is dedicated to the truth.

CHAPTER 30 - THE GIZA PLATEAU

The sound of running water drew my attention to a pool of water, and to a waterfall that flowed into it. Standing naked in the flow of the water, bathing, was Crystal. As I drew closer, like the Pleiadean Emissary at Abu Ghurab, she morphed into a billion shimmering points of light and became the water, transmuting and transporting, this time down into the pool.

Eager to follow her, to be with her, Nemo appeared in the water and swam after her. Beneath the surface, the pool led down into a dimly lit cave and subterranean tunnel; it was as if I was back beneath the altar at Abu Ghurab following in the 'fin'steps of Nemo who had swished away down one of the passages that shot off from the main well chamber. I wondered where Crystal was headed, where she was leading me.

Moments later the tunnel opened into a massive underground lake, strangely illuminated by parts of the rock, where Crystal and Saeed stood talking beside the entrance to another descending passage. As I joined them, Saeed thrust a bag of papyrus scrolls into my hands.

'You go on, I will stay here and hold them back.'

'No, they'll kill you.'

Crystal took charge.

'They will kill him anyway. Unless you delay them, they will kill you both, and then all your efforts will have been in vain; this is the only way to get the scrolls out.'

Nemo started leaping out of the water as the lake started churning, something big and ominous was rising to the surface. Meanwhile, back up through the darkness of the previous tunnel, I could hear them coming, their shrieks, their hisses, their growls. Crystal barked her command.

'Go!'

I slung the bag over my shoulder and embraced Saeed.

'Shukran, Ahoya. May Allah be with you.'

'It is Allah who has brought me here. Now GO!'

As I looked around for Crystal, she was once again naked, this time frolicking in the water with Pernille and Bill. I knew where I wanted to be, with Crystal, but, at the same time, I knew where I *had* to go, further into the unknown. I took off down the tunnel as fast as I could, left, right, the passage lined on all sides, the ceiling, floor, and both walls, with perfectly-machined red granite; it was as if I was descending beneath a pyramid. Deeper and deeper I ran, into the earth, into the underworld. Turning a corner I was suddenly confronted by a giant three-headed snake, similar to the ones I had seen on the walls of the tombs in the Valley of the Kings, blocking the path.

All of a sudden I could barely move, my feet were going in slow-motion and there was nothing I could do to escape. The serpent fixed its gaze on me, flicked out its poisonous forked tongue to taste my fear, and slowly closed in for the kill.

Curling its massive body around me like an enormous anaconda, the snake gripped me tighter and tighter; I was totally defenceless, all I had were... the scrolls. I worked one arm free, reached behind into the bag, took one out and, like David and Goliath, hurled it with all my might, striking one of the serpent's heads in such a way as to render it unconscious. A second scroll went straight down the throat of the second head, causing it to choke and collapse. That left the third head, the central one, but well-aimed third and fourth scrolls struck the beast in each of its blood-red eyes, blinding it.

The beast released its grip and suddenly I was free and able to run. I picked up the scrolls and bolted past the serpent, deeper into the underworld. I may have escaped temporarily but I knew the giant snake would soon recover and be right behind me; time was of the essence and I would need all my skills and wits to complete my mission. However, no sooner had I turned the next corner than the passage was blocked by a massive portcullis.

'Feel the stone.'

I placed my hands on the stone and started toning, willing for it to open.
'Ahhh.'

Behind me I heard the hisses of the serpent as it closed in. Why wouldn't the stone move? I shifted the tone and sound.
'Awww.'

I heard a rumbling sound stirring deep within.
'Wake up, sleepy head, or you will snore your way through your date with destiny.'

Bang, suddenly I was back in the here and now, although it took a few seconds before I could put the pieces together as I was a little the worst for wear; a slight hang over or dehydration keeping me below my peak. Then I connected the voice to the person and to the final explosive events of the previous evening; it drew my attention the fact my one-eyed pajama python was already up before me

Crystal was just coming out of the bathroom, drying herself with a towel having just had a shower.
'The bus leaves in ten minutes.'

I dragged myself out of bed. I wasn't sure if last night was just a one night stand sort of thing, or if the beginning of something more long lasting, or even the continuance of something that had been going on for numerous lifetimes, so I wasn't sure exactly how to react. In the end I went with my gut, wrapped my arms around her naked body and kissed her.
'Good morning, Queen of the Nile.'
'Good morning;...'

What I initially didn't realize was that my erection was once again pressing against her. She kissed her fingers then patted it on the head.
'...I think you'd better save your energy for later, it could be a big day.'

I gave her another kiss and jumped in the shower.

As I used the flowing water to fully awaken and refresh my body, I realized I had never been so happy in my life. Then the parametres of my predicament clicked in, I still had to get out of Egypt alive. No problem, a visit to the pyramids and Sphinx, followed by a quick car trip to Alexandria, and by sunset I would be safely on Bill's yacht and making my way to Greece. All I had to do was keep a low profile.
'You have five minutes, I will be downstairs waiting with the others.'

I turned off the shower.
'Crystal, what are your plans after today?'

'In what way?'

'Where are you headed?'

'I have a flight booked back to Germany tomorrow night, although there are several other alternatives presenting.'

'Such as?'

'We can talk about this later; get dressed and get that cute butt of yours downstairs, or you will miss the bus.'

Crystal left the room and I quickly dried off, threw on my clothes and went to exit.

'Shit, I almost forgot.!'

I briefly contemplated leaving my backpack behind and returning after visiting the Giza Plateau to pick it up, then heading off to Alexandria, but that may not have been Saeed's plan, he may have wanted to get moving straight away, so I picked it up, tossed it over my shoulder, and made my way down to the lobby of the hotel.

I was only a few minutes late, but everyone was downstairs waiting, including the ladies of Diane's group, all dressed in white; it looked like a convention of nuns or high priestesses. Bill and Saeed were amongst them, and, once a head count and roll count was done, the ladies filed out of the lobby and aboard the bus waiting outside. Pernille and Crystal decided to join them on the bus, and who were Bill and I to tell them otherwise. Instead, Bill and I left them to their goddess work, jumped in the minivan with Saeed, and both vehicles set off for the stables.

'Did you get a good night's sleep?'

'Like a baby.'

Bill chuckled away.

'What, you dribbled all over your pillow and wet the bed?'

If only he knew!

Even at 4:30 in the morning Cairo was a bustling metropolis. We passed a boy, probably no more than ten or eleven years old, riding an old bike. On his head was a sheet of plywood, about the size of double doors, stacked to the brim with various types of freshly baked breads; it looked like he had a golden pyramid on his head. I watched transfixed as he rode along the street, dodging dogs, cows, donkeys, cars, buses, taxis, death!

He was no different to me, or to anyone really; death was always just a moment away, a swerving truck, a runaway bus, a heart attack, cancer, lightning strike, a bee sting, the Secret Police, and yet he happily went about his life, as simple as it seemed to be. By the look on his face I could tell he never complained about his life, that he made the most of what little he had.

'Hey, Bill, do you ever regret walking away from the priesthood?'

'Every day! Every day I look at my bank account, every day I travel the world first-class and stay in the world's top hotels, every day I make another million; are you serious?'

'Silly question, hey?'

'Actually it's not, and if you'd asked me the question nearly thirty years ago when I turned my back on the church, I would have given you a totally different answer.'

'So why did you really leave?'

'I couldn't stay; the deeper I got into it, the more I felt I was drowning…'

I knew exactly how he felt, until I arrived in Egypt I felt I was struggling just to keep my head above water, that any second the undertow was going to suck me down. Bill continued.

'...Do you know that there are around forty-two thousand different denominations of Christianity alone, *forty-two THOUSAND,* all believing they have the corner on truth, all believing they and only they understand what the scriptures really mean. But the reality is there are way too many contradictions within them for anyone to understand, so all they do is debate and disagree, because it's not the word of god, it's the fabricated delusions and dogma of a system of control for the feeble-minded and easily influenced. Let me give you an example:

Deuteronomy 22:23-24 says, *"If within the city a man comes upon a maiden who is betrothed, and has relations with her, you shall bring them both out of the gate of the city and there stone them to death: the girl because she did not cry out for help though she was in the city, and the man because he violated his neighbours wife."* Clearly God doesn't give a shit about the woman, the rape victim, he's only concerned about the wrong done to the other man.

Deuteronomy goes on to say in lines 28-29, *"If a man is caught in the act of raping a young woman who is not engaged, he must pay fifty pieces of silver to her father. Then he must marry the young woman because he violated her, and he will never be allowed to divorce her."* Now tell me, what sort of fucked up lunatic would force a rape victim to marry her attacker? Certainly not the god I wanted to speak for.

There were so many, but, ultimately the big one I couldn't get over was this one, Deuteronomy 17:12, *"Anyone arrogant enough to reject the verdict of the judge or of the priest who represents the LORD your God must be put to death."* How fucked up is that, disagree with the priest and you MUST be put to death.

No, that wasn't the path for me, and I've never looked back, NEVER regretted my decision to leave. Sure there were times I wondered not only what lay ahead, but how in the hell I was going to get there. When my folks said I had rocks in my head, they were right, and I started to listen to them, to what they were saying to me. That's why I got into Geology, there's an energy in rocks, Alex, they've been around for millions of years, they've seen and heard it all. I didn't just study what they were, what they were made up of, I tuned in to how they felt, how they made me feel.'

I shook my head and laughed.

'Feel the stone, hey!'

'Yep, it led me to gold, to money, to Egypt, and to Pernille; there was no way I could have predicted that when I left the church nearly thirty years ago.'

It got me thinking about my journey, about the 'drama' in my life, from teaching, through two failed marriages, my false imprisonment and the battle to clear my name, my trip to Egypt, meeting Crystal on the felucca, *"Feel the stone",* she said, and finally my predicament with Kareem's papers and the Secret Police; the next twenty-four hours were going to be pivotal in my life.

One hump or two

We'd only been travelling ten minutes at the most when we pulled up at the site of the stables, situated somewhere to the southern side of the Giza Plateau. It was still dark as we made our way down an alley to a covered outside area and were welcomed by the owner of the stables and his two sons. They had prepared a modest but traditional Egyptian breakfast for us all and once he had personally welcomed each and every one of us, invited us all to take a seat and make ourselves comfortable.

Crystal and Pernille were inseparable so I tried to grab the seat on Crystal's other side, only to be pipped-at-the-post by Diane and several of her group. In the end I sat opposite her in the circle; it looked like the female version of the Knights of the Round Table. Then I did a head count; nine women, exactly the same number as the nine maidens of Avalon, and the muses, the nine daughters of Zeus, the nine Valkyries of Norse mythology, the furies, the harpies, the nine prototypes of the human race, the seven pleiades of Atlas… plus two.

I hadn't bothered before, but now it seemed more relevant; there was Diane, Caucasian, white skinned, one Asian lady, yellow skinned, one African-American, black skinned, one brown, one coffee. Last night in the circle Diane said something about them all being initiated as daughters of Aset, of Isis; was it possible this was a reunion of the nine maidens of Avalon? And was that a meeting of the descendants of the original prototypes of the human race?

As we tucked in to breakfast I looked around to figure out which one of the women would have been Morgan le Fay, the great sorceress and Arthur's half sister. My first thought was Crystal, was it her? It had to be, surely. Would that mean I was Arthur? It didn't feel right; watching Bill's affability, he was more the King Arthur type. And Pernille? Yes, I could just see Bill as King Arthur, and Pernille as Guinevere. No, that was purely romantic conditioning based on the modern story of Camelot; Pernille had to have been of the *sang réal*, and, looking at her and Crystal interacting, they had to have been sisters on more than one occasion, so Pernille was possibly Arthur's 'forbidden' sister, Morgause. Was Diane the third sister, Elaine, or possibly even Igraine, Arthur's mother? And where did that leave me; if I wasn't Arthur, was I Arthur's father, Uther Pendragon, or perhaps even Myrrdyn?

A shiver when up my spine, and, right at that moment, Crystal looked straight at me.

'What do *you* think, Alex?'

'Sorry, what do I think about what?'

'Free love.'

Hell, she was putting me on the spot. Was she wanting me to agree, or to declare my undivided monogamous devotion? I took the non-committal humorous approach.

'Free love, it's better than having to pay for it.'

'Do you have some sort of problem with prostitution?'

'No, share the love I say, keep the economy ticking over.'

'Have you ever used a prostitute's services?'

I think she was enjoying watching me squirm.

'I've paid more than once for sex; two marriages, two ex-wives, both of whom took the car, cleaned out the house, and left me sucked dry. I paid more than my fair share, and I got well and truly screwed in the process.'

Bill was the only one who laughed; I think the other women were all either unhappily married or unhappily divorced. Thankfully Diane took the pressure off me.

'There's no doubt that "prostitution", as we would call it now, not only flourished in ancient Egypt, whether it was being carried out at one of the well-established pleasure houses, or under the sacred guidance of the priestesses in the temples, but it was an accepted part of everyday life.'

That was a big statement, but, having been thrown a lifeline, I was not going to stick my neck back on the chopping block. Fortunately Bill did.

' *"An accepted part of everyday life"*, what exactly do you mean?'

'The Ancient Egyptians were totally comfortable with their sensuality and undoubtedly loved and celebrated life to the fullest. They believed that life, sexuality, and rebirth, were elements that all went hand in hand and had an important part in the scheme of everyday life, and so, like the waters of the Nile, erotica flowed through all levels of ancient Egyptian society, and not just through the women, but through the men as well, who were not afraid of demonstrating their love.'

'In what way?'

'Through love poems and erotic texts; there are numerous examples from ancient Egypt, poetry, erotic dreams, in books of wisdom, and in the tales of the gods. Let me read you one…'

It seemed I didn't have to wait to raise the topic of ancient Egyptian love with Crystal; it was being discussed over boiled eggs and hibiscus tea, like discussing the latest 'Mills and Boon' over tea and scones. And now it was about to become a poetry-reading session.

Diane took a large workbook from her bag, yes, the bag with the hand-painted death mask of Tutankhamen I had given her way back at Karnak, and opened it up.

'…It's an extract from a 3,000 year-old papyrus from the 21st Dynasty.
"She is one girl, there is no one like her. She is more beautiful than any other.
Look, she is like a star goddess arising at the beginning of a happy new year;
brilliantly white, bright skinned;
with beautiful eyes for looking, with sweet lips for speaking;
she has not one phrase too many…"

What the hell, was this some sort of joke? It was almost an exact copy of the poem I had written for Crystal back on the banks of the Nile after visiting Kom Ombo. I looked at her and she smiled and raised an eyebrow.
"…With a long neck and white breast, her hair of genuine lapis lazuli;
her arm more brilliant than gold;
her fingers like lotus flowers, with heavy buttocks and girt waist.
Her thighs offer her beauty, with a brisk step she treads on ground.
She has captured my heart in her embrace.
She makes all men turn their necks to look at her.
One looks at her passing by, this one, the unique one."

The ladies went into a fervour of compliments, commenting how good it would be if modern men would get back in touch with their feminine side. At the request of several of the other ladies, Diane passed the book around.

Meanwhile I was left scratching my head; the poem was almost exactly the same as the one I'd written a week ago, and that didn't make sense, I hadn't even told Crystal about it, let alone given it to her. Unless…

While I was trying to fathom the implications, Bill got back to basics.

'I'm sure they didn't just write poetry, if you'll excuse the pun, how was sex actually physically handled in their everyday life?'

One of the other ladies responded.

'It was all about fertility, and about big families, because infant mortality was high and you wanted someone to look after you when you were old. So, for the most part, despite the fact that polygamy wasn't illegal, just expensive, marriage was voluntary and monogamous.'

'And no one fooled around, there were no affairs?'

'There probably were, but given adultery was considered a serious crime and carried such severe punishments as having your nose cut off, then people either thought twice about straying, or spent a lot of energy keeping it a secret.'

'So no one lived in sin?'

I rejoined the conversation.

'Remember what Pieter said, Bill, Sin was the Akkadian god of the moon in Sumer, Assyria and Babylonia, the husband of the sun-goddess, so there was no "sin" in ancient Egypt.'

'True, well said.'

Diane added her thoughts.

'Also, adultery could lead to the situation were the paternity of any child birthed was in question, and, as the ancient Egyptians were preoccupied with their bloodlines, it was a major issue.'

'That explains why they were so incestuous.'

'Actually it was really only the royal families that inbred, and it was done primarily to secure the royal blood line and preserve peace and legitimacy, rather than for any perverted reasons.'

'And in the temples?'

'It depends which temples you refer to. I am not at liberty to reveal the practices in the Temples of Aset, however in the Temples of Amun there were numerous different practices over time.'

'Such as?'

'In one period, a woman would go into the temple, have sex with whomever she pleased until menstruation, after which there was a celebration. Then she was married.'

I couldn't resist.

'No wonder she celebrated, all that unprotected sex and no pregnancy.'

Once again I drew numerous looks of disdain; I had to learn to keep my mouth shut. Fortunately Bill once again came to the rescue.

'I remember something in Barbara Thiering's book, "Jesus The Man", where she talks about how with the Essenes there were two marriages, the first when the woman is still a virgin, or supposedly so, and the second marriage ceremony, the binding one, taking place after she has conceived, after she has proved she is fertile. Now, we know that many of the Jewish rituals came from Moses, from his time in ancient Egypt, so, is it possible there was a similar two-part marriage ceremony in ancient Egypt?'

'It is not only possible, it's highly likely.'

'But what if she didn't menstruate, what if she fell pregnant, and wasn't married?'

Diane was clear.

'Then, most often, once the child was born, the woman became a priestess.'

I could see straight through that.

'So it was all a scam, a way for the Amun Priests to have unlimited sex, then "sanctify" the abuse by "sanctifying" the women, by turning them into priestesses, or servants of the temples. And what happened to the children?'

'The females were raised by the Daughters of Isis, the males as Amun priests.'

'Indoctrinated and conditioned from birth.'

'Exactly.'

And then I totally understood what was *really* happening, and I couldn't keep quiet.

'Wait a minute. You said, *"a woman would go into the temple, have sex with whomever she pleased until menstruation"*, right?'

Diane was curious.

'Yes.'

'Then you're not just talking about women, you're talking about young girls, really young girls if they're pre-menstrual….'

Several of the women gasped.

'…The Amun Priests were all paedophiles; they used their positions and influence purely for their own sexual gratification.'

I couldn't believe it, nothing much had changed in over four-thousand years, and it had a ripple effect through everyone, everyone except Crystal that is.

'There was even more to it; once the girls came of age, became sexually mature, the Amun Priests permitted the Dracos to perform genetic experiments on them.'

There was at least five to ten seconds of poignant silence, as each person fully absorbed what that meant for them, before several of the women spontaneously burst into tears; clearly they were reawakening to their abuse back then. As was the case in the Luxor Temple, the remainder of the Daughters of Aset instantly circled the wagons, supporting their sisters; it was clear that was the signal that breakfast was over and it was time to move on.

At that very instance our hosts hastily returned, believing there was something about breakfast that had displeased the women. After Diane reassured both the women and our hosts that everything was perfect, our hosts invited us to 'saddle up'.

Horses for courses

Bill and I stood back allowing the ladies to have first choice, most of them, excepting Crystal, Pernille, and two other woman, selecting horses. Soon enough, the ladies were all sorted and it was Bill and my turn.

'What do you think, Alex, horse or camel?'

'When in Rome.'

'One hump or two?'

'No need to be greedy, one is plenty.'

Our mindless banter rapidly running out of steam, Bill and I climbed aboard our faithful chargers, Bill turning to our host.

'What is my camel's name?'

'This Queen Elizabeth.'

'Queen Elizabeth? The first or second?'

'Does it matter, Bill, either way you're humping royalty.'

'And what's your camel's name?'

'I'm going to call her Geraldine?'

'Let me guess, your ex-mother-in-law?'

'Yep, spot on, although the camel is better looking and has a much better personality and disposition.'

Precariously perched atop my ship of the desert, Saeed came up beside me.

'Indy, you are sure you wish it to do this, to go to Giza, there are not many tourist, you will be very easy to be seen?'

'I take your point, Ahoya, but it's something I have to do. You're not coming with us?'

'Not this time, no; there are many thing that I must arrange it before we drive to Alexandria.'

'When is that?'

'I will meet you in front of the Sphinx at 12pm.'

'High noon; how appropriate. 12pm Egyptian time or Western time?'

'This time, my friend, most definitely western time; from there we shall all drive it to Alexandria to get you on to Mister Bill's boat and ready to leave at the setting of the sun.'

'Safely out of Egypt to Greece.'

Saeed paused, as if for dramatic intent, then spoke clearly and deliberately.

'Indy, please, be very careful, the vulture he can spot it the dead carcass from several mile away.'

'Well, I'm not dead and I don't intend to end up that way for at least another fifty years, so don't worry, everything will be fine.'

Leaving Saeed behind, our little nocturnal caravan, in two lines of six with our hosts' two sons walking alongside and Bill and I appropriately bringing up the rear, slowly plodded off into the relative silence of the night, the mild Giza air tinged with excitement and expectation.

We made our way out of the stables and westward along the outer perimeter of the Giza walls erected by our anti-hero Zahi Hawass following the Luxor Massacre. The walls were basically huge concrete barriers, probably bigger than the Berlin wall, and supposedly designed to stop anyone from sneaking in during the middle of the night and damaging the pyramid and Sphinx; yeah, sure!

The locals had clearly not been happy about the construction of the wall as numerous breaches and sections of compromised wall were located at various intervals along the perimeter, testimony to the locals' determination to have continued free access to the plateau on the other side.

'Hey, Bill, do you know much about the Giza Plateau?'

'A little.'

By the wry smile on his face, "a little" meant a lot.'

'Do tell.'

'Geologically speaking, the plateau consists of thick sloping layers of limestone, marl and slate in various formations, the base being the Mokattum Foundation.'

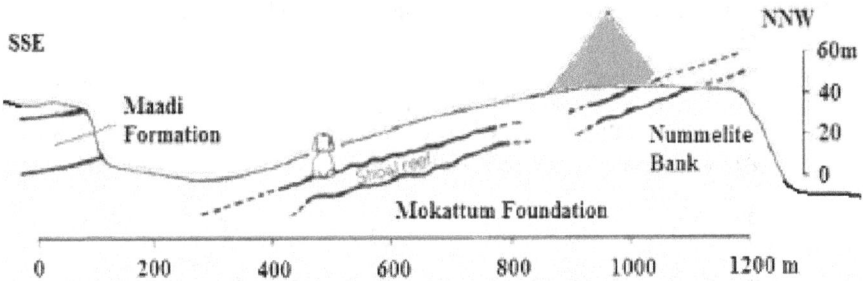

'Sloping layers, that means some sort of geological upheaval, right?'

'Sure does; originally the layers are laid down flat over millions of years, then at some later time, an earthquake or continental shift forces the ground out of kilter, creating the sloping layers.'

'Or a pole shift?'

'Yes, or a pole shift.'

'And the differences between the layers are signposts of the shift from one period to another, some other geological activity, right?'

'Yep. For instance the limestone tells us that the plateau was once the ocean floor.'

'And the intermediary layers, especially the thin ones, like layers of ash, often indicate volcanic activity?'

'Alex, you're starting to sound like an expert.'

'And the top layers, the latest layers, they show the most recent activity, including any deposits made by the ash from volcanic erupts or deposits from tsunamis, which would include marine creatures from the Mediterranean.'

'That they would.'

'I'm thinking the experts haven't really had a good look at the different rock strata and what's there, and more importantly, what's not there.'

'What's not there?'

'Yeah, for instance the action of large amounts of water to wash away and carve out those deeper, older layers. By comparing what layers *are* there, surely they could figure out *when* the other layers were washed away.'

'I'm sure they could, maybe the wadi holds the key?'

'What do you mean?'

'Giza can be subdivided into two groupings of monuments separated by a wadi, or valley. The larger grouping consists of the three "Great" pyramids, the Sphinx, and their temples, and the private mastabas of the nobility, all mostly made from limestone quarried and transported to the site. The second grouping, located on the ridge to the southeast, on the other side of the wadi, in the Maadi Formation, contains a number of private tombs, belonging to citizens of various classes, simply carved out of the rock.'

'I doubt we will get to see the second group, but I bet they're like the so-called tombs at Aswan. Wadi Hillal and Amarna.'

'So, what are you on to, what do you think you'll find here at Giza?'

'I'm not sure, but I know I'll know it when I see it.'

'Not if it's underground you won't; unless you find a way to get *beneath* the plateau.'

I looked across at Bill.

'Is there something you're not telling me, Bill?'

'I was going to talk about it yesterday, when you mentioned about the secret entrance in the south face of the Great Pyramid and the underground chambers, but we got sidetracked.'

We suddenly reached the end of the Berlin Wall; it just stopped, as if anyone seriously wanting to destroy the pyramids would not think to come in from the desert. It made a farce of the wall being for security reasons; it was like building a prison with no doors. Anyway, once past the final section of wall, we headed out into the Sahara Desert.

'Well, Bill, now it's just you, me, Queen Elizabeth, and Geraldine the troll-faced camel.'

'You don't think much about your ex mother-in-law, do you?'

'Actually I have a lot to thank her for; she thought she was doing the right thing interfering in her daughter's marriage, but then again Hitler thought he was doing the right thing invading Poland. In the end I don't blame her, I take full responsibility myself for not seeing the apple didn't fall far from the tree and like mother like daughter. If it wasn't for Geraldine sticking her nose in and getting in her daughter's ear, I wouldn't be here in Egypt discovering the astonishing things I'm discovering and meeting the amazing people I'm meeting, like yourself for instance. And for that I will be eternally grateful. That said, now what were you going to tell me about what's *below* the Giza Plateau?'

'Well, in ancient times the Giza Plateau was known as "Rostau", supposedly because the plateau is composed of limestone, which creates natural crevices and pockets in the stone. But "Rostau" also means the "mouth of the passages" or the "abode of Osiris", the same name as a region of the ancient Egyptian underworld known as the Duat. So the "mouth of the passages" is clearly a reference to the entrance to a subterranean cave world beneath the plateau, and ancient funerary texts clearly allude to the existence of that subterranean world being in the vicinity of the Giza pyramids.

Now there's been heaps of reports, going back thousands of years, of cavities and underground tunnels here, but if there is any sort of man-made underground complex here, or a Hall-of-Records, unfortunately they haven't been found yet.'

'Or they have been found and the-powers-that-be are keeping the discoveries a secret.'

'Now *that* I do believe, because in 2006, a team from the National Research Institute of Astronomy and Geophysics in Cairo, led by Doctor Abbas Abbas, performed extensive ground penetrating radar scans of various sections of the Giza Plateau.'

'I've seen them, Frank showed me some.'

'Seriously, the scans?'

'Yeah, he had a whole file on them. As far as I can remember, most of the scans were in the area between the Great Pyramid, the Pyramid of Khafre and the Sphinx.'

'That's right, and they discovered numerous cavities deep within the bedrock, including the Osiris Shaft, or Tomb of Osiris, which Hawass totally took the credit for discovering.'

'And no doubt robbing.'

'No doubt at all. Also, several of the cavities had tunnels at least three to five metres wide coming off them.'

'Who knows where they lead?'

'Hawass says they're just natural fissures in the bedrock, that there's nothing there.'

'Yeah, right, that's why he dug a fucking enormous hole in front of the Sphinx, supposedly for the Red Bull games, and then robbed the underground chambers in the middle of the night in April 2010. These other reports, what do they say?'

'According to a recent report by a British explorer by the name of Andrew Collins, who, after reading the forgotten memoirs of the 19th Century diplomat and explorer, British consul general, Henry Salt, and apparently tracking down the entrance to a mysterious underworld, confirmed there are tunnels in the limestone bedrock beneath the pyramid field at Giza that lead to a lost underground complex.

In his memoirs, Salt apparently writes about how in 1817 he and Giovanni Caviglia investigated an underground system of catacombs at Giza for a distance of several hundred yards, discovering four large chambers with further passageways leading off them. Salt wrote that the caves were tens of thousands, if not hundreds of thousands of years old, highly dangerous, with unseen pits and hollows, and had a delicate ecosystem populated by colonies of bats and a species of venomous spider he tentatively identified as "the white widow".

Collins claims he located the entrance to Salt's "lost catacombs" in a supposedly unrecorded tomb to the west of the Great Pyramid, and, inside the tomb, discovered a crack in the rock that led into a massive natural cave, but went no further. Interestingly, Zahi Hawass dismissed the discovery, claiming, "We know everything about the plateau" and "There are no new discoveries to be made at Giza".'

'Of course he'd say that, he doesn't want anyone to know the truth…about anything!'

'What's even more interesting is that Collins proposes the caves, the "lost catacombs", may well have existed prior to the pyramids being built, and both inspired the development of the pyramid field as well as the ancient Egyptian's belief in an underworld. And he may be right, because there are apparently several places on the plateau where the limestone pavement surrounding the pyramids was built over pre-existing crevices and holes in the limestone bedrock.'

'Then, after the circle in the king's chamber, we've got to find a way to get under the plateau and check it all out.'

'And how do you propose to do that, we don't even know where to start looking?'

'Yes we do; somewhere west of the Great Pyramid, Salt's unrecorded tomb.'

'Alex, if it's unrecorded and Hawass has discounted it, then it's hardly going to be highlighted with neon signs or a trail of bread crumbs.'

'I know, but that's half the fun, right, half the adventure, finding it. Besides, I might be able to find more clues about it in my notes or on the net. So, are you with me?'

Bill nodded.

'Life is for living, not for sitting on your ass watching it go by.'

Speaking of sitting on our asses, or rather our camels, we'd been riding for well over half-an-hour and my butt cheeks were definitely starting to feel the pressure; if we didn't stop soon to stretch our legs and shake the stiffness out I was going to be walking around like a duck for a week at least. I was just about to ask how much longer we had to go when one of the ladies near the front of the caravan announced the appearance of our destination.

'There they are!'

Through the pre-dawn light slowly creeping out of the darkness and the haze of the pollution, the silhouette of the Giza pyramids magically and majestically appeared on the horizon. We were still probably over a mile away but already they dominated the skyline. Thankfully, a few minutes later, we stopped at a raised part of the desert that gave a spectacular view of the pyramids.

We all dismounted, THANK GOD, some of the ladies taking the opportunity to snap photos of themselves, the pyramids, their camels or horses, and any and all combinations of the above. I took the opportunity to stretch the stiffness out of my body, get some blood flowing back into my butt and casually saunter across to reconnect with Crystal.

'How are you enjoying the ride?'

'It is not as exciting or enjoyable as the one last night, but it is the perfect way to start today, although I will definitely need a massage later on if you happen to know someone with an available, sensitive and willing pair of strong hands to get right into my butt cheeks.'

I don't know if it was what she said, or the way she said it as she looked suggestively into my eyes, but instantly I felt that within my trousers the order had gone up to make camp and the tent pole was being erected post-haste.

'Well, I haven't had too much practice lately, and I don't want to stick my nose in where it's not welcome, but I'd be more than happy to look into it for you.'

By the smile on her face, she not only got my double entendre, but clearly appreciated it; Green light!

'Come on, Crystal, I want a shot with you and me with the pyramids in the background.'

Detour! Pernille had unknowingly interrupted our oral intercourse, "flirtus interruptus", but it was just as well, because it would have been rather embarrassing to sport an erection in the midst of the ladies; even more uncomfortable to have had to ride on a camel with one.

I remembered, as a school kid on the bus, getting spontaneous and uncontrollable erections due to the vibrations through the seat, which was not helped by the getting on and off of numerous schoolgirls from the local catholic girls school. Many days I had to walk down the aisle of the bus clutching my school bag to my waist and groin to cover my "situation".

'Come, we go now. Imshee, Imshee.'

My buttocks temporarily relieved, the call of our guides indicated it was time to get back aboard Geraldine for the final onslaught. I took the opportunity to check some of my notes on the Giza Plateau. The first note related to the "age" of structures on the plateau.

> "The tomb of Djet, on the outskirts of the Giza plateau dates from the 1st Dynasty, and jar sealings discovered in a tomb in the southern part of Giza mention the 2nd Dynasty Pharaoh, Ninetjer."

That got me thinking, the 'mainstream' position was that the plateau had been occupied since the 1st Dynasty and that the great 4th Dynasty pyramids were built on top of those earlier dynasties, over and obliterating existing 1st and 2nd Dynastic tombs, which would have been built less than four-hundred years earlier. That didn't sit well with me. If "Djoser's" step pyramid was the first pyramid, and I totally ruled that out based on what I had seen at Saqqara, then all the next owners moved southwards, Sekhemkhet, Snefru, possibly Khaba and Huni, before suddenly shifting north to the Giza Plateau with Khufu, then off to Abu Raoush for Djedefre, then back to Giza. No, too messy, it didn't make sense, and the evidence I had seen didn't support the 'mainstream' view.

Wasn't it more logical to see that the Great Pyramids were already there, and that the early dynasties, the 1st and 2nd Dynasties, simply built their communities around the pyramids because they had some religious or practical significance to society and/or life? Soon enough, I would find out for myself.

Looking up, I noticed our caravan had morphed from two single lines into more of an amorphous wave, most likely so everyone had a clear view of the approach to the pyramids. Inching ever closer, one camel-pad-print at a time, I overheard several of the ladies discussing how the pyramids were built.

Their theories covered the usually touted ones including; the bases were prepared and then the stones, each averaging around seven tons, were levered into place one at a time, which was totally ridiculous, or that the Egyptians had built a long sloping ramp, or one that wrapped around the pyramid, and then hauled the stones up the ramps and into place using sledges, rollers and then levers, which was equally as ridiculous.

I was taken slightly off guard when Pernille brought me into the conversation.

'What do you think, Alex?'

'Me? Well, firstly, I think all the conventional theories have major flaws and impossibilities that rule them out. Take the ramp idea for instance; firstly you would need to build a ramp over a mile long and several times bigger in volume than the pyramid itself; where do you get the materials? Then you would need maybe a hundred men to pull each block, weighing say ten ton, probably a lot more, but lets say its only a hundred men. As they get closer to the top end of the ramp, they run out of room to pull, they can't keep walking in thin air to pull it, and there's not enough surface area on the stone, or room behind it, for a hundred men to get behind it and push it. And how do they get the stones around corners, let alone get them to the corners?

As for the lever idea; firstly, where do they find wood strong enough to lever ten ton blocks, my guess is the wood would either snap like a toothpick or be too massive to be practical, besides the Japanese tried to duplicate the levering of blocks in the 1980s and failed miserably.'

Then Crystal brought me back to the question.

'OK, that's your reasoning on how they *weren't* built, what's your understanding of how they *were* built?'

'Firstly I don't think they were built by the ancient Egyptians at all, not the dynastic ones that is; everything about the early dynastic Egyptians points towards them being a "recovering" civilization, not an advanced civilization, to a civilization trying to emulate and repair rather than one that made such rapid technological advances. I think to find out how the pyramids were built you need to find out *who* built them, and *why* they were built, and to do that I think you need to go back way before the early dynastic period, in fact way before the last pole shift, to a race of beings we call the Annunaki, who were not only responsible for building the pyramids, which were not originally tombs, rather energy generators and amplifiers, but who were also responsible for the very creation of the human race through genetic engineering.'

I expected all sorts of reactions and objections, but there were none forthcoming, just nods and acknowledgements, followed by a reiteration from Crystal.

'So, how were they built?'

'Everything about ancient Egypt, and by ancient Egypt I mean pre-dynastic, pre pole-shift ancient Egypt, comes back to vibration, so the simplest theory is that they used some sort of sonic saw or laser to cut the stone, and levitation to transport them and lift them into place. Even now, scientists in laboratories are proving it can be done; by using lasers to cut metal and sound waves to levitate objects.'

One of the ladies fired me a question.

'And you think the pyramids were built as energy generators and amplifiers?'

'Yes.'

Another joined in.

'What sort of energy?'

'I'm not sure, maybe fusion; but I'm sure they used the vibration of the stone, particularly red granite as a part of it.'

'Do you think it had something to do with magnetism; the Great Pyramid is perfectly aligned to true north.'

'I'm sure it does, the magnetic field of the earth is just one big torus running through north-south, and whole universe is one big electro-magnetic pea soup.'

'Do you believe that the Great Pyramid incorporates codes, also hidden in the Bible, about prophecies concerning the future of the human race?'

That was a curly one; and, for a moment, I wondered if I was about to offend someone.

'No, I don't buy into that. Sure there are sacred geometries incorporated into its design, like pi and phi, but I think they relate directly to harmonic relationships and the function of the pyramids rather than any occult meaning. As to any secret Bible codes, why would you put them in one structure tens-of-thousands of years, maybe hundreds-of-thousands of years before *'The Bible'* even exists, and not incorporate them into any other pyramids? No, I just think the religions have an agenda and are trying to claim "ownership" of the pyramids for their "God". What do you think, Bill?'

'That certain information may be "hidden" in *'The Bible'* is a distinct possibility, but then you must ask yourself the questions, *who* is hiding it, *how* is it hidden, and, most importantly, *why* are they hiding it? Remember, over the past two-thousand years, *'The Bible'* has been translated through several languages and undergone significant editing and manipulation to suit the doctrine of the day. At best, *'The Bible'* today is a compilation of short stories, based on a common but broad theme and on threads of truth that date back and find many of their origins right here in ancient Egypt. So why read the book, with all its distortions, half-truths, and even lies, when we are all about to see the real thing for ourselves and make up our own minds about what rings true?'

The ladies all nodded; clearly they respected Bill's perspective. I, on the other hand, was still under the spotlight.

'Do you think the positions of the Giza Pyramids relates to the stars?'

'Definitely. You know, as little as twenty years ago, the explanation put forward by most of the early Egyptologists for the 'random' positioning of the three pyramids at Giza, as to why they weren't in a straight line, or clustered around the largest one, or grouped in any kind of expected symmetrical way, was that it had something to do with the sloping terrain, or it was simply the way the construction had worked out, and some Egyptologists still stick to that belief, that it was some sort of "oversight", or error. This so called 'error', meaning the third pyramid was positioned nearly a hundred metres to the southeast, is of a magnitude totally not in keeping with the mathematical skill of the ancient Egyptians, who were accurate to within miniscule fractions of an inch. But, in the early 1990s, a Belgian named Robert Bauval put forward a different idea.

After looking at an aerial photograph of the Giza Plateau, Bauval noticed that the Giza pyramids were arranged just like the three stars of Orion's belt in the night sky, Alnitak, Alnilam, and Mintaka. He thus proposed, that in light of the fact that the constellation Orion was sacred to the Egyptians, and who believed it was the home of the god Osiris, that the pyramids were deliberately built to represent Orion's belt. Now, when Bauval came out with his perspective, he was ridiculed and bashed from pillar to post by the 'establishment', whereas now it's almost entirely accepted as a given that's what the pyramids represent. It goes to show that the Egyptologists on the whole are not only guessing, but they are resistant to any ideas that conflict with their beliefs, especially if they come from an 'outsider', someone without any letters after their name.

That said, I don't think Bauval got everything right; he tried lining up shafts in the king's chamber with other stars and put forward a lot of other theories piggybacking on the Orion alignment, but many of them fall short. However, he opened the door for others, and the work of Wayne Herschel goes a major leap further and aligns all the pyramids along the Nile with stars in the Milky Way along the Galactic Equator. I was only directed to it a few days ago but I strongly suggest, if you're not already familiar with it, you should check it out.'

The discussion was curtailed by our arrival at the southwest corner of the third of the "Great" pyramids, the smallest of the three, the Pyramid of Menkaure.

'This Pyramid of Menkaure, son of Khafre, six pharaoh of four Dynasty. Please to get off and walk around...'

He pointed clockwise...

'...We wait with horse and camel on east side...'

...then east.

'...please to be ten minute.'

It was all very exciting, here we were, the Giza Plateau.

Everyone dismounted and formed themselves into three independent but intertwining little explorative parties; Bill, Pernille, Crystal and I, in one, Diane and two ladies in another, and a group of four ladies in the third.

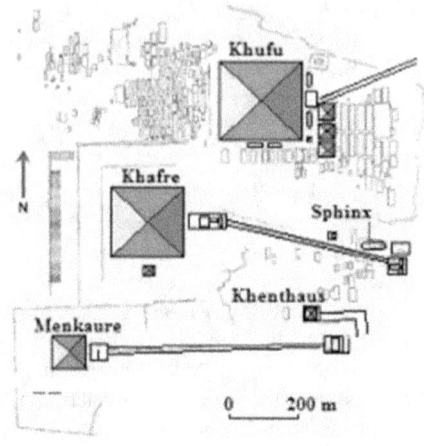

While the other two groups followed our guide's directions and slowly headed north, clockwise around Menkaure's pyramid, I instinctively headed in the other direction, south, to do a little loop and check out the three 'queens' pyramids that stood in a row along the south side of the Pyramid of Menkaure and that were once surrounded by a common perimeter wall. They had been inspirationally named G3a, G3b, and G3c; G obviously meaning Giza, 3 referring to the third pyramid, that of Menkaure, and a, b and c, to each of the smaller satellite pyramids.

The Pyramid Complex of Menkaure

Oriented north-south, G3c had a base of around thirty metres and was made of mud-brick, but was in pretty poor condition; it looked like the ruins of a step pyramid or one with a four-step core but without any casing stones. I read my notes out loud, mainly for the benefit of Bill.

'G 3c was never completed; no casing stones were added, nor was its burial chamber, constructed under the northwest part of the pyramid, ever finished, and no burial was found within. The owner is thus not known but presumed to be a consort of Menkaure.'

There was, however, clear evidence of a small north-south mortuary temple that would that once have been squeezed in front of the east side of this pyramid.

'What have you spotted, Alex?'

'Would you built a temple beside an unfinished pyramid, especially in such a tight space?'

'Of course not.'

'So the pyramid must have been completed at some time in the past, right?'

'It's logical.'

'So what happened to it?'

'Your Thera tsunami perhaps?'

'I don't know what the subterranean chambers are made of, but the evidence above ground shows the damage to the pyramid probably occurred *after* the Mortuary Temple had been built. Which means, if, as was the case elsewhere, the mortuary temple was an Old Kingdom addition, then the damage to the pyramid post-dated the Old Kingdom. Further, the mud-brick superstructure was most likely a New Kingdom repair job, thus pointing the finger of blame for the damage directly at the Thera tsunami.'

'Clear as day.'

The next pyramid, G3b, looked almost identical, including having the remains of a small mortuary temple to the east, however I gleaned a little more information from my notes to support my thoughts.

'Listen to this, Bill…

"Like G3c, the burial chamber was constructed under the northwest part of

the pyramid, and was likewise not finished; it lacks a barrier in the descending corridor and the bones of a young woman were found in the pink-granite sarcophagus which stood against the west wall of the burial chamber".'

'Well, there's your proof; a red-granite sarcophagus.'

'I think it's fair to assume G3c probably has one as well, which means they had to be pre pole shift. And the fact the mortuary temple was squeezed in and is orientated north-south, shows in was added after both G3b and G3c were built.'

Pernille chipped in.

'What about the female bones, do you think she was one of Menkaure's consorts?'

'I doubt it. She was probably just a later addition when the damaged structure was usurped and converted into a tomb, possibly during the Middle Kingdom, or more likely during or after the New Kingdom.'

That brought us to G3a, the easternmost of the three queens' pyramids.

'Partly made of granite, like the main pyramid, G3a, with a base of 44 metres, height of 28.4 metres and slope of 52° 15', is the largest and only "true" pyramid of the three satellite pyramids.'

'Partly made of granite? Does that mean they stopped half way, or they repaired the original damaged structure as best they could with mud-brick?'

'My point exactly, Bill, and the fact they used mud-brick tends to make me think the repairs were done after the Thera tsunami, or else they would probably have been made using limestone.'

'Anything there about the burial chamber?'

'The substructure consists of an entrance situated in the middle of the north wall, a little above ground level, which leads via a descending corridor equipped with a barrier, to the burial chamber, dug from the rock and under the centre of the pyramid. The burial chamber was originally equipped with a pink-granite sarcophagus, embedded in the floor next to the west wall.'

'More evidence.'

'Yep.'

Once again Pernille was keen to find out more.

'Who did it belong to, who was buried here?'

I scanned my notes, to no real avail.

'They don't know, but at least they do concede that it's not impossible that the pyramid was originally simply a cult pyramid and later transformed into a tomb.'

Bill chuckled.

'Which is half right.'

'Better to be half right than all wrong I suppose.'

Crystal was quick to remind us.

'There *is* no right or wrong, just different perspectives. The question is one of whether your perspective serves you or limits you.'

And, that said, she started making her way back to join the other ladies, Pernille right behind her. I wanted to complete my survey, so quickly headed to the east side of G3a. Sure enough, there was the evidence of a mortuary temple there as well.

"G3a had a small, east-west oriented mortuary temple partially built of limestone and hastily finished with mud-brick."

It was clearly oriented east-west because there was room for it to be built out in that direction, unlike the other mortuary temples of G3b and G3c which were block by G3a and G3b respectively.

"The west end of the temple was dominated by a large, open courtyard with niches in its northern wall; on its south side, a row of wooden columns. A small cult chapel with an entrance adorned with deep, double niches to either side, led into an offering room that included a false door."

Wooden columns? No, that indicated to me that the Mortuary Temple was clearly an Old Kingdom, possibly 6th Dynasty, addition. Suddenly Bill tapped me on the shoulder.

'You know we're at the far end of the Giza diagonal; on the southwest edge of the Mokattam Formation...'

He pointed to the ridge to the southeast.

'...See over there, where it dips down, that's where the Mokattum Formation disappears below the younger Maadi Formation on top.'

'Got it.'

'I can just see the water of your Thera tsunami gushing through here, knocking the tops off the little pyramids, and carving out the wadi that stretches to the northeast.'

'So can I, Bill, so can I.'

'Come on, let's catch up with the girls; who knows what other titbits are waiting around the next corner.'

'It's tidbits, Bill, not tit-bits.'

He just chuckled away.

'I know; but you look for whatever you want, I know where my buns are buttered.'

So did I. I wrapped an arm around his shoulder, and together we set off along the southern face of Menkaure's pyramid in pursuit of the girls.

Several layers of unfinished pink-granite casing stones, most likely from Aswan, rose from the base up to a height of about maybe fifteen metres.

'More red granite, Alex.'

'Yeah, and definitely not just there to make repairs.'

'What do your notes say about the main pyramid?'

Turning the corner to the west face, I flicked the page.

'*"The rock base of Menkaure's pyramid had to be carefully prepared, particularly around the northeast corner, leaving it two-and-a-half metres above the base of the adjoining pyramid of his father, Khafre."* Do you think there's anything in that, Bill?'

'Of course, but I don't think it's anything particularly profound; it's easier to raise one corner than it is to lower three. What else does it say?'

'Named "Menkaure is Divine", the Pyramid of Menkaure, with a base of 108.5 metres, occupies a mere quarter of the area consumed by the pyramids of Khafre and Khufu. It has a slope of 51° 51°20'25" and once rose to a height of 66.45 metres, representing only about 1/10th of the volume of Khufu's pyramid. However, despite being the smallest of the three Giza pyramids, it is also the most unusual.'

'And why is that?'

'It has a core of local limestone blocks, with the first sixteen courses of the exterior casing made of unfinished pink granite from Aswan. Further up, the uppermost portions, like several Pyramids at Dahshur, are made of brick, and the casing was probably made in the normal manner of fine, Tura limestone."

'That hardly sounds like a normal building project, now does it?'

'One theory is that Menkaure died before his pyramid could be completed, and the remaining construction was hastily done, to finish it in time for the burial, by his son, Shepseskaf.'

'So Shepseskaf, stricken with grief, tells the workers to forget about the thousands of limestone and red granite blocks they've already quarried, or are currently quarrying, and quarry a load of other rocks instead? Does something about that sound totally illogical and insane, or what?'

'And how would the people see Shepseskaf, the cheapskate son who penny-pinched on his own father's eternal tomb? I don't think so.'

'So what are your thoughts?'

'I haven't seen or read of any evidence to the contrary, so I'm pretty convinced the Pyramid of Menkaure was not built by Menkaure, instead, it sounds like what you might finishing up with if the top of the pyramid had have been washed completely away by a tsunami, and then was rebuilt during some later period using stone and inferior technology.'

'That it does.'

We caught up with Crystal and Pernille as we rounded the corner of the pyramid to the north side, where there was a large gash in the middle of its north face. Pernille was quick to comment.

'What happened there?'

Of course I had the answer at my fingertips.

The vertical scar in the north face was created at the end of the 12th Century when the Muslim, al-Malek al-Aziz Othman ben Yusuf, Saladin's son, attempted to demolish the pyramid. After eight months of painstakingly slow demolition work, thankfully he gave up, but not before leaving the telltale gouge in the pyramid.'

'Wouldn't it have been much safer to start down at the base, or easier to start with the edges?'

Pernille was right; it made no sense to start so far up the face, unless…

'You know, Pernille, I think you've got a good point; I don't think they were just trying to destroy the pyramid at all, I think they were trying to find the entrance, which they must have known from other pyramids was in the centre of the north face.'

She pointed to the actual entrance to the pyramid, just above the current ground level, around which were gathered Diane and all the other ladies.

'So why didn't they just break in through the entrance that's there?'

Bill was right on to it.

'Because they didn't know it was there, because it was buried below thirty-or forty-odd feet of sand and silt. I've seen old photos and sketches from the 19th Century that show the sand levels much higher than they are today; they must have been even higher in the 12th Century.'

As we joined the rest of the group, I noticed there appeared to have been considerable reconstruction of the façade and entrance, including a modern metal staircase leading up to it, however the entrance was closed and we had no permission or time to explore it. Diane turned to me.

'Alex, the ladies are curious to know what's inside this pyramid, do you have any notes or pictures?'

'At your service ladies.'

The Pyramid of Menkaure was once believed by Manetho to have belonged to Nitocris, daughter of Psamtik I.'

'That is not correct….'

Crystal was quick to set me, and everyone else, straight.

'…You must not always believe what you read. Nitocris was the daughter of the 6th Dynasty pharaoh, Pepi II. Psamtik I did not rule until the start of the 26th Dynasty, over fifteen hundred years later.'

'So which is true?'

'Neither...'

Given Crystal had told me she was Nitocris in a previous life, I wasn't about to question her.

'…Why don't you stick to the physical facts, they have served you well so far on this journey, have they not?'

She was right, again.

'OK, the facts it is! *"Access to the inner chambers was originally via an entrance in the centre of the north wall, about four metres above ground level, that led via a descending corridor, partially lined with pink granite, and sloping down at an angle of around 26 degrees, for 31 metres through the masonry core to the chambers below. This 'lower corridor' terminates in a room 3.63 x 3.16m with panelled walls and niches. At the beginning of the next corridor, there is a barrier made of three granite blocks that were lowered into place after its completion."*

Bill was doing my thinking for me.

'That red-granite corridor and those granite portcullises are totally in keeping with your theory, Alex.'

One of the ladies enquired what my theory was, to which I dutifully replied.

'I'm convinced these subterranean chambers are much older than the construction times attributed to them. This pyramid may well be known as the Pyramid of Menkaure, but, as far as I'm concerned, the evidence makes it pretty clear he wasn't responsible for its construction.'

'Really! Please, keep reading.'

'The following corridor continues at a slight downward angle until it comes out in a relatively small, east-west oriented upper antechamber with undecorated walls, the east end of which is located directly under the vertical axis of the pyramid. Here, another passageway known as the 'upper corridor' runs back above and over the 'lower corridor', through a short horizontal section, before climbing in a north-south direction into the pyramid core, where it terminates.'

'Why would it do that?'

'I think it's something to do with the addition of a later entrance at some time after the pyramid was damaged and partially buried by a massive tsunami…'

I pointed to the damaged face.

'…and I think that's what the huge gouge is all about; I think they were looking for this second entrance.'

As I kept reading the truth was unfolding before my eyes.

' *"There is a rectangular indention in the west section of the antechamber floor, suggesting that a sarcophagus may have once been intended for this room."* And that would have made the design of the substructure consistent with most of the substructures of the other pyramids, especially those at Saqqara and Abusir; a descending passage leading to an east-west antechamber and burial chamber, the latter containing a sarcophagus set in the floor against the western wall. But there's more to it.

"In 1835, Richard Vyse unearthed the remains of an anthropoid wooden coffin, with Menkaure's name on it, in the antechamber; inside, were human bones. The coffin is now in the British Museum." Clearly that's why the pyramid was attributed to Menkaure, but the coffin could have been placed there anytime. In fact,

"Most scholars today believe the coffin was placed in the pyramid during the Saite period, thousands of years later, and the bone fragments confirmed this when they were carbon dated them to the Coptic Christian period two thousand years ago." So, we know something strange was going on.

"From here, the substructure underwent significant changes in three phases, during which the original plan was enlarged." I think this second stage happened after the pyramid had been badly damaged by a tsunami that struck Egypt, either during the last pole shift, or most likely at the end of the 17th Dynasty around 1600 BC.'

I quickly showed them the photos and diagrams so they had an idea what I was talking about, then got back to the notes.

' *"From the middle of the floor of the antechamber, another granite corridor has been cut out that leads downward to a short horizontal passage and on to the actual burial chamber. Cut into the northern wall of the horizontal passage wall, just before the entrance to the burial chamber, is a short flight of steps that leads to an area cut out of the bedrock that is sometimes known as the 'cellar', which contains six small, deep niches, possibly used to store funerary equipment and supplies."*

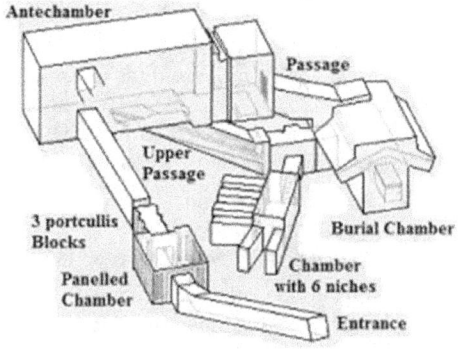

I think, by looking at its position and its rough finish, this side cellar was clearly the last addition; dug out once the subterranean chambers were usurped to use as a tomb. But the descending granite corridor itself could be a much earlier modification directly related to the creation of the "burial" chamber, or main resonance chamber as I now like to call it.'

'And the chamber itself?'

' *"The rectangular burial chamber, 6.59 x 2.62 metres and 3.53 metres high, and oriented north-south, lies 15.5 metres beneath the foundation level of the pyramid's base. It is completely lined with pink granite, including the gabled ceiling, constructed of nine pairs of enormous granite blocks hollowed out from beneath to make a round, barrel vault."* Now this would have been a massive effort, probably impossible with today's technology, first having to lower massive blocks of granite down narrow corridors, and then lift them up into place.

"It required a large descending tunnel to be built from the western part of the upper antechamber, from which visitors today may actually view the top of the vaulted burial chamber." I don't think there's any possible way this chamber was constructed by the dynastic Egyptians, the logistics are just to complex.'

'Did they find anything in the chamber?'

' *"On the burial chamber's west wall was a magnificent, dark basalt sarcophagus decorated with niches in the style of a palace façade. The sarcophagus was empty, and its lid was missing, however, fragments of the lid were discovered, indicating it was ornamented with a bold concave cornice."*......Basalt hey, Bill, what do you make of that?'

'Interesting, very interesting, I'd like to check that out.'

'Well you'll need a deep sea submersible… *"Unfortunately, the sarcophagus now lies at the bottom of the Mediterranean, sinking on October 13, 1838, with the ship Beatrice as she made her way between Malta and Spain, whilst taking it from Egypt to the British Museum in London."* …A convenient cover story?'

'Probably, or else someone would have tried to find it by now and salvage it; it would be worth a fortune, and who knows what else was on board, what other priceless treasures?'

'Mental note to self, do a search to find the manifesto of the Beatrice.'

'If you find anything, let me know, I might have a few spare quid to put into a search and salvage operation.'

'You're on!'

'Hang on,…'

Bill was suddenly musing over something.

'…How did they get the sarcophagus *out*, there would barely have been enough room to negotiate it around inside the chamber, let alone lift it up the various passages and around the corners; certainly not out through the lower entrance.'

Pernille was right with him.

'They must have used the upper entrance, maybe that's the reason why it's so damaged?'

'Meaning Vyse lied. Now, why would he do that? Is there any mention of *how* he moved it through the passages?'

I quickly scanned the notes.

'No, I don't think so.'

'Then he may well have used levitation.'

One of the ladies chipped in.

'Just like that guy in Florida who built the castle out of huge blocks of coral?'

'Yes, Edward Leedskalnin, a Latvian; no one knew how he moved around massive coral blocks up to thirty ton, but he did it all on his own, obviously by levitation.'

'There's some belief he was a reincarnated Atlantean.'

Another of the ladies contributed her thoughts.

'Or part of a secret order.'

Even I could put two and two together.

'The Followers; Vyse was Illuminati!'

'Very likely, and that raises the questions of why he *really* wanted the sarcophagus, and whether it actually sank to the bottom of the Mediterranean.'

'You've lost me.'

'As we know, the sarcophagi were not for burials, but rather used as resonance boxes.'

'They used them for regeneration…'

And suddenly it hit me.

'…Vyse wanted it to prolong his life.'

'Highly likely, or for some sort of spiritual awakening.'

Pernille was already streets ahead.

'I get it. You lie down in the sarcophagus, somehow it gets stimulated and resonates, triggering sympathetic resonances in your own body, in your DNA; a spiritual awakening.'

'Exactly. And that means the Beatrice may never have sunk the way we've been told, that it simply sank somewhere between Malta and Spain; it may well have sailed to a different destination, possibly to south France, which, as we know, was at one time a stronghold of the Cathars. There, the sarcophagus would have been unloaded, along with who knows how many other priceless treasures, then the Beatrice was either decommissioned or, more likely, taken somewhere between Malta and Spain and scuttled.'

'But what about all the crew, they would have said something.'

'Unless they were all paid off, or, more likely, killed.'

'What, all of them?'

'Alex, remember, we're talking about the same people who have instigated innumerable wars throughout the last thousands years at least, who control and promote the current global drug industry, both legal and illegal, who were responsible for the atomic bombs on Hiroshima and Nagasaki, and the whole 9/11 conspiracy; a boat-load of common sailors "drowning" in the middle of the Mediterranean would hardly even be noticed, especially back then. Was there any mention of survivors? Even of any bodies found?'

'I don't think so.'

'Not one; don't you find that even slightly suspicious?'

'Now that you mention it. Quite a scam, use the British Museum's funds, the people's money, to move it, then steal it from right under their noses and give them a token wooden coffin as compensation.'

'Of course, it's just a theory.'

'Of course.'

'It would make a mission to find and raise the Beatrice a waste of time and money.'

'Which is perhaps why they haven't bothered to look for it.'

We raised our eyebrows and laughed, moving on towards the eastern side of the pyramid; the ladies seemingly genuinely excited that they may well have been part of some potential new discovery. So was I!

Our guides were waiting with the camels and horses, beside the entrance to the ruins to the Mortuary Temple, on the pyramid's east side. As the ladies set about mounting their faithful steeds I took the opportunity to whip over and do a quick once-over of the temple. I had a theory, if there was any granite it would be closest to the pyramid and indicative of a much older structure, limestone probably related to the Old Kingdom, and any mud-brick would be attributable to later repairs most probably in the 19th Dynasty. Time to test the theory.

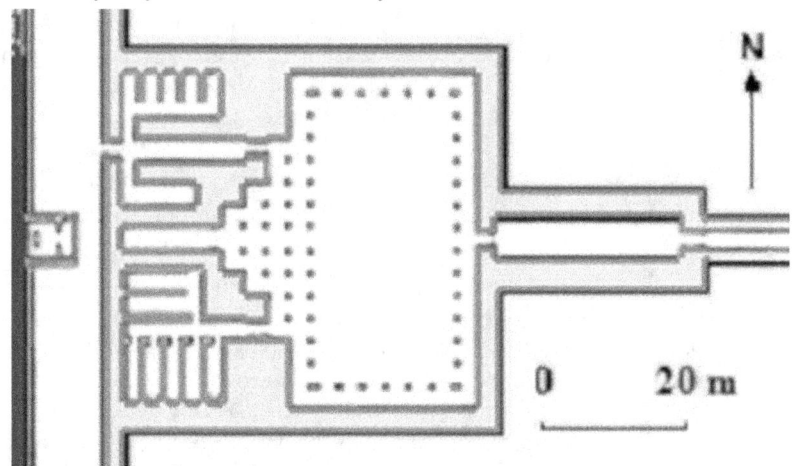

Menkaure's Mortuary Temple, whilst fairly well preserved in places, and appearing to have an almost square ground plan, was still hard to clearly define, so it appeared I might have to rely quite a bit on my notes. I started at the entrance.

The entrance corridor led to an open porticoed courtyard.

"The inside wall of the courtyard was made of crude red mud-brick plastered with a thin layer of limestone and decorated with niches."

It was probably a later addition, possibly by Menkaure, or his son, Shepseskaf, but more likely a 19th Dynasty repair to the damaged temple.

The western wall of the courtyard gave way to a portico of pillars that led to a long offering hall that probably once contained a statue of Menkaure at the western end of the hall. In this western part of the temple the foundations and the inner core were made of limestone.

"Menkaure began with core blocks of locally quarried limestone, the heaviest of these, t the northwest corner of the temple, the heaviest known at Giza, weighing some 220 tons."

I had to see it, so I made my way to the northwest corner, discovering sections of flooring and walls of red granite.

"The heaviest granite ashlars imported from Aswan weighed more than 30 tons."

The evidence was mounting.

"A limestone altar and fragments of a seated statue of Menkaure, rendered in pink granite, were found in the five, two story magazines that form a north-western part of the mortuary temple."

The statue was probably the one that once stood at the end of the offering hall. And then I found the monolithic limestone foundation stone; it was enormous; there was no way the Egyptians of the 4th Dynasty could move such massive blocks. To me, this was clear evidence this part of the temple was pre-dynastic and pre pole shift. With time of the essence, I moved quickly on to the courtyard surrounding the pyramid, as the mortuary temple was not built adjacent to his pyramid's east wall.

Immediately in front of the pyramid's east wall I found the remains of a small red-granite platform that probably once supported a false door, again of red granite, though there was no trace of it. The question was, did Menkaure build it, or was it already there when he claimed the pyramid as his own?

"An inscription on one of the fragments of a stela found in the mortuary temple says that Shepseskaf 'made it (the temple) as his monument for his father, the king of Upper and Lower Egypt'. Other elements found within the temple date beyond the reign of Shepseskaf, including the stelae of Merenre I and Pepi I."

I'm not saying Shepseskaf didn't complete or augment his father's temple, or that the temple wasn't further usurped by Merenre I and/or Pepi I, after all, it seemed to be a common practice of ancient Egypt pharaohs, but couldn't the Shepseskaf stela just as easily have been referring to the stela itself, and not actually to the temple?

"Many Egyptologists believe the whole mortuary temple was originally meant to be constructed of pink granite, but left incomplete because of the sudden death of Menkaure, and completed by his son, Shepseskaf, using mud-brick."

I didn't buy it; I agreed that the "original" temple was probably red granite, but not the extensions Menkaure was making. And to think Menkaure's son would be such a skin-flint as to finish the job in mud-brick was ludicrous. Suddenly a whistle pierced the air.

'Hey Alex, better get on your bike or you'll miss the bus.'

The others were all aboard and only Bill remained on the ground.

'On my way, you get going, I'll meet you at the causeway.'

To complete my mini-expedition, I only had to explore the southwest section of the temple, really just to see if there was anything of importance I might have overlooked.

"The southwest part of the temple remained uncompleted."

As I made my way back through it, and through the courtyard, I formulated my own conclusions.

My theory was that the temple *was* completed, though smaller and earlier, and not by Menkaure, but before the pole shift. Then it was partially destroyed by the Osireion tsunami, after which, during the Old Kingdom, it was extended and reconstructed, with limestone by Menkaure, who had claimed the pyramid as his own. Possibly because of Menkaure's death, the extended temple was completed by his son, Shepseskaf, and, following the Thera tsunami, was repaired in the New Kingdom with mud-brick, possibly by Khaemwaset. And the evidence I had seen with my own eyes totally supported that belief; it didn't disprove the 'experts' theories at all, but it made a hell-of-a-lot more sense.

Catching up to the caravan, I climbed aboard Geraldine and we continued on our trek.

'Anything interesting?'

'Of course; more evidence supporting the tsunamis.'

'You know, Alex, you should write a book about all this, and, if you do, I'll put the money up to get it printed and distributed.'

'Wow, you'd do that?'

'Just make sure you're on my boat tonight in one piece.'

'That's the plan.'

From the Mortuary Temple, a causeway, almost completely covered in sand, led over six hundred metres down to the Valley Temple. While the caravan made its way down, I checked my notes.

"The 660 metre mud-brick causeway leading from the Mortuary Temple to the Valley Temple had floors made of limestone blocks and highly compressed clay mixed with limestone fragments. The walls, made of mud-brick and a little more than two metres thick, supported a roof, made of either wooden beams and mats, or a vaulted roof of brickwork, depending on which theory you believed."

I was hardly likely to believe either, but what I did consider was, that like those at Saqqara and Abusir, the limestone 'floor' may have been the ceiling of a subterranean tunnel. That notion was further supported, irrespective of the roof theories, by the later addition of mud-brick walls.

"The causeway was never completed; work seemingly stopped at the point where it meets the west side of the old Khufu quarry. From there to down to the valley temple, the causeway was probably never more than a construction ramp for delivering stone and was most likely completed by Shepseskaf."

Not completed? What an idiotic statement; the whole purpose of the causeway was to connect the valley temple with the mortuary temple, and if there was a valley temple, there HAD to be a causeway. However, if the bottom section had been washed away by the Thera tsunami surging through the wadi, then it may also have washed away part of the walls and roof of the upper section that were added during dynastic times.

I assumed we were heading to the valley temple, but that was not the case, as, just before the end of the causeway, we detoured off to the left, towards the Pyramid of Khentkaus I.

Just to be sure I wasn't missing anything, I checked out my notes on the Valley Temple of Menkaure.

"The valley temple, situated at the mouth of the main wadi, was completed in at least two stages; the west part of the limestone block base and lower part of the core of the temple's north wall probably completed during the Menkaure's reign, while the remaining clay masonry of crude mud-brick is attributable to his son, Shepseskaf."

Given what I was now aware of, that didn't ring true; the two stages may have been true, but one was pre-tsunami, probably pre-dynastic, the other post-tsunami repairs most likely done by Khaemwaset in the 19th Dynasty.

"The entrance to the temple led to a square antechamber flanked to each side by four storerooms. The antechamber was adorned with four columns; the alabaster bases, pressed into the clay floor, still in situ. Beyond was a huge open courtyard, its inner walls decorated with niches.

A path, paved with limestone slabs, ran from the antechamber through the centre of the courtyard, to a low stairway, which in turn led through a portico with two rows of wooden columns to an offering hall, in which an alabaster altar once stood. To the north of the offering hall were twelve storerooms, and, to its south, five additional storerooms where numerous statues of Menkaure were found."

Again, just because statues of Menkaure were found there doesn't mean Menkaure was responsible for the construction of the temple; it seemed to be a common error of assumption not only made by the early Egyptologists, but accepted and perpetuated by the modern ones.

"More recently, a small brick structure with a platform, low benches, together with a basin and a small drainage canal, was discovered at the northeast corner of the temple."

Given its location, and the materials from which it was constructed, it was clearly a much later addition, probably post 19th Dynasty, and of no real interest to me.

"Perhaps as early as the 5th Dynasty, the temple was badly damaged by water after a particularly heavy rain tore away the temple's west side."

A particularly heavy rainfall, are they serious? Did they actually look around and see where Giza was, on the edge of a massive desert? Something "tore away" the temple's west side? That can only mean a massive flood. And a flood of that magnitude would not be the result of a "particularly heavy rainfall": a tsunami, yes, heavy rainfall, no.

And as to it being as "early as the 5th Dynasty", do they mean sometime, anytime, *after* the reign of Menkaure? If they did, then the Thera tsunami would definitely fit the bill. Wake up and smell the hibiscus tea, guys, the evidence is all there, all you have to do is just shift your perspective. And that's exactly what I did next.

As obvious as the testicles on a prize bull

As I looked further east, out and over the perimeter wall we had all traversed the outer side of earlier in the morning, my eye was once again drawn in the immediate distance to Bill's Maadi Formation.

We'd slipped past it in the darkness of the pre-dawn, but now it loomed large, not only in the distance, but also in my mind. It didn't look like a 'natural' outcrop of rock, but, I was no expert, so how was I to know. I decided to bring Bill in on my thoughts.

'Hey, Bill, that Maadi Formation of yours, that's it over there, right?'

'Yep, it's called Gebel Gibli.'

'Does anything about it look unusual to you?'

'In what way?'

'I don't know, the layers, the exposed face, the cave underneath?'

'No, not really?'

'Then why is there a protective fence around it, like the one around the plateau?'

'That's a very good question, my friend.'

'If Hawass went to all the trouble of arranging the Luxor massacre just so he could erect this perimeter fence, and he included a fence around that rock outcrop, then he must have known something the rest of the Egyptology fraternity knows nothing about.'

'It's probably not even on the map.'

The second Bill said it, I instantaneously had a flash.

'Wait a minute, maybe it is…'

I dived back onto my iphone and logged online to Herschel's website, hiddenrecords.com.

'…I remember seeing an image on Wayne Herschel's website of the Giza Plateau that showed the position of the three pyramids, but it also showed….'

I found the image.

'…yes, here it is.'

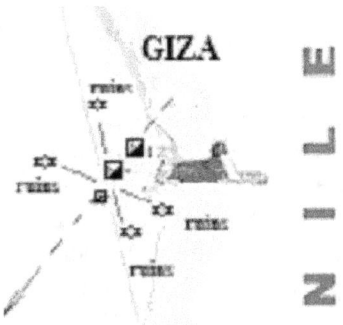

I quickly showed the image to Bill.

'Now that *IS* interesting.'

'Herschel was pretty spot on when he figured out that the pyramids all lined up with stars in the Milky Way. Listen to this:

"He overlaid a transparency of the stars onto a map of the pyramids, and all the brightest stars within the known constellations were represented in one complete three-hundred-and-sixty degree ring along the Milky Way."

We were almost at the next landmark on our trek, the Khentkaus pyramid, and it must have sparked Bill's thinking.

'Do you think the Pyramid of Khentkaus I could represent Betelgeuse?'

'It's possible, but I think it's too close, and too obvious. If it was, Herschel would have clearly identified it, but he doesn't. Instead he says:

'*"All of the brightest stars all had pyramid counterparts on the ground, however, there were some important stars for which pyramids were apparently missing. In Giza for example, Herschel found four potential, as yet unrecognised, pyramid ruins on an antique early map."* Here, check this out!'

I handed the iphone to Bill so he could have a more detailed look.

'Oh, wow, you're right, it's twice as far out as the Khentkaus pyramid; the map does seem to indicate there might be something where the Maadi Formation is; it corresponds exactly with the position of the star Betelgeuse.'

'Not just there, but there are three other locations around Giza as well, including the one to the west, Rigel, do you think it could be the entrance to Salt's lost catacombs?'

'I don't know, I guess it's possible, although it might be too far out as well, like the one to the north, they might be buried under the expanding metropolis.'

That got me thinking.

'I wonder if the site to the north is the same location where some people were digging under a house?'

'What did they find?'

'Who knows; statues, gold, we'll never know, because, according to both Abdo and Saeed, Zahi Hawass supposedly took over the excavation and the whole thing became a covert operation that not even the mainstream Archaeological community knew about. When the house collapsed, about ten people died and Hawass buried all discussion or mention of it as well.'

'Who knows if we'll ever find out the truth about what's under the ground here?'

'Well, apparently there's something about it Kareem's papers.'

'Even more reason for you to be on my boat tonight.'

'Don't worry, I'll be there.'

'Famous last words!'

Bill was only joking, but it did put me a little on edge, causing me to look around to see if suddenly the Secret Police were about to leap out from behind a ruin or sand dune and whisk me off to oblivion. Thankfully, the cupboard was bare, and my attention was distracted by the ruins of the Pyramid of Khentkaus I.

The Pyramid of Khentkaus I

Initially I thought we might have stopped to give it the once over, but I was wrong, we were just a ship passing in the night.

"Khentkaus I was a queen during the 4th Dynasty, although it's possible she was the lady 'Redjedjet' mentioned in the Westcar Papyrus, as the name Khentkaus never appeared in a cartouche. She may even have taken on kingly titles, even though some of her titles are ambiguous and open to interpretation.

The title 'mwt nswt bity nswt bity' should be read as 'The Mother of two Kings of Upper and Lower Egypt', however others have interpreted it as 'the King of Upper and Lower Egypt and the Mother of the King of Upper and Lower Egypt'."

Who and what she was didn't seem to be of much relevance to the issues I was focused on, but I took it on board anyway.

"Khentkaus was most probably Menkaure's daughter. She may also have been married first to her brother, or half-brother, Shepseskaf, and later to Userkaf and may have been the mother of both Sahure and Neferirkare Kakai."

It all went to show how much guesswork and speculation the Egyptologists indulged in.

"The pyramid complex of Khentkaus I consists of the pyramid (LG100), a chapel, a solar boat, the pyramid city, a water tank and granaries, and a valley temple."

I knew what I was looking for, red granite, and I knew where I was most likely to find it, in the "burial" chamber, but as we made our way between the pyramid to the left and its accompanying city to the right, and, as we were unlikely to stop and explore for ourselves, I double-checked my notes for anything of relevance.

"The small valley temple of Khentkaus, referred to as the 'washing tent of Queen Khentkaus', was constructed of mud-brick and connected to the valley temple of Menkaure. The floor is the opening of a limestone drain, covered by arched sections forming an almost circular stone pipe, which runs downwards under the ground for a distance of 7.20 m, emptying into a large, rectangular basin."

That must have been the small structure discovered at the northeast corner of Menkaure's valley temple, and, though the limestone seemed to indicate an Old Kingdom origin, possibly attributable to Khentkaus, the mud-brick could still have been a 19th Dynasty repair job.

"Immediately east of the pyramid, a causeway, connecting the valley temple to the pyramid chapel, was flanked on both sides by a city; constructed towards the end of the 4th Dynasty and functioning well into the 6th Dynasty. Laid out along several streets, and divided into groups of houses containing their own magazines and granaries, the city was constructed from unbaked mud-brick, with the surfaces covered in a yellow plaster. Near the end of the causeway, it turns south, giving the settlement an inverted-L shape; the southern extension consisting of some larger, more important houses, possibly for the priests."

Something about that didn't ring true; that there'd been a settlement during the 4th to 6th Dynasties was highly probable, the settlement would almost certainly have lasted well into the 17th Dynasty. But a tsunami through that area at the end of the 17th Dynasty meant the mud-brick structures seemed to me more likely to be attributable to the 19th Dynasty.

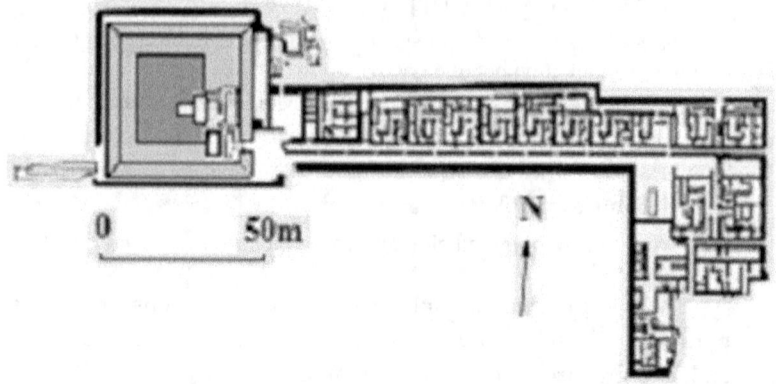

The other thing that stuck with me was that these were the first above-ground, "real" dwellings I had encountered or read about since those on Elephantine Island, before this, they were all determined to be mastabas or tombs. My trips to Meidum, Dahshur, and especially Saqqara, changed my thinking on that!

Khentkaus's tomb is actually neither a pyramid nor a mastaba:

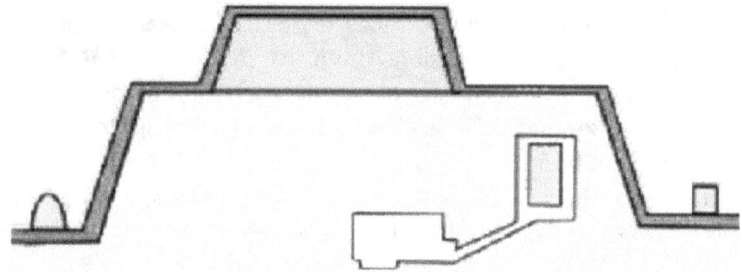

"It was cut out of the natural bedrock into the shape of a cube, the surrounding stone used for the nearby pyramids. This cube was encased in white limestone with a slope of about 74°, the same as the layers of some earlier step pyramids, and topped with a slightly vaulted structure built in masonry."

I had a different theory; the subterranean chambers were constructed before the pole shift, and, when the water gushed through, it carved out the wadi alongside the original subterranean chambers. Then, at a much later date, the exterior was carved into its current shape and the stone 'mastaba' constructed on top. Whether this was done during the reign of Khentkaus, or rather dynasties earlier, and Khentkaus usurped the structure, was undeterminable.

"The entrance, located in the South corner of the substructure's East face, opens to a chapel consisting of a main hall and an inner shrine; the floor covered in Tura limestone. The walls were covered in reliefs, however, like most of the tomb's internal structure, they were very badly damaged in ancient times."

By ancient, did they mean by a tsunami that flooded the area around 1600 BC, or were they referring to human intervention? Without seeing it for myself it was hard to be sure, but just looking at the state of the rock and pillars made me lean towards the tsunami.

"A 5.6 m long passage cut in the floor of the inner chapel, and lined with red granite, leads down below the main structure of the pyramid to the burial chamber, which is large and resembles the burial chamber of Shepseskaf in Saqqara. The burial chamber, also lined with granite, possibly housed an alabaster sarcophagus, as many pieces were found in the sand and debris filling the chamber.

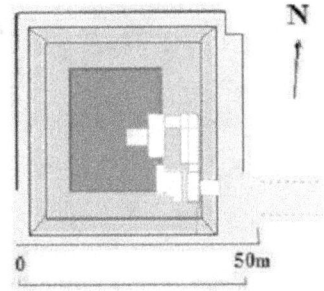

A small scarab made of a brown limestone, and believed to be from the 12th Dynasty, was also found in the chamber, leading some to believe that Khentkaus's tomb was reused for other later tombs."

Well, I think that's a given, even Jack the blind miner could work that out.

The caravan plodded on, towards the Valley Temple of Khafre, past Khentkaus, and through another section of the plateau filled with numerous 'underground' dwellings, many of which were not only carved out of the bedrock, but lacked any form of markings or ornamentation.

Others were extended and augmented with limestone and other materials, all showing faint signs of various decorative hieroglyphs; who knows when any of them were first carved out of the stone? But one thing was certain, there was no way this was conceived as a necropolis; it looked more like the layered terraces of seaside resorts in Spain, Italy or Greece!

As soon as we arrived beside the Valley Temple our guides brought the caravan to a halt and everyone started to dismount; it was 6:49am, the sun was slowly climbing in the east, and it seemed this was the end of the ride. I bid farewell to Geraldine and joined Bill in slipping the guides a little extra baksheesh; tourists had been few and far between and Bill wanted to give them enough to tide them over for at least the next few months.

Large blocks of limestone and granite were strewn across the ground to either side of what I first thought was a raised limestone walkway about eight-feet wide, running parallel to, and about ten metres from, the temple wall. I quickly figured out it was not a walkway at all but rather the lower section of what was once a massive perimeter wall that surrounded the temple and made from enormous limestone blocks that must have weighed a hundred ton or more each; this was going to be interesting.

The Pyramid Complex of Khafre

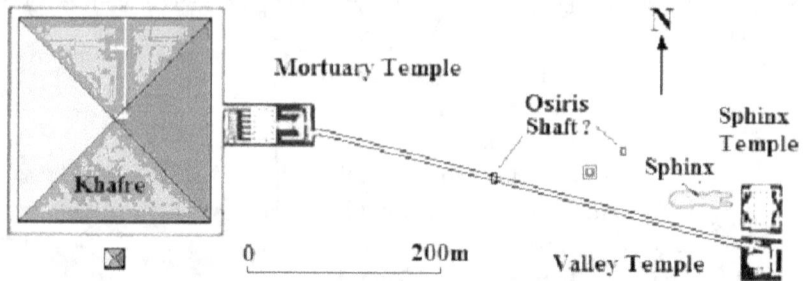

Mortuary Temple

Osiris Shaft ?

Sphinx Temple

N

Sphinx

Khafre

0   200m

Valley Temple

Having been met by the local guardian, we all made our way around to the entrance of the temple, which was fronted by a large terrace paved with limestone slabs. Scattered around the terrace were numerous large blocks of limestone and granite.

Running across the terrace were two causeways that led from what would have been the Nile, or a canal running off it, to each of the two temple entrances.

"The causeways passed over tunnels, framed with mud-brick walls and paved with limestone, and with a slightly convex profile, that formed a narrow north-south corridor or canal."

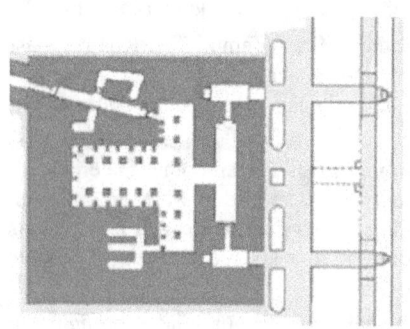

I scratched my head trying to figure it all out; were the causeways built over the channel, or was the channel built under the causeways, and, in either case, why? It made sense that if you were to build the channel first, it would be level, however the channel ducked under each of the two causeways so it musty have been a later addition, and the fact it wasn't level meant it wasn't for water, it was for people, which raised the issue of why an "underground" corridor was needed, other than for covert reasons.

Aligned east-west, the temple was almost square, its core walls built of huge blocks of limestone, now heavily weathered, that must have weighed as much as one-hundred-and-fifty tons. The inner core was covered with slabs of red granite, no doubt quarried from Aswan. Bill was standing beside the outer wall, running his hands over the slightly-inclined lower level of granite slabs that remained.

'Hey, Alex, massive blocks of red granite, you know what that means?'
'Yep, pre pole shift.'

The others were all filing into the temple; it was time for me for me to do likewise.

"The two temple entrances were sealed by huge, single-leaf doors, probably made of cedar wood and hung on copper hinges. Each of the doorways was protected by a Sphinx, the northern-most dedicated to the goddess Bastet, the southern dedicated to Hathor."

The sphinx's probably sat in the niches about five metres above the ground, if that was in fact what the niches were originally for, and not just usurped.

Leading from the two entrances into the Valley Temple was a long, north-south antechamber, its walls lined with polished red granite and its floor paved with white alabaster. Just inside the northern entrance, a 'shaft' in the floor had been turned into a makeshift wishing well; no doubt a passive scam concocted by the local guardians to coerce tourists into parting with their money. Was the shaft originally part of the antechamber? It was hard to tell: probably.

The antechamber led to the heart of the temple, a T-shaped hall adorned with sixteen monolithic red-granite pillars, several of which looked they had broken at the bases and been restored. Totally devoid of any decoration, yet remarkably well preserved, straight away the Valley Temple reminded me of the Osireion at Abydos, the perpendicular antechamber, the row of five pairs of monolithic red-granite pillars down the centre of the main hall; the only thing missing was the shallow rectangle in the centre of the floor that probably held a massive altar.

The pillars supported an architrave of similarly massive blocks of red granite that would have supported the roof. In the centre of it all, the ladies had gathered together and were toning. Not sure if we were invited or not, Bill and I hovered around the outer parts of the hall. Like the antechamber, the walls of the main hall were also sheathed with slabs of polished red granite and the floors paved with white alabaster. Amid all the red granite, I was surprised to find a solitary slab of black granite, in the shape of a trapezium, used in the lower section of one of the walls.

I put my hands on it and did a little toning of my own, tuning in to the stone. Within a few breaths Nemo appeared behind the stone in a dark descending staircase; it seemed the black slab was a door. Before I could venture down and explore where it led, Bill called me over.

'Hey, Alex, what do you make of this?'

I wandered over to where Bill was looking at the floor; there was a row of rectangular depressions evenly spaced along the wall and around the hall.

'My guess is that there were once statues in here.'

Bill slapped by shoulder.

'Dah! There were, twenty-four of them, supposedly all representations of Khafre, made from diorite, slate and alabaster. But that's not what I was talking about. I'm talking about the floor, or rather the floors, "plural".'

'There's two floors! There's another floor underneath.'

'My thinking exactly...'

Bill took off on an inner lap of the hall, checking out each of the statue holes enroute.

'...It's clear that the upper floor, the one of alabaster that involved the statues, has been laid over the top of a previous floor that appears to be made of red granite.'

'Just like the floors in the inner sanctuaries at Dendera and at Edfu.'

'That's right, it is. And if the current alabaster floor dates back to the Old Kingdom, to the 4th Dynasty, then that means the floor beneath must be earlier, but how much earlier? And why the need to "resurface" it?'

'Do you think it's because, just like in the Osireion, there's actually a recessed rectangle in the middle of the floor where an altar once stood?'

'If there is, and there was an altar there, it might explain why the ladies have paused here to have a little choir meeting.'

There being nine of them, the ladies started to make complex harmonies, every now and then creating one that caused the group to shimmer and the space within the temple to vibrate and 'come to life'. Each time they created a certain combination, a certain harmony, I noticed how the group seemed to glow and shadowy white spectres appeared in and over each of them, like they were expanding into ten-foot higher versions of themselves. That's what it was; I could see their higher consciousnesses, like the outer shells of nine Russian dolls.

Following the statue spaces, Bill and I had made our way around to the south end of the 'T', where, opposite the black door, a 'real' doorway led into the south side of the temple. Unfortunately, entry was blocked by a modern locked gate.

'I wonder what's in there they don't want us to see?'

'No dramas.'

"The line of statues continues along the cross of the T-shaped hall ending at a doorway that leads to a corridor and three storage chambers, and from which a ramped stairway winds clockwise up and over the top of the corridor to the roof. On the south side of the roof was a small courtyard, situated directly over six storage chambers also built of pink granite and arranged in two stories of three units each, embedded in the core masonry of limestone. Symbolic conduits lined in alabaster, run from the temple's roof courtyard down into the deep, dark chambers below, and run through the entire temple."

'Any thoughts?'

'No.'

'You?'

'Store rooms? Light shafts? Air shafts?'

Both in the dark, we moved on, following the ladies, who had concluded their rehearsal and were now flowing like a wisp of white smoke out of the temple westward via the opposing corridor at the northern end of the 'T'.

The passage, paved in alabaster, led past two more locked gates, one to either side; the one to the right presumably a staircase up, and the other, to the left, which was of more interest to me, presumably led to a staircase down, that led to ????…an extensive underground network of ancient tunnels perhaps?

The Causeway

The western end of the passage opened onto a causeway, the main one at Giza, attributed to Khafre, running about five-hundred metres from the Valley Temple up the slope to Khafre's Mortuary Temple and pyramid.

Stepping out onto the causeway, off to the right we were greeted by the Sphinx, gazing mystically off to the east; the Great Pyramid over its shoulder in the distance. The poor old thing looked like it'd had more patch jobs than a favourite hand-me-down family teddy.

I wanted to find a way down into the enclosure and have a good sticky-beak around, however, it seemed the plan was to bypass the Sphinx and save it as a special treat for after our time in the Great Pyramid, so I snapped a few shots and moved on.

Like the causeways at Abusir and Abu Ghurab, despite what the Egyptologists speculated, there appeared to be no significance to its east-south-east direction, or to it detouring because the Valley Temple was built out of alignment due to the presence of the sphinx; it could have just as easily gone directly east and to the left of the Sphinx, but it didn't. My guess was the causeway didn't run exactly along the east-west axis of the pyramid and mortuary temple because it quite simple ran directly to what would have been the water's edge when the valley temple was built.

"Archaeologists believe the causeway was probably a covered corridor built of limestone and lined on its exterior by pink granite blocks. Within, it may have been decorated with reliefs."

Now *that* was interesting. My take was that if it *was* lined with red granite, then it confirmed the whole complex was pre pole shift, because why would you make a simple causeway out of limestone, then line it with a 'high-end' finish such as red granite, unless there was some functional purpose for the granite being there. I also felt that the lining, just like with the Valley Temple, would not only have been on the exterior, but it may well have lined the interior. Of course, there was always the possibility the causeway was *still* a tunnel, and what we were trekking on was the roof.

As to there being reliefs, if there were, my thinking was the reliefs were probably dynastic additions carved into the limestone. But the obvious elephant in the room was that the walls and ceiling were gone, some might suggest pilfered away to build the local mosque, I would suggest that was *after* they had been knocked over and washed across the Giza plateau by the tsunami.

Looking back and to the left, to the rear of the Valley Temple, I noticed a large opening in the rear wall, right of centre, which was clearly a doorway; there was no sign of it from the inner hall. Doorways have a habit of leading from somewhere *to* somewhere else and this was a very big and prominent doorway. Was it part of one of the six 'store-rooms', or did it indicate something else?

Given the rear wall was completely of limestone, did it mean the whole rear section of the temple was missing, swept away, and that the Valley Temple was possibly even more similar to the structure of the Osireion, with an antechamber at each end? Was there also once a trench running around the perimeter of the inner hall, beneath where the statues had been placed?

That got me thinking in the other direction; did that mean there was an as yet to be discovered causeway and pyramid complex somewhere in the desert to the west of the Osireion? Surely Herschel's star maps would hold a clue, that is, if they stretched back up the Nile that far.

While I had my head in the stars, meanwhile Bill was looking around, including off to the right and back to the rear of the Sphinx.

'What are you looking at, Bill?'

'The ass of the Sphinx.'

'I didn't know you were that way inclined.'

'Look who's talking, I've noticed you appreciate a nice piece of ass just as much as I do, if not more.'

We both looked ahead on the causeway to Crystal and Pernille.

'Guilty as charged! But what's the big attraction to the Sphinx's ass?'

'Back in the 1930's, there was a guy called Baraize who was responsible for excavating the Sphinx and making repairs. In the course of his work, he discovered two apparently dead-end subterranean passages, the entrances located at the Sphinx's rear, just north of centre, and the other on the northern flank. He took heaps of photos, sealed the entrances with blocks and cement, and they were pretty much forgotten until the late 1970's when the SRI conducted research using resistivity technology and the rear shaft was rediscovered, along with several other anomalies.'

'The SRI?'

'SRI International; once known as the Stanford Research Institute. They're an independent, non-profit research institute based in California.'

'California again, and independent; are we talking Illuminati here?'

'Is the Pope a Catholic?'

'What did they find?'

'They didn't actual do any excavations, but the shaft was investigated in 1980 by Hawass and Mark Lehner, who reported the shaft went up and down but led nowhere.'

'Mark Lehner, I've heard of him, he's an Egyptologist, right?'

'A pretty famous one at that; he's a part of AERA, the Ancient Egypt Research Associates.'

'Are they associated with the Cayce group, ARCE, the American Research Centre in Egypt?

'I believe they are.'

'Then if Lehner is buddies with Hawass, and connected to ARCE, that says it all; Lehner must be Illuminati as well?'

'Unfortunately, I tend to agree; to have the access he has, Lehner must be, either that, or he's an innocent puppet.'

'So, do you think Hawass and Lehner are lying about the shaft?'

'Either they are, or Borris Said is, and my money is on the former.'

'Borris Said?'

'Doctor Borris Said actually. According to a tomograph scan done by him, there's a tunnel running from a seven-metre-deep shaft at the rear of the Sphinx that leads directly to a room in the middle of the Khafre causeway, most likely the Osiris Shaft, and from there on to Khafre's pyramid.'

'The Osiris Shaft, the one discovered by Hawass?'

'Actually Hawass didn't discover it, the opening and first two levels were found back in the 1930s, Hawass was just the first to fully excavate it, to pump out the water from the third level.'

I saw a large opening up the slope and to the right of the causeway.

'Is that is over there?'

'No, that's too big, I think that's Campbell's Tomb; it was discovered and excavated back in the 1830s. It took several years to dig out the sand, but eventually they found an almost square shaft, about nine metres by eight metres, and more than thirty metres deep, surrounded on all sides by a deep trench; that adds up to at least ten-thousand ton of limestone dug out!'

'It must have been important. Did they find anything else other than a deep hole?'

'At what they thought was the bottom, they discovered a number of sarcophagi, interestingly enough, now that I think of it, one of them was made of basalt and is now in the British Museum. But the excavation apparently only revealed the upper parts of the tomb, which consisted of a secondary burial generally agreed to be from the 26th Dynasty.'

'And the lower level, or levels?'

'I don't remember reading anything about them ever being excavated?'

'But I'm sure they were.'

'They had to have been.'

I wondered if that was what Mark's associates caught Hawass removing from beneath the plateau back in April 2010. The vulture strikes again!

'And the Osiris Shaft?'

'Although there are some reports are it's supposed to be about thirty metres down the slope from Campbell's Tomb, which would put it over...there!...'

He pointed directly north of where the caravan was, to another anomalous excavation.

'...Hawass, on the other hand, says the opening to the Osiris Shaft lies near the western wall of a north-south tunnel that runs under Khafre's causeway, which correlates Said's claim and would mean its somewhere up there.'

Now he was pointing in the direction we were heading. Suddenly something

Frank had showed me came to mind.

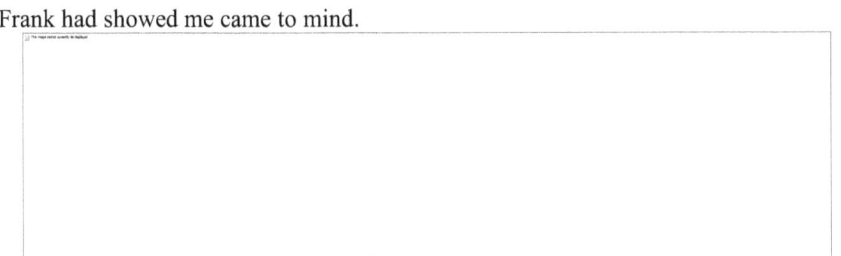

'Actually, Bill, Frank showed me a series of ground penetrating radar scans of the plateau done in 2006; I'm sure they also indicated there was a shaft was about half way up the slope, directly under the causeway, and particularly in line with the centre of the Great Pyramid?'

'You may well be right, but I bet there's hundreds of undiscovered tomb shafts here on the Giza Plateau.'

'You think the other directions could be a red herring to throw people like us off the trail?'

'It's possible.'

'Let me check.'

Loading my iphone up with pdf files on ancient Egypt before I left was the best move I had made; a few flicks and once again I had the information I needed.

The Osiris Shaft

'The "Tomb of Osiris" was excavated in 1933–34 by Dr Selim Hassan, who reported; "Upon the surface of the causeway they built a platform in the shape of a mastaba, using stones taken from the ruins of the covered corridor of the causeway. In the centre of this superstructure they sank a shaft, which passed through the roof and floor of the subway running under the causeway to a depth of about nine metres".'

'That's very telling, I read somewhere that Giza's been under close scrutiny by the Egyptian authorities since Hassan's time, and yet, though Hassan's report mentions some sort of superstructure in the shape of a mastaba, Hawass doesn't mention it at all, and, looking up ahead, I can't see anything even vaguely like a mastaba on the causeway, so, what happened to it?'

'Harvested to build houses?'

'I don't think so, not in the 20th Century. It means the entrance to the Osiris Shaft must be directly beneath the causeway up ahead, and definitely not the one over there east of Campbell's Tomb.'

'It sure does, and it also raises the question of whether the tomb was deliberately built through and under the causeway, or if the causeway was built over the top of the previously existing subterranean chambers.'

'Now that *is* a good question. What came first the chicken or the egg? It makes no sense to dig the shaft through the causeway, they could just as easily have dug it to either side, nor does it make sense to build a causeway over an existing subterranean chamber.'

'Unless you didn't know it was there?'

'Good point.'

'What do you make of the subway they dug through?'

'Nothing extraordinary, I think that's what Hawass was referring to, a small tunnel, an underpass, burrowed beneath the causeway as a shortcut for people get from one side of the causeway to the other; Hawass found another one under the ruins of the causeway of the Khufu Pyramid.'

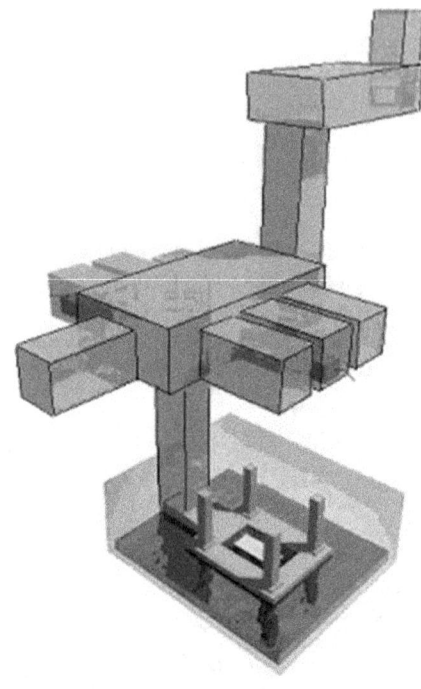

'Which pretty much reinforces the causeway was not for people, or else they would simply have put a doorway in, a crossing, right? Clearly the causeway was intended to transport something impervious to people traffic, something like water for instance.'

'Agreed! The question is, why didn't they just start digging down from the floor of the subway? Why would you need to dig down through the causeway as well?'

'Maybe the answer is under the ground?'

I flicked the page.

'At the bottom of the first shaft is a rough-cut rectangular chamber thirteen feet wide, twenty-eight feet long, and nine feet high; empty. In the floor of the eastern side is another shaft that descends about fourteen metres and terminates in a spacious chamber twelve feet wide, twenty-two feet long, and seven feet high, which was probably the original chamber. At some later stage it was expanded with the addition of seven smaller burial-chambers off three of the walls, each of which contains a sarcophagus.

OK, two questions, how did they lower the sarcophagi down there, and second, how did they get them into the side chambers? I can go with them being lowered down, just, but how do you slot a massive block weighing several ton into a closed space?'

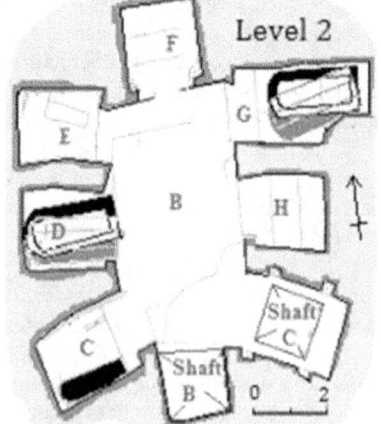

Bill had started "thinking".
'Wooden rollers perhaps?'

I wasn't so easily convinced.
'Let's just say the jury's out.'

'Yes, they are. Those notes you were reading, they're from Hassan's report, right?'

I double checked.
'Yep, from 1944, but I have a diagram by Hawass.'

I handed it across to Bill who nodded and went further into one of his "deep-thinking" modes.

'According to Hawass, there were only three sarcophagi found, two of them made of monolithic basalt and containing badly decomposed skeletal remains, whereas Hassan said there were seven, which no doubt included the sarcophagus he had seen in the lower, third level. That means that somewhere between say 1935 and 1999 at least three sarcophagi have just disappeared.'

He handed back the iphone.

'You think Hawass stole them?'

'Does a bear shit in the woods? He was at Giza from what, 1972? If it wasn't him it must have been the tooth fairy or the Easter bunny.'

'Couldn't it just as easily have been Hassan, couldn't he have been on the take as well?'

'Of course, no one gets a concession to excavate in Egypt unless they come under the umbrella of the Illuminati masters.'

'Oh, Randy would love all this. But couldn't the sarcophagi have been removed during the Second World War, or the six-day war, or anytime since 1935?'

'Sure, but I doubt it. I think it was a question of technology and visibility; the Giza Plateau was too public, that was until Hawass put the walls up in 1999. Suddenly he starts excavating the Osiris Shaft, clearing the second level and pumping the water out of the third level.'

'More than just a coincidence.'

'Hawass says he cleaned out all the side chambers and that all he discovered, apart from the skeletal remains, were some shards of pottery, ceramic beads, and shabtis, and, that based on stylistic grounds, they were all dated to the 26th Dynasty.'

'You believe Hawass?'

'About the remains he said they found belonging to the 26th Dynasty, sure, about everything else, about as far as I could throw a fully grown blue whale.'

Fortunately I had more notes on the shaft.

'Well; listen to this, it's by someone who supposedly snuck down into the Osiris Shaft after Hawass had pumped it out, and put his observations and photos up on a website.

"The room to the left had space for the sarcophagus of a child. Next, I found an enormous black sarcophagus leaping out of the left middle room, large enough for a bull. It was a magnificent, majestic work of art, and stood in excellent condition; its lid slightly opened, revealing the sarcophagus was empty."'

'Don't get too excited, Alex, that's pretty much what Hawass said, and obviously the skeletal remains had been removed..'

'Hawass didn't say anything about a sarcophagus for a child though.'

'True; maybe he removed it shortly after, besides all your visitor says is that he saw "the space" for a child's sarcophagus.'

'What about this? *"It also looked as if there might be a further entrance behind it".*'

'Is there a photo?'

'No.'

'Then what looked like an entrance could have been a shadow, a further niche, or maybe it was an entrance to somewhere else, or maybe your visitor was projecting what he wanted to see.'

I held up the iphone for Bill to see.

'What about this photo, look at the ledge of the niche, doesn't that make rollers unlikely.'

'Not really, you just use different diameter ones, then lever the end of the sarcophagus up to remove them. Getting them out would be a reverse of the process.'

'And that's where Hawass comes in, when he pumped the water out of the lowest level.'

'If the third level *is* the lowest level; who knows for sure.'

'You think there's more?'

'Possibly.'

I went back to my notes.

'Hassan's report says that through the clear water in the lower level he could see *"a colonnaded hall with side chambers containing sarcophagi"*.'

'That's interesting; Hawass didn't say anything about side chambers or sarcophagi "plural". I think it's the third level that holds the most interest.'

'According to Hawass's notes, *"there are seven little niches carved into the walls around the opening to the third shaft"*, which he believes were used as anchor points for wooden braces used to lower a sarcophagus down the shaft to the lowest chamber.'

'I agree, but I think the sarcophagus they lowered may have been the one originally in the second level, before the additional niches were excavated.'

'That makes sense.'

We reached the mid-point of the causeway where it aligned with the centre of the Great Pyramid, a neat 'hole' cut into the ground and a slab to one side.

'By my reckoning we should be right over it.'

'The Osiris Shaft?! Under here?...'

Suddenly I couldn't pass up the opportunity to at least check it out for myself.

'...Stop the world I want to get off!'

The message rapidly filtered through to Diane who brought the whole procession to a halt.

'What is it, Alex?'

I waved them off.

'It's OK, you all go on and I'll catch up with you at the top end of the causeway, next to Khafre's pyramid, or before you reach the entrance to the Great Pyramid.'

Bill decided to come with me.

'I can't let you go wandering around on your own, you might fall down an unknown tomb shaft and be lost forever, then who am I going to get to write about the missing wreck at the bottom of the Mediterranean?'

We bid the ladies adieu and they plodded on, leaving Bill and I perched atop the causeway. I immediately started looking down the first shaft and around for signs of the mastaba, while Bill headed straight off the beaten path, looking for the 'subway'.

'Here it is.'

I clambered down to join him, following inside as electrical cables led the way along the floor to halfway through the tunnel where the shaft penetrated the causeway and a barred section and locked gate marked the location of the entrance to the Osiris Shaft. I rattled the door and tried the lock.

'Damn it! No go.'

Beyond the gate, the cables, along with a ladder, disappeared down the shaft and into the depths of the Giza Plateau; clearly there was still work going on down below.

Looking around, I noticed, at the top of the barrier, several bars were bent back, obviously by someone eager to either see the subterranean chambers without authorization, or, more likely, to do a spot of opportunistic treasure hunting.

I looked at Bill, raising my eyebrows at the possibility of making an unauthorized visit of our own, and he was quick to respond.

'Don't even consider it! If you think I'm going to get through that gap let alone climb up there, you've lost your marbles. And if you think I'm going to let *you* do it, you're even crazier; God knows what would happen if you got caught.'

'I wonder what's *really* down there?'

As I looked for information on my phone, Bill knelt down and drew a picture in the sand.

'The tomb is about a hundred feet down and more architecturally complex than the previous chambers. Rough-cut, it's approximately thirty-feet square, and, around the edge is a narrow ledge carved into the rock. In the centre is a large rock-carved rectangular 'island', with a trench running around it that seems to have been deliberately designed so that the groundwater would fill it, and which, during Hawass's excavations, remained filled with water.

At the four corners of the island are the remains of four rough-cut, square pillars, now almost completely destroyed. In the centre of the island, a shallow pit had been excavated that contains a basalt sarcophagus, the lid of which was found in the floor of the shaft indicating someone had been down there previously, before the chamber was flooded.'

'And, as we know, basalt is probably connected to the pre pole shift civilization.'

'Except that skeletal remains were found inside the sarcophagus, which, together with amulets and other artefacts found at Level 3, all dated to the 26th Dynasty.'

'That just proves the tomb was probably just usurped?'

'Oh, I'm sure it was...'

Bill got to his feet.

'...In fact Hawass believes the Osiris Shaft is what Herodotus was referring to when he said, *"Khufu was buried on an island in an underground chamber, located in the shadow of the Great Pyramid and fed by a canal from the Nile".'*

'You think this was once the tomb of Khufu, and not the Great Pyramid?'

'Probably, the Great Pyramid certainly wasn't a tomb.'

'Agreed. I don't think any of them were.'

'Come on, we'd better catch up with the girls.'

Bill walked back out of the tunnel and, very reluctantly, after one last wistful look back down the shaft, I followed him. As we made our way through the ruins, my mind was still ticking over.

'But even Khufu could have had his tomb usurped by a succession of pharaohs, right up to the 26th Dynasty.'

'True, and that's what doesn't make sense, because it would imply the causeway, which was built over the top of the tomb, was built after the 26th Dynasty, and we know that's not the case. Which brings us to the most interesting unexplored feature of the tomb.'

'And that is?'

'There's a narrow carved tunnel in the northwest corner of the chamber that extends twenty-odd metres in the direction of the Great Pyramid. Initially it's barely large enough for a child to crawl through, and further along, about six metres in, a branch splits off. A remote camera was sent ten metres into the branch before it became too narrow and muddy for the rover to go any further. Hawass says the tunnel follows a natural fissure in the rock and that there are no networks of secret passageways; I'm not so sure.'

I double-checked my notes as Bill led the way through the ruins and on towards Khafre's pyramid. I flicked back to my other page.

'Hey Bill, what do you make of this? *"The water in the tomb was illuminated from underneath. It showed that below the stone sarcophagus, and below the water, is another stone sarcophagus, shiny blue in colour. Underneath that sarcophagus is a huge cleared vertical shaft submerged in water. Off that shaft are tunnels going west to the middle pyramid, and east to the Sphinx. What is below that is not known."*

'Now that's *very* interesting. Add to that the fact that the sarcophagus has apparently been carbon dated and the results are so off the accepted Egyptological chronology that they're not being released, and you have a inconsistency of evidence that can't, or won't, be explained by Hawass or his clutch of Egyptologists.'

'I didn't think you could carbon-date rock.'

'You can't, but apparently when the layer of dirt was removed from lid of the sarcophagus they found ingrown shells, like coral, embedded into the basalt; they must have carbon-dated the coral.'

'You're right, that *would* be interesting.'

And then, I heard a noise that caught my attention.

'Hey, Bill, do you hear that?'

'What?'

'That humming noise.'

He focused his attention, but it was barely audible, and at first I thought maybe I was hearing things, but then I heard it again.

'That! Hear it?'

'That low pitched sort of droning sound?'

'Yes, what do you make of it?'

'It reminds me of the sound you make when you blow across the top of a bottle, just much lower; you can hardly hear it.'

I zeroed in on the direction of its origin, further west, from a group of dwellings half-buried beneath the sand.

'It's coming from somewhere over there.'

We altered course, heading past several buildings filled with rubble and, most of all, sand. It was unbelievable to think that most people were led to believe the Giza Plateau consisted of three big pyramids and the Sphinx, but little else; clearly there was a hell-of-a-lot more here worthy of exploring, almost all of it below the surface.

The buildings reminded me a lot of the images I had seen of the abandoned and desolate ruins of Pompeii and Herculeum, although instead of being buried in ash, Giza was buried in sand. There were also parts that looked like Swiss cheese, strange intertwining shafts and chambers forming a honeycomb effect; the sound was coming from them. As the breeze was gently blowing across and through the cavities it was producing a low-pitched humming sort of sound.

'That's a Helmholtz resonance.'

'A what?'

'A Helmholtz resonance; it's the phenomenon of air resonance in a cavity, like an ocarina, or when you blow across the top of an empty bottle.'

'Do you think its deliberate, or just accidental?'

'I don't think there's anything "accidental" on, or under, the Giza Plateau. Maybe they used these buildings and shafts the same way honeycombed cavities are used as Helmholtz resonators in architectural acoustics?'

'How would that help?'

'By building a resonator tuned to the problem frequency you can reduce undesirable low frequency sounds, even eliminate them. If the pyramids were resonators attuned to specific frequencies, then other frequencies would interfere with their function; I suppose the shafts and chambers were used as a massive earth-based isolators or acoustic insulation for the pyramids.'

'Bill, if that isn't the most far-fetched idea I'd heard on the trip, it's certainly close to it. But, given everything else I'd discovered or heard on this trip, it makes total sense. The problem is, how would you test it?'

We made our way up to the top end of the causeway, where the ladies were just finishing their exploration of the Mortuary Temple that sat just east of Khafre's Pyramid. Now it was our turn.

The Mortuary Temple of Khafre

The causeway entered the mortuary temple near the southern end of its eastern facade. The core of the temple was built of megalithic blocks of limestone, the largest an estimated four hundred tonnes. Alas, most of it was in ruin, though, now having a fair idea of the basic structure of these temples, it was still possible to make out its rectangular floor plan.

The entrance led through to a small antechamber, once adorned with a pair of monolithic red-granite pillars, and flanked by several small chambers, two granite chambers immediately to the left of the entrance, and, at the other end of a short corridor running along the front of the temple, four more chambers lined with alabaster. The erosion to the limestone was obvious and extensive.

'Alex?'

'Definitely water damage. Definitely pre pole shift'

The antechamber led to a transverse hall, with recessed bays, which once contained fourteen massive granite pillars similar to those in the Valley Temple. At either end of the hall were two long, narrow chambers. The transverse hall led to a rectangular second entrance hall that once had an additional five pairs of granite pillars.

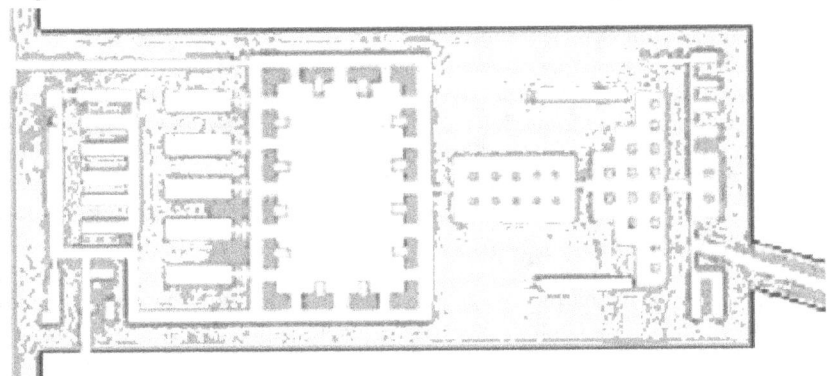

Beyond the entrance halls was once a large, open courtyard situated in approximately the middle of the temple; virtually nothing remained so Bill headed right and I went left.

"Oriented north-south, and paved in slabs of alabaster, along its sides once ran a covered ambulatory with a flat limestone roof made of slabs supported by broad pillars of pink granite. The lower part of this ambulatory was formed by a dado in red granite and limestone and covered by brilliantly coloured reliefs, of which only fragments remain."

Five, long niche chapels were next, and, beyond that, five 'store rooms'. While Bill, who was eager to catch up with the ladies, took a corridor that led from the northwest corner of the courtyard directly to the paved pyramid enclosure, I took a southern corridor that led to a long narrow north-south offering hall located in the west part of the temple that contained a false door positioned on the west wall, precisely on the pyramid's long axis. I met up with Bill.

'I find it hard to accept this was originally designed as a mortuary temple.'

'I'm with you on that; I'm even more convinced the structure had some functional connection to the real purpose of the pyramid.'

Khafre's pyramid was once surrounded by a huge, stone perimeter wall, a length of which was clearly visible to the south and comprised massive blocks maybe ten metres long.

Within the walls and around the pyramid was an open courtyard about ten metres wide, paved with irregular-shaped slabs of limestone, which encompassed the four sides of the pyramid. I knew now the irregular shaped stones were part of a advanced plan to reduce vibration. Rather than head straight after the ladies, who were now heading off along the south side of the Great Pyramid, I decided to do a quick lap clockwise around Khafre's pyramid.

After a little concern about my diverting from the agenda, Bill, who had unofficially assumed the role of my bodyguard, tagged along.

'It looks like the girls are taking the long way around, so as long as we're not too long; five minutes max.'

I hustled around to the south side, where, aligned with the centre of the pyramid, were some core blocks and, around them, the twenty-metre square outline of the foundation of the remains of an almost completely destroyed small binary pyramid, which, in turn, was once originally surrounded by its own enclosure wall. Bill was right behind me.

'Do you have any notes about the substructure?'

A quick flick on the iphone.

'Khafre's satellite pyramid has a simple substructure consisting of a descending corridor that leads to an underground chamber with a T-shaped ground plan. Possibly for one of Khafre's consorts, the tomb contained bits of wood, pieces of ritualistic furniture, carnelian beads, fragments of animal bones and vessel lids.'

'Nothing about red granite though?'

'Nope. But I wonder if the location of the binary pyramid relevant to the main pyramid has any significance?'

'What do you mean?'

'Some of the binary pyramids are to the southwest, some to the southeast, others are situated to the northeast; this one is directly south?'

'Maybe it's some reference to their orbital direction around the main star relative to the galactic centre?'

'Bill, that's brilliant, if they do a study and prove it's true, you might get a Nobel Prize for science.'

'If we don't get back to the girls by the time they head inside the Great Pyramid, I might need another one, for peace.'

We moved on to the western side of the pyramid only to find it was fenced off, supposedly because of the danger of falling stones, which were strewn across the courtyard. Suddenly, Bill was in his element.

'Look at how the layered limestone of the Nummelite Bank has been cut away and reinforced with mud-brick to form the perimeter wall. And look at the erosion underneath, it's definitely not because of wind and sand, that sort of erosion is caused by large quantities of water.'

I initially thought Bill's reference to the 'Nummelite Bank' might have been to some ancient Egyptian treasury built into the wall. That's when I noticed something, rather innocuous at first, but then extremely unusual; not that there were entrances in and *under* the perimeter wall, but that they had electric cables going in, and an air conditioner. I pointed it out to Bill.

'What do you make of that, Bill?'

He dragged himself away from manhandling the wall and turned his attention to the barred 'window'.

'Hmmm, must be important; the only need for an air conditioner would be if you were spending lots of time very deep beneath the surface. I wonder what's in there, and why the officials haven't told us anything about it?'

'You know the answer to that; there must be something valuable down there.'

'Or something they don't want us to know about.'

'Such as an underground network of tunnels.'

'Maybe even a forgotten underground city?'

I ignored the signs of falling rocks, and the potential danger, and easily scaled the pyramid to gain access to the western side.

'What are you doing, Alex? What if you get caught?'

'I want to see what the fuss is all about. Besides, the quickest way back to the girls is the most direct route.'

Bill looked around, then quickly followed.

There were several other man-made cavities in the western wall, the majority of which were 'sealed' with piles of blocks and stone. As to the rocks strewn across the courtyard, something didn't make sense.

'Most of these pieces seem to be red granite, which means they would have been part of the lower course of casing stones, and not from the upper casing, which would have been Tura Limestone. So they would hardly have "fallen" say twenty feet and tumbled another sixty.'

'They could have been scattered by stone thieves during their pilfering of the limestone.'

'Or, they could have been deliberately scattered as an excuse to fence off the area from prying eyes.'

'Like the 'wreckage' outside The Pentagon when the 9/11 "jet" supposedly crashed into it?'

'Exactly! And if rocks are falling from the western side, how come it's amazingly only happening from the western face and not the entire pyramid?'

I didn't have any notes on it, but I did find another piece of interesting information.

'Here's a good one for you, Bill. *"West of Khafre's pyramid, beyond the outer perimeter wall, are the ruins of a storehouse that contained long, mostly east-west oriented rooms".*'

'Nothing unusual about that; they could even have been office buildings.'

'Hang five; I'm not finished yet. *"Interestingly, a great number of mollusc shells were found here, suggesting that the surrounding area was, rather than arid desert as it is today, a kind of savannah with the corresponding flora and fauna".*'

'Molluscs, hey, well, there's more proof for your tsunami, unless of course the buildings were an oyster farm. How could they even suggest it was a savannah, really; are they serious?'

We'd reached the northwest corner when Bill, deep in thought, tossed in another bombshell.

'You know, according to Collins, the entrance to Salt's "lost catacombs" is west of the Great Pyramid, which puts it somewhere just over that wall. If the catacombs head down under the ground, which catacombs tend to do, they'd most likely be somewhere behind that wall.

I didn't have anything about it on my iphone, so I logged on to the web.

'What should I search under?'

'Try "Tomb of the Birds".'

Seconds later I pulled up Andrew Collins' website.

'Here it is, the Tomb of the Birds; NC2. NC2?'

'North Cave 2, original isn't it!'

'Dah! Anyway, it says that Collins discovered the lost tomb in January 2007, then returned in March 2008, thanks to sponsorship from ARE, the Association for Research and Enlightenment, in the USA. ARE, isn't that Edgar Cayce's group?'

'Yep.'

'Jesus! Hang on;... *"The rock-cut tomb is generally accepted as being an Old Kingdom construction".*'

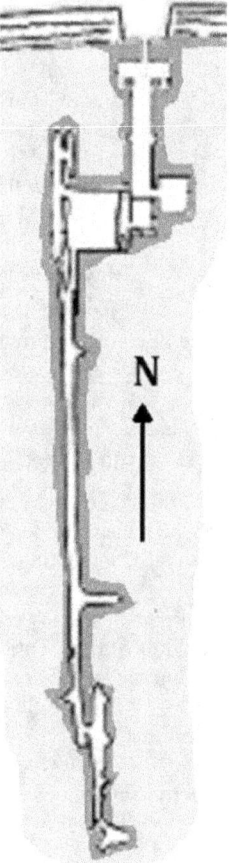

N

'No, it's got to be earlier than that. It may have begun as a natural cavity, and had a façade and tomb dug out during the Old Kingdom, but the caves must have been accessible long before then.'

'What makes you say that?'

'The Giza Plateau is basically limestone, which, over time, gets dissolved by the Carbon Dioxide content of rainwater that takes the path of least resistance as it traces through natural faults in the bedrock. Clearly there was a time in the past when the plateau was fully saturated, either under water or continuously subjected to torrential rains.'

'Or from a massive tsunami?'

'Possible, but unlikely, as the water would most likely recede fairly quickly. The sort of saturation we're talking about takes place over hundreds, possibly tens-of-thousands of years. Initially, the rainwater would pass through the fissures beneath the water table, carving out phreatic passages and circular caves.'

'Phreatic passages?'

'That's where the water flowing through a fault passes beneath the water table, moves slowly, dissolving the rock, enlarging the cracks and fissures to create circular tube-shaped passages. Then, when the rainfall eased, and the water table fell, the passages became vadose in shape, or V-shaped, meaning they were eroded by the flowing water rather than dissolved, and that's what we see in the caves below Giza.'

'How do you know?'

Eager to keep moving, Bill headed off along the north face of Khafre's pyramid.

'Collins took dozens of photos; you should be able to see them on his website, and those images are supported by some other pretty compelling evidence.'

'Such as?'

'In 1977, the SRI and the Ain Shams University here in Cairo, using ground penetration radar, detected the presence of previously unknown subterranean chambers near Khafre's Pyramid. One was situated beneath Belzoni's Chamber, inside the structure, while another was found six metres deep beneath the pyramid's northwest corner, where they also discovered localized faulting...'

As I followed, Bill, who was muttering away as if on autopilot, he wandered over to the perimeter wall, closely examining the way it had been eroded and reconstructed.

'...Collins backs it all up with radar satellite imagery that shows geological faults that extend hundreds of metres from the position of the tomb to beneath Khafre's Pyramid, precisely where Collins says the tomb and catacombs are.

And yet, despite all this, Hawass first denied the existence of any natural cave system, then went about fitting a metal gate across the entrance and excavating the site himself. And he's still not released any details of what he found.'

'That's no surprise. What are your thoughts about what's inside?'

He made his way across and along to the entrance to Khafre's pyramid.

'Well, according to medieval sources, the Pyramid of Khafre is supposedly the site of the Cave of Hermes.'

'Hermes, the Greek personification of Thoth?'

'The one and only; keeper of ancient records and guardian of ancient wisdom.'

'So what's inside?'

'The cave supposedly contains not only the earthly remains of Thoth, but also the so-called Emerald Tablet on which was written the secrets of creation. Now if the Tomb of the Birds was found to have been filled with thousands of mummified ibises, that would support that speculation, but, until the powers-that-be reopen the Tomb, we may never know.'

We stopped outside Khafre's pyramid briefly taking it all in.

The Pyramid of Khafre

Named "Khafre is Great", with a base of 216 metres and a slope of 53°10', meaning that, even though now the capstone is missing, it once rose to 146 metres; it was definitely impressive. So much so that, although it is smaller and sits on bedrock 10 metres higher than the Great Pyramid, and it has a steeper angle giving it the illusion it appear to be taller, because of its shape, position and remaining upper casing stones, early on I'd often confused it with the Great Pyramid.

And, like the Great Pyramid, and Abu Raoush, it sits on an outcrop of bedrock that was incorporated as part of the core to both increase the stability of the pyramid, as well as to conserve the amount of building materials needed for its construction. However, due to the slope of the plateau, the northwest corner was cut 10 metres into the rock substrata and the bedrock fashioned into 'steps', while the opposing, southeast corner was conversely built up, using mammoth blocks of stone, probably quarried from the northwest.

The base established, the core of the pyramid was then built in horizontal courses of locally quarried limestone blocks, those at the bottom very large, up to 2.5 tons each, and often with no mortar between them, but, as the pyramid rose, the stones became smaller. For the first half of its height, the courses are rough and irregular and do not always run exactly horizontally, but a narrow band of regular masonry is clear in the midsection of the pyramid, possibly to bring the structure back into alignment. However, the four corner angles were not quite aligned correctly to meet the pyramid apex, so there is a very slight twist at the top.

The bottom course of casing stones was made out of blocks of Aswan red granite weighing up to 2.5 tons each, but the remainder of the pyramid was once cased in blocks of Tura Limestone, which became considerably smaller towards the apex, with the top third still remaining.

Looking at the scene before me, it could have been so easy to suggest that most of the casing stones were simply washed away by the tsunami. However, the truth be told, a large part of the pyramid casing, probably from the south face, was removed between 1356 and 1362 for use in the Mosque of al-Hassan. Despite that, most of the casing stones were still in place as late as 1646, when John Greaves, wrote, "the surface was smooth and even, free of breaches of inequalities, except on the south", and have since been harvested to build structures in Cairo.

It was all so surreal. But while the superstructure told part of the story, what I really wanted to know was what was underground.

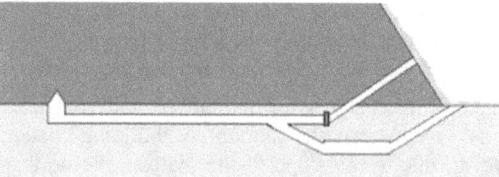

The pyramid had two entrances, offset 12 metres east of centre, both of which apparently led to the burial chamber. One was about 12 metres up the face of the pyramid and the other opened at the base of the pyramid. Bill turned to me.

'Which entrance do you think is the original one?'

'Going by the other pyramids I've seen, the lower one, but I'll check. *"Located 12 metres up the north wall of the pyramid's face, the "upper entrance", discovered by Belzoni in 1818, led to an "upper" descending passage lined in pink granite that descends to join with a horizontal passage at the base of the pyramid and cut from the bedrock".'*

'There's your red granite again.'

'Sure is, and, as expected, there's more. *"At the transitional point where the descending and horizontal sections meet, is a barrier made of pink granite, which grave robbers managed to dig around in antiquity. The passage continues south after the barrier, eventually arriving at the burial chamber, which lies on the vertical axis of the pyramid".*'OK, I've changed my mind, the red granite tells me *this* was the original entrance.'

'And the one here in the ground?'

' *"The oldest of the two entrances is located in the ground to the north of the pyramid."* Well that's wrong for a start. *"Carved completely out of the bedrock, the passageway descends to a horizontal corridor, off which, to the west, is a small chamber, 10.41 x 3.12 x 2.61 high, cut from the bedrock and with a gabled roof, where part of the burial equipment was possibly stored. The horizontal corridor continues on, then ascends to intersect with a horizontal passage, shared by the "upper entrance" that leads to the burial chamber."*

It's pretty obvious that the lower entrance and passage were cut to create a new access to the chamber, probably after something went wrong in the main "burial" chamber.'

'What do your notes say about the burial chamber?'

'Carved out the bedrock, the burial chamber has a rectangular, east-west oriented, 14.15m x 5m x 6.83m high, which places it at a right angle to the passage system. The chamber's gabled ceiling, located above the pyramid's base, is built from enormous pented, limestone blocks.

There are shaft entrances high up in both the north and south walls of the burial chamber that, at first, appear similar to those in the Queen's and King's cambers of the great Pyramid, but are rather short, horizontal openings that could have been used to reinforce a wooden structure inside the tomb.

On the wall of the burial chamber is Arabic graffiti that probably dates from 1372 C.E., and the reign of the Great Emir Jalburgh el-Khassaki, during which the pyramid was apparently opened.'

'I don't think when the pyramid was breached is really important now, more what they found and what they removed.'

'Near the west wall of the burial chamber, almost directly under the vertical axis of the pyramid and sunk partially in the floor, stands a blackened red-granite sarcophagus, in which Belzoni found the bones of an animal, possibly a bull.'

'That's very interesting.'

'The bull bones?'

'No, I'm more interested in the blackened sarcophagus; I'd read somewhere it was made of black granite, but a blackened red-granite sarcophagus would imply some extremely high temperatures. The question is, red or black?'

'The lid of the sarcophagus was found in two pieces close by.'

'Broken or fractured?'

'What's the difference?'

'Broken by vibrational force, or fractured by impact; it could tell a lot about what really went on inside these sarcophagi and chambers.'

'Another small pit in the floor nearby most likely contained the canopic chest. Apart from that, no positively identifiable remains of the king's mummy or his other funerary equipment were found within the pyramid.'

'Because it wasn't a tomb, and I think we both know Khafre didn't build this pyramid.'

Somewhat miffed, Bill walked off, heading towards the Great Pyramid, me right with him.

'The Egyptologists seem pretty sure he did.'

'They've just accepted it as so, even though the evidence is overwhelming that Khafre wasn't responsible.'

'And what evidence is that?'

'Firstly, what evidence *is* there supporting Khafre was the original owner?'

'Ah, I'm not sure.'

'Exactly, because there is none, nothing has been found in or on this pyramid with Khafre's name on it. The only thing found attributable to Khafre was a diorite statue, discovered by Mariette in 1858, of Khafre on his throne with the protective outstretched winds of the falcon god, Horus, sheltering his head from behind. However it was discovered in the Valley Temple, and, as we've discovered, the statues there were probably a much later addition.

The Egyptologists had already made the mistake of tagging the Great Pyramid as belonging to Khufu, so, when they found Khafre's statue in the adjoining Valley Temple, they perpetuated and compounded the error by claiming the Second Pyramid belonged to Khufu's son, Khafre. And that's it. So let's look at the other "evidence".

Firstly, there's a large double mastaba, G 7130-40, in the East section at Giza that belongs to Khafkhufu, which may well have belonged to Khafre before he prematurely assume the throne upon the unexpected death of his elder brother, Djedefre. Second, the Egyptologists claim Khafre deliberately built the Second Pyramid on higher ground and in the central position to outdo his father, despite the conveniently overlooked fact that it was another four years before Menkaure even assumed the throne, let alone built his pyramid, so there was no "central" position.'

'And, assuming the pyramids were built in succession, it totally negates the whole Orion alignment proposition, or if it does take into account the star maps, it means that Sirius, Abu Raoush, should have been built first, before Khufu, and by Snefru, not after by Djedefre.'

'Precisely!'

'All the pyramids had to have been planned, and possibly built, at the same time, otherwise Abu Raoush, being the first and not 'finished', meant the others wouldn't have been started.'

'I like your thinking.'

'And if Khafre really wanted the higher ground, why didn't he just usurp his elder brother, Djedefre's, unfinished pyramid at Abu Raoush?'

'A very good question.'

'I've got a few more. If the position was important, and the higher ground was an issue, why didn't Khufu build his pyramid on the higher ground in the first place, or at Abu Raoush? And if Khafre really wanted to outdo his father, why is the interior of his pyramid so simple?'

'The sort of questions the Egyptologists can't answer, or just fob off.'

We crossed the modern road and headed up through the Great Western Cemetery, if that's what it really was, recently opened after being closed for over a hundred years. It was supposedly the final resting place of 5th Dynasty viziers, high court officials, grand royal architects, and their families. It was somewhere here that a forty-six-hundred-year-old female mummy was discovered, encased in a completely unique plaster 'wrapping' that has never been seen or found anywhere else. That should have raised all sorts of questions for the Egyptologists, but it seemed to have been pushed to one side.

There were fifteen mastabas accessible; the structures all in tidy, well-defined rows, or streets. It amazes me that there hasn't been a single Egyptologist who has questioned the real function of these buildings. Isn't it poignant that no cities, no towns, no houses have been found here of any substance, and yet there are rows upon rows of tombs, tombs built *above* the ground.

One of the "tombs" we past belonged to the vizier and master builder Senedjemib-inty, "Overseer of All Royal Works," who served under Djedkare. We didn't have time to enter any of them, but if they were like the structures at Saqqara it confirmed my thoughts they were not tombs but administration buildings.

Has the 'romantic' notion of discovering "tombs", or labelling obvious dwellings or administration buildings as tombs, over-shadowed logic, common sense and simple observation? It would appear so.

Leaving the Cemetery, we crossed the road and made our way to the Great Pyramid.

'What about the Tomb of Thoth?'

'It's possibly somewhere back *under* "Khafre's" pyramid?'

'At the end of the Tomb of the Birds?'

'Perhaps, more likely even deeper below the second pyramid.'

'You sound like you know something!'

'I know someone does.'

'Who?'

'In more recent times, Mark Lehner and Hawass, under the "auspices" of the American Giza Plateau Mapping Project, set up acoustic sounding equipment in the upper chamber of the second pyramid and detected two large anomalies below it, one twenty-one metres deep and another at thirty-three metres, that were either definite man-made chambers or caverns with strong signatures. Either way, the chambers would be an amazing discovery.

Additional tests in the horizontal passageway revealed the presence of another anomaly about four metres deep, which they thought could be a tunnel or passageway that might lead to the even more chambers.'

'And what have they done?'

'The EAO supposedly gave permission for a small bore hole to be drilled down through the bedrock and a camera inserted to determine whether the subterranean spaces were manmade or not, but unfortunately, no funds were available, so, as far as I know, the anomalies have never been investigated.'

'No funds, seriously?'

'Well, that's what they say.'

'Another cover up.'

That made Bill laugh.

'Alex, you sound too much like a conspiracy theorist.'

'Come on, Bill, if it looks like a duck, walks like a duck and quacks like a duck.'

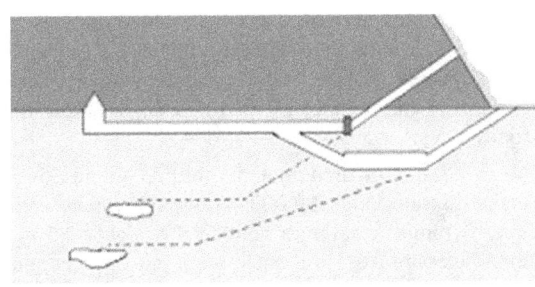

'Then it ain't a flock of seagulls, that's for sure!'

We turned the northwest corner to find the ladies milling around on the ground outside the entrance; it was time to turn my attention to the Great Pyramid.

CHAPTER 31 – THE GREAT PYRAMID

Located in the supposed geographic centre of the land mass of the earth, the Great Pyramid of Khufu covers more then 6 hectares, or 13.5 acres. With a base of 230.38 metres, and a slope of 51°50'40", it originally rose an awe-inspiring 146 metres above the Giza Plateau. The only surviving structure of the Seven Wonders of the Ancient World, "Khufu's Horizon" was constructed from an estimated 2.3 million limestone blocks weighing from 2 to 15 tons each, with an average weight of 2.5 tons; I'd been fascinated by it for years, and I wasn't the only one.

Rather than use metric or imperial measurements, Flinders Petrie, who based his measurements on the work of John Taylor, a 19th Century eccentric Brit and one of the founders of modern Pyramidology, and Professor C. Piazzi Smyth, a British Israelite and the Scottish Astronomer-Royal, suggested, from his survey and studies, that the pyramid was originally 280 cubits high by 440 cubits long at each of the four sides of its base, and there is a lot of evidence supporting the use of the Egyptian cubit, or pyramid inch.

But the reality is, the unit of measurement is perhaps not as relevant as the *ratio* of one measurement to another; the ratio of the perimeter to height of 1760/280 cubits equating to 2π to an accuracy of better than 0.05%, corresponding to the common approximation of π as 22/7. So, clearly sacred geometry was intrinsic to the pyramid's design, and that raised the issue of harmonic relationships as well, but was it a deliberate part of the construction, or an accidental by-product?

According to Herodotus, the Egyptian priests told him the Great Pyramid was built for the pharaoh Cheops, Greek for Khufu, and that it had taken 400,000 men, working in three-month shifts of 100,000 men at a time, twenty years to build, building in steps and using lifting devices made of timber that raised the stones from one step to the next. Now, that might be what Herodotus said, even what Herodotus was told, but it doesn't mean it's true.

If they used 400,000 men, where did they all live, and there would've had to have been a support environment, family, shops, etc; we're talking about over a million people, at least. So, where's the evidence for a city that size? There is none. So, let's ignore the number of men needed, let's say it's irrelevant, let's just look at the stones.

It's estimated that 5.5 million tonnes of local limestone, 8,000 tonnes of Aswan granite, and 500,000 tonnes of mortar were used in the construction of the Great Pyramid, creating a volume of roughly 2.5 million cubic metres. If 2.3 million stones averaging 2.5 ton each, were put in place, and set with mortar, over 20 years, that means 115,000 per year, or 315 blocks a day. Let's then assume they only worked during the daylight hours for 12 hours a day. That means 26 stones were placed every hour, or, a 2.5-ton block of stone, lifted, placed, positioned and mortared, non-stop, without accidents or delays because of weather, *every two-and-a-half minutes*!

If that's not incredulous enough, the base of the pyramid is level to within 1.5 cm over 13 acres, and the only difference in the length of the sides was 4.4 cm over 230.38 metres; that's a 0.002% error margin, that's ridiculous!

I didn't buy either of the "ramp" theories: that a long angled ramp was built and the stones dragged up the ramp, the ramp would have taken even more material that the pyramid, and there was no evidence to support it. Besides how did they get each block to the end of the ramp, they would have run out of space to pull it, and definitely not have been able to push it. The other ramp theory, the winding one, although it may have taken less material and less space, was just as ridiculous for the same previous reasons. The "ramp" theories led nowhere.

In addition, the sides of the base are closely aligned to the cardinal compass points; not exact, but within three to four minutes of arc, though that's based on true north, not magnetic north. I wasn't as convinced about the relevance of the alignment, as, if I theorized, the pyramid was built before the last pole-shift, then it could account for the discrepancy. What I was sure of was that at some time it definitely had a functional relationship to the electromagnetic field of the earth. What that meant, I wasn't sure, perhaps the answers were inside?

No sooner had we started along the north face than Bill tucked in close to the pyramid itself, glaring along its face.

'Nope, still can't see it.'

'See what?'

'The concave faces; the pyramid actually has eight faces, not four.'

'Frank said something about that back in Dahshur, about the Red Pyramid.'

'Yeah, that has it as well, so does Menkaure's Pyramid.'

'What exactly is it?'

'Each of the four sides is indented along their central line from the base to the top, dividing each side into two adjoining right-angle triangles, and the whole pyramid into an eight-sided structure.'

'How come no one's mentioned it, or studied it?'

'They have; it was first mentioned in the late 1700's, then Flinders Petrie measured and reported it in the early 1900's, but it wasn't until 1940, when a British Air Force pilot called Groves, who was flying over the pyramid and took a photo, that real proof was established, and it was rediscovered.'

'But there must have been tens, hundreds of millions of people who have been here since 1940, how come no one's noticed it?'

He squinted and looked again.

'The displacement has such an extraordinary degree of precision that it's supposedly only visible at certain times of the day, and from the air.'

'Maybe that's why planes aren't allowed to fly over the top of it?'

'I'm sure that's one reason.'

'So why do you think it was built that way, or do you think it was an accident?'

'Some accident, especially on all four sides; no, it's a deliberate part of the design, which means it must've had some functional purpose.'

'Such as?'

'I'm no expert on sacred geometries, so there may be something peculiar to the eight sides, but my guess, since it's all about vibration and resonance, is that it either helps to focus the energy or insulate and negate extraneous vibration, or, maybe it works to absorb or buffer the inner pressures created within the pyramid. The problem with the latter is that there's nothing for the pressure to be dispersed *onto*, nothing at the corners to brace against, so, if it was the latter, then you would expect that over time the pyramid would "spread", but it hasn't, so, to tell you the truth, I don't know. But it must be something to do with the vibrational physics of geometric solids.'

'And I thought all the mysteries were inside.'

'I think the answers are.'

And that's what we were about to do, enter one of the world's greatest mysteries; the other being the Sphinx just down the slope, but I'd get to that later.

As we traversed further along the courtyard beside the north face, the questions kept coming back, as they had for decades, 'who really built the Great Pyramid, and why?' Certainly I didn't concur with the self-appointed 'experts', the mainstream Egyptologists, who believed *"the pyramid was built in the Old Kingdom by hundreds of thousands of slaves, as a tomb for Khufu, second pharaoh of the 4th Dynasty"*; the evidence to support that concept was scant at best, and easily misinterpreted, and I was pretty sure Bill was in my camp on that, but, to be sure, without divulging my conversation with Frank and Mark about who Khufu was, I tossed out a few teasers to Bill to get his thoughts.

'Who was this Khufu anyway, and what do the Egyptologists propose made him so special that he instigated the creation of such a uniquely monumental structure?'

'There's a report by a 14th Century Historian, Al-Maqrizi, that Khufu, or *Sarjak* as he was called by the biblical Amalekites, didn't just build the Great Pyramid, he built all three of the pyramids at Giza, supposedly to protect his treasures and books of wisdom after he'd had repeated nightmares in which the earth turned upside-down, the stars fell down and people were screaming in terror, and after receiving a warning from his prophets about a devastating deluge that was coming that would destroy Egypt.'

'The earth turning upside-down, the stars falling, a devastating deluge; that sounds more like an imminent pole-shift caused by a passing brown dwarf. And the books of wisdom point to Thoth. So the information is right, it's just been *attributed* to Khufu. Or do you think Khufu was a reincarnation of Thoth?'

'I guess it's possible; we know Imhotep was around then.'

'Imhotep, of course! He lived for at least four-hundred years, from Djoser to Huni, so who's to say he wasn't around fifty years later when Khufu assumed the throne?'

'He may well have still been around, but I'm not convinced he *was* Khufu, advising him perhaps.'

'What do we know about Khufu?'

'Well, Khufu, or Khnum-Khufu as he was originally called, was Snefru's successor, and it would be logical to assume, as it was traditional that the eldest son or a selected descendant inherited the throne, that Khufu was Snefru's son. However, according to the Egyptologists, the latest research indicates that although Khufu was most likely the son of Queen Hetepheres I, he may not necessarily have been Snefru's biological offspring.'

'That doesn't bother me, Bill, Khufu probably got the job because he was the son of the *sang réal*. He may have been the son of Hetepheres I and Imhotep?'

'It certainly fits in with your theory.'

'But basically, as usual, the Egyptologists are just guessing?'

'I think they would called it "making educated deductions".'

'You can call a fart a "passing of intestinal gas" but it's still a fart, and it still stinks. The Egyptologists are like amateur detectives trapped in a crowded elevator when someone lets go of a rancid SBD and everyone speculates with their eyes and noses as to who was the perpetrator. You can point the finger of blame as to who you think is responsible, problem is, by then, the scent of truth has wafted far from its source.'

That amused Bill.

'True.'

'Anything else?'

'He apparently had four wives, including Meritites I and Henutsen,…'

'Who were probably also his sisters or cousins.'

'…Possibly. And had numerous children, including his sons and successors, Djederfre and Khafre, and daughters, Meritites II, Hetepheres II, who later married Djederfre, and Khamerernebty I, who married Khafre.'

'The family that stays together plays together.'

'I'm not sure how long he reigned, maybe you've got more information about him in your notes?'

'Way ahead of you, Bill.'

I'd already found a file about the Great Pyramid and it's supposed builder.

'There's a bit of a discrepancy depending who you believe; anywhere from the Royal Canon of Turin citing twenty-three years, to Herodotus, fifty, and Manetho, sixty-three.'

I kept reading.

'Despite his long reign, apart from a few finely-polished limestone relief fragments from his pyramid temple and causeway depicting Khufu's name only appears in a few inscriptions found on a few limestone walls at the site of the ancient eastern port of Wadi al-Jarf on the Red Sea coast, and in buildings at el-Kab and on Elephantine Island.'

'He was hardly a world beater.'

'And, even though the earliest examples of imprinted papyri ever found in Egypt, a collection of hundreds of papyrus fragments discovered in June 2011 at Wadi al-Jarf by a couple of French Egyptologists that date to the 27th year of Khufu's reign and describe how the central administration sent food and supplies to the sailors and wharf workers and provide a new insight into the everyday lives of people during the 4th Dynasty, not much is actually known about Khufu himself; in fact the little that is known about him comes from inscriptions here at Giza or from later documents."

'You'd think someone responsible for the building of one of the ancient wonders of the world would be more famous than Ramses II, that he'd have temples and massive statues everywhere.'

'Yes, you would, wouldn't you, but it seems the opposite is true.'

'Though part of the Palermo Stone mentions the creation of two oversize standing statues of Khufu, one made of copper, the other of pure gold, neither of which has ever been found, the only completely preserved three-dimensional depiction of Khufu is a three-inch-high ivory figurine that depicts the king, wearing the Red Crown of Lower Egypt, seated on a short-backed throne, a flail in one hand, the other arm resting on his leg. Although it was found in a temple ruin at Kom el-Sultan at Abydos in 1903, it possibly comes from a later period, probably the 26th Dynasty.'

I did a quasi double-take.

'The 26th Dynasty, that's nearly two thousand years later? How does that figure?'

'According to the Egyptologists, the Giza Necropolis fell into disuse, and outright abuse, during the Middle Kingdom, which is when the pyramids and tombs suffered frequent plundering and destruction.'

'Or, most of the destruction attributable to the Middle Kingdom was in fact caused by the Thera tsunami, that washed most of the Middle Kingdom away, leaving only the major structures, which had been usurped during the Old Kingdom anyway.'

'That's totally logical, but, according to the thinking of the Egyptologists, the plateau then experienced a revival during the New Kingdom, particularly during the 18th Dynasty, when religious devotion centred on the Sphinx, and the pyramids again became the flavour of the month.'

'That would make sense; it's after the tsunami. I mean, wasn't that when Thutmoses IV *dug* the Sphinx out of the sand?'

'Sure is, about two-hundred years after. And, fifty years before that, Amenhotep II built the temple facing the head of the Sphinx.'

'Exactly, because the Sphinx had been buried by the tsunami, most of the pyramids and definitely their temples would have been as well. And if civilization was trying to rebuild after the disaster, most people would have been killed and most of the knowledge, lost or buried,...

And then I remembered something from earlier in the trip.

'...if the knowledge was even *there* before the tsunami.'

That threw Bill.

'OK, now it's my turn to be lost.'

'Think about it; when the Hyksos invaded Egypt towards the end of the Middle Kingdom, and occupied northern Egypt from say the middle of the 13th to the end of the 16th Dynasties, they had a different religion and didn't bury their dead kings the same way as the Egyptians. Not only would they have eliminated all traces of the previous religion, but it would also explain why no 15th or 16th Dynasty tombs or mummified pharaohs have ever been discovered, they didn't know how to do it.'

'Right, now I'm with you, go on.'

'Then, about a hundred-and-fifty years after the tsunami, civilization recovers, working its way back *down* the Nile from Luxor, rediscovering the Sphinx and the temples around the pyramids. Amenhotep II builds a temple, his son, Thutmoses IV, digs out the Sphinx and uncovers the mortuary temple beside the Great Pyramid. He finds it was attributed to Khufu, and the 18th Dynasty do exactly what modern day Egyptologists have done, just assume Khufu had built the pyramid.'

'That's brilliant! And, logically, it persisted into the Late Period, into the 26th Dynasty, as is evidenced by the Inventory Stela, which dates from then and tells the story of how Khufu built the Great Pyramid.'

I was still reading.

'And it explains why numerous 26th Dynasty figurines and more than thirty scarabs with Khufu's name on them have been discovered, and why Khufu was still being worshipped two thousand years after his reign.'

'Not only that, Khufu's influence perpetuated through the Late Period, through the Ptolemaic Dynasty and into the modern period, the earlier historians, such as Diodorus and Herodotus, painting Khufu as a heartless heretic and sacrilegious tyrant, whereas modern Egyptologists tend to portray him as inquisitive, reasonable and generous. The truth is, there's no evidence either way.'

'Well, I think that pretty much closes the case on Khufu, that he's not the one responsible for building the pyramid, but it doesn't explain *how* the pyramid was built.'

Just as we approached the ladies, Diane emerged from the group and crossed towards us.

'Ah, just in time, we're all set to go in...'

It was 7:27.

'...We've sorted it all out with the guardians; the ladies and I will head into the Queen's Chamber first; unfortunately, gentlemen, that part of proceedings is ladies only.'

Pernille gave Bill a huge hug; I raised an eyebrow at Crystal.

'More secret women's business, hey?'

Before Crystal could respond, Diane answered.

'I'm afraid so, but don't fret, we'll only be about ten or fifteen minutes, and then we'll continue on into the King's Chamber where we'll have the best part of an hour to do what we need to do. So, either you can wait out here for fifteen minutes, or go ahead into the King's Chamber and wait for us.'

I looked at Bill...

'Your call.'

...but there was something else on his mind, and for once it wasn't Pernille.

'Actually, Diane, do you think it's possible for Alex and I to visit the Subterranean Chamber while you're all in the Queen's Chamber?'

'I'm not sure, I'll ask.'

As she walked away towards the guardians, I turned to Bill.

'The Subterranean Chamber?'

'Why not?'

'It's not like visiting the tombs in the Valley of the Kings, you know, or just popping down into the crypts at Dendera, or wandering through the corridors of the Serapeum, or visiting the chamber inside the pyramid of Sahure.'

'I don't expect it would be.'

'I'm just saying I've been inside the pyramid at Meidum and Teti's pyramid at Saqqara, crawled through the passages and tunnels of the Red Pyramid and Bent Pyramid, this is far more challenging than those, far more imposing, this is under millions of tons of rock.'

'Six million, actually.'

'What?'

'The Great Pyramid is comprised of an estimated *six* million ton of rock, and that doesn't include the forty-five to fifty metres of natural bedrock between it and the Subterranean Chamber.'

'It doesn't bother you?'

'Alex, I've been a mile underground in coal mines and gold mines, this will be a walk in the park; unless of course *you're* a little apprehensive or claustrophobic?'

Before I had time to answer, Diane called back.

'No problem, William, one of the guardians will take you down.'

'Brilliant, thank you...'

He turned back and put me on the spot.

'...So, are you with me? Leave no stone unturned I say.'

'That's just the sort of thing I'd expect from a Geologist.'

'Well?'

'Sure, I mean what can happen, apart from an earthquake hitting and entombing us in the bowels of the earth forever.'

Like a mother hen, Diane gathered her brood.

'Right then, off we go.'

Single file, like an albino snake on Vallium, the ladies slowly filed up the makeshift staircase built into the lower courses of the pyramid and towards the modern entrance.

Bill took the time to examine a fragment of one of the tens of thousands of slant-faced, but flat-topped, casing stones of highly polished white Tura limestone that once covered the pyramid; some, at the base, 12 ft long, 5 ft high by eight ft long and weighing as much as 20 ton.

'You know, Alex, most of the casing stones and inner chamber blocks were fitted together with such an extremely high level of precision that the mean, average gap between the stones is only half a millimetre; that's amazing!'

'Especially when you consider thousands of men were supposedly using ropes to pull them up ramps on sleds or rollers, levering them with wooden fulcrums and putting them in place one every two-and-a-half minutes.'

'It just doesn't add up, does it?'

'It can, if you're a corrupt embezzler wanting to fiddle the books.'

'But what I find really interesting is that Flinders Petrie found a different orientation between the core stones and the casing stones of one-hundred-and-ninety-three centimetres plus or minus twenty-five centimetres.'

'Which means?'

'I don't know. Petrie suggested there was a redetermination of north made after the construction of the core, but that a mistake was made, and the casing was built with a different orientation. But I don't think any mistakes were made building the pyramids.'

'A redetermination; a re-measuring of north?'

'Yes.'

'About two metres difference; as if the poles were moving, or had moved slightly?'

'It's possible. Or it might just be something to do with magnetic north versus true north? Trouble is, with almost all the casing stones apparently loosened by a series of earthquakes in the Middle Ages, and many of them harvested and carted away to build mosques and other buildings, we may never know.'

The inner truth

The ladies were, one by one, disappearing within the pyramid, through the modern entrance, an opening supposedly cut straight through the masonry in the 9th Century by Caliph al-Ma'moun, who instructed his men to tunnel into the pyramid from a point at the centre of its north face, about seven metres up.

Once through the outer casing, they dug about 27 metres straight in, without success, before one of the men supposedly heard the thud of something heavy falling within the pyramid not too far away. They altered course to the left and ran into the granite blocking stones at the base of the Ascending Passage. Unable to move the stones, the men kept digging, up beside them through the softer limestone of the core, until they eventually broke into the interior of the pyramid via the Ascending Passage.

Ten metres above the modern entrance and just over seven metres east of the centre-line of the pyramid was the original entrance.

'Hang five, Bill, I'm just going to have a quick look at the original entrance.'

'Right behind you.'

We scrambled up the rock to where the original entrance descended into the pyramid. To the left of the walkway was a carefully shaped piece of red granite with two perfectly drilled holes in it. I pointed it out to Bill.

'Hey, Bill, how hard would it be to drill a hole about two inched diameter, six inches into a block of granite?'

'With copper chisels, fucking impossible!'

'Then I guess this is just a figment of your and my imaginations.'

'That looks like it could be part of a hinged-door mechanism; there would have been another one of these on the other side. Reportedly, before 1356 when the casing stones were first stripped away, there was once a swivelling fulcrum door-stone, weighing around twenty tons, that covered the "Entrance" and was so well balanced it could be opened by pushing out from the inside with minimal effort, but when closed, was such a perfect fit that there was barely a crack around the edges to gain a grasp from the outside.'

While Bill gave it the once over, a finger in the hole here, a caressing fondle of its curves there, I extended my view upwards, above the locked door to the descending passage, to a huge squared limestone block, and above that, to where four huge gabled stones capped the entrance. They created a triangle-shaped cavity in which a wave pattern was carved into the stone. I scrambled up for a closer look.

'What do you make of it, Alex?'

'It's symbolic, that's for sure, but symbolic of what?'

'A sine wave?'

'Possibly, although it's not exactly a sine wave; too irregular.'

'Well, waves are usually symbolic of water.'

Note time!

'Inside one trough of the carved wave pattern, archaeologists discovered a remarkable set of four symbols that are not Egyptian hieroglyphs nor do they correspond to any type of known glyphs.'

'That's interesting! A code perhaps; maybe it's an indication of a sonic lock?'

'If it *was* an "entrance", but, given the pyramid wasn't a tomb, I don't think it was an "entrance" at all; the descending passage is much too small to walk through, let alone transfer a sarcophagus or any large funerary items, and the massive limestone block, which by the position of the gabled blocks would appear to be where the entrance should be, makes absolutely no sense at all in being where it is.'

Bill started poking around.

'It does look like there was a small chamber here though, between the descending passage, the block, and the outer fulcrum door.'

'If these gabled stones worked the way the others did, to relieve pressure, then maybe the parting of the stones triggered the fulcrum door to open to release waste.'

'Hang on, Alex.'

Bill pulled out a cross-section diagram of the pyramid.

'I thought so. Look at that, the entrance is below the level of the Queen's Chamber.'

'And?'

I could see it, but I didn't get the significance until Bill pointed it out.

'It's an overflow valve; the wave form is a symbol for water.'

'I get it! If the whole pyramid is a hydrogen reactor, then it's logical that water would be a by-product.'

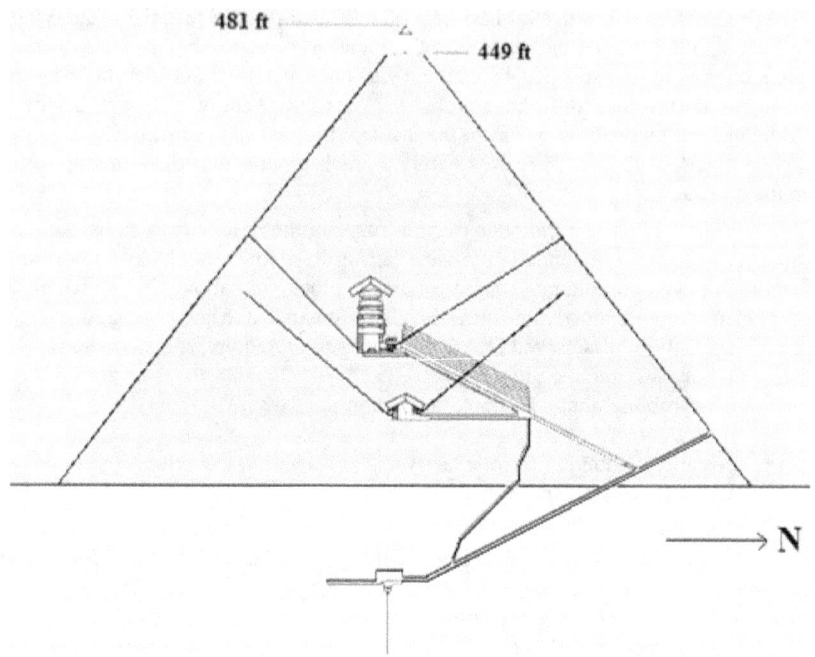

481 ft

449 ft

→ N

'It flows down the Well Shaft and drains out of the Subterranean Chamber, but, if there's excess, it could back up and flood the Queen's Chamber, so the so-called entrance is a release valve; when the water level rises, it builds up the air pressure in the top of the Descending Passage and triggers the gabled stones to part, the fulcrum door to open, and the excess water to drain out, thus keeping the Queen's Chamber 'dry' to continue functioning.'

'Brilliant!'

Bill went into one of his deep-thinking modes, staring at his diagram.

'You know what all this means, don't you, Alex?'

'What's that?'

'If this isn't the entrance, then where is it?'

I got it; I mean I *really* got it.

'Whoa, that's big; it confirms there has to be another entrance, the one on the south face discovered by the Followers in 1976.'

'Possibly, but I think it might be a bit high for a day-to-day entrance, after all you'd have to scale four-hundred feet of slippery polished limestone.'

'So where?'

Bill pointed straight down.

'From below, from the underground tunnels.'

'Then, what are we waiting for, let's go and check out the Subterranean Chamber.'

Once again I led the way, this time down the courses of rock and back to where our guide was awaiting at the modern entrance. As we climbed down, my mind was racing; most of the debate around the Great Pyramid centred, not on its entrance but, around its internal structures, and I think I'd read them all.

'Some 'scholars' believe that the pyramid's internal structure was developed in three stages, representing three different phases in its construction, that first the burial chamber was planned for the subterranean chamber, then they changed their minds and decided on an internal chamber, but abandoned the 'Queen's Chamber for some reason and built the King's chamber.'

'Their thinking is, that because pyramid building was a new thing, they were still working out what they wanted; what a load of bollocks!'

'Other self-appointed experts believe that it was all done according to a unified plan.'

'I agree.'

'But they think that the underground chamber was a backup burial site to be used in case the king met an unexpected death.'

'A backup burial site for an unexpected death; are they serious?'

'Further, they believe that the Queen's Chamber was never intended as a burial chamber, and that the niche in the east wall indicates that it had some special, unknown function, though they have absolutely no idea what.'

'That's the problem with false premises, they lead to false conclusions.'

As Bill and I took our first steps inside the superstructure, I couldn't help but think; it was not only time for me to see the evidence for myself and formulate my own opinions, but to look for signs of a secret entrance or entrances.

The Al-Ma'moun entrance led horizontally into the body of the pyramid. Obviously Al-Ma'moun's men were all short-asses because every few feet I had to duck my head so as to avoid sconing myself on a section of rock they'd left in place. Still, it was much easier than the constricted entrances to Meidum, Teti, or the Red and Bent Pyramids.

Having safely negotiated the obstacle course, we arrived at a junction where Al-Ma'moun's tunnel met a staircase that led up to the Ascending Passage and, in the other direction, the Descending Passage.

'Last chance to back out.'

'Lead on, Macduff!'

'No, my friend, after you.'

Going down

Our guide unlocked the mesh door that blocked access to the Descending Passage and motioned for us to enter, which we gratefully did, me first, followed by Bill, with our faithful guide bringing up the rear. As soon as I looked down into the abyss I thought; maybe this wasn't such a good idea after all.

We'd entered the Descending Passage right where the Ascending Passage split off from it, about 28 metres from the outside world, which meant we still had about another 80 metres to go!

Similar to the descending passages in the other pyramids at Meidum, Dahshur, and Teti's passage at Saqqara, the descending passage here was tight; barely a metre wide, maybe a little bit higher, and at an angle of 26°31'23". The difference here was it disappeared into the depth so far I couldn't see the end. Eager to explore, Bill gave me a prod.

'Let's go, we don't want to keep the girls waiting.'

I adopted the bum-crawl slide-scramble technique and led they way down into the gates of hell. At first, we made our way through the masonry of the core of the superstructure, then down through the bedrock into the earth beneath the pyramid to the subterranean chamber. In an effort to keep my mind off the descent, I turned my thoughts to the passage itself.

'Do you think there's any significance to the angle of the passage; twenty-six degrees is about half the pyramid's slope of fifty-one degrees?'

'I'm sure there's a functional reason why it's the angle it is, the ascending passage has approximately the same angle, but, whether they're directly related to the angle of the pyramid or not, I don't know. What I do know is that the passage was important enough that they built it to within an accuracy of one-fifth of an inch over one-hundred-and-fifty feet and a quarter-of-an inch over the full length, and to within three-tenths of an inch for the roof.'

'Meaning the floor and walls were more important?'

'It would appear so. Which would be the case if you were creating a conduit for a fluid such as water. If we have time after the circle, on the way to the Sphinx we should try and check out the Trial Passages to the east of the pyramid.'

'Trial passages?'

'Yeah, they excavated an almost identical plan of this part of the interior, not the chambers, just the passages.'

'Why would they do that if the passages were simply just to get from point A to point B?'

'Obviously they weren't just passages, they had a function, so, whatever the reason, they excavated the alignment of the Ascending and Descending Passages to make sure they worked.'

We passed under where the bottom end of the Well Shaft intersected the Descending Passage and arrived at the end of the Descending Passage, where thankfully it levelled out, although it continued on for another 8 to 9 metres, meaning it was still an effort to deal with the low ceiling.

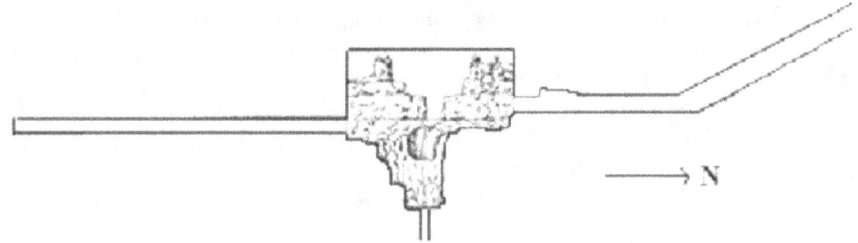

'Hey, will you look at that!'

In my eagerness to get to 'higher ground', where I could stand up, I'd actually almost gone straight past it, a chunk of what was once part of a shaped piece of red granite, tucked into an unfinished niche to the west of the passage.

'Now that's interesting, I wonder where it came from.'

'It was supposedly found by Flinders Petrie about half way down the Descending Passage and just below a huge diagonal of limestone that's now missing.'

'Given the trend to dump rock downwards into the subterranean pit rather than haul it out up the passage, it means the block must have originally been somewhere back up the Descending Passage, at least half-way or higher.'

Bill was scratching his chin again, he wasn't so sure.

'But where, and, more importantly, why?'

'Maybe it was part of a portcullis, up near the junction most likely, if not that, perhaps it was part of the original entrance.'

'Not part of a portcullis, not in the Descending Passage anyway, there was no sign of it and it wouldn't make sense if the Descending Passage was an outlet for surplus waste water. And I doubt it was part of the entrance for the same reasons, unless it was part of the door hinge mechanism, which it doesn't seem to be. I think it might have been dumped down the Well Shaft and made its way progressively all the way down here.'

'From?'

'The Antechamber.'

'Do tell.'

'One step at a time, Alex, let's wait until we get there. Let's focus on the Subterranean Chamber first.'

'No worries.'

Having made a note of the block, we quickly moved on and into the Subterranean Chamber, where finally I could stand up.

The pits

Probably because it appears to have the 'classical' substructure, of a descending corridor leading to a subterranean chamber carved out of the solid bedrock, some Egyptologists suggest the Subterranean Chamber was intended as the original burial chamber, and that later Khufu changed his mind and wanted it to be higher up in the pyramid.

Thirty metres below the ground, the 'unfinished chamber', 14 metres east-west, 8.3 metres north-south, and 3.5 metres high, looked more like a quarry, or some strange underground mini hillside dwelling, than a standby burial chamber; although there weren't any, I felt like I was in the bat-cave.

If it was planned as a tomb, then there were some major inconsistencies and flaws; firstly, there was no way they could have lowered a sarcophagus down the Descending Passage, through the horizontal section, and in via the narrow opening, it was way too small. Secondly, it would have meant they would have had to carve a sarcophagus out of the bedrock, which was inconsistent with the use of granite for sarcophagi. A tomb, no!

The first thing I encountered was a semicircular modern metal fence tucked against the eastern wall that surrounded the pit, a square-cut shaft six feet wide, dug in the floor of the chamber, centred halfway between the north and south walls. The diagonally-set shaft disappeared straight down into the earth; the bottom of which was apparently filled with rubble and debris.

'Where do you think it leads?'

'That's a good question. It's supposedly at least sixty feet deep, but no one really knows; they haven't completely cleared out the rubble. My guess is it eventually connects to an underground river.'

'Or more underground tunnels?'

'Which might explain why they haven't cleared it out and fully explored it.'

'Or that they *have* fully cleared it out, *and* fully explored it, but that they filled it back in again so no one knows the truth.'

'It's a possibility. In 1992, a team, headed by a French engineer called Jean Kerisel, used GPR to scan the area around and under the Subterranean Chamber. Under the horizontal passage and niche they detected what they thought could be a corridor, about one-point-six metres high and oriented SSE NNW, and at a depth that would correlate with an extension of the descending passage, that rises slightly and opens into the pit. However, when they returned later that year, they used micro-gravimetry to confirm the discovery but detected nothing, indicating the passage had been filled in.'

'They made the mistake of telling Hawass about it.'

'But it wasn't a complete loss; what the micro-gravimetry *did* detect was a large anomaly west of the horizontal passage and just after the descending passage ended, about six metres before the entrance to the chamber. It was estimated to be a vertical square pit about one-point-four metres wide and at least five metres deep; now it could just have been a naturally occurring grotto created by underground water dissolving the limestone, and Kerisel was apparently keen to do some drilling to further investigate the findings, but the work has never been performed so we're left in the dark.'

'Kept in the dark, more like it, like a mushroom, kept in the dark and fed bullshit.'

I turned my thoughts back to the pit; diagonally set, it dropped about six feet down where the opening narrowed to about four feet wide.

'If it was just a drainage shaft, why did it need to be square, wouldn't a round hole have been just as good, especially for water?'

'Maybe it was easier to cut.'

As we slowly circled the pit, I noticed something more of interest, perched precariously on the ledge of the pit.

'Speaking of easier to cut, look, there, another piece of red granite; do you think it was washed down here as well?'

'Definitely.'

'It looks like it's got holes drilled in it.'

'Yes, that *is* interesting, which means the stone may well have been part of the lowering system of the three portcullises in the Antechamber.'

I was impatient.

'OK, what's the deal with the Antechamber?'

'I'll have a better idea when we get there, but basically there've been four fragments of red-granite blocks discovered in and around the pyramid, each just over twenty inches thick, that match the dimensions of the portcullis grooves in the Antechamber, which are twenty-one inches wide; this one, the one outside in the niche, another in the Grotto above, and another outside. Three of the four blocks have three-and-a-half-inch holes drilled in them, this one has two, which is exactly the same diameter as the channels for the ropes in the south wall of the Antechamber.'

'So they smashed the portcullises in the Antechamber to gain access, and tossed the pieces down the Well Shaft?'

'It's the most likely scenario, although the portcullises may not have been originally smashed, they could have been fractured by an explosion in the King's Chamber.'

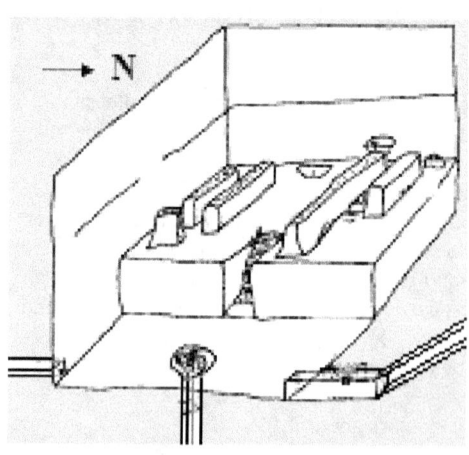

'Which would make sense if the pyramid was a power station and it went into meltdown because of a pole shift.'

'Possibly.'

I looked off to the west, something didn't add up.

'So if we assume the pyramid *was* a power generator, that this wasn't ever intended to be a burial chamber, and the entrance was an overflow valve, then it makes sense that the water flowed down here, then down the pit to a subterranean river or lake, right?'

'Probably.'

'So why the need for all this terracing?'

Bill walked up the ramp and starting looking around.

'Initially, I would've agreed, there appears to be no need for it. My original thinking was that only the eastern section first existed, then it was extended westward and upward, creating the terraces, possibly for the workers who were assigned to repair the pyramid.'

'It's their tea room...'

That gave Bill a good chuckle.

'...and now?'

I joined him as we wandered around as best we could, as, while the eastern half of the chamber averaged around four metres high, the western half, about six foot off the ground, was less, barely half that, maybe 6 feet. The top level contained a number of east-west ridges that reached up to, but didn't connect with, the ceiling. Bill was running his hand over one of the ridges.

'Well, actually being here, I'm not so sure. Just before the trip I read a website by a guy called John Cadman, who proposed that the Subterranean Chamber functioned as a Hydraulic ram pump. His evidence was pretty compelling, he even made up models to prove his theory, and now that I'm here, and I've heard all your thinking about the pyramids being power stations, I'm inclined to believe him; I think this was a brilliant natural pump that pumped water from the Nile into the Great Pyramid.'

'Wow!'

We made our way back down the ramp, the only other point of interest remaining in the chamber being a small square hole, just like the entrance, but maybe half the size, about 2 ½ feet square, immediately opposite, tucked away in the eastern corner of the south wall and almost hidden behind the metal fence. Just like the entrance, it was also a step above the chamber floor. It led to a horizontal tunnel that supposedly ran 53 feet to a vertical wall, a dead-end.

I knelt down and took a look inside.

'You know, Bill, the knowledgeable scholars have proposed this is a corridor that was originally intended to lead to a second subterranean chamber, but that for some reason the idea was abandoned.'

'Maybe they couldn't find any dwarves to use it. Seriously, how could any intelligent educated archaeologist propose that the ancient Egyptians dug a corridor out of the bedrock, fifty feet long, but only two feet high? If it was meant as a corridor, but unfinished, it would have been built to its full size from the beginning.'

'So what do you think it is, where does it lead?'

'I don't think it leads 'to' anywhere, I think it leads 'from' somewhere.'

'But it's a dead-end.'

He looked down the shaft.

'It *appears* to be a dead end. Cadman suggests that at the end of the end of the shaft is a vertical surface that correlates to the back side of a check-valve, and that the shaft continues beyond it.'

'A check-valve?'

'By adjusting a "valve" at the end of the shaft, the backpressure can be varied, changing the compression wave's velocity and frequency. This creates a standing wave in the subterranean chamber, a pulse frequency that is transmitted through the bedrock to the Antechamber of the King's Chamber, which is directly above. Basically, Cadman was saying that the Great Pyramid was an acoustic generator and amplifier than ran on water.'

'Free energy.'

'Yep. Of course, if the Well Shaft is a drainage shaft, leading into the horizontal passage, then this drain could be exactly the same, just draining from some as yet undiscovered room in the southern part of the pyramid.'

'The secret entrance in the south face had a number of rooms off the descending staircase; it could be one of those.'

'It probably is; the shaft has to come from somewhere. Come on, we'd better get going, we can mull it all over on the way.'

As we made our way back into the horizontal passage and up the Descending Passage, I couldn't believe not only how all the pieces were falling into place, but how easily and obviously they fitted. How was it the Egyptologists were so blind?

Onward and upward

After what seemed a small eternity trudging back up the slope, we finally bid the Descending Passage farewell and headed for the Ascending Passage.

Originally, the Ascending Passage was supposedly accessed through a hole in the ceiling of the Descending Passage about 28 metres down from the 'entrance'; well, not so much accessed, as connected, because access could never have been an issue given the three, 1.5 metre long, massive seven-ton 'portcullis' blocks of red-granite that filled the lower end of the Ascending Passage. Access now was via a modern set of steps that led from Al-Ma'Moun's tunnel, up and around the portcullis blocks and into the Ascending Passageway.

Bill paused on the steps to examine and admire the granite blocks.

'Well, here they are, the three seven-ton granite portcullis stones that supposedly sealed off the entire arrangement of upper chambers; some say they were built in-situ, others that they were slid into place.'

'What're your thoughts?'

'I'd never really considered it; that is until we figured out that the entrance wasn't an entrance at all.'

'Because if the entrance wasn't an entrance, then there was no real need to seal it the way they did.'

'Exactly. Besides, if the blocks were slid into place, then the only exit for the builders would have been through the Well Shaft, and digging an escape shaft basically defeats the purpose, as anyone could simply travel the reverse route.'

'And, given we now know the Well Shaft was for drainage, most probably from the Queen's Chamber, it means these portcullis blocks must have some other "functional" reason for being here, other that just to "seal" the passage. The question is, what was it?'

Bill was carefully scrutinizing both the stones and the passage.

'Unlike the rest of the Ascending Passage, which is gun barrel straight, here at the bottom end it tapers inwards slightly, which would have required extremely accurately cut blocks, which means the granite blocks fit almost seamlessly into the passage, except that Petrie reported a four inch gap between the bottom block and the next one up.'

I looked closer.

'It's closed now.'

'Probably because the passage has been opened up on this side and it's slipped down, maybe dislodged by the blasting...'

As he groped and prodded the joints, that far-away look of deep contemplation came over his face again.

'...But what's really interesting is, that unlike the lower end of the second block, which is smooth, the upper end of the lowermost block has a fractured irregular appearance, which is not what you would expect if you wanted the stones to abut tightly; as always, there must have been a reason.'

'Which is?'

'I'm not one-hundred-percent sure, but I think I'm getting to it...'

He shifted his attention to the top block.

'According to Petrie the present top stone is not originally where it was either, it was about two feet further up the passage where it was held in place by a coarse red plaster.'

'So the plaster gave way.'

'Probably when Al-Ma'Moun's men were smashing their way in; the vibrations loosened the cement, causing the top block to slide down, knocking the second block further down the passage and possibly dislodging the limestone ceiling slab in the Descending Passage that hid the "entrance" to the Ascending Chamber.'

'Or it dislodged when the pyramid blew up?'

'Alex, that's brilliant.'

'Really?'

'Really, a stroke of genius, but it's just the beginning, it doesn't explain the blocks themselves, just why they're where they are now.'

Like a spectator at a fast-forward tennis match, Bill did a quick back-and-forward examination of the top blocks.

'Look, both the second and third blocks don't have smooth ends, they're roughened, wavy; I think we're on to something.'

It reminded me of something I'd read in '*The Giza Power Plant*'.

'Smooth bottom and rough top, that's just like the slabs in the Relieving Chambers above the King's Chamber; Dunn thinks they're to fine tune the vibrations in the King's Chamber.'

Bill was suddenly glowing.

'That's it; it's all to do with frequency. The blocks are there to either dampen unwanted vibrations or create interference patterns, or to focus a specific frequency.'

'Interference patterns, I remember Dunn saying something about the Ascending Passage being to create interference patterns so that the pyramid wouldn't overload, but I don't remember how.'

'I'm not sure either, perhaps the sound from the Grand Gallery, or maybe the Queen's Chamber, echoes down the Ascending Passage where it hits the irregular surface of the top block. Maybe it's not reflected but is absorbed by the stone, which transmits it on to the next gap. Any excess vibration is passed on to the second block through the gap, and the process is repeated for the third block, passing any unwanted vibrations ultimately into the Descending Passage so as to keep the system from overloading. Or maybe the three stones vibrate; somehow creating an opposing interfering wave that negates the original signal.'

'That's pretty out there, I mean it's simple, but how in the hell would you test all that to see if it worked?'

'Maybe that's what the Trial Passages east of the pyramid were for?'

Before I could say any more, Bill headed off into the Ascending Passage.

'You know, this passage might look the same as the Descending Passage, but there's a huge difference between the two of them.'

'And what's that, it's got the same dimensions as the Descending Passage; 1.1 metres wide, 1.2 metres high, and it rises at almost the same angle of 26°30'. The only difference I can see is that the Ascending Passage, at 39 metres, is thankfully shorter at a little over one-third the length.'

He got to a specific spot and stopped.
'These...'

I climbed up beside him.

'...The passage is supported by a regular series of stone "girdles", each one hollowed out of a slab of red granite; four single ones, and three "half girdles" made of two stones combined for the same purpose. The corridor was laid through them.'

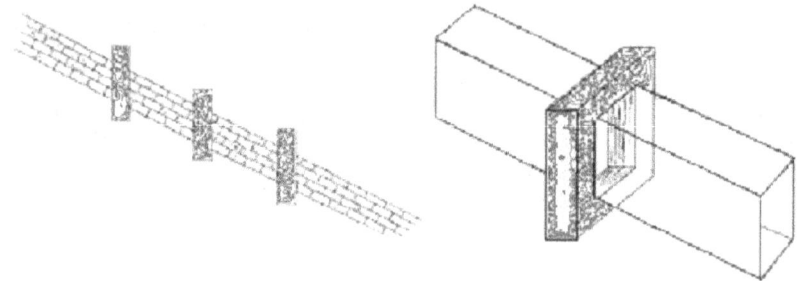

'Why; there had to be a reason?'

'That's right, and it had to be more than just structural, or else the Descending Passage would have had them as well; it had to be specific to the *function* of the Ascending Passage...'

He moved on to locate the next ones.

'...The fact they're made of red granite and not limestone means it must have something to do with the three blocks at the bottom, and that means its something to do with frequency.'

'Well, thirty-nine metres divided by seven girdles is one roughly every five-and-a-half metres.'

'Except it's divided by eight, seven girdles means eight division of roughly one every four and seven-eighth metres; that's if they're evenly placed.'

'What do you mean?'

'If it's all about frequency, that means it's all about wavelength, so the girdles might be placed strategically to create interference waves that negate all unwanted frequencies, or a standing wave, a set frequency, that feeds back into the Grand Gallery.'

Bill was like a man on a mission and forged on, leading the way to the point where the ascending passage levelled off; the junction between the foot of the Grand Gallery, the low horizontal passage that led to the Queen's Chamber, and the Well Shaft. As I reached the level ground, the ladies' guide sitting patiently outside the chamber waiting, Bill turned to me.

'From the murmurings leaking out from the Queen's Chamber, it sounds like the ladies are still going. Good, that gives us more time to check things out.'

'Such as?'

'Well, the Well Shaft for instance.'

To the right-hand side was a hole cut in the wall, covered in chicken wire. This was the start of the Well Shaft, an accurately-cut, 28-inch-square, vertical shaft, built and lined with regular blocks of limestone, that then follows an irregular path down through the masonry of the pyramid to the Grotto, and then on through the natural bedrock for a total of over 200 feet before it connects with the Descending Passage. I took a look down.

'If you think I'm going down there, forget it!'

'You don't have to, we know all about the Well Shaft.'

'Do we? The Egyptologists say, it was dug by tomb robbers?'

'Their standard answer for everything; blame the tomb robbers! They *may* have dug in, but, if they found anything, how did they get it out, and it doesn't explain why the original shaft was there to begin with, so I think we can safely dismiss the "tomb robbers".'

'Other Egyptologists say the Well Shaft was dug to provide air for the builders.'

'No, that makes no sense, because the builders would have obtained their air from the open Ascending Passage.'

'What about as an escape route for the workmen who lowered the granite plugs into place?'

'We've dismissed that too, it's illogical and impractical. The top part of the shaft is rough cut *out* of the original limestone blocks, meaning it was done *after* the construction, not part of the original design. That excludes the option it was an escape shaft and *includes* the probability it was done after the pyramid short-circuited. No, the original purpose of the shaft was simply drainage, *but* it's the Grotto and the *widening* of the shaft that I'm interested in.'

'What's so interesting about the Grotto, isn't it just a small cavity that marks the boundary between the natural bedrock and the masonry above?'

'Exactly, the question is, why is it there?'

'Well, I guess if the Well Shaft was just a drainage channel, then there's no need for the Grotto at all.'

'Precisely, it's not in the *original* design and construction, so, as you said, there's no need for it at all.'

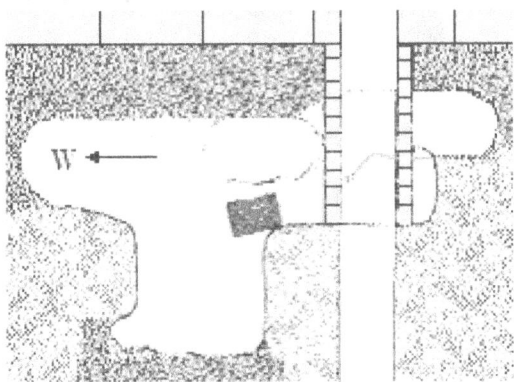

'You think it was excavated later?'

'Yep, had to be! Here's my thinking. The pyramid was supposedly built on a natural high point on the plateau, twenty-five feet higher than the pyramid's base, yet deliberately over the opening to a natural fissure that runs from the Grotto deep into the bedrock; it was the perfect drainage option to the underground water table.'

'Or a supply *from* the water table!'

'True. In either case, if they had wanted a chamber where the Grotto is, they would have built one, and lined it with limestone, but they didn't, because they didn't need one.'

'So why is it here?'

'My guess is, there may have been a leak at the junction between the upper limestone blocks and the bedrock and the drainage water may have seeped laterally, initially dissolving the bedrock. Then, after your tsunami short-circuited the pyramid, they sent workers into the pyramid from either the "entrance" or some other as yet undiscovered subterranean entrance.

They tunnelled up the Well Shaft from the Descending Passage, hacking into the masonry and widening it to it's current width of around twenty-eight inches, and expanded the Grotto to use as a sort of halfway station.'

'Another tea room; gee, they had it easy!'

'A tea room with a large red-granite block in it.'

'In the Grotto; from one of the portcullises originally in the Antechamber?'

'Most likely, it would have been dropped down the Well Shaft when the workmen entered the inner chambers to repair them.'

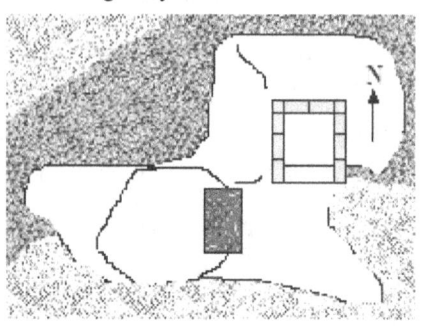

'Then it was just pushed to one side, into the Grotto, out of the way.'

'Which makes me think the portcullises may well have been fractured *before* the repairmen entered, because surely they would have left them intact if they could have, as they were crucial to the pyramid's function.'

Bill took a look down the horizontal passage.

'Sounds like the ladies are winding up.'

Sure enough, one by one, the ladies started to filter out of the tiny entrance to the passage, silently climbing the steps that led to either side of the Grand Gallery and waiting for the others.

We smiled at each of the ladies as they emerged, but they opted to stay silent, some holding their finger to their lips indicating for us to do the same. Naturally we obliged, but, when Pernille emerged, one of the last to do so, and Bill went to hug her, she smiled, shook her head and lovingly fended him off. Bill got the message straight away and backed off; clearly something profound had transpired within. When Crystal followed, next in line, I respectfully gave her the silent treatment, although she was so focused she didn't even make eye contact.

Diane was the last to emerge, joining the others in the lower part of the Grand Gallery. As she ascended the steps of the ladder, Bill gave me the head-nod to duck into the Queen's Chamber, which we did, leaving the ladies to commence toning.

The Queen's Chamber

The entrance to the misnamed Queen's Chamber was southward, between the ramps and through the horizontal passageway, a back-breaking 1.1 metres high for most of its 45.72 metre length. As we crawled along, Bill filled me in on some interesting facts.

'You know, Alex, in March, 1985, two French guys, Gilles Dormion and Jean Patrice Goidin, noticed that the limestone blocks in the walls of this horizontal passage were in a cross-shaped pattern, which was different to the other patterns in the pyramid...'

Rather than run my eyes along the floor, I started focusing on the walls.

'...Eighteen months later, thinking there might be a storeroom behind the wall that could contain the pharaoh's treasure, Dormion returned and, using a micro-gravimeter, discovered evidence of a cavity behind the west wall of the passage. Ah, here they are....'

He stopped in the passage.

'...The Egyptian Antiquities Organization gave Dormion permission to drill three small one-inch holes in the wall, these ones here at the base, plugged with metal caps. The first and second holes revealed nothing unusual, but the third hole, which was drilled at an angle and over two-and-a-half metres into the wall, revealed a cavity filled with very fine quality sand.'

'Maybe a maintenance corridor?'

'Could be? But something's behind there.'

Hardly overwhelmed by the three small metal-capped holes at the base of a wall barely a metre high, Bill moved on, and I was quick to scamper after him.

'I think I remember reading something about that, but I thought it was a Japanese crew.'

'No, the Japanese came just after that, in January 1987. They were from Waseda University and followed up on Dormion's findings, using GPR to scan the floors and walls of both the horizontal passage and the Queen's Chamber.'

'And did they find anything?'

'They confirmed there was a cavity behind the west wall, probably a concealed passage, that ran parallel to the horizontal passage from the north wall of the Queen's Chamber for thirty metres before it either came to an end or turned west, away from the horizontal passage. Not only that, they believed they detected another cavity, about one-and-a-half metres beneath the floor, that might be as much as three metres deep and that's probably filled with sand.'

'Sand-filled cavities would definitely help dissipate extraneous vibrations.'

'They would, but most Egyptologists believe sand was used to buffer the effects of *external* vibrations, earthquakes, rather than internal vibrations.'

Thankfully, about five metres from the end of the passage, there was a step down in the floor, after which the passage sloped downward about sixty centimetres to the floor level of the chamber. I couldn't stand up completely, but at least I could walk.

'So what happened?'

'They moved their equipment into Queen's Chamber, where they discovered the presence of a cavity about three metres behind the western part of the north wall of the chamber.'

'What did the Japanese do then?

'Nothing. Well, nothing that we know about, because, just after the Japanese announced their findings, Zahi Hawass closed the Great Pyramid for six months, supposedly for maintenance.'

'Ah, Zahi Hawass, the vulture strikes again!'

Located at the 25th course of masonry and precisely in the centre of the pyramid's east-west and north-south axes, the Queen's Chamber was made entirely of bare and, apart from some more modern graffiti, uninscribed limestone blocks. Measuring just under six metres north-south by a little over five metres east-west, it was over six metres high to the centre of its gabled ceiling. The limestone floor was rough, uneven and looked more like the substratum of the chamber flooring.

It was mainly because of this that some Egyptologists had claimed the chamber was unfinished, that the builders changed their minds and built the King's Chamber instead. Others speculated that the floor was once covered in red granite and that it had been stolen. Seriously? Why on earth would you break into a pyramid to steal the granite floor slabs; as souvenirs? Especially when there were far more accessible sources of red granite elsewhere on the plateau, the Valley Temple of Khafre for instance.

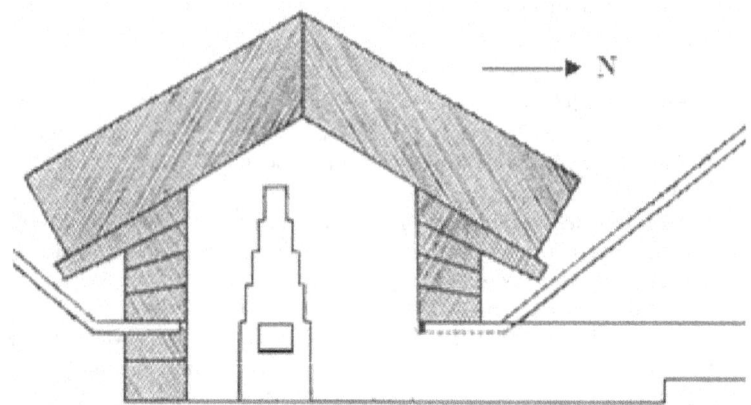

None of the conventional theories gelled with me, simply because if they built the pyramid from the ground up, with the Queen's Chamber in mind as the prime 'burial' chamber, then the position of the Ascending Passage and the extensions of the north and south shafts made no sense.

'It looks baked and battered, more like the inside of an old potter's kiln; which is totally in keeping with Christopher Dunn's belief that the Queen's Chamber was a 'chemistry lab' for producing hydrogen gas that travelled out the horizontal passage, up the Grand Gallery, and into the King's Chamber.'

'Hydrogen gas? Interesting!'

Bill headed straight for a corbelled niche in the southern half of the eastern wall, possibly because it looked a little bit like a chimney. Nearly five metres high and about a metre deep, it reminded me of the shape of the chambers in the pyramid at Meidum and inside the Red and Bent Pyramids.

The niche contained a small horizontal "tunnel", 38 feet deep, with a flat level floor, an almost perfect right-angled left hand side, and ending in bulb shaped cavern. Bill was giving it the quick once-over.

'That's interesting, the Egyptologists believe this niche once housed a statue of the king, which is ridiculous, and that this tunnel was hacked by treasure hunters, which may be true, however, going by the different sides of the tunnel, it shows two things; one that it was an original part of the design, and two, that, just like the Well Shaft, it was hacked at some later stage to widen it, either to search for treasure, which I think is highly unlikely, or, to gain access to whatever was at the other end of the tunnel so as to repair it.'

'What do you think was there?'

'No idea, but whatever it was, or is, it had something to do with whatever the function was of whatever was in the niche. Either something was brought into the chamber via this tunnel, or taken away; the key is the top of the tunnel. We know the water went out via the Well Shaft, and if it was a chimney or outlet for other gases, you would expect it would work contrary to the purpose of the horizontal passage, so it must have been bringing something in.'

'Such as?'

'The obvious thing is water.'

'Sea water?'

'Water from the Nile most likely; pumped up from the Valley Temple via the Causeway and Mortuary Temple.'

'But if these pyramids were built *before* the last pole shift, isn't it possible that the Nile was part of the oceans, that the Nile was filled with salt water?'

'It's possible, why?'

'Well, Dunn says they found lots of gypsum in here, Calcium sulphate, and that gypsum is produced from sea water.'

'It's also produced by the action of sulphuric acid on limestone,…which would probably release hydrogen gas as well.'

'Would it produce Hydrogen Sulphide as well, rotten egg gas?'

'Probably, why?'

'Because the early archaeologists reported a foul stink of sulphur in this chamber, they thought it was because someone had burned sulphur in here to get rid of bats.'

'Sulphuric acid; I'm no chemistry expert, but if you want to run a hydrogen fusion reactor, you need a regular source of hydrogen, and, although water is surely one of the best options, the other choices would probably be hydrochloric acid and sulphuric acid.'

'After *his* investigation of the pyramid, Dunn came to the conclusion that diluted hydrochloric acid was pumped in through one shaft and a hydrated Zinc chloride solution in through the other, which produced the hydrogen gas.'

Again deep in thought, Bill shifted his attention to the shaft in the southern wall.

'Which brings us to the real function of the shafts.'

'You don't buy into the theory they were aligned with stars?'

'Of course they were aligned with stars; everything is aligned with something, my ass is aligned with the Sphinx, but it doesn't mean the shafts were designed that way, nor that what they align with now is what they were aligned with when the pyramid was built. Some speculators have suggested the north shaft was aligned with the circumpolar stars, Minoris, Ursa and Beta, and that the southern shaft is aligned with Sirius, but I think they're trying to force explanations based on their theories when the evidence just doesn't support it.'

'What makes you think that?'

'For starters the shafts were only discovered less than a-hundred-and-fifty years ago, in 1872 by a British engineer called Waynman Dixon, who speculated there might be shafts similar to those in the King's Chamber. Originally bricked over, Dixon found a slit in the brickwork in both walls, and broke them open, discovering they each travelled horizontally for about two metres, hollowed out of the rock, before they started climbing upwards at about thirty-five degrees.'

He crossed the room to the site of the northern shaft.

'Inside the lower part of the northern shaft he retrieved a small black diorite ball, a wooden slat and a bronze hook, no one having a clue what they were doing there, and which eventually finished up in the British Museum. But that's just it, they were obviously part of the original design, and hardly relevant to the issue of star alignment, they had a functional purpose for being in the shaft.

Secondly, the shafts aren't completely straight, or uniform, as you would expect if they were targeted on any particular star, the cross section of the shafts are sometimes oval, sometimes domed, sometimes rectangular, and they have "detours". For instance, the north shaft bends after about eighteen metres.'

It supported my belief the shafts must have been made as the pyramid went up; the builders surely wouldn't have continued making the shafts after the decision to abandon the chamber.

'Finally, in late March, 1993, a German engineer by the name of Rudolf Gantenbrink used a crawling robot called Upuaut 2, which was fitted with a camera, to explore and video the shafts. Approximately twenty centimetres wide, the north shaft travelled for seventeen metres before it made a turn that Upuaut couldn't negotiate.'

I remembered I'd read about it in Dunn's book.

'Wasn't it blocked by a pipe or something someone had thrust up there in modern times searching for treasure.'

'That's right, and Gantenbrink didn't want to risk Upuaut getting stuck as well.'

'So he turned his attention to the southern shaft, right?'

'Right; which was quite a different story…'

Bill crossed back to the opening to the southern shaft. I considered telling him I'd read all about it, but Bill was deep in thought and I didn't want to interrupt him.

'…Gantenbrink observed that, about sixty metres up the shaft, the fairly-uneven, rough-hewn, and yellowed limestone walls changed to highly-polished fine white Tura limestone for five metres before, about sixty-five metres up the southern shaft, the walls of the passage revealed stress-reliving construction techniques of vertically-laid blocks rather than horizontally laid blocks, at which point the shaft was "blocked" by a limestone "door", seemingly free of any mortar, with two heavily corroded copper "handles" sticking out of it.

Hawass's explanation was that the fittings weren't handles; rather they were most probably hieroglyphic signs, "symbols of the magic power that enabled the soul of the king to pass through the blockage".'

'Spiritual door knobs!'

'Spiritual door knobs from a spiritual knob-head!'

As I laughed, Bill started on a circuit of the chamber, scrutinizing the gabled ceiling and running his hand over the walls and floor, checking out their condition. I thought he was going to keep talking about the function of the "handles", and their relationship to the "hook" discovered by Dixon, instead he went on a different tack.

'Dormion also suggested there was another undiscovered room, beneath the floor, which he believes is the actual burial chamber of Khufu, and that it might contain a treasure which could rival or exceed that found in Tutankhamen's tomb.'

'Did he find any evidence from his scans?'

'Not that I'm aware of.'

'Then I think he's dreaming.'

'Don't write him off so fast, he's been working in the pyramids for more than twenty years, and, to his credit, in 2000, his radar analyses at Meidum led to the discovery of two previously undetected rooms.'

'OK, I'll give him the benefit of the doubt. So, what happened with Gantenbrink and the door in the shaft?'

'He was scheduled to meet with the Minister of Culture about the discovery, but it never happened. A press conference was scheduled, but that didn't happen either. Incredibly, but perhaps not surprisingly, a full week after the discovery, not a single word had been said to the press.'

'They hardly wanted to let the truth get out before they'd had a chance to get in there themselves and rob whatever was behind the door.'

'Exactly! Not only that, despite the fact the pyramids belong to the world, it doesn't matter who you are, a tourist, a scientist, or a documentary-maker; everybody pays. And part of "the deal" is that all media announcements must come from official Egyptian channels, and that no commercial use is made of the research.

So, when nothing had happened about the announcement, Gantenbrink, perhaps naively and totally unaware of the whole Illuminati agendas and rigid Egyptian protocols, broke the story himself in The Daily Telegraph on the 7th of April

1993, and from there it quickly spread across the world.'

This was all new to me, I was glad I'd let Bill waffle on.

'Considerable speculation followed, with some believing that there might be a serdab with a statue of the king behind the entrance, while others, like Bakr, called it a big hoax.'

'That's right, I remember it now, there was a huge stink about it at the time, then, all of a sudden, it died down; today's news, tomorrows fish-and-chip wrapping.'

'Well, clearly by breaking the story, Gantenbrink had broken the rules. A week later, the Egyptian government told him to pack up his robot and get out of Egypt; they claim he leaked too much information to the press for their liking.'

'So that was it?'

'No, Gantenbrink was just an innocent pawn caught in the middle of a complex web of intrigue and deceit, he had no idea the inconvenience he'd created; he just wanted to get the discovery out to the world. His subsequent requests for a license to re-investigate the northern shaft, with a modified robot that could successfully navigate the bend, was flatly refused; he even offered to supply the camera and train an Egyptian technician, but to no avail.'

'Why not?'

'Hawass used the excuse that it was the German Institute in Cairo, and not Gantenbrink, that had the concession to the Great Pyramid, and that the Institute wasn't interested in completing the work on the shafts. Because Gantenbrink was an individual, and the antiquities law in Egypt only allows for concessions to be granted to institutions, it was impossible to assign the concession to him, so Hawass decided that the Supreme Council would do the work instead.'

'How convenient, especially when it was really Hawass who set the rules.'

'He used to; Hawass had a huge influence on the laws relating to archaeological digs in Egypt. He would lobby the government for new laws and often get them.'

'But he's such a hypocrite; he calls for the death penalty for anyone who takes artefacts out of Egypt, and yet he's the biggest thief of them all.'

'Ironical, isn't it, which makes the Gantenbrink incident even more interesting because it was around the same time Hawass was sacked as well.'

'That's right, wasn't Hawass sacked by Doctor Bakr because he supposedly stole a valuable statue?'

'Possibly, but it makes more sense it was because Hawass let the cat out of the bag.'

It all made sense.

'But Hawass didn't take it lying down, he went above Bakr's head; he flew to America to meet with his Illuminati masters. Hawass probably said it was Bakr's fault, because Bakr was in charge of the media releases, and, three months later, Hawass is not only miraculously reinstated, but promoted to Chief Inspector, and Bakr is fired instead.'

'It sounds pretty straight-forward to me.'

'Gantenbrink wouldn't have had a clue what was really going on...'

Having concluded his examination, Bill nodded then made a beeline for the entrance.

'...We'd best get going, I'll fill you in on the rest along the way...'

Following right behind, we clambered back into the confines of the horizontal passage.

'...And that's how it stayed, at least officially, until 2002, when the National Geographic Society created a similar robot, specially designed to ascend the southern shaft and drill a three-quarter-of-an-inch hole through "the door".'

'And?'

'The block was only about six centimetres thick, and, when they inserted a miniature fibre-optic camera into the space, it revealed another rough-hewn blocking stone, with cracks all over the surface, lying about twenty centimetres beyond the original southern shaft door.'

'No secret chambers or treasure?'

'Nope.'

'So that was it?'

'No, a few days later they sent the robot up the northern shaft.'

'Don't tell me, they discovered the same thing.'

'More twists and turns, but, yep, about sixty-five metres in they hit another "door", again with the remnants of two copper "handles" sticking out.'

'And that was in 2002?'

'Yep.'

'The very same year Hawass became Secretary General of the Supreme Council of Antiquities and built the walls around the Giza Plateau.'

'Just a coincidence?'

'Of course, just like it's a coincidence that night follows day.'

We emerged from the other end of the passage back to where there was an almost seamless transition from the Ascending Passageway to the Grand Gallery.

'And was that the end of it; nothing's been done since?'

'Who knows what they've done behind closed doors? But the investigations apparently started up again in 2011 with the Djedi Project, who penetrated the door in the northern shaft then used a fibre-optic endoscopic "snake" camera to view all around the narrow empty space they discovered behind it.

Interestingly they discovered a number of what they called "faint quarry marks" or "hieroglyphs" written in red paint, although the symbols didn't correlate with any known hieroglyphs.'

'I wonder if they correlate with the ones inside the wave pattern at the entrance?'

'Now, that *would* be interesting!'

The Grand Gallery

Ahead of us, still toning, the ladies had made their way slowly to the top of the Grand Gallery, which certainly was an architectural masterpiece.

Nearly 50 metres long and from 8.48 to 8.74 metres high, the gallery rose at the same angle as the Ascending Passage. It's size was extraordinary, but, most impressive, was the corbelled ceiling, which was much like the chambers in the pyramid at Meidum and the Red and Bent Pyramids but on a much more grandiose scale. At the base it was about two metres wide, but, just over two metres up the side walls, the slabs of stone corbelled inwards by three inches on each side for each of the seven 'steps', so that at the top it was only a metre wide. The construction is apparently so precise that not a piece of paper or a needle can be inserted between the stones. The ceiling stones, rather than flat, were all angled towards the King's Chamber.

The fact the walls were completely bare, not a single relief, image, or hieroglyph, to me somewhat betrayed the naming of it as a "gallery", especially as, according to the majority of Egyptologists, the purpose of the gallery is supposedly to divert the weight of the mass of stone above the King's Chamber into the surrounding pyramid core. But, if the diversion theory were true, why the need for such accuracy, and wouldn't there be a gallery on all four sides of the pyramid?

As the ladies continued toning, their dulcet tones resonating and reverberating through the pyramid, every now and then, one or two of them shifted pitch, creating a new chord and causing the gallery to somehow come to life. The more I listened, the more I looked, the more I kept coming back to *'The Giza Power Plant'*, that this was a resonating chamber.

Low ramps about half-a-metre wide ran along both sides of the gallery, leaving a central gully about a metre wide between them. Each ramp contained 27 regularly spaced slots, alternating large and small, which corresponded with right-angled niches in the side walls. The Egyptologists didn't have much of a clue what they were for, but seemed to believe the central gully was for storing the portcullis blocks before they were slid down into the Ascending Passage, and the slots held wooden beams to initially restrain the blocks. What, all 27 slots? That's 27 portcullis blocks; I don't think so. Yet another wild speculation that didn't make sense; why, because you had the whole Ascending Passage to do that if that's what you wanted.

Eager to rejoin the ladies, Bill had started up the left hand steps to make the ascent along the left hand ramp. I paused momentarily to try my hand, or rather my larynx, joining the others in toning.

I focused on the pitch that seemed to cause the gallery to pulsate and suddenly found my voice box was doing things it had never done before, like it was turning upside down; it was as if my larynx was not mine, but that of another entity. I felt as if my voice was underpinning the harmonic chant of the whole group, like a sonic foundation for what was to come, the rich resonating sound cascading up and down the Grand Gallery.

'Is something wrong?'

Bill had stopped and was looking back at me.

'No, just testing the acoustics.'

'Hmmm, yes, remarkable!'

I climbed the opposite staircase and made my way up the right side of the gallery.

'You know Christopher Dunn figured out this was a massive resonating chamber that had a whole series of your Helmholtz resonators in it.'

'Did he just? Helmholtz resonators! Where?'

'Suspended seven deep in each of theses slots.'

Bill looked around, up and down the gallery.

'Interesting! Plausible; hollow vessels, like ocarinas, probably made out of pottery, although they may have been carved out of diorite, granite would make sense, schist, basalt, quartzite, even crystal, suspended throughout the gallery. Very plausible!'

'Do you think there's any significance to there being 27 rows of them?'

'I'm sure there is; twenty-seven is three cubed.'

'What does that mean?'

Bill chuckled away.

'I've got no idea, but the seven layers deep might refer to the seven notes within a musical scale; you know, doh, re, mi, fah, soh, la, and ti, with no need for the octave as it would be duplicated by the first resonator.'

'Well, that's blindingly obvious then, isn't it Fraulein Maria; seven steps, seven notes!..'

As I started to sing a medley from *'The Sound of Music'*, I remembered something.

'...Hey, weren't most of the other big pyramids constructed in seven steps?'

'I do believe they were.'

'So what about the smaller pyramids, the ones with four or five steps?'

'Maybe they just functioned on the pentatonic scale; doh, re, mi, soh, la?'

'Could it really have been as simple as that?'

'It's possible.'

As the last of the ladies ducked down and disappeared into the narrow antechamber that led to the King's Chamber, and the sound of their toning stopped, Bill started musing over the ramifications of the function of the Grand Gallery. Standing on the step at the top of the gallery, I took the opportunity to check out another key structural element.

The Relieving Chambers

Reaching the upper end of the gallery, on the right-hand side of the southern wall, near the roof, was a hole. There was no way of getting up there to check it out, but the opening apparently led to a short tunnel and to the lowest of five Relieving Chambers, so named because they supposedly relieved or distributed the weight of the blocks above the King's Chamber away from the chamber to prevent it from collapse, although that theory had more holes in it than bullet-ridden Swiss cheese.

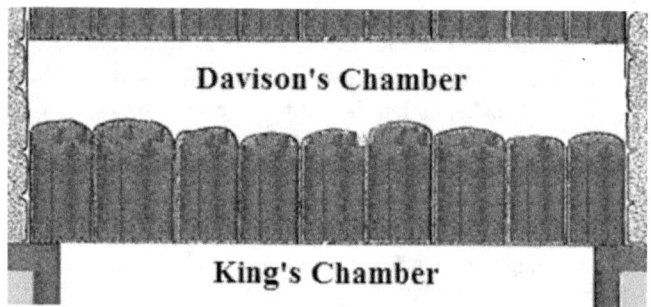

For instance; the Queen's Chamber, positioned lower than the King's Chamber, has far more weight bearing down upon it from the masonry above, and yet it has no relieving chambers, just its gabled ceiling. The Relieving Chambers had to serve some other purpose.

From my previous research, I knew the lowest chamber, called "Davison's Chamber", after the 18th Century English diplomat who visited it, was low, only a few feet high, with it's flat ceiling consisting of 9 huge blocks of red granite, weighing up

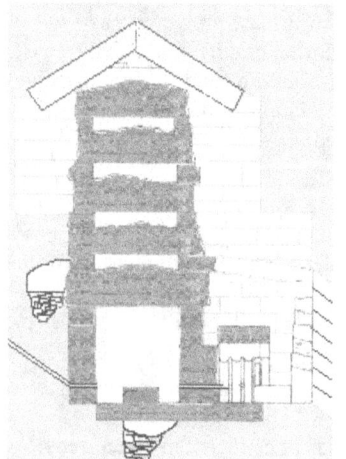

to 70 ton each, square-cut on three sides and roughly cut on top. Why granite, why not limestone?

The existence of Davison's Chamber excluded the possibility the ceiling stones held up the weight, in fact, it confirmed they were "free-standing", meaning they were free to vibrate. The arrangement of the ceiling stones, side on, confirmed there was a functionality to them that had nothing to do with bearing the weight of the pyramid above.

I knew the use of red granite had major significance, and that its significance was relevant to vibrational frequency, but why exactly was it used here. I could understand it being the floor, that was the ceiling of the King's chamber, but why was it used as the ceiling of Davison's Chamber? And there were more chambers, discovered in 1837/38, when Vyse used blasting powder and dynamite to reveal four more "Relieving Chambers", one atop the other, above the King's Chamber.

Vyse named the four chambers, in order from lowest to highest, "Wellington's Chamber", after Duke Wellington, "Nelson's Chamber", after Lord Nelson, "Lady Arbuthnot's Chamber", after Lady Ann Arbuthnot, and, finally, the largest, "Campbell's Chamber", after the Scottish diplomat and amateur archaeologist, Patrick Campbell.

It was in one of these chambers, "Campbell's Chamber", that Vyse supposedly discovered a cartouche, believed to be that of Khufu, on one of the southern roof blocks.

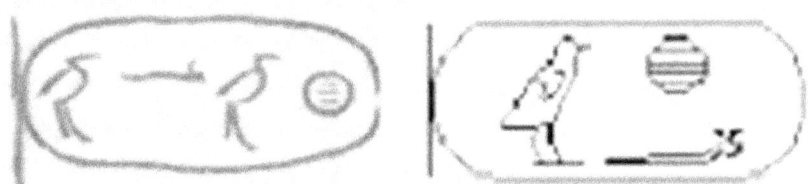

It wasn't exact, and yet it is from that one solitary scant unreliable skerrick of information, that the Egyptologists have formulated their whole history concerning the Great Pyramid, and have done so despite the speculation, as early as when it was first "discovered", that it was Vyse himself who painted the cartouche. One of Vyse's staff even noticed that the paint of the cartouche was still wet.

Later investigations by Zecharia Sitchin in 1980 came to the conclusion the name was initially spelled incorrectly and later corrected, and the kind of red ochre paint used for the cartouche was still in use in 1837. Despite that, many Egyptologists have refuted the evidence and clung to the Khufu attribution as fact, claiming that there is no reason why Vyse would do such a thing. Really? So, why *would* Vyse fake a cartouche?

Vyse had invested considerable time and money blasting up from Davison's Chamber only to find nothing in the next three chambers. It is logical to assume that by the time he reached Campbell's Chamber, he was frustrated and realized, by its gabled ceiling, that he'd reached the end of the line, and that it too was empty. Remembering that these early 'archaeologists' were actually treasure and glory hunters, it's logical to assume, that hoping to claim some sort of glory, that, while Vyse was up there on his own, he deliberately forged the markings, if only to save face. All that aside, there have supposedly been other markings discovered in some of the other chambers.

Another cartouche, apparently on the south wall of "Lady Arbuthnot's Chamber", apparently belongs to "Khnum-Khuf", which is nowadays believed by many Egyptologists to be Khufu's real name.

Or is it just that they are trying to fit the evidence to their theory rather than let the evidence speak for itself? Just because you find a name scrawled in the attic of a building doesn't necessarily mean that the owner of that name is necessarily the one who built the house. I think we colloquially refer to such scrawls as graffiti, and there were hundreds of examples of it all over the monuments of Egypt, of people who had visited the monuments and left their calling card; "Foo was here".

Is it possible that Khufu, or rather someone from Khufu's era, perhaps a repairman, visited this extremely inaccessible location? If so, why? Was it to make repairs after the pyramid had short-circuited during the pole shift? That's what Dunn proposed in *'The Giza Power Plant'*, and, whilst he didn't consider a pole shift as the cause, I believed he was spot on about the 'explosion' within the King's Chamber, and about the repairs made.

However, there are other, unforgeable marks located behind the blocks, only visible through cracks in certain stones, which are reportedly of the same ilk as those inside the wave motif at the entrance and behind the door in the northern shaft of the Queen's Chamber. What their story is, remains to be revealed.

Overall, the whole structure, from the bottom of the King's Chamber to the top of Campbell's Chamber, is about twenty-one metres high. Each chamber had a rough-cut uneven floor formed from the red-granite block of the ceiling of the chamber below, indicating the floor was not meant to function as a floor per se? I could understand its use as the ceiling of the King's Chamber, but why use red granite for the ceilings and floors of the additional four chambers?

And, why the need for the ceilings to be cut smooth, the exception being the final, top chamber, "Campbell's Chamber", having a gabled saddle roof made of limestone blocks? Sure, it was consistent with the gabled ceilings in other pyramids, but why the shift to limestone here? It confirmed the use of red granite for the floor/ceilings of the other chambers had a definite functional purpose.

Dunn suggests in *'The Giza Power Plant'* the purpose of the Relieving Chambers was to create amplification of a frequency through sympathetic vibration, and I agree. Each stone would have had pieces removed from its roughened top surface until it was 'tuned' to the desirable matching frequency of the King's Chamber. It would also explain the tunnel leading from the top of the Grand Gallery; it was a conduit for the sound produced in the Grand Gallery. And then the bleeding obvious it hit me!

'Hey, Bill, the sound wasn't propagated through air, it was through hydrogen gas, the hydrogen produced in the Queen's Chamber; the whole Grand Gallery would have been filled with hydrogen gas!'

'Of course, it wasn't a fusion reactor at all, at least this one wasn't; the whole structure was attuned to the subatomic spin resonance frequency of hydrogen.'

'OK, Dunn said something about that, and I sort of followed, but why hydrogen, why not just normal air?'

'Normal air is too impure, it's made up of around seventy-eight percent Nitrogen, twenty-one per cent Oxygen and one percent of other gases like Argon, Carbon Dioxide, Neon, Helium, Methane, and a whole range of other inert gases; each one having its own different spin resonance frequency. Hydrogen gas, which is the simplest of all gases, consisting of two protons and two electrons, would easily have been excited by the numerous Helmhotlz resonators in the Grand Gallery which would have been attuned to the frequency of hydrogen in such as way as to encourage the electrons to jump to a higher shell.

The excited gas would have risen up to the top of the Grand Gallery, in through that hole up there is the south wall, along the tunnel and into the Relieving Chambers where it would cause significant sympathetic vibration in the forty-odd blocks of the floors-stroke-ceilings of the Reliving Chambers and thus create a downward acoustic pressure into the King's Chamber below.'

'I'm guessing it would also have travelled down the Ascending Passage, where it would similarly stimulate the seven girdles, as well as the three granite portcullis blocks.'

'Ultimately creating a long chamber resonating with a specific frequency, which would channel through the upper tunnel into the Relieving Chambers.'

'Brilliant.'

'Wait, there's more. Some of the vibration here in the Grand Gallery would also have been reflected by the ceiling tiles directly towards the entrance to the King's Chamber, travelling in and through the antechamber, and on into the King's Chamber.'

'A double whammy!'

'Yep.'

I wasn't sure if it was exactly what Dunn had suggested, it sounded similar, but different; the principle was the same though.

'Bill, I think you're a fucking genius.'

He gestured for me to enter the antechamber.

'Couldn't have figured it out without your input.'

The Antechamber

Bill led the way, ducking down and entering the narrow passage and antechamber that connected the Grand Gallery to the King's Chamber.

Barely a metre high and wide, there was no way this was ever intended to be an access for funerary artefacts let alone humans.

After just a metre it opened into a small confined section where I could stand up; it felt like I was standing in a chimney. Looking up, the southern wall, which was incomplete in that it only went about halfway up, was made from one, or possibly two slabs of granite.

Referred to as a 'leaf' by the Egyptologists, though why I could never understand, it created a partial partition between this part of the 'antechamber' and the following section. The 'leaf' sat in a groove, cut into the surrounding walls, that only went partially down the wall; clearly this block was never intended to be a portcullis, otherwise it would have fully sealed the space. But it didn't, so it was never intended to be a portcullis. That raised the question, what *was* it for?

In the centre of the north face of the leaf was a small oval-shaped knob. At first I thought it might have been a raised cartouche, or, as some have suggested, a 'boss' for making the slab easier to maneuver. I took another look. To create the 'boss' meant removing about an inch of the surface of the entire slab, except for the 'boss'. That was an extraordinary amount of work just to create a 'handhold' when surely it would have been much easy to carve a "handhold' *in* to the slab? No, the 'boss' had a function, what that was, I had no idea.

I ducked under the leaf and moved into the second part of the 'antechamber', the section that, according to the theories of the Egyptologists, supposedly once housed three monolithic red granite portcullis blocks, about four feet by six feet and just over twenty inches thick.

The southern wall contained four long thin vertical grooves, about 6½ inches apart, most likely for holding and guiding ropes. It explained the 3½-inch holes drilled through the red-granite fragments found in the pit of the Subterranean Chamber, the one in the horizontal passage outside it's entrance, another one inside the Grotto, and possibly the one outside the main entrance; all parts of the smashed 'portcullis' blocks. That the holes were precision-drilled 6½ inches apart, with some jewelled tubular drill capable of cutting through granite, and that they aligned perfectly with the vertical grooves in the southern wall, confirmed the fragments once belonged in the antechamber.

But then something didn't add up, it was the ropes with the grooves; there was no way the ropes could have run up the groves, the portcullis blocks would have jammed under the lower part of the southern wall. Then I figured it out. The grooves *were* for the rope, but not for its length, rather for the knot where the rope was passed through the slabs; it would have stuck out. Problem solved.

In the adjacent walls were four twenty-one-inch-wide grooves, three of which were probably intended to hold the massive granite slabs, each weighing two ton, similar to the leaf, but, more than likely with a different function. It was from here that the various granite fragments, all around twenty-one-inches thick, most likely originated, as part of a portcullis system.

And that was the predominant theory proposed and accepted by the majority of Egyptologists, that the antechamber once housed a 'portcullis' system, that, during the life of the pharaoh, used ropes and pulleys to hold the three portcullis blocks up in the opposing vertical grooves, and were lowered to form a barrier after he had been entombed. As I examined the grooves I contemplated the reliability of their theory.

There were all sorts of problems with the 'accepted' theory; primarily that it didn't explain *all* the features inherent within the antechamber. For example, the main problem as I could see it was that the antechamber hallway was only a metre square, and it would make it almost impossible to move anything of substance into the King's Chamber.

My next thought was, if the pyramid wasn't a tomb, rather a power plant as Christopher Dunn suggested, then these portcullises really weren't portcullises, they had some other function. Dunn speculated they were acoustic filters, or 'baffles', that could be adjusted to ensure that a specific frequency or harmonic chord could be focused into the King's Chamber free of any interference waves. He goes on to suggest the 'baffles', rather than portcullises, would have been adjusted when they were installed. I wasn't so sure.

Whoever built the pyramid had extraordinary knowledge and the skill to make precise structures of amazing complexity. If they wanted to have a specific frequency they surely would have constructed it in a fixed way, not with three variable slabs. That left only one option; the 'baffles' were constructed to regulate the input *during* the operation of the power plant, and that's when the next question arose.

If the Queen's Chamber, Grand Gallery, and King's Chamber were all filled with hydrogen gas, how did anyone get in to make any adjustments; there was no clear access, and no air to breathe? There had to be an adjacent control room, and that control room had to be accessed somehow, from some tunnels or staircases as yet undiscovered, or rather discovered but not made public. Why? Because the staircases led to other rooms the puppet-masters didn't want us to know about. The evidence from the 1976 expedition was becoming even more relevant.

I was a little caught up in my thoughts when Bill popped up next to me having returned from the King's Chamber.

'You joining us?'

'Sure. But, before we go, do you know if they've done any scans here in the antechamber for other adjacent rooms?'

'Yep, when the SRI did their scans back in 1977 they spent a night collecting data from the King's Chamber and the antechamber.'

'Did they find anything?'

'That's a good question, Alex. They supposedly found an anomaly just over seven metres beneath the floor, about halfway between the King's and Queen's Chambers.'

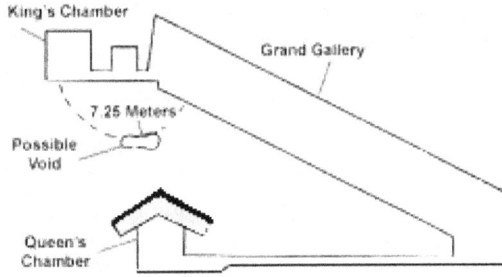

'Did they do anything?

'Another good question; the "official" report is that the SRI suggested it was just a void created by the change in plan in building the pyramid, or a large crack, and the Egyptians took the view, that as the pyramid was a tomb, they knew all there was to need to know, that there were no more mysteries, and it would be a waste of time to investigate further.'

'They're just scared the truth might come out and ruin their reputations.'

'Probably.'

'Was there any mention of rooms to the side of the antechamber?'

'Not that I know of, why?'

'I think there has to be a control room to the side where they would've adjusted the blocks that were once in here while the pyramid was operating.'

'Now that's interesting; Come on, I think you might find what's next door might suggest you're right.'

Bill ducked back down and led the way into the King's Chamber.

The King's Chamber

Set in the 50th course of the pyramid's masonry and made entirely of Aswan red granite, the King's Chamber measures 5.2 metres north to south, 10.5 metres east to west, by 5.8 metres high. There are 21 stones comprising the floor, 101 comprising the walls, and 9 huge beams, each weighing between 50 and 80 ton and with a combined weight of over four hundred tons, forming the flat ceiling. I had dreamt of this moment for over twenty years, and now it was about to come true.

As I followed Bill into the low connecting tunnel, I stubbed my foot on the floor; it seemed the builders had left a ledge of just under an inch between the floor of the antechamber and the slightly higher floor of the King's Chamber. An oversight? An accident? A miscalculation? I doubted it.

'Alex, just in time...'

In the centre of the room Diane and Pernille were lighting several tea lights on the floor, Pernille having placed her newly acquired crystal ball, nestled in a scarf, in the centre of them. The other ladies were dispersed around the room, mostly around the sarcophagus. Diane was calm, yet methodical.

'...We're just waiting for the guardians to turn off the lights at 8:00 am and we'll get started. You might want to take the time to have a quick look around.'

I checked my iphone 7:52 am; I figured I had time to look around at the same time as I got Bill to show me what he wanted.

Apart from the sarcophagus in the western end, the chamber was empty: a massive empty stone room. There basically wasn't anything else to see, all the walls were bereft of images, nothing, not even a calling card from Foo; the only points of interest were the entrances to the north and south shafts.

There's been considerable speculation about the purpose of the shafts in the King's Chamber as, unlike the Queen's Chamber shafts which both terminated at

Gantenbrink's 'doors', the King's Chamber shafts continued through to the outside of the pyramid. The various theories include:

- ventilation shafts, which would be ridiculously superfluous to a dead pharaoh, and much easier to have constructed horizontally,

- some ritualistic purpose associated with the ascension of the dead pharaoh's spirit to the heavens and showing his path to the afterlife,

- alignments with specific star systems such as, depending whose theory you want to believe, to Orion's belt in the ancient skies, or Sirius, or the circumpolar stars.

None of the mainstream theories stood up to close scrutiny, primarily because the northern shaft doglegged its way around the Grand Gallery before rising towards the surface. As it was closest to the entrance, being just over a metre along the north wall and about a metre from the floor, I was quickly drawn to its small rectangular opening.

About 8.4 inches wide by 4.8 inches high, Dunn suggested in '*The Giza Power Plant*' it was almost exactly attuned to the frequency of hydrogen, around 1.42 Giga hertz, or a wavelength of around 8.31 inches, which, given the evidence I had seen with my own eyes, I was inclined to accept.

Beyond the opening, the north channel, only 5 inches high x 7 inches wide, twisted and turned then ascended at an angle of approximately 31°, and for over 235 feet in length, before emerging 53 metres up the surface of the north face.

There had to be some reason why the north shaft was so closely aligned and integrated into the structure of the Antechamber and the Grand Gallery. Dunn thought it was to do with transmitting atomic hydrogen from the universe but I wasn't so sure, that could have been done from shafts in any direction. Close, but no cigar; well, as far as I know.

'If it's not the shafts, then what's the big surprise, Bill, the sarcophagus?'

Keeping his voice low so as to not disturb the others, he pointed back at the tiny entrance.

'No. You see the entrance?'

'Hardly a grand entrance fit for a king.'

'Exactly. That's because it wasn't an entrance, well, not for people, it used to be sealed by a granite block.'

I looked around for it, not really sure what Bill was getting at.

'Yeah? Where is it?'

'I don't know, it used to be on the floor, next to the sarcophagus, up at the other end of the chamber, but it disappeared in 1998 during Hawass's "renovations".'

I dived into my iphone.

'Hang on a sec, I think I've a photo of it.'

'According to reports, the block's dimensions exactly matched those of the entrance, which means it probably slotted snugly in the corridor, sealing the chamber.'

'So, they pushed it into place before they lowered the portcullis blocks, what's unusual about that?'

'That's just it, it had to have been pushed into place from *inside* the King's Chamber.'

'How do you figure that?'

'The cross-sectional area of the section of corridor between the Grand Gallery and the portcullis chamber is smaller than that of the corridor between the portcullis chamber and the King's Chamber; it doesn't make sense it would be stored in the portcullis chamber, there's just not enough room, and there's no indication of the use of any mortar to seal it in place.'

I found the image I was looking for.

'Here it is! Yep, there was a block beside the sarcophagus...'

I handed the iphone to Bill.

'...You can see where Al-Ma'moun's men must have smashed the outer end and sides of it before finally pushing it into the chamber.'

'And that's where it must have stayed for over twelve-hundred years, until Hawass moved it...'

He handed me back the phone.

'...The question is; why did he get rid of it?'

'Spring cleaning?'

'I doubt it; I think he had other things on his mind.'

'Such as?'

'That's what I wanted to show you, come, take a look at this.'

He led me up towards the sarcophagus, and pointed at the wall.

'Sorry, Bill, what am I supposed to be looking at?'

'The wall; look at the lowest stone second from the left.'

I crouched down for a better look. It was "different", there was a noticeable gap between it and the surrounding stones that had been plugged with mortar, badly I might add. And it was fractionally out of alignment; that was inconsistent with the rest of the whole pyramid, in fact it was often said that the joints in the pyramid were so perfect that you couldn't insert a razor blade into them. I compared the other stones around it in the wall.

'No, all perfectly fitted, seamless, except this one.'

'Surely, if the lowest block was put in place first, it would've been aligned to the two blocks beside it, and the block on top aligned as well, but here, all the others are in alignment with each other *except* this one, which means it was either added later, or ...'

'It's moved.'

'Sure it's moved, because it was *meant* to move. Take a look at the stones on top of it; the bottom one isn't even load-bearing. In fact, the very top stone is more like a door lintel, bearing the entire weight of the ceiling stones.'

Bill was right; it looked like a slightly skew-whiff doorway.

'It's another entrance, just like the main one!'

'Certainly looks that way...'

It had to be, and it made sense that it connected to the room that contained the controls to the ropes and pulleys in the antechamber.

'...See the cracks in the centre of the second stone; they're a sure fire indication there was a space between the two blocks, and that the lower stone is free standing, meaning it was mobile.'

'If this was a door, or an access portal, why would the ancient Egyptians put the sarcophagus right in front of it?'

'They didn't, it used to sit between the north and south shafts, lifted slightly off the floor by a small piece of flint under one end.'

'That would free it up to resonate as much as possible and for as long as possible with only a minimal dampening effect from its contact at the other end.'

'Exactly, and the end probably acted as a harmonic node for the sarcophagus anyway.'

'A resonating box within a resonating chamber.'

'Within a resonating superstructure.'

'So why is it here?'

'Hawass moved it, to cover up the stone and the floor, to cover up the "renovation work" they did back in 1998.'

'Renovation work? What exactly was this "work" they supposedly did?'

'Who really knows? Officially it was to reconstruct the floor in the northwest corner of the King's Chamber; for years there was a modern grille covering the excavation done by Al-Ma'moun's men.'

'Why did Al-Ma'moun specifically dig here, did he know something?'

'My guess is, he did; the movable block in the lower layer must have been a clue that there was another chamber behind the wall and, either he made a mistake and ordered them to dig down, or, and this is strictly my belief, having broken in, he knew how thick the walls were and decided it would be easier to try and tunnel underneath, through the floor and limestone foundation.'

'Or...'

And the idea hit me suddenly.

'...Do you think he might have actually had a floor-plan? After all he seemed to know exactly where to break *in* to the pyramid, exactly level with the intersection of the Ascending and Descending Passages; surely that was more than just a coincidence? It was like he'd already been inside and knew exactly where to target to circumnavigate the blocks at the bottom of the Ascending Passage.'

'That's an interesting thought; I don't think anyone's every considered that before. It's possible.'

We turned our attention to the open sarcophagus, the southeast corner of which looked broken away. About 2 ¼ metres long, around a metre wide and weighing about 3.75 tons it had to have been put in place before construction of the chamber was finished as it was way too big to have been brought in through both the Antechamber corridor and the Ascending Passage.

'And how long did it take Hawass to fix the floor?'

'He shut down the pyramid for eight months?'

'Eight months! To re-block and reconstruct a section of floor less than six metres square? I smell a rat, or rather a vulture!'

'I think Hawass was just another puppet in a long line of marionettes.'

'What makes you think that?'

'The fact he was sacked in '93 and then quickly reinstated; the same as recently. Besides, the whole "renovation" saga goes way back to 1966, way before Hawass was even on the scene.'

'You've lost me?'

In between making our way around the sarcophagus, closely examining it, Bill filled me in.

'It all started back in 1966 with the Joint Pyramid Project, when a team from the University of California, led by Dr. Luis Alvarez, together with a group of Egyptian physicists from the Ain Shams University, and archaeologists from the then Egyptian Antiquities Organization, supported by, amongst others, the Smithsonian

Institute, IBM and Hewlett-Packard, used cosmic-ray detectors designed by the US Atomic Energy Commission, to scan the Pyramid of Khafre for more chambers.'

'That's quite a pedigree of Illuminati-controlled organizations, but, Luis Alvarez, isn't he the guy who came up with the idea that the dinosaurs were all wiped out by an asteroid sixty-five million years ago?'

'That's him.'

'How did *he* get involved?'

'Alvarez was also a giant of physics; you know was aboard the Enola Gay when it dropped the bomb on Hiroshima, he even worked with the Warren Commission on the investigation into the assassination of JFK.'

'No way! Shit, then he's about as straight as a dog's hind leg; if Randy was here, he would be like a pig in shit. So, what did they find?'

'Well, the first thing of interest is that the experiment had to be delayed because of the outbreak of the Six Day War.'

'Surely you're not suggesting the Six Day War was just a diversion, that they actually went into the pyramids during the war so that no one would notice?'

'Whether it was deliberately planned, or opportunistic, I can't say, but I wouldn't put it past them either way.'

'But that was Khafre's pyramid, right?'

'Yep, officially, but it doesn't take too many brains to consider they would have taken the opportunity to scan the Great Pyramid as well.'

'What were the results?'

'*That's* where it gets interesting.'

Bill started fingering one of the three holes that had been drilled into the top edge of the western side. As he did, I sprouted what the Egyptologists had concluded.

'Pinion holes, to hold the lid in place?'

He wobbled his head.

'Well, yes and no, that's what the 'experts' say, but without a lid to cross-reference then the pinion holes could have been drilled for anything; they've never found any other sarcophagi with them.'

'And because the lid has never been discovered, nor any fragments of it, nor any mummy, it of course raises the question of whether it actually was a sarcophagus and whether there actually was a lid; there probably was, but then again there possibly wasn't.'

'I think it's fair to assume there *was* a lid, the question is, why would you need pinions to hold a two-ton lid in place inside a chamber where there is supposed to be no movement? Pinions would only be necessary, and make total sense, if the coffer was designed to vibrate, resonate, and you didn't want the lid to move laterally. That said, I think one thing is certain, it wasn't a sarcophagus.'

'You know, Bill, Christopher Dunn deduced the coffer was machined from one single block of Aswan red granite using high-speed machinery.'

Bill took a closer look at the stone.

'I agree, there's no way they could have done this with copper chisels and diorite pounding stones, to even suggest that is asinine. But this surface is hardly finely-cut, I think it might have been once, but, well, now it looks cauterised.'

'Cauterised?'

'Burned, melted; the granite looks like it's been burned by extremely high temperatures, like it's been baked.'

I had a closer look myself, running my hands over the surface.

'Yeah, it's darker than the chamber walls, which look like the inside of an oven; Dunn even speculated the broken corner wasn't so much broken, as melted.'

'I tend to agree. All of which supports that the chamber was filled with hydrogen and some extremely high-temperature explosion took place.'

'A fusion reaction?'

'I don't think so, but something pretty catastrophic happened here, that's for sure.'

'Did the scans done by Alvarez give any clues?'

'Not really; the information collected from the detectors was recorded on magnetic tapes and, when they analysed the tapes back at Berkeley University, they found that each time they ran the tapes through the computer, although it was scientifically impossible, different patterns appeared, supposedly indicating something weird was going on.'

'You think they deliberately scrambled the results?'

'Of course, but only after they'd discovered the truth. Later on, when they adjusted the data, it supposedly revealed Khafre's pyramid had nothing but a solid core.'

'If they didn't find anything, what makes you think they're hiding something?'

'If they didn't find anything, why did the SRI and the Ain Shams University come back in 1977 and do acoustic sounding, resistivity *and* magnetometry surveys, not just of Khafre's pyramid, but *then* specifically targeted the Antechamber and King's Chamber of the Great Pyramid for two nights?'

'Good point.'

'That was followed by Hawass becoming Chief Inspector at Giza in 1980.'

'And the following year Sadat was assassinated because he knew too much.'

'Then, five years later, when there's talk of the possibility of new rooms inside the Great Pyramid, Hawass again suddenly closes the pyramids for six months, again supposedly for maintenance. How does it take six months to "maintain" a stone monument that has been around for maybe hundreds-of-thousands of years?'

'Not only that, the following year, because of his "maintenance work", Hawass was rewarded by being made General Director at both Giza and Saqqara, and given a professorship from the University of Pennsylvania.'

'Rewards for his efforts no doubt. But then there was the Gantenbrink saga, in 1993, and that put a spanner in the works that nearly cost Hawass his position.'

'Until the puppet-masters bailed him out. Then, two years later, Hawass expels all the foreigners from Giza, becomes Undersecretary of State at Giza, and after that, there's the Luxor Massacre.'

'The following year, Hawass shut the whole pyramid down again, this time for eight months, but not before, on the 1st April 1998, a team of researchers, led by Simon Cox from University College in London, apparently took some covert video inside the pyramid that showed secret

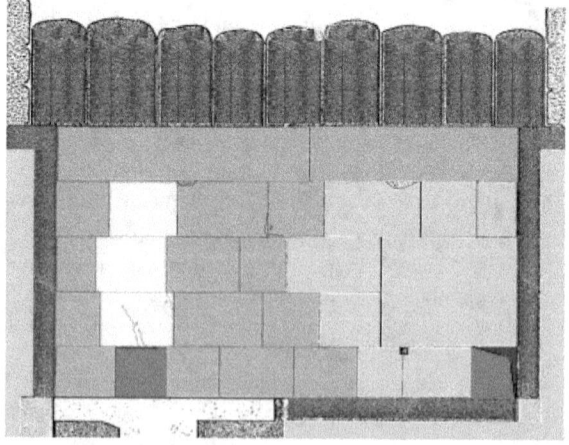

excavations of a tunnel which they believed from their discrete inquiries was discovered by sonar and led to three previously unknown chambers.'

'Whereabouts?'

Bill pointed back out of the chamber.

'In a wall inside the antechamber.'

'I knew it!'

'Cox stumbled across a rusty old rectangular metal grille, about three-and-a-half feet by two-and-a-half feet, fixed with new mortar. Modern electric cables ran along the ceiling, clearly indicating that lighting and/or machinery was being used.'

'I didn't see any grille.'

'No doubt it was replaced by the original blocking stone when they'd finished. Anyway, shining his torch inside, Cox saw a tunnel, high enough to stand in, with two stairs leading up.'

'The tunnel must have led to the control room.'

'Possibly...'

By then, Bill had shifted his attention to the south of the western wall, to a crack in the last stone of the second layer.

'...Look over here. Whatever happened in here, it had enough force to fracture the whole stone.'

I examined the fracture; it ran the full span of the stone from top to bottom.

'Some have suggested it was caused by an earthquake?'

'Possible, but highly unlikely. Whatever happened here not only fractured this stone, it caused the walls of the chamber to shift *outwards* by a few centimetres.'

'Didn't al-Ma'Moun and Vyse both use explosives?'

'Sure, but not here, not *inside* the chamber, and I doubt they had the ability to localize the effects anyway. Besides, why would they go to the trouble of trying to repair the crack by sealing it with gypsum? The repairs are obviously post-event, but they must also have been before Al-Ma'moun blasted his way into the pyramid.'

'Khufu?'

'Possibly, maybe even earlier.'

'Which means if the pyramid short-circuited because of a pole-shift it may have taken the return of Imhotep to know how to fix it.'

'That's an interesting concept!'

And then I noticed the bleeding obvious.

'Hey, Bill, if this crack extends through the whole block, then that means this corner is exactly like the entrance, that this lower square block is most likely free standing,

'Which means there could be even another corridor and chambers beyond it.'

'Exactly. The plot thickens!'

'It does indeed.'

We moved on and reached the location of the cup-shaped opening to the southern shaft, the channel of which measured about 8 inches high x 12 inches wide, and rose at an angle of 41° for 175 feet before appearing 71 metres up the southern face of the pyramid. It was here that Gantenbrink had installed a ventilation fan to regulate moisture in the chamber so as to minimize the damage caused by the excessive moisture produced by the breath and sweat of visitors.

Perhaps the most remarkable aspect of the southern shaft, although it had been long-removed to the British Museum, was an iron plate, about 10 inches long, 3 ½ inches wide, and up to 1/5th of an inch thick, discovered in 1837, in a joint in the masonry at a point where the southern shaft exited the pyramid. Tests on the badly corroded plate detected the presence of gold, indicating the plate was possibly once gold-plated. The question is: what was it doing inside the shaft; surely it had absolutely nothing to do with any star alignment?

As I touched the wall beside the opening, I suddenly remembered the vision I'd seen at Karnak of alien satellites orbiting in a grid-network around the planet. Frank had even confirmed NASA knew about them, that the whole shuttle program was designed to bring them down to earth to study. Of course! The shafts weren't targeted on distant stars, their position would change with the orbit of the earth and with precession, the shafts were targeted on satellites and the gold-plated plate was part of a receiver or transmitter of microwave energy. Christopher Dunn had proposed it in *'The Giza Power Plant'*, and I think he hit the nail on the head. The northern shaft probably received relayed solar energy which was amplified in the King's Chamber using the frequency of hydrogen, then converted into piezoelectric energy, microwave energy, by a crystal sitting inside the granite coffer, and transmitted via the southern shaft, to a satellite for distribution around Egypt and possibly even the whole planet.

Then I thought: What if the satellite network was also in place to protect the planet in some way from the effects of the passing of Nibiru, a type of force-field? If that was the case, then was it the presence of the brown-dwarf that had caused the pyramid to overload and short-circuit? Something had to have been the cause.

Meanwhile, while I'd been preoccupied with the southern shaft, Bill had moved past the shaft and was staring at the ceiling in the southeast corner. I joined him.

'That's quite a series of fractures.'

'Maybe one block could spontaneously crack, but for all three to crack in almost exactly the same place is so far beyond the mathematical realms of probability it's impossible. Those cracks could only have happened if all three blocks were lifted into the air, then crashed back down. I can't begin to comprehend the necessary force required to lift three seventy-ton blocks of granite high enough into the air for them to fall and fracture the way they have; those blocks are at least two-and-a-half metres deep.'

'Dunn says they found a fine black powder in the space above, in Davison's chamber, and analysis showed it was the cast off of shells and skins of insects.'

'Exuviae.'

'That's it!

'Except it wasn't from insects, it was from the nummulitic limestone sides of Davison's Chamber, the limestone being made from fossilized seashells, calcium carbonate.'

'That's what Dunn says.'

'He's right! The explosion in the King's Chamber was so massive, so intense, it pushed the walls out, lifted the ceiling blocks into the air, shook the surface of the limestone loose, and the intense heat caramelised the calcium carbonate powder in the air, baked the surface of the chamber walls, and melted the outer surface of the sarcophagus.'

'Which is exactly the conclusion Dunn came to.'

'Which makes absolutely no sense if the pyramid was a tomb; what could possibly explode in a burial chamber?'

'A rancid post-mortem pharaonic bowel eruption perhaps?'

'It would give new meaning to the mummy's curse, but, no, I think we can rule out mummy farts as the cause. Anyway, sometime later, repairers entered through the main entrance...'

'Or from some as yet unknown entrance, the one discovered in the south face in 1976, or even a subterranean entrance.'

'True. They probably realized it would be easier to cut up through the limestone bedrock of the Well Shaft than try to bypass the blocks at the end of the Ascending Passage...'

'Isn't it more likely they didn't want to disturb the Ascending Passage because of its function?'

'Brilliant! That makes a hell-of-a-lot more sense. Then, once they exited the Well Shaft, they made their way into the King's Chamber, plastered the gaps in the walls and ceiling, and hoped for the best.'

'Which raises the other issue of why they would go to all the trouble to force their way in to make repairs if the chamber was just a tomb? And why build almost the entire pyramid out of limestone, then just the floor, the walls, the doorway, and the ceilings above the King's Chamber out of red granite?'

'That in itself is clear evidence the King's Chamber had a specific function, and that function related to the properties of red granite.'

'And, if the King's Chamber had a specific function related to red granite, then so did the whole pyramid, and so did all the other subterranean chambers made of red granite. Sure there may have been secondary functions, but those functions surely would have related to, or derived from, the properties of red granite. The question is; what are those properties?'

Bill ran his hand over the wall.

'First, red granite has a high thermal conductivity; moreover, it's rich in quartz, which, as we know, when pressure is applied, can generate voltage.'

'But where would the pressure come from?'

'The obvious source would be from the energy of excited hydrogen, that could produce an incredible amount of piezo-electric energy, which is clearly why the room had to have sealed surfaces, to contain the hydrogen, and possibly to keep the resonance constant as well.'

'Do you think they were successful?'

'Who knows, it depends when the repairs were made, and who made them.'

'What we do know is that after Moses stole the crystal from the coffer and was chased out of town, and then the Thera tsunami hit, the pyramid ceased to function and took on a totally different meaning in the light of the 18th Dynasty onwards.'

Suddenly the lights went out, leaving just the few tea lights in the centre of the chamber illuminating the room. For some reason I checked my iphone; 8:08 am, the guardians were obviously running on Egyptian time.

'All right, everybody, let's get started....'

The initiation

Diane had taken a position in front of the coffer, Crystal to her right and Pernille to her left. Lit by just a few tea lights in the centre of the room, they cast large shadowy spectres on the western wall. My mind instantly turned to the Annunaki; it was as if I could see them manifesting before my very eyes.

'...William, Alex, if you would be so kind as to take a place on either side of the room; Alex, perhaps if you take the centre of the south wall, and, William, if you could take the opposite position against the north wall.'

Unsure what was about to transpire, I assumed my allotted position, cleared my mind totally, and just opened my heart to the moment.

'Daughters of Aset, you have come here to take your final initiation, your final awakening. To assist you, and ground you through this passage, we welcome our brothers, William and Alex, and thank them for their love and service...'

Service? I didn't know what or why I was here, but I was, and, given the smile of confirmation on Crystal's face, I was sure there must have been a reason for it.

'…The great search for light, life, and love, merely begins here on the material plane. Carried to its ultimate destination, its final goal is complete oneness with the consciousness of the universe.

She who would follow the pathway of the goddess, must extend their consciousness beyond the darkness, into the void, must be open like the flower of life that blossoms through all time and space; beyond the nine interlocked dimensions, beyond the nine cycles of space, beyond the nine diffusions of consciousness, beyond the nine worlds within worlds…'

At first, Diane's words seemed cryptic, but, when she mentioned the flower of life, somehow I knew that she was speaking of quantum physics and of multiple dimensions of existences. For some reason, I took out my iphone to record her, closed my eyes and let go.

Next she started talking about the 12 pyramids on the Giza Plateau and that each pyramid had its own tone. 12 pyramids? In my mind I wandered off and did a quick count: there was Menkaure's Pyramid, which had 3 smaller pyramids, Khafre, which had one, and Khufu's Pyramid, which I was pretty sure had 4 satellite pyramids; that made eleven. Where was the other one; was it Khentkaus II, or possibly the Sphinx?

But then I had a thought; maybe the smaller pyramids weren't part of the 12, maybe the 12 were only all the large pyramids, all the major stars in the sky. As Diane continued, I counted them off starting at Sirius, Abu Raoush, and working back up the Nile; there was Abu Raoush, the three at Giza, the two pyramids at Zawiyet el-Aryan and the five at Abusir, at least 12 at Saqqara, six at Dahshur, 2 at Mazghuna, 2 more, at El-Lahuna and Lisht, and one each at Meidum and Hawarra. T least 35 pyramids. Far too many; I brought my thoughts back to Giza. As I did I heard the tail of Diane's oratory.

'…so each of the twelve pyramids here at Giza has its own specific tone, its own vibrational identity, and you, Alex, as the keeper of those tones, know those tones, and now is the time for you to sing them.'

My mind did a double take, 'What the fuck?', and then suddenly from within me a voice started to tone. My throat started doing back flips again, like it had in the Grand Gallery. This time not only were there notes, but words as well, ancient subtle variations on Ut, re mi, fah, soh, la, ti.

Though I recognized them as the white notes of a musical C major scale, they weren't the exact pitches you'd find on a piano, which is what they call 'even-tempered', these notes were natural harmonic frequencies, which vary slightly from the even-tempered system. They were the notes Bill and I had mentioned less than half an hour ago in the Great Gallery, and as I toned them, I had visions of the Grand Gallery 'turning on', 'lighting up'.

Then, after the first 7 notes were toned, the being I now was returned to the tonic and added in each of the chromatic notes related to the tonic, the black notes on the piano; di, ri (mor), fi, si, and ta. As I toned each note I had visions of other pyramids coming to life, being switched on, and 'downloads' of who I really was, why I was the one who was toning these notes and why they were being toned at this time, which was not just to reactivate the 12 pyramids, but to send out a beacon, a series of calling cards out across the cosmos saying, 'Yoo hoo, we're back online, and we're open for business'. And to whom were these messages being broadcast? To the star races genetically connected to the human race: the '12 Tribes of Israel'.

I'd often wondered how I'd known the reason the pyramids were different angles was because they had different vibrational base key frequencies. Now I knew, all the pieces totally dropped into place; because I was there when they were built.

The notes having been toned, the keys turned in each of their respective locks, who I was, the entity within me, then started to speak.

'I was once a mighty king, of a race not known to most of you. Full of pride was I, full of ego was I. Then I surrendered all to my people and, together with my queen, I travelled amongst my race; a vagabond was I, a hobo was I, a wandering minstrel was I, poet, prophet, pauper. And I was humbled. Eventually, I was liberated of all ego and thus my people were set free to travel both illusions: time and space. Then one day, millennia ago, I was invited to share this journey with others beyond my race. This is how I know you all; for as a Vagabond king, a wandering minstrel, I walked amongst each and every one of your races: each of your twelve tribes.

There are many other tribes for whom I have strummed my lute and sung my songs, retold my tale in both prose and poetry, but it is because of your twelve tribes that I am here. Each of your twelve tribes is of the one, yet different, similar, like the facets of a cosmic diamond. Like notes of chords of music they are; each resonates as part of a mighty symphony, yet each has its own sound, its own colour, its own distinctive resonance and vibration.

Your twelve tribes have been scattered to all the corners of the universe, and, as such, overtime, have lost connection to the cosmic orchestra, instead distracted to play your own tunes, and as such, whilst you believe you are all in tune, in reality you are playing out of time and out of tune with each another.

As both composer and conductor, this planet was created to bring those notes and chords back together to sound as one. And so it was that you, the instruments, the kings or queens of each of the twelve tribes, volunteered to forgo your egos and incarnate here on this planet to retune your race and reunite with your brothers and sisters in the cosmic orchestra.

So as not to forget this reunion, the great architect, the great composer, Thoth, along with a wise and mighty representative from each of the twelve tribes, constructed these twelve pyramids to hold the sacred tones of their origins in eternal memory: separate, yet linked together. The pyramids completed, into each was intoned the resonant history and wisdom of one of the twelve tribes.

As this one had walked many lives with all of the twelve tribes, recorded their songs, their wisdom and hearts, this one was entrusted with all of the sacred tones of each of your twelve tribes, of each of the twelve pyramids; to carry them through the nine dimensions of time and space until such a moment as it was deemed to be.

That time has come, for these twelve tribes are now to remember both who they truly are and that the twelve tribes are all key chords in the symphony of the One, not in discordant conflict, but in intricate harmony. Today, each of the twelve tribes, through you, their kings and queens, come together for their people here in the King's Chamber: the heart of the Great Pyramid, the conductor's podium. Today each of the twelve sacred tones has been sounded, awakening the twelve tribes across the planet, across the galaxy, across the universes.'

As suddenly as it started, it was over and there was a noticeable silence that followed. But then Bill started toning. By now, I knew I'd shared many lives with Bill, as warriors, brothers, priests, leaders and wise men; we'd both sat at Arthur's table, though it was nothing like the fables described, and both lived several lives both in and before ancient Egypt. What came out of his mouth was extraordinary. Firstly he began an octave below the tonic of the notes I had just toned. Then, from this note, probably a low C, he proceeded to make amazing sounds, often split harmonics that would take years to learn how to do.

My eyes still closed, I was compelled, in a low-toned 'Oumm', to provide harmonic support for Bill, a sort of tonic grounding, but the octave above. Next, as they had in the Grand Gallery, all the ladies joined in, first in higher octaves, then each quickly shifting to different pitches, 5^{ths}, 3^{rds}, then more complex harmonies, 7^{ths}, 9^{ths}, however this time they had tuned into the notes that my entity had toned, each finding their own 'home' frequency.

The cluster chords they were creating sounded astonishing; exactly what I would describe a choir of angels to sound like. Then, above the chord, like a thread of gossamer, floated the most beautiful soprano voice; I opened my eyes and looked for its source.

The ladies had all moved into the centre of the room, joined hands, and formed a circle around the tea lights and Pernille's crystal ball. It may well have been the flicker of the tea lights, or an optical illusion, but it looked as if the crystal ball was full of flickering flames, those flames, like silhouetted sprites, dancing on the walls of the chamber behind the ladies.

The soaring voice belonged to Pernille, and she wasn't just toning a pitch, completing the chord, she was singing a melody that seemed to either shift with the flickering in the crystal ball, or cause the ball to react; either way, they were in total sync.

The ladies split into three groups of three, 'headed' by Diane, Crystal and Pernille. Then one of the ladies from each group went one way, and one the other, forming another three groups of three, Diane, Crystal and Pernille anchoring each group. As they mixed, the chords changed and the crystal ball reacted, sending out glorious patterns and swirls. After a minute or so, the ladies rotated again, creating different triads and different patterns. It was as if the crystal ball was receiving the sonic input and transforming it into visual light and projecting the images onto the walls; it was breathtaking.

Finally, the ladies all gathered together in the centre in one group-embrace and returned, one voice at a time, to the unison note, as if to come to the resolve that though it is our unique differences that define us, ultimately we are all the same, all frequency, and that though it is our unique differences that interact to create the vitality and diverse possibilities of life, ultimately we are all one. That was also the view of the entity within me.

'Today for the first time in millennia, the twelve tones have sung as one, and the angels cried such was the beauty of that sound. For each of you, kings and queens of your respective tribes, your journey has just begun; for it is time for you to go forth, as vagabonds, as wandering minstrels amongst your people to remind them of their part in the cosmic symphony. Sing your hearts out my dear friends, for your cosmic kin sing with you all.'

Then the choir dispersed, and Diane, who had picked up Pernille's crystal ball, led them up to, and around, the coffer. Not wanting to step out of line, Bill and I held our positions against the wall, leaving Diane to continue.

'Daughters of Aset, you are now invited, each in turn, to lay down in the womb of initiation to complete your rebirthing, your re-membering, and your reawakening...'

Pernille was the first to step inside and lay down, Diane handing her the crystal ball.

'...As you do, close your eyes and relax, clear your mind of all thoughts, and centre your soul-force in the place of your consciousness, for you must be pure in mind and in your purpose to achieve your desire to re-member who you truly are and why you have incarnated at this time on earth. Place in your mind the image you desire, picture the place you desire to see, vision the Hall of Amenti as described by Thoth.

Long with the fullness of your heart to be there, to stand before the Lords of time and space. Once before them, in your mind, command the words we have rehearsed that you be granted entrance to the realm of wisdom and the great mysteries of life.'

As soon as she finished speaking, Diane started toning directly into the coffer, the others following suit. As before, they all started on the same pitch, then, as Diane shifted, they all shifted, creating the most amazing chords. The whole room was pulsating, I couldn't see into the coffer but, though the only illumination was from the tea lights, I was sure there was a white glow with golden flickers emanating from it.

After about a minute, they stopped toning, Pernille stood up, absolutely glowing, handed the crystal back to Diane, they exchanged positions, and the whole process began again. I looked across the chamber at Bill, who was transfixed by the whole thing. He looked at Pernille in absolute wonder, admiration and devotion; how could you blame him; she was radiating, she looked ten years younger.

Was that the secret to these sarcophagi, they somehow recalibrated and rejuvenated your physical body, or was it just an illusion. Certainly Pernille's energy had changed. I remembered the disheartened and downtrodden woman I had seen on the Felucca who was hoping to rekindle a relationship long-mummified and long-entombed; I wondered where Jacques was, probably back in Zurich preparing the divorce papers and cutting her out of everything. Asshole!

I glanced back across at Bill, the quirky rolly-polly, down-to-earth gold-miner in the mohair body stocking; he was so different to Jacques. Sure he didn't have the Armani suits, the suave European smell of success, or the arrogant supercilious sneer, but Bill was genuine, loving, and he was worth bazillions! I was so happy for both Bill and Pernille.

Diane emerged, similarly enlightened, and handed the crystal ball to Crystal, who took her place within the coffer. As the Daughters of Aset once again began toning, I could feel my whole body quivering in antici.....

And then it was my turn to stand in awe, with my jaw dropped down so far it could have been the floor of the subterranean chamber, as, like Venus emerging from the oceans, Crystal slowly emerged from the coffer; she wasn't just glowing, she was radiating. It was as if she *was* the crystal ball, golden shafts of light were shimmering in all directions from her.

Crystal handed the ball to the next woman and the process was repeated, and so on for all of the women, each time, they emerged from the coffer with a distinct change in their very being; some were crying, some on a cosmic cloud-nine, others almost in catatonic shock.

When the last of the woman had taken their turn inside the coffer, Diane turned her attention to Bill and me.

'Would you gentlemen like a turn? I'm sorry, we can't let you use the Lamp of Isis, but you *can* experience the next best thing.'

Bill and I looked at each other, then nodded.
'Sure, thanks. After you, Alex.'
'No, Bill, age before beauty.'

He laughed.
'Well, I can't argue with that one.'

As Bill climbed into the coffer, Diane began giving him instructions.

'Just close your eyes and relax, clear your mind of any thoughts, and centre your soul-force in the place of your consciousness. Allow it to take you where it will.'

Bill dutifully closed his eyes and the ladies began their chorus. After about 15 seconds, Diane leaned in and muttered something, I couldn't quite hear so leaned in to make out what she was saying and see how Bill was travelling. Diane had finished saying whatever it was, as, motionless, arms across his chest like a departed pharaoh, Bill looked like a deceased emperor lying in state. Either that, or it was a scene from a horror movie, 'The Revenge of the Zombies', 'Curse of the Bogans', or 'Back to the Planet of the Apes'.

The ladies stopped toning and, after few seconds, Bill slowly opened his eyes. 'Whoa, that was extraordinary.'

I leaned in and helped him to his feet.
'What happened?'

He climbed out and gestured for me to take his place.
'Best you find out for yourself.'

I handed him my iphone and took off my backpack, passing it to him. Then I realized the iphone was still recording, so I took it back and climbed in, lying down in the coffer and resting the iphone on my chest. For some reason, I rapped the granite side of the coffer, which let out a dull resonance.

'Now, close your eyes and relax, clear your mind of any thoughts, and centre your soul-force in the place of your consciousness. Allow it to take you where it will.'

I did just that and Diane started toning; exactly same frequency as that of the coffer, and on which the others based their tones. No sooner did they start than the whole box began shimmering in sympathetic vibration, the air pulsed and warped; it was 'alive', like it had a consciousness all of its own.

I soon found a short, simple but distinctive melody, which oscillated around the base frequency, running not just through my head, but my whole body. Somehow I knew what this meant; it was programming the coffer, or rather unlocking its message, so that anyone who lay in the coffer after this moment, and who hummed or toned the base frequency, would be similarly activated with the love and spiritual consciousness and the awakening that each one of us, Bill, me, and the Daughters of Aset, had enacted and experienced in our time here.

Not only could I hear it, but I could *feel* it, in every cell of my body. Even though my eyes were closed, lights started flashing before me, like bolts of lightning going off inside my head, but in a multitude of colours.

'Mekut-El-Shab-El Hale-Sur-Ben-El-Zabrut Zin-Efrim-Quar-El....'

Diane was whispering into the box, it was probably what she had done to Bill, although rather than a whisper, it was booming around and through me.

'...Edom-El-Ahim-Sabbert-Zur Adom.'

I had no idea what it meant, but suddenly it was like someone had switched one of those fast-forward montages where every frame of film has a different image, 24-frames a second, except a hundred, a thousand, times that, probably more. It was as if I'd opened a massive zip file from within the DNA of my entire body and released the history of every atom within it. Not only did my life flash before me, but my *lives* flashed before me, ALL of them; it was too much to comprehend.

And then it was over; the ladies had stopped singing, and, when I opened my eyes, the modern lights had been turned back on; clearly our time was up.
'Perfect timing. Right then, ladies, our next stop is the Sphinx.'

Bill gave me a helping hand out of the coffer, and it's just as well he did, as the brief but powerful effects of my time inside had left me slightly disoriented. As I hit stop on the iphone recording, Bill handed me the backpack.

'Pretty amazing, huh!'

'I don't know where to begin.'

Crystal stepped forward and placed a finger on my mouth.

'He who talks does not know; he who knows does not talk.'

I knew what she meant, basically, shut up and allow the magic to do its work. I nodded, leaving Diane, like a muted Pied Piper of Hamlin, to lead us all out of the King's Chamber.

The last to leave, I took one last look around the room; was my business finished here? I had stumbled over some of the secrets to this pyramid, but had I discovered them all? Closing my eyes, I did a quick scan of the room, clearly 'seeing' the other, 'secret' rooms behind the walls. But something was pulling my attention down, below the floor, way below the floor, below the Subterranean Chamber to the ancient chambers discovered in 1976; it seems my journey was incomplete. The question was; how was I meant to get there?

I made my way out through the Antechamber and followed the others as we silently descended the Grand Gallery. Except for the Descending Passage to the Subterranean Chamber, as far as I knew, the only other way down below the pyramid was via the secret staircase that opened from high on the southern face of the pyramid.

That posed several problems; firstly, I had no idea which stone in the face it was that opened onto the staircase, secondly, even if I knew which stone it was, I didn't know the words to open it, thirdly, the local authorities were hardly going to allow me to scale the pyramid.

I contemplated the possibility there may have been something about it in Kareem's papers, but then concluded it was unlikely, and that even if there was, the information would be in Arabic and there would be no way I could translate it, or trust it to anyone else at this stage of proceedings. Despite my recently acquired insight, I still felt I was flying blind.

I followed Bill as we took our last look at the entrance to the Queen's Chamber and the Well Shaft, then climbed down the narrow Ascending Passage and out of Al-Ma'Moun's tunnel to the outside world. It was just after 9:00 am and a handful of tourists were waiting to make the trip inside; they had no idea what really awaited inside.

Out in the open

Moving past them, I spotted evidence of a shaft just outside the entrance, in the paving of the limestone courtyard. Was it part of the original design, or a later excavation? As we climbed down the stones of the face of the pyramid, I pointed towards it.

'Hey, Bill, do think that's relevant?'

Bill made a beeline straight for it.

'Possibly. You remember I was telling about that website, about a guy called John Cadman, who proposed the Subterranean Chamber was a Hydraulic ram pump?'

'Yeah.'

'Well, he seemed to think this was a well shaft that played an important part in the overall function of the pyramid. Cadman proposed that the space where we are, between the pyramid and the enclosure wall, was filled with water from the Nile.'

To the north and to the east, I could see the remains of the original fine Turah limestone enclosure wall that lay about 10 metres from the base of the pyramid, and that enclosed the now familiar limestone-paved courtyard.

'What, like a moat?

'Yes, and that this was a well shaft that headed straight down, to a lateral tunnel that connected directly to the Nile, and was instrumental in maintaining a stable water level.'

'Interesting. What do you think?'

'Again, it's possible, and it would be consistent with the pyramid's function as a power station.'

'Maybe that's why the Supreme Council and Hawass have tried to pretend it's nothing, pretend it's not important?'

'Speaking of important.'

Bill took a few steps away, then stop to pick something up that had caught his eye.

'There you go, Alex...'

He handed me part of a broken shell and continued walking after the ladies, picking up more fragments as he meandered and handing them to me.

'...Now, according to some experts, and as theorized by certain Arabian historians, the presence of sea shells here at the base of the pyramid indicates the pyramid could have been built before a great flood, like the one at the end of the last ice age about twelve thousand years ago.'

'And it could have, it fact it probably was, but the shells could also be as a result of the Thera tsunami.'

'That they could. So, how are you going to tell the difference?'

I gazed down at the assorted fragments in my hand.

'Carbon dating?'

'Probably, as shells are composed of Calcium Carbonate, $CaCo_3$, and that contains Carbon, I suppose you could. The problem is though, that whilst you could work out *when* the sea shells lived, you couldn't derive when or how they got *here*.'

'But if the shells dated to 1600 BC and not 10,000 BC it would be pretty strong evidence they arrived courtesy of the Thera tsunami.'

'You would think so, especially if you Carbon-dated a dozen of them and they all came back with the same date. Of course, they might just be the remnants of a giant clambake; a massive celebratory pharaonic beach party held by Apopi or Ahmose.'

I looked again at the broken fragments in my hand, like pieces of an enormous jigsaw. They were part of the evidence, part of the big picture, the question was, where did they fit in, assuming of course, they *did* fit in at all?

Either way, I couldn't believe that for the last fifty years millions of people, scientist and Egyptologists included, had been trampling around the Giza Plateau all over billions of sea shell fragments, and not one of them had thought to pick up a sea shell, realize the glaringly obvious that it was hundreds of miles to the ocean, that it didn't originate here, and have the shell radio-carbon dated!

That bizarre anomaly racing around in the head, I instinctively put a few of the shells in my pocket, where, along with my fragments of granite, I discovered the shell Crystal had given me on the river bank at Silwa Bahari, half way between Kom Ombo and Edfu; I must have subconsciously slipped it into my pocket as a keepsake. I pulled it out and compared it to one of the fragments Bill had just handed me. Now, if they carbon dated both of these, and they came back with the same date, *that* would be compelling.

'Hey, Alex, check this out.'

Having moved a few steps ahead, Bill had stopped and was once again examining the ground. We were about 70 feet along from the northeast corner of the Great Pyramid, where, lo and behold, a massive stone about 4 foot by 10 foot, and who knows how deep, was imbedded at an angle into the foundation.

'What do you make of it?

Bill fervently scratched his chin, before crouching down to make a closer inspection.

'Well, the joints are very precise, so it's no arbitrary or random placement, and, looking around, it seems as if this is the only stone in the foundation perimeter that's not set at a right angle to the normal construction angles, which means it must have had some sort of specific function, otherwise why set it at an angle.

What's interesting is, that by its position, the stone would've been covered by the casing stones of the pyramid, but now, since the casing is gone, it's accessible.'

'Perhaps the casing was build over it?'

'Or, the original pyramid, wasn't a pyramid at all, but something smaller, like a Ziggurat?'

'That would be a game changer! And the stone?'

'Well, the only thing it could be, is an entrance to a subterranean corridor.'

'A secret door that leads to the subterranean chambers, or into the unknown inner chambers of the pyramid.'

'It's hardly very secret; but certainly it's become unnoticed and unconsidered.'

Without the magic words, 'open sesame', we hustled on to catch up with the ladies, who had just turned the corner and were heading down the eastern side of the pyramid. Off to the left, to the north east, was part of a cyclopean stone wall, the so-called 'Wall of the Crow', a huge gateway about 3.5 metres high and bridged by massive limestone slabs, which was perhaps the original entrance to the Giza plateau, and part of the enormous wall that once surrounded the entire Giza Complex.

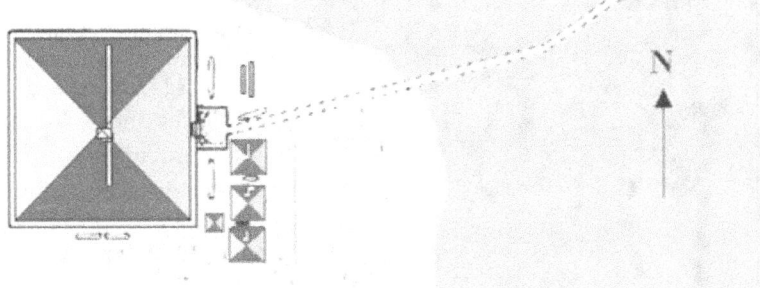

Continuing down the eastern side, along the foundations of the enclosure wall, we passed the first of three shallow boat-shaped pits discovered east of the pyramid, two flanking the mortuary temple, 8 metres deep, 7.5 metres wide and 52 metres long, and one north of the causeway.

Boat pits, sea shells; I was still confused about the boat pits.

'Hey, Bill, if the pyramid wasn't a tomb but rather a power station, which the evidence seems to support, then the notion of the boats being boats for the afterlife of the pharaoh seems untenable.'

'So what were they then, and why were they buried?'

'Good questions.'

I delved into my notes for clues to an answer.

"A further two pits were discovered south of the main pyramid, the south-eastern pit, discovered in 1954 and covered with slabs of stone weighing up to 15 tons each, contained 1,224 pieces of cedar wood, the longest 23 metres long, the shortest 10 centimetres.

The pieces were entrusted to a local boat builder who, over the next 14 years, worked out how the pieces fitted together and reassembled them to recreate the 43.6 metre long sea-going cedar-wood boat that now resides in a special boat-shaped, climate-controlled museum above the boat pit to the south of the main pyramid."

'That's a hell of a jigsaw puzzle!'

'Sure is!'

I continued on.

"During construction of the museum, the south-western pit was found, containing yet another boat, which was deliberately left unopened until 2011 when excavation began."

'I'm not sure how, but the fact that these boats were sea-going vessels may well support your thoughts about them being pre-tsunami, but couldn't they also possibly have been pre pole shift?'

'Of course! The clue has to be the 15-ton slabs. I'm convinced that it's highly unlikely the 4th and 5th Dynasty civilizations had the capacity to move such massive blocks, and that has me leaning to a much earlier pre-dynastic civilization.'

'I wonder if they've actually done any radio-Carbon dating on the cedar that made up the boats, or have they just assumed the boats belonged to Khufu and left it at that, another case of history by speculation and assumption?'

'Bill, you're a genius; that would be a major piece of the puzzle.'

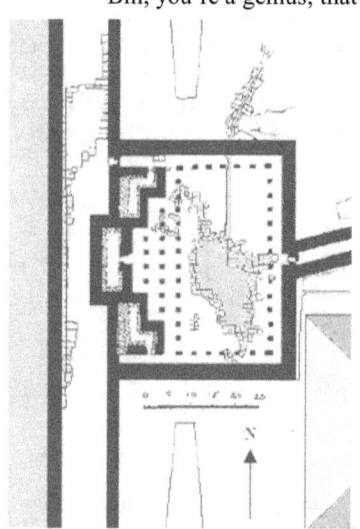

Speaking of puzzles, beyond the first boat pit were the remains of the 'Mortuary' Temple. It once measured over fifty metres north-south and forty metres east-west, although now the only thing left was part of the basalt paving of the courtyard.

Like the floors at Niuserre and Sahure, the basalt floors were constructed from irregularly sized and shaped slabs of basalt.

"The basalt blocks showed clear evidence of having been cut with some kind of saw with an estimated cutting blade of 15 feet (4.6 m) in length, capable of cutting at a rate of 1.5 inches (38 mm) per minute."

I wasn't sure what that meant, so I showed it to Bill, who raised an eyebrow.

'That's impressive, even by today's standards, and this was supposedly when, 2500 BC? I don't think so!'

Though there were no columns or fragments of any columns, there were sockets in the floor, which most-likely held the numerous red-granite pillars that would have comprised the colonnade that surrounded the open court.

At the western end of the temple, where there ought to be the inner sanctuary, was a recess and signs of an outer wall. To either side were irregular 'L'-shaped rooms. As far as I knew, no other temple had this arrangement of rooms.

"The portals were made of red granite, the ceiling stones made of white limestone. The interior walls were made of limestone and were carved with fine reliefs. This temple is the first known temple to make use of limestone, granite and basalt."

That was if it pre-dated Sahure and Niuserre; it may well have been contemporary with them, especially if they were all pre-dynastic and pre pole shift.

As Bill moved on to catch up with the ladies, I looked towards the east, along the scant remains of what would have been an 825-metre-long causeway, to where the valley temple once would have lain. Although there are unconfirmed reports of the location of the basalt paving and limestone walls, officially, it hadn't been discovered, but, if anything remained, it was beneath the sprawling metropolis of Giza, buried somewhere beneath the village of Nazlet el-Samman, where, coincidently, Hawass had clandestinely appropriated the fateful local excavation.

"Khufu is depicted in several relief fragments made of finely polished limestone. Some of them originate from the ruined pyramid temple and the destroyed causeway, where they once completely covered the walls. One of the relief fragments shows the king with the double crown and impaling a hippopotamus."

Although they were in no great rush, and in fact were just ambling along in two's and three, sharing their experiences within the King's Chamber and the coffer, the ladies had still moved some distance ahead, and I hustled to rejoin them, moving past the southernmost of the two flanking boat pits, to where a small pyramidion sat, 'reconstructed' from fragments discovered in 1991, that supposedly belonged to a small satellite pyramid just outside the southeast corner of the enclosure wall of the main pyramid.

I actually wasn't so keen on the term 'reconstructed', I preferred reassembled, as, unlike the other pyramidions, that were made from one solid piece of granite and fractured and fragmented, this pyramidion was constructed from five deliberately shaped pieces of stone that had been reassembled into the shape of a pyramidion; by that alone, it wasn't contemporary with any of the other pyramidions at all, it had to have been created much later, using far inferior skills.

Beyond the pyramidion were the scant remains of the satellite pyramid to which it supposedly belonged. Along with the pyramidion, the first course of stones was discovered in 1991 by a team clearing the area.

The area now cleared, all that remained of the pyramid was a T-shaped trench that included a small descending passage and chamber. Had the whole pyramid simply been swept aside by the tsunami? That's what it looked like.

The rest of the group had paused briefly beyond the satellite pyramid, outside what turned out to be the 'tomb' of Seshemnefer IV, apparently an official who lived during the 6th Dynasty and bore the title "Secretary of all the king's secret orders". Again, I wasn't that interested or convinced it was a tomb; given its close proximity to the main pyramid, I figured that like the other 'tombs' it was more-than-likely actually an office.

Having regrouped, the ladies were discussing their options; some wished to visited the boat museum at the base of the southern face of the pyramid, whilst Diane, who had seen the boat before, along with Crystal, Pernille, and one of the other ladies, were more intent on continuing straight down to the Sphinx.

As for me, whilst I was keen to spend some time with Crystal to discuss the goings-on inside the King's Chamber, I also wanted to make the most of my time at Giza while I had the chance, and wanted to do a quick circle back up via the Queens' pyramids, then down through the eastern 'cemetery'.

Amid the constant chattering of the ladies, Bill leaned in and whispered behind his hand.

'Sometimes you've got to wonder how they ever find the time to breathe.'

'Didn't you know, Bill, a woman can take a snatch breath.'

That sent Bill into a fit of hysterics, and he still hadn't recovered by the time the ladies had decided to split, and meet in front of the Sphinx in 30 minutes. That decided, I felt it was OK for me to head off on my little detour as well. Fortunately Diane was extremely obliging.

'Not a problem, Alex, we shall meet you in front of the Sphinx.'

'If it's OK, I'll come with you.'

Bill, having somewhat recovered, was looking to Pernille for permission. She just smiled and nodded with her head indicating for him to go. That done, we all went our separate ways.

I wanted to talk to Bill about what had just happened in the King's chamber, to get his thoughts on it, and on his experience inside the granite coffer, but I wasn't sure where to start. Before I new it, we arrived at the first of the 'Queens' Pyramids, the southernmost one, labelled GI-c and attributed to Princess Henutsen, one of Khufu's wives.

Made of mud-brick, although it was badly damaged, it was still the most intact of the three. To the east, there was evidence of the remains of an adjoining chapel or mortuary temple, so I checked my notes and read them aloud to Bill.

'At the end of the 18th Dynasty a temple was built for the goddess Isis beside Henutsen's satellite pyramid, G-I-c. It was extended during the 21st Dynasty and again in the 26th Dynasty.'

'Sounds plausible.'

'Except, it also says here there was a stele found around here that said "Khufu erected one of these Queens Pyramids for Princess Henutsen beside the Temple of Isis, and archaeologists have confirmed that the southernmost of the three satellite pyramids is indeed dedicated to Henutsen".'

'That casts a different shadow on things; firstly, that though it confirms there was once a Temple of Isis here, second, that it existed before this satellite pyramid was built, which means the satellite pyramid may even have been deliberately built as an annex to the original Temple of Isis.'

'What came first, the chicken or the egg?'

'Exactly, and unless they can definitely prove Khufu built the Temple of Isis, then he probably didn't build the Great Pyramid either.'

'Well, apparently the stele also says that Khufu described that the Pyramid and Sphinx were already present at Giza during his reign.'

'There you go; you would think that if the part of the stele referring to the Temple of Isis and the satellite pyramid of Henutsen proved to be true, then the rest of it must be true as well, including the fact that Khufu described that the Pyramid and Sphinx were already here when he ruled the roost. However, despite that, and the fact the satellite pyramids are unquestionably inferior in design and construction to the Great Pyramid, the "experts" still insist Khufu built them all. I don't even think Khufu was actually a pharaoh.'

'I'm with you on that.'

We made our way around to the north face.

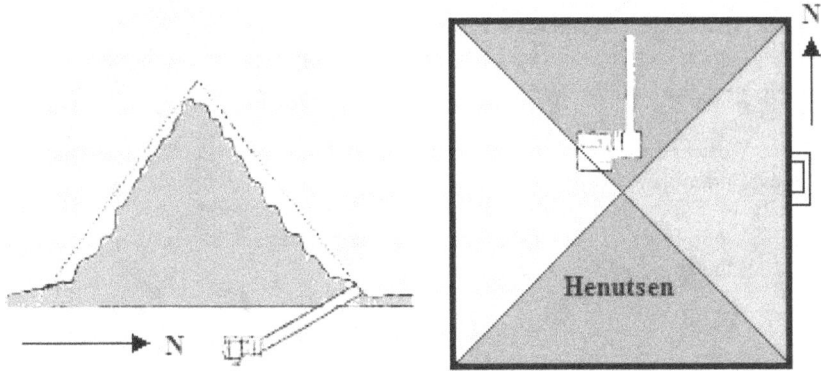

'Henutsen's pyramid consists of a sloping descending passageway that leads from the opening to a main chamber after taking a short right angle turn. The chambers are subterranean and their interiors are carved into the bedrock of the plateau.'

Bill peered down into the opening.

'Any mention of red granite?'

'Nope.'

'Because if the chamber *was* built by Khufu, there probably wasn't any.'

The next pyramid, the central one of the three, GI-b, also made of mud-brick, had been ascribed to Meritites, thought to have been Khufu's sister as well as his wife. It was more damaged than Henutsen's, perhaps only reaching just over half its original height.

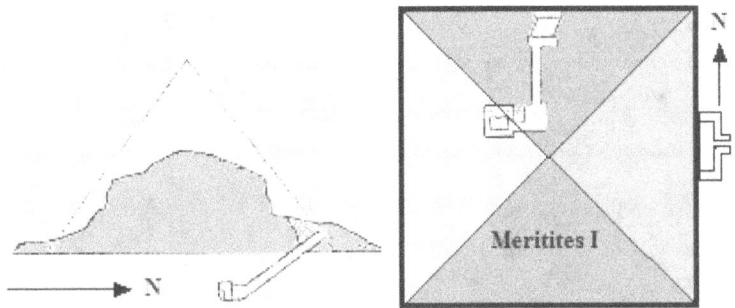

In fact it looked more like it had been constructed as a step pyramid, which supported my theory it was either a later addition, or part of a repair project.

According to the accompanying diagrams in my files, Meritites' pyramid had almost exactly the same internal design of corridors and chambers as Henutsen's.

'Meritites' Pyramid has the same design; a descending corridor with a right hand turn into the main chamber, which, according to the photo in the file, looks more like a sunken Jacuzzi than a burial chamber.'

As we headed north through the remains of a mortuary temple or chapel on the east side, I showed the image to Bill who nodded then shrugged his shoulders.

'Unfortunately we can't get inside to check it out for ourselves.'

'It seems pretty certain though that there was no red granite in there.' All in all, it strongly suggests that the "Queens" Pyramids of Henutsen and Meritites were contemporary with each other.'

'Actually all it shows is that the subterranean sections were contemporary with each other, and the superstructures were contemporary with each other, but were the superstructures contemporary with the subterranean elements, *that's* the big question.'

We continued on, to the northernmost and most damaged of the three 'Queens' Pyramids, GI-a, loosely attributed to Hetepheres I, who was either the sister and wife of Snefru and mother of Khufu, or Snefru's mother, wife of Huni and Khufu's grandmother, although the way the ancient Egyptians interbred she could have been all of the above and then some.

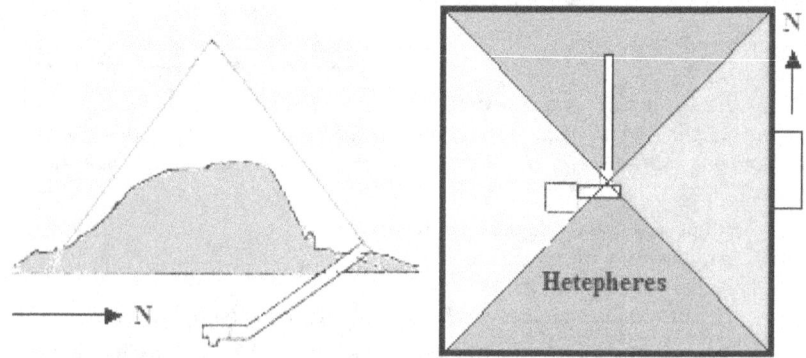

Again there were the scant remains of a chapel or mortuary temple to the east, and, like the other two 'Queens' pyramids, it consisted of a sloping descending passageway that led from the opening, via a right hand turn, into to a subterranean main chamber carved out of the bedrock of the plateau.

'*The pyramid acquired its identity from the intact tomb of queen Hetepheres I, G 7000x, discovered nearby by accident, in 1925, hidden beneath the paving around the east of Khufu's pyramid. The burial was intact and contained many precious funerary goods, although the carefully sealed coffin proved to be empty.*'

'That's interesting; do they say what the sarcophagus was made of?'

'No.'

'Yet another empty "sarcophagus", this one in an intact tomb,...'

Bill shook his head.

'...You would've thought the Egyptologists would have got the message by now, they weren't sarcophagi.'

'Another appropriated vault?'

'That's what it appears to me.'

'It makes a mockery of this satellite pyramid being for her burial then, doesn't it?'

'Oh, I'm sure the experts can come up with a reason.'

Then I read something that caught my attention.

'Hang on; listen to this. "*The northernmost pyramid, GI-a, was probably originally intended to be built slightly east of its present location. This is evidenced by the levelling of the rock at that original location and the beginnings of a substructure. However, this apparently would have interfered with a shaft cut for the reburial of Queen Heterpheres and so the pyramid was moved slightly west*". What do you make of that?'

Bill started looking around and wandered off, first to the east, then north.

'I don't believe for one minute they made mistakes about where things were built, not the original structures anyway, so I wonder if it's related to the position of the Trial Passages?'

'Trial Passages, what are they?'

'Come over here.'

He led me across the remains of the causeway, past another boat pit, towards what looked like the entrance to a subterranean tomb that headed north.

'This must be them, the so-called "Trial Passages"; an almost identical replica of the junction between the ascending and descending corridors in the Great Pyramid....'

I took a few steps down the ramp to examine the surface paving, which looked as if it had been broken away.

'...They were discovered by Perring and Vyse, but Petrie was really the first to write about them; tagging them as Trial Passages for the Great Pyramid, mainly because, although the passages were shorter in length, at about twenty metres, they were full size in width and height and duplicated the junction between the horizontal corridor into the Queen's Chamber heading into the Ascending Passage and the Descending Passage...'

Bill continued on, northward across the ground, and I scrambled up to follow him, looking for a file about the Trial Passages on my iphone.

'...Just like the passages in the Great Pyramid, the passages here are oriented north to south, although here they're cut entirely from the bedrock; cut carefully and well squared, there's even the constricting of the Ascending Passage where the three portcullis blocks are located...'

As I followed him, I almost fell ass-over-tit down a vertical shaft in the middle of nowhere. Without stopping, Bill stated the bleeding obvious, tossing the words back over his shoulder.

'...That would be the vertical shaft; as far as we know, it's the only feature which is not an exact copy of the passages in the Great Pyramid. It's analogous in size to the Well Shaft of the Grand Gallery, but it's not in the same position.'

Bill stopped before reaching the tomb of Hetepheres I, at the northern entrance to the Trial Passages, the rock levelled to either side and which, although cut in angled steps that once formed the foundation of some stone superstructure, showed definite signs of having been 'reconstructed'. As he did, I found a file reference to the passages actually written by Petrie and read it out to Bill.

'The passages have a total length of 22 metres and a total vertical depth of 10 metres. At the north end there is an opening in the bedrock, which is cut in steps. This becomes a sloping passage 1.05 metres wide and 1.20 metres high, which continues at an angle of 26°30'.

From the north entrance of this passage, a second passage, of almost identical cross-sectional dimensions, begins. This second passage ascends southward at approximately the same angle as that by which the first passage descends. At 5.8 metres from its beginning, this second passage reaches the surface of the bedrock and widens into a corridor which is open to the sky. A square shaft, about 0.72 metres width, was cut vertically from the surface of the bedrock to the point where the two passages meet.'

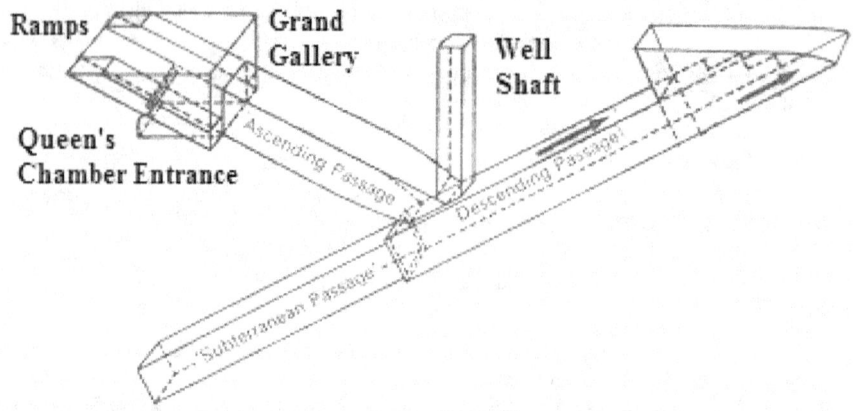

'Not only that, but some parts of the passages were even encased with mortar.'

'Seriously? Why would you bother to do that if it was just a trial passage, especially if it's supposedly just for burial?'

'Exactly; either they had to test the acoustics of the passages in the Great Pyramid, which of course is highly possible, or the "Trial Passages" were not "trial" passages at all, rather, actual functional substructures in their own right.'

'You think there may have been another pyramid here, a fourth queens' pyramid perhaps?'

'I guess it's possible, the passages lie on the same north-south axis as the queens' pyramids, and the surrounding rock around the north entrance was levelled, but if there was a pyramid planned, my guess is it was never built, which means the passages were more-than-likely independent of what was built, or planned to be built, on top.'

To make matters even more confusing, about six metres west of the Trial Passages, and running parallel to them, was a long, narrow trench, about three-quarters of a metre wide and seven-to-eight metres long. The rough-cut northern end was only around six inches deep and it sloped down to a depth of around eighteen inches at the well-cut southern end.'

'Another "trial" passage?'

'I doubt it.'

'A failed attempt at a descending passage for the abandoned fourth queens' pyramid?'

'No; the slope is too shallow for a normal descending corridor.'

'Then…?'

'I haven't got a clue, although it's almost exactly equal in width to the vertical shaft in the Trial Passages.'

'Which means?'

'Which means that there are many unsolved riddles here on the Giza Plateau, and no greater one than the Sphinx. Come on, we'd better get going.'

The Eastern Cemetery

Rather than go back the way we came, we decided to cut through what had been labelled the Eastern Cemetery; a series of parallel rows of flat-topped Old-Kingdom mastabas that supposedly contained the remains of Khufu's favourite children, princes and princesses, his favoured servants, as well as esteemed court officials ranging from Khufu's reign on and into the 6th Dynasty.

'Bill, can I ask you something?'

'Sure, fire away.'

'It's about what happened in the King's Chamber.'

Bill had a little chuckle.

'That was quite a speech you gave in there; *"A wandering minstrel I a thing of shreds and patches"*. Next!...'

I was amused by his obscure reference to *'The Producers'*, and the way he could always see the lighter side of everything.

'...Seriously though, it was pretty mind-blowing; nine dimensions of time and space! If that's so, then we've only scratched the surface in understanding the universe. And then there was the big one, the notion that this planet, and the human form, were actually created to reunite the star races scattered to the far reaches of the universe by the reptilians; the Twelve Tribes of Israel. It's like a plot from Star Trek or Stargate.'

'But the Twelve Tribes of Israel come from *'The Bible'*, right?'

It was Bill's area of expertise, and, by the look on his face as he paused outside the entrance to two 'tombs' just east of the satellite pyramid of Hetepheres, he was off in another brain-space again.

'Well, that's where they're first mentioned, the Tribes of Israel being the traditional divisions of the ancient Jewish people, but it doesn't mean that's where they come from. In fact, most modern scholars don't generally accept the biblical proposition that the twelve tribes are simply sub divisions that developed naturally from patriarchal roots, and neither do I, especially since our discussions about Moses and Joseph being one and the same person.'

'What do you mean?'

Bill took a quick glance at his watch and took off down the stairs into the 'tomb' of Idu, an official who lived during the 6th Dynasty and the reign of Pepi I. Right behind him, we arrived at a large, empty, almost-square room. Although Bill scanned the walls, it was clear his mind was somewhere else.

'Traditionally, *'The Bible'* holds that the Twelve Tribes of Israel are descended from the sons and grandsons of Jacob, those being Reuben, Simeon, Judah, Issachar, Zebulun, Benjamin, Dan, Naphtali, Gad, Asher, Ephraim and Manasseh. But the first mention of the term 'Israel' actually comes from Egypt, from a stela created by Merenptah.'

'The son of Ramses II?'

'Yes. It celebrates his victories in Canaan around 1206 BC; including a phrase something along the lines of: *"the people of Israel are laid waste, its seed is not"*.'

'Which means?'

'Well, firstly, it means the *"people of Israel"* must have been around significantly long enough to have established their presence and nomenclature, which would take more than a few generations at least. Add to that the fact Moses kept the Israelites in the desert for forty years, and we're probably looking at maybe a hundred to a hundred-and-fifty years time frame at the bare minimum.'

'Which puts them back around the time of Akhenaten. And from there it's not that hard to connect it to the Exodus and to the Thera tsunami.'

'It all seems to fit.'

'And secondly?'

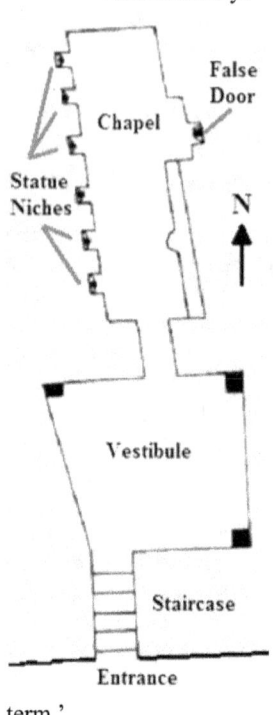

False Door

Chapel

Statue Niches

N ↑

Vestibule

Staircase

Entrance

Bill moved on, through a short corridor into a long north-south rectangular room; the west wall of which was adorned with a series of six niches, each containing a statue carved from the bedrock. Even though I later discovered the experts had speculated the statues, which included a smaller one closest to the door, either depicted Idu at various ages in his life, which didn't seem apparent, or Idu and members of his family, which made even less sense, there was nothing to convince me this was a tomb, a place of offering, yes, probably even an office, but not a tomb.

As if inspecting a military parade, Bill ambled along the line up of statues.

'The second point about the Israel stela is, that though it says, *"the people of Israel are laid waste"*, it also says, *"its seed is not"*, which seems fairly obvious that as far as Merenptah was concerned, the core threat from *"the people of Israel"* still existed.'

And then an idea flashed through my head.

'Hang on, Bill, does the stela actually say "Israel"?'

'Apparently, why?'

'Then the term "Israel" must be an Egyptian term.'

'I've never thought of it that way; you're right, it must be. Although, according to the Hebrew Bible, the name "Israel" supposedly comes from a name given to Jacob by God after Jacob wrestled an angel all night on the shores of the Jabbok river and had *"striven with God and with men, and had prevailed".'*

Turning our attention to the opposite wall, the explanation seemed obvious.

'Remember, Bill, all the early chapters of the Old Testament were written by Moses, by Joseph; he still had to create a legitimacy to his right to rule, and that meant not only linking his father, Jacob, to Abraham, which he probably made up as well, but what if Jacob was really Joseph, leading his family out of Egypt in the Exodus, and, while being chased by Kamose, there was a battle beside a river, which would be a logical place to be trapped or held up? Maybe it was even just before they crossed the Red Sea at Nuweiba.

Then, to the Egyptians, Kamose would have been an "angel" of God, of the murdered pharaoh and of the new pharaoh, Ahmose. So, was the term "Israel" coined by Ahmose, by God, the pharaoh, in reference to those who fled Lower Egypt led by Moses/Joseph.'

Bill stood before the eastern wall, which contained a false door stela, painted to simulate granite, with an image of Idu from the waist up, arms extended, upturned palms, in the bottom half of the false door, as if he was rising like a zombie from the grave to receive his offerings.

'So, what you're suggesting is, that the term "Israel" really means something like "murdering thieves"?'

'Too far fetched?'

'Not to me, I love it, it's as logically conceived and factually sound as all the other theories, probably more so, but I'm sure historical theologians and Jews all over the world won't be as open minded.'

Chuckling away under his breath, Bill led the way out; through the 'antechamber' and back up the stairs to outside world. I did one last scan of the walls; there was Idu wearing a wig and wide collar, and his wife, Meretites, shown sitting opposite each other at an offering table, and, apart from a few funerary scenes, generally the scenes included men and cattle returning from the marshes, the preparation of food and drink, music with dancers, persons bringing offerings to Idu and his wife, Meretites, and children playing games. A tomb? Nup!

Just to be sure, before I left, I did a quick check of my files. To my surprise I did find a folder on the Eastern Cemetery at Giza. Inside were a number of paragraphs on the Mastaba of Idu, G7102, most of which I brushed aside, however, one did stick out like dog's balls.

"Just inside the entrance, on the right hand side of the west doorjamb, in one vertical line, is a curse that reads: 'As for every man who shall enter this tomb, not purifying him(self) as the purification of a god, one shall make a punishment for him because of it evilly (or painfully)'."

'Brilliant! Just as I attack the whole state of Israel, I wander into a tomb with a curse on it.'

I rubbed my hand down over the doorjamb as I exited.
'No offence, Old Boy.'

It wasn't really the sort of curse that said "Do Not Enter, or else", this one seemed to actually welcome entrance so long as you were appropriately purified, which on second thought supported my belief it wasn't a tomb at all.

By the time I'd reached the top of the stairs, Bill was disappearing down the stairs to the adjacent tomb, G 7101, that of Meryrenefer, better known as Qar, who was either Idu's son or father, the experts didn't know, although they were sure he was another

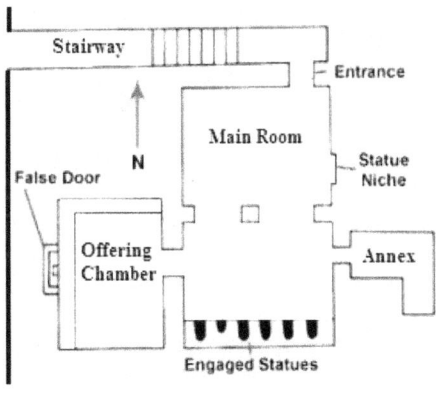

official from the 6th Dynasty and the reign of Pepi II, which more-than-likely made him Idu's son.

The stairway led, via a small entrance corridor, to the main room, which was divided in two by a single central freestanding pillar and two engaged pillars. The pillars supported an architrave richly decorated in carved hieroglyphs.

Bill was standing before a seated statue of Qar that was carved into a niche in the eastern wall just along from the entrance, but clearly his mind was still mulling over the discussion in the previous mastaba.

'You know, Alex, the whole story of the Twelve Tribes of Israel has Joseph's, or rather Moses', dirty rotten hands all over it. Until now, all of the traditional beliefs, that see the twelve tribes as one nation as early as their enslavement in Egypt, or of the wanderings in the desert, were regarded as having no actual basis in fact, but now, the pieces seem to make perfect sense, although *now* they paint a very different picture altogether.'

'In what way?'

Bill moved on, going from element to element, niche to panel, panel to panel, past the pillars, their numerous faces covered in various images of Qar at different stages of his life, and into the second half of the main room.

'Remember, this is the time when Lower Egypt was ruled by the Hyksos, the invaders from the east, and it's possible that Jacob, who came from the east, was possibly a ruler or rich landowner; he may even have been related to Apopi.'

'OK, how is that significant?'

'Jacob had four wives, which means he must have had money, but two of them, Bilhah and Zilpah, were actually handmaidens to his wives, which means there was a class system, and that rather than being sold into slavery, it's more likely that Joseph, as the first-born of Jacob's second wife, Rachel, who may also have been from a significant family, was gifted to the pharaoh as a peace offering, a potential son-in-law for Apopi's daughter, or to secure trade relationships.'

'Normally that wouldn't make much sense, but if, as you suggest, Jacob was somehow related to Apopi, it's far more plausible.'

We past by a small annex in the eastern wall and stood before a row of statues carved into the rear wall, once again either representations of Qar at various stages in his life, or, more-likely, of Qar and his family, including his young son. Though we'd stopped to take them in, Bill was still on a roll.

'Then, at some point, Jacob and his other sons go to Egypt, supposedly because of the famine in Canaan, which was most-likely caused in part by the ash fallout from the Thera eruptions. Now, according to 'The Bible', Jacob and his sons didn't recognize Joseph, but that doesn't ring true if Jacob knew Joseph was gifted to Apopi, in fact it's not only probably the reason Jacob went to Egypt in the first place, but it explains how Jacob and his sons got such easy access to Apopi and to Joseph.

And it would definitely explain why they were taken in; remember we're talking about Jacob, four wives, eleven sons and a daughter, and maybe twenty or thirty grandchildren. That's perhaps fifty or more mouths to feed, and I'm sure Apopi wasn't that obliging to everyone that landed on his doorstep asking for help.'

'It all seems so obvious.'

'I guess the big mistake in studying history is to only believe what is written down, and not look at who wrote it, why they wrote it, and whether it corresponds to other events and to common sense.'

In the western wall was an opening that led to what had been labelled an offering room, which could well have been a later addition; there was no way of really knowing. Facing the entrance and on the door jambs were coloured, though faded, depictions of Qar, his hands gesturing as if inviting us in to make an offering.

I followed Bill inside.

'So, everything is all happy families until the shit hits the fan when Joseph sends two of his brothers to Upper Egypt to get the resurrection rituals from Seqenenre Tao.'

'Most likely Simeon and Levi, yes.'

'You said something about that on the felucca. How do you know it was Simeon and Levi and not two of the other brothers?'

'Moses own words, Verses 5-7: "Simeon and Levi are brothers; tools of violence are their weapons. Oh my soul, do not come into their secret. Let not my honour be united with their assembly. For in their anger they killed a man, and in their self-will they hamstrung a bull. Let their anger be cursed, for it was fierce; and their wrath, for it was cruel. I will divide them in Jacob, and scatter them in Israel". Most theologians suggest it was the massacre of the people of Shechem, but, the more I think about it, it had to be the murder of Seqenenre Tao.'

Within the offering room, a false door of Qar was set into the western wall, surrounded by numerous scenes of offering-bearers and offerings to either side.

'So, basically, Joseph blamed them for the whole civil war, for the need for the rapid Exodus, and for having to tough it out in the wilderness of Saudi Arabia for 40 years.'

'Yep., for destroying his cushy lifestyle.'

'And when he was writing his memoirs, as Moses, he made himself out to be the hero and pointed the finger of blame at his brothers.'

'Alas, that's human nature.'

'Especially for a megalomaniac…'

We started to make our way out of the 'tomb'.

'…But why did Joseph lead them south east, why didn't he just lead them back east back to Canaan?'

'Maybe their escape route was cut off, but probably because he knew from Jacob it was in famine, and because they were following the ash cloud from Thera as a "sign from heaven" leading the way.'

'So they crossed the Red Sea and finished up in modern day Saudi Arabia.'

'Or, as it was known then, Midian.'

Bill slowly circled the outer room, like a hungry shark looking for vulnerable prey, moving wall to wall, register to register, as if he was speed-reading, searching the funerary images, offering lists, purification tent, embalming-house, and processions of men towing the funerary boat containing Qar's sarcophagus toward his tomb, for a missing clue. He was still thinking, and I was still asking questions.

'All six-hundred-thousand of them?'

'No, I don't buy that either; the logistics of moving six-hundred-thousand people, of controlling their movements, would be nearly impossible.'

'Especially if you were being pursued by a fully-armed and pissed-off Egyptian Army.'

'Exactly. I think the theologians and "scholars" have selectively over-exaggerated a touch. The texts actually say six hundred "Elef", or "clans", or families, and I think a family simply meant a household, maybe ten people at the most, and that brings the figure down to a very plausible six-thousand, a figure Moses could control to some degree.'

'And he led them wandering through the desert for 40 years?'

'Well, that's the next big issue isn't it, forty years in the desert? Suddenly Joseph and his Habiru family are all on the run; they have no government, no judicial system, no code of laws, no method of settling disputes, and most of all, no homeland. As the "highest ranking" outcast, Joseph sits in judgment, taking the leadership role and leading them out of Egypt. But where? You would have to ask, why stay in the desert, and, how did they survive there for forty years? I think it's just a romantic notion, a fiction created by Moses to make them look good, but I don't think that's what happened at all.'

'So, what's your take?'

It pushed Bill into deeper contemplation.

'Let's take as a given that Joseph knows Canaan is in famine, so going there's not an option. But, as Vizier of Lower Egypt, he must have known the Midianites and indeed have had some sort of relationship with the Midianite king, so, knowing Canaan was in famine, I think he knew exactly where he was leading them, to Midian…'

The revelation struck him like a lightning bolt and he bolted out the entrance, up the stairs and out of the tomb, and I was right behind him.

'But wasn't Joseph sold by his brothers as a slave to the Midianites? Why would he go back there?'

Bill continued to unravel the course of events.

'Well, I think we've pretty much established that Joseph *wasn't* sold into slavery, I think that's just creative story-telling by Moses to make Joseph even more of an innocent victim.'

'So why the Midianites?'

A grin came over Bill's face; he had the answer.

'I think Joseph/Moses took refuse with the Midianites, which is probably how he came to marry Zipporah, daughter of "Jethro", who was also known as the High Priest, Reuel, but who must really have been the Midianite king or, more-likely a son of the king. Joseph *was* the vizier of the Egyptian pharaoh and he probably bullshitted the king into believing he was an emissary from Apopi, and it would have been a fait-de-compli if the Midianites were at war or on poor terms with Seqenenre Tao.'

'It also explains even more how and why he adopted the Midianite god of storms and war, Yahweh, the lord of the Midianites, a vindictive god that punishes disobedience, as the new Almighty God of the Hebrews.'

'It sure does.'

We continued on our way through the cemetery, through the remains of several other mastabas, heading further east towards a few other 'tombs'. Whilst there was clearly a defined regularity to the structure and arrangement of the mastabas above the ground, the same couldn't be said about the chambers cut out of the bedrock beneath, which seemed architecturally unrelated to the superstructures above; clearly they were not from the same periods. I didn't have time to turn my attention to contemplate it as, once again, Joseph/Moses was the prime topic for pontification and discussion.

'The traditional belief painted in *'The Bible'* is that during the chaos and disorganization of the desert wanderings, the leadership of the people was vested in the "princes" of each of the tribes, and the elders, with Moses left alone to serve the people and settle disputes.'

'The "princes" being Joseph's brothers, who by Joseph marrying a Midianite princess, could, by association, also be seen to be princes.'

'Exactly. They met and legislated for the entire people, the system built upon the premise each "tribe" would govern itself.'

'Because like any squabbling family, the brothers were competitive and probably couldn't agree, and would not allow themselves to rule over each other.'

'So Moses solves the problem by making them autonomous, but with himself presiding as Chief Judge over larger disputes. Interestingly though, it supposedly wasn't Moses who organized the Twelve Tribes of Israel in the desert, but rather his father-in-law, Jethro, the 'shepherd', the 'keeper of the flock' who did it.

Exodus 18:24-26; *"Moses listened to his father-in-law and did everything he said. He chose capable men from all Israel and made them leaders of the people, officials over thousands, hundreds, fifties, and tens. They served as judges for the people at all times. The difficult cases they brought to Moses, but the simple ones they decided themselves."*

'Jethro probably saw all the infighting and came up with the solution.'

'Yep. So Joseph gave them what they wanted, power; he picked men he could trust, namely his brothers, and put them in charge of everything.'

'It's logical, and politically wise; better the devil you know.'

Bill counted them off as best he could.

'Levi was put in charge of the priesthood, Dan, the path of law and order, of the judiciary, Gad was appointed a General and put in charge of the army, Asher was given control of prosperity and pleasure, the Treasury and whorehouses...'

'The whorehouses?'

'Most definitely; the Temples of Isis, or whatever the goddesses were called in Midian, after all, what self-respecting corrupt government doesn't have close control and involvement with the boudoirs of the people?'

I put on my best Bon Jovi impression,...

'It's all the same, only the names have changed.'

...to which, Bill quickly responded.

'Don't give up your day job.'

My rock career in tatters, I quickly returned to the discussion.

'What about the other brothers?'

'Issachar, being the scholar, was put in charge of Education, Zebulun, the merchant, would have been in charge of business and trade, whereas, according to Moses, Joseph not only survives, he thrives. He achieves greatness through his challenges, overcomes all adversaries and becomes a great leader, saving his entire generation, and despite his corrupt environment, he maintains his spiritual integrity.'

'Self-praise is no reward, he just created a corrupt 'Boy's Club'; hardly a democracy. Joseph simply did what any other self-serving megalomaniac would do.'

'And there Joseph stayed, in Midian, while Ahmose and Amenhotep I invaded Canaan to the north. For forty years he stayed there, in the "desert", or until he died, plotting and planning, building his troupes. He changed his name to Moses, possibly to impress Jethro or to give more legitimacy to his standing amongst the Midianites.'

'Maybe it was bestowed upon him by the Midianites, by the Midianite king, as a title, when he married princess Zipporah?'

'That would make sense as well. And once he had the Midianite king in his back pocket, probably using the old "I had a dream" scam again, he would have appointed his brothers and sons to those various positions, spreading his power. Eventually Jethro would have died, and, if he did so without any sons, Moses would have taken the opportunity, like all good megalomaniacs, to seize power.'

'Why not Reuben, wasn't he the eldest son of Jacob?'

'I don't think that had any relevance once they left Egypt and Joseph had positioned himself as top-of-the-tree by marrying Zipporah. Besides, Reuben was only Joseph's *half*-brother, and, as Joseph learned in Egypt, it was all about the maternal line, so Joseph believed *he* was the eldest, which he was in his own way. So Reuben's place as *head* of the "Twelve Tribes" was usurped by Joseph, and that played a decisive role during the periods of the settlement and the Judges.'

'You're talking about Rachel right, who bore Joseph, who was supposedly Jacob's favourite wife, and how all Joseph's eleven brothers were apparently all jealous of Joseph, including his actual full brother, Benjamin?'

'Yep, and that's exactly what you'd expect to read if the whole story was written by Joseph, or, rather, Moses, because Joseph was the eldest of Rachel's blood line and there were no DNA tests back in those days, the only way you could really know who belonged to who was through the maternal line. It all totally supports the theory that "The *story* of Joseph" was actually written in the 5th Century BC as a way to validate the dominion of the *House of Joseph* over the other tribes of Israel and link the Abraham-Isaac-Jacob period found in Genesis with the subsequent story of Moses and the Exodus.'

'And the common denominator, the link in the chain, is Joseph/Moses.'

'Exactly!'

It had answered some questions, but the issue of the "Twelve Tribes" was still on my mind.

'Bill, do you think Joseph really had eleven brothers?'

'It's hard to say, it's possible; the names of some of the tribes actually correspond to the names of ancient sites in Canaan that existed before the time of Jacob, such as the mountains of Naphtali, Ephraim, and Judah, the desert of Judah, and Gilead. With the passage of time, those who dwelt in these areas would have just assumed the names of the localities.'

'So it's a matter of which came first, the chicken or the egg?'

'I'm afraid so.'

'But isn't it just as possible the regions, the Twelve Tribes of Israel, were named after Joseph's sons and brothers, like *'The Bible'* says?'

'Yep, at the moment there's no clear evidence either way. All we can say for certainty is that after forty years, and following Moses' death, a new generation, led by Joshua, Ephraim's son and Joseph's grandson, invaded Canaan and "reclaimed" the Promised Land, supposedly in accordance with the promise made to Abraham by God, with each tribe allotted an individual territory in which to settle.'

We arrived at G 7140, the mastaba of Khufukaf I, a priest and apparently a son of Khufu, and Bill headed straight inside. I took a moment to pause for a second to catch my bearings.

"On the back of one of the casing stones displaced from the east face of the mastaba-style tomb of Khufukaf I are quarry marks that appear to contain a date indicating that it was built in the 23rd year of Khufu's reign."

Well, that told me a lot. Firstly, that the superstructure, the mastaba only *appeared* to have been constructed during Khufu's reign. It probably was, but it also meant that only the superstructure could be dated to then, not the rest of the structure. And what if the casing stone was part of a later restoration? That would make the internal elements much older. Best head in and have a squiz for myself.

A short entrance corridor led to a rectangular vestibule, the walls of which were covered in very refined and perfectly preserved bas-reliefs, including scenes of two large representations of Khufukaf on either side of the door, to the left with his mother, Henutsen, and with his son to the right. In other scenes, Khufukaf and his wife, Nefretkau, posed in a number of different costumes, and Khufukhaf was receiving offerings, such as a lotus flower, from a young woman, presumably one of his daughters. Although there was little or no trace of colour, the large-scale figures were remarkably well crafted.

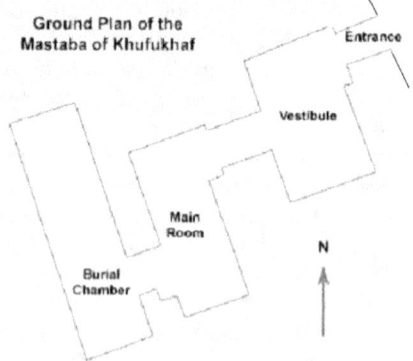

Ground Plan of the
Mastaba of Khufukhaf

Entrance

Vestibule

Main
Room

Burial
Chamber

N

Meanwhile, whilst I thought we'd covered the whole Joseph/Moses issue, Bill was still muttering away to himself as he scanned the walls..

'The question is, why did the Israelites wait forty years before invading Canaan, invading during the famine would have been ideal?'

Straight away I had an idea.

'The famine would have been over once the Thera tsunami hit, then it would have been a matter of rebuilding, and Ahmose would have been in charge of that. Besides, the Israelites would have had to regroup first, build up the numbers, that would have taken at least a generation, maybe two.'

'True.'

'And maybe it wasn't forty years, maybe it was actually fifty years.'

'What makes you say that?'

'Ahmose ruled for twenty-six years, which was followed by the reign of Amenhotep I of twenty-four years, a total of fifty years. It would make strategic sense for the Tribes of Israel to wait until Amenhotep I had gone, leaving the inexperienced Thutmoses I in charge, before they decided to invade Canaan.'

'Oh, wait a minute…'

Bill was running something through his mind as he hustled off, beyond the vestibule, through a second slightly wider corridor, to what was supposedly the main room, or chapel, longer but narrower than the first.

'… Towards the end of their supposed forty years wandering in the wilderness, during the time of the Judges, the Israelites were apparently so severely oppressed by Midian, for seven years, their crops destroyed, that it reduced them to such extreme poverty that they were obliged to seek refuge in caves…'

He stopped before a false door.

'…Which means Moses must have had a falling out with the Midianites. Well, not all the Midianites, as according to Judges i. 16, the Kenites, the descendants of Jethro, surrendered its identity by attaching itself to the Israelites. *"In this instance, which occurred in the period of the Judges, the Kenites, descendants of Jethro the Midianite, attached themselves to the Israelites in the wilderness of Judah, south of Arad".*'

'That makes perfect sense if Moses had infiltrated and taken over the family of Jethro, the Kenites.'

'I don't think the Kenites surrendered at all, I think they were usurped, it was a coup; Moses just wrote it with that slant to make himself look good. I think the real reason for the falling out of favour was because the Israelites once again fell into idolatry, and the clues are to be found hidden elsewhere in *'The Bible'*, Numbers 25. verses 1-5 to be precise.

"While Israel remained at Shittim, the people began to play the harlot with the daughters of Moab. For they invited the people to the sacrifices of their gods, and the people ate and bowed down to their gods. So Israel joined themselves to Baal of Peor, and the Lord was angry against Israel."…'

'The "Lord", being Moses himself.'

'That's the way I see it. *"And the Lord said to Moses, 'Take all the leaders of the people and execute them in broad daylight before the Lord, so that the fierce anger of the Lord may turn away from Israel'. So Moses said to the judges of Israel, 'Each of you slay his men who have joined themselves to Baal of Peor.'"*'

'So "God", i.e. Moses' massive ego, told Moses to order the deaths of all who had bowed to the false gods, as a way of regaining control of the people.'

Bill briefly skirted along the northern wall, which contained a procession of people, over five panels, bearing offerings from the possessions of Khufukaf, his wife, nefret-Kau, embracing his arm.

'Yep, if it worked once, why not use it again.'

'Like Bush and his claim of weapons of mass destruction, and the "Axis of Evil".'

'Exactly. But I don't think that's all there is to it. I think Moses had an even bigger plan.'

Still deep in thought, he headed down along the east wall, which depicted, in faded colours, numerous offerings in three registers. Not wanting to interrupt him, I took the opportunity to refer to my notes.

"There were models found of a beer vessel just a few centimetres in height, which bore the same offering spells as the carved and painted two dimensional representations on the walls. Yet, there was also found in the tomb an actual beer vessel."

Scanning the reliefs didn't convince me it was a tomb; it could just have easily been a place of celebration, or a place to bring offerings to a high official.

'Moses was supposedly ordered by God to punish not *just* those who had "strayed" but *all* the Midianites, and I think the real motivation can be found in the Book of Genesis; the Midianites were the descendants of Midian, who was himself a direct son of Abraham through his wife Keturah, and thus racially akin to the Israelites as descendants of Abraham, and therefore legitimate threats to the right to rule.

And so Moses, or Gideon, depending on which part of the Bible you read, is called by God to deliver Israel from Midian's armies and dispatches an army of twelve-thousand men, led by Phinehas the priest, against them. The Midianites are defeated, their cities set on fire and all the cattle and goods are seized. Then all the males are killed, including their five kings, Evi, Rekem, Zur, Hur, and Reba, and the women and children taken captive. Now, you would think that would be the end of it, and if it was just about "worshipping false idols", it might be, but, no, Moses doesn't stop there, he goes even further, and that's an indication of his true motive.'

Then he just disappeared, through a beautifully carved doorway in the south of the western wall, its jambs and lintels decorated with bas reliefs and texts.

There was no way I was going to let him leave it at that, and dived in after him, arriving, via a third short corridor, to the supposed burial chamber, a long narrow rectangular room, undecorated, and most probably dating to a later period.

'According to Numbers 31: Verses 17-18, Moses ordered the Israelites to slay every Midianite male child and every woman, sparing only the female children. *"Now therefore, kill every male among the little ones, and kill every woman who has known man intimately. But all the girls who have not known man intimately, spare for yourselves".*'

After which, Midian is said to have been *"subdued before the children of Israel, so that they lifted up their heads no more",* and according to the Book of Judges, largely disappeared from the biblical narrative.'

'Of course, kill all the men, all the scribes, and I guess you kill the written history as well.'

'It not only insured the extermination of the Midianites and thus prevented them from not only *"ever again seducing Israel to sin",* but from writing their version of events and from claiming a legitimate right to rule.'

We both scanned the blank walls and gabled ceiling.

'Genocide, fratricide; hardly the acts of a just man and hero to millions. But I guess the Jews and Christians would say, "That's OK, he was just doing what God told him to do".'

'But wait, there's more, Numbers goes on to say in verse 35, to share *out* the thirty-two *thousand* girls, virgins who have never slept with a man, as plunder.'

'That's sick, if someone did that today we'd call them the head of a paedophile ring, string him up by his balls with rusty piano wire, and slowly cut his cock off with a dull kitchen knife.'

'Careful, Alex, you're talking about a religious icon revered by millions of Jews and Christians around the world. It may well have been a horrible thing for the girls, but at least their lives were spared.'

'Spared, so that at the age of ten, or eight, or even six, they could be married off, enslaved, and raped, by the very men who had butchered their mothers and fathers. I can see now where the Islamic practices got their beginnings, where they get their reward of virgins; the practice was barbaric then, and it's barbaric now.'

'I agree, but at that time and in that culture, the reality of taking women as wives as a by-product of war was a necessary if somewhat unfortunate evil.'

'Perhaps, but that doesn't mean it should be condoned today, nor condoned in the past.'

'It just goes to show you what some people say is acceptable in the name of "God", and the astonishing lengths to which they will go to defend their religion and its idols.'

'Geez, Bill, imagine a paedophile getting up in court charged with multiple counts of raping a six year old girl and using as a defence that, "it's OK, I married her" and "God told me to do it", then citing Moses or Mohammed as a "previous case and ruling" justifying his actions.'

'It gives a new slant to the term "Blind Faith", that's for sure.'

'The world is fucked, no, people are fucked for letting it happen!'

Somewhat angrily, we made our way back out of the 'tomb'. As we did Bill tossed in an aside to lighten the mood.

'You know, circumcision was apparently practiced by the Midianites way before it was adopted by the Israelites.'

'If the Israelites were all circumcised as slaves, I still can't figure why they would keep the practice?'

'Because of Moses: he turned it into a ritualistic commitment to Abraham. In effect the Jews were still being marked as slaves, and still are; slaves to Moses' twisted megalomaniacal fantasies.'

'Moses was fucked! I can't believe so many people on the planet are so blind.'

'Alex, until this trip, both you and I were part of that group.'

'Yeah, well that's going to change. When I get out of Egypt, *with* Kareem's papers, I'm going to blow the lid on it all; I'm going to write that book!'

'What will you call it?'

'I don't know; how about "The Curse of the Pharaohs", or "The Mummy speaks. Dead men do tell tales"?

'Brilliant, and I'll put up the money to print it, distribute it, and publicize it.'

As we exited the tomb, Bill stopped and held out his hand.

'Deal?'

'Deal!'

We shook hands, and continued on our way, passing south of the huge tomb of Prince Ankh-haf, G 7510, and by G 7530-40, the 'tomb' of Meresankh III, the daughter of Kawab and Hetepheres II, children of Khufu.

'Do you think we have time for one more tomb?'

I looked around: Diane's group were held up, exploring the temple in front of the Sphinx, while the others had still not emerged from the boat museum.

'It would appear so, Lead on Macduff.'

Once again, Bill led the way, this time into the 'tomb' of Meresankh III, down the short entrance stairway and into a large rectangular room, what proved to be the main chamber, oriented north-south; it was the first substructure we'd explored that actually aligned with the superstructure. Close to the doorway were a number of texts, most likely Meresankh's name and her titles.

Heading clockwise, on a small part of the eastern wall just to the left of the entrance, the wall was divided into five panels that showed the sculpting and painting of statues of the Meresankh, who eventually married her half brother, Khafre, and died at about the age of 50, which meant the tomb probably dated to late in Khafre's reign. Below these scenes, other men were carving the sarcophagus and false door whilst gold workers were smelting gold to make a palanquin.

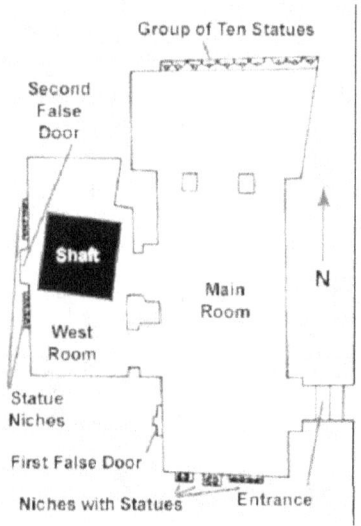

Adjacent to these scenes, on the south wall, were three niches that contained six high-relief engaged statues of six men, presumably either scribes or priests, or possibly even sons of Meresankh. It got me thinking about the Twelve Tribes again.

'Hey, Bill, do you think the Twelve Tribes of Israel originated with the sons of Jacob, or with the individual territories that were established after Canaan was invaded?'

Bill stopped before an incomplete false door on the western wall, that depicted Meresankh seated at a table, and slowly turned to face me.

'That's a good question; some would suggest it was when the Israelites asked for a king.'

'They *asked* for a king?'

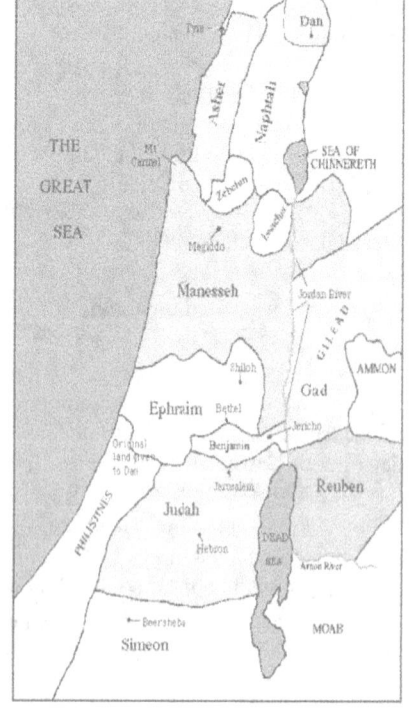

'According to 1 Samuel it was *"because they wanted to be like the other nations"*, although the Israelites generally used the term *nagid*, which means "leader", rather than the actual term for king, which was *melech*. I think it's reasonable to deduce from that they were looking more for a leader to unite the tribes, which means there was probably still ongoing internal squabbling amongst the tribes, and they called on Samuel to appoint someone because they couldn't agree. Although it is possible Saul was made a king at Gilgal after leading the army to victory against the Ammonites, I doubt that was the reason, more a confirmation.

In any case, according to 1 Samuel and Acts 13, *"God gave them Saul, the son of Kish, of the family of the Matrites"*. But I think the real reason was because Saul was also a member of the tribe of Benjamin, Jospeh's younger full-brother, which infers that Joseph himself never had any sons, although we know he had Ephraim and

Massanah. Either way, it's clear that the Samuel's selection of Saul in "being told by God to appoint Saul", as *'The Bible'* would imply, was no random act, but a deliberate political appointment, and if Ephraim and Manasseh were alive, dare I say an unpopular one.'

'Unless by "God" you mean Moses?'

'Well, it's possible; Moses was either dead, or a very old man by then, possibly on his last legs, and, possibly Ephraim and Manasseh had died, having no children of their own, though I doubt it. In any case, Samuel passed the baton to the lineage of Joseph's only full-brother, Benjamin, or rather to one of Benjamin's direct descendants, Saul, who became the first king of a united Kingdom of Israel and Judah.'

'So that's when the Tribes became united?'

Bill laughed.

'Yeah, about as united as the knife-wielding faceless men of the back-benches of both sides of Australian politics.'

He headed into the first of two large openings in the western wall. It led to an adjoining offering room, smaller than the main room, but also oriented north-south.

On the western wall were two more niches, flanking a second false door, each niche containing a statue, presumably of Meresankh III and her mother, Hetepheres II. It raised the question of whether the 'tomb', if it was a tomb, was just for Meresankh III, or originally for her mother, Hetepheres II, and Meresankh III was added later. On the small eastern wall were agricultural scenes.

'Now it gets really interesting!..'

Once again Bill was trawling his vast Biblical knowledge and reviewing his understanding of it.

'...Do you know the story of David and Goliath, Alex?'

'The shepherd boy who killed Goliath with a sling shot?'

'That's him. The Philistines had returned with an army to attack Israel, but, having massed on a hillside opposite to the Israelite forces, they supposedly suggested that to save lives on both sides, it would be better to have a proxy combat between their champion, Goliath, and someone of Saul's choosing.'

'And Saul chooses a shepherd boy? It doesn't make sense.'

'But David supposedly has faith in God's power to defeat his enemies.'

'I don't care how much you believe in God, it still doesn't make sense that Saul would put his whole kingdom in the hands of a kid, especially up against a giant like Goliath...'

Suddenly a thought took me on a different tack.

'...Wait a minute, do you think Goliath could have been Annunaki?'

'Now that's an interesting concept!' He did have six fingers and toes so I guess it's possible, although this was maybe five hundred years later, so it's more-likely he was a half-breed offspring, or some throw back to the interbreeding of the Gods with man.'

'Jesus!'

'Speaking of Jesus, you know he was supposedly of the lineage of David, of the tribe of Judah?'

'How can that be if Jesus was Caesarion? Or did someone just fabricate the lineage to justify some prophecy?'

'That's another great question.'

'Surely the lineage of Jesus, if it wasn't though Caesar, must have been through the female line, through Cleopatra and the Ptolemies? Well, not exactly the Ptolemies, but well, somehow through the women. So how do you get from David to

Cleopatra?'

'First, let's ask why Saul selected a simple shepherd boy to represent his entire army, and sent David into battle, dressed in Saul's own armour, for a one-to-one fight to the death, against a giant bone-crushing thug like Goliath.'

'It would've, or should've, been certain death.'

'Exactly. So, it was a pointless ploy.'

'Maybe it was a delaying tactic?'

Bill was on to something, I could tell.

'Or, it wasn't the Philistines who suggested the one-to-one battle at all; it was Saul who suggested it.'

'Why the hell would Saul do something stupid like that, and then put up a kid; he might just as well have surrendered then and there?'

'Maybe it was a delaying tactic, but maybe David, because of his lineage, was a possible threat to Saul's position as ruler, he used the opportunity to eliminate him?'

'Which is exactly what the situation was with Caesarion and Octavian.'

'A coincidence?'

'No fucking way!'

'And so History repeats; Tiberius uses the Pharisees and Sadducees to try to eliminate Jesus, just as Saul used the Philistines to try to eliminate David.'

Suddenly I had flashes of images of Bill, as David, up against Goliath, with Saul, Jacques, scheming in the background. Shivers when up my spine like someone had just walked over my grave. And that's just where we found ourselves, standing before a large square shaft that descended about five metres to what was supposedly the burial chamber of Meresankh III.

The first thing that struck me was that the shaft was dug offset to the north-south axis of the room, a dead giveaway the shaft was not contemporary with the offering chamber that surrounded it, and that it had more-than-likely been usurped from an earlier period.

'You got any notes about Meresankh III's tomb?'

Bill had caught me a bit on the hop, but I quickly found the file and read aloud from my notes:

'*"Discovered within the burial chamber was a black granite sarcophagus decorated with the palace façade, presented to Meresankh by her mother, Hetepheres II. Within the sarcophagus was the mummy of Meresankh, which has since been transferred to the Cairo Museum."* What do you make of that, Bill?'

'The sarcophagus may well be from the Old Kingdom, but it could just as easily be even earlier, and have been usurped by Hetepheres II to bury her daughter. It's hard to say without examining it, but if the sarcophagus has the same sort of primitive scratchings on it as those in the Serapeum, then it would support the hypothesis that the sarcophagi date to a much earlier period...'

He looked up from the shaft towards the northern wall, which was covered with unpainted images of food and wine being prepared for a banquet, while, above, musicians, singers and dancers entertained Meresankh, who sits holding a lotus flower and watching over the proceedings.

'...One thing I'm pretty certain of is, that these chambers above, and the mastaba, came much later than the burial shaft.'

We made our way through the second opening and back into the main chamber, but I hadn't finished with Saul and David.

'So Saul appoints David as his champion, and against all the odds, David defeats Goliath with a single shot from a sling, which supposedly hits Goliath smack between the eyes, knocking him out, or disorienting him. Goliath falls forward and David seizes the opportunity, decapitating Goliath with his own sword. And all the amassed hordes of Philistines who are sitting by waiting to see David dismembered, all they do is sit back and say, "Good shot, Young Whipper Snipper, well played Old Chap. Well, fair's fair, we'll just be on our bikes now, on our horses, and leave you to it. Sorry to have caused you any bother". Come on, the whole thing has to be made up.'

'I agree.'

Bill was scanning the walls again, which were decorated with various scenes of agricultural production, offerings, hunting, fishing and nautical scenes, along with many of Meresankh's relatives, including her mother, father and children. In one scene, Hetepheres II, wearing a black lappet wig and clad in a long white tunic, stands in the front of a boat, her back to Meresankh, who is wearing a hair-band around her black hair and a blue bead net over a white garment. They are gathering lotus flowers and catching birds with nets. In other scenes, Hetepheres had blond or red-hair which seemed very unusual for the period. Obviously it was part of his thinking process.

'The questions thus becomes; how and why did David *really* ascend the throne? Even before he was anointed king, David was referred to as a "future" *nagid*, or military commander, so I don't think he was a boy at all; a young man perhaps, probably a captain. Saul would have concocted the one-to-one battle with Goliath hoping to eliminate David, but David probably used his wits and defeated Goliath, and I'm sure a battle ensued and David led the Israelites successfully into battle...'

Bill turned his attention north, to the northern end of the chamber where two square pillars divided the main chamber into two; the additional section beyond about a third the size, but wider. Clearly the pillars were part of the original north wall, and the additional space was a later extension.

'...In any case, with David getting public acclaim, Saul had no choice but to change tack, and, so, supposedly in return for his victory over Goliath, Saul offered his daughter, Merob, to David as a wife.

However, according to 1 Samuel, David was too humble to accept, and wasn't interested in the arrangement, so Merob was married off to a different man. The way I see it, I think David knew exactly what Saul's motives really were, to keep your friends closer and your enemies closer, and David wasn't going to have a bar of that.

Even when Saul's other daughter, Michal, fell in love with David, and Saul repeated the offer, David again turned it down, this time claiming he lacked the wealth of a suitable husband.'

Depicted on the pillars were images of Meresankh, shown facing into the tomb and dressed in an elegant white robe, her two sons, Duaenre and Niussere, the latter of whom would eventually rise to the throne of Egypt, standing at her feet. As he scanned them, Bill continued to unravel the past.

'Not to be defeated, Saul persuaded David that the dowry would only be a hundred Philistine foreskins, secretly hoping that David would be slain trying to achieve the tally.'

'What was the big preoccupation with circumcision? Was Saul literally taking the piss out of David?'

'As I said, it's all about slavery.'

'So what did David do, did he tell Saul he was a wanker, or did he wander up to a hundred Philistines and say, "Hey, Phil, flop your chop out for me and, for a quick snip off of your fan belt, I'll convert you to the faith"?'

'Actually, David apparently considered Michal to be worth twice as much, as he obtained two-hundred foreskins and was consequently married to Michal, although

I'm sure he obtained them from dead soldiers.'

'He went around chopping the foreskins off dead soldiers?'

'Probably.'

'I can just imagine David leading the troupes into battle, then, as part of his victory lap, he stops to fondle the snags of a few dead soldiers. "Hey David, what you doing?" "Oh, nothing, just getting a few souvenirs for my betrothed." Do people actually believe this crap?'

'Word for word.'

'I don't know who was more screwed up, Saul for suggesting it, or David for following through.'

'Or Moses for coming up with the idea in the first place.'

'Exactly! Which reminds me, have you heard the one about the rabbi and the Catholic priest who were having lunch at the local pub, and when the rabbi takes out his wallet to pay, the priest sees it and says; "What an unusual wallet". The Rabbi says, "Yes, it is made from one hundred foreskins; we don't waste anything in the Jewish religion". Slightly uneasy, the priest gives the wallet a quick once-over and says, "What's the point of having a wallet made out of a hundred foreskins?" The rabbi smiles and replies, "Because, when you rub it, it expands into a suitcase".'

It sent Bill into a fit of hysterics, and he kept laughing as we moved beyond the pillars, into where the room had been extended and widened. On the rough-cut northern wall of the extension, a large niche was carved out of the bedrock that framed ten large statues of various women, sculpted in high relief and decreasing in size from right to left. There were no individual inscriptions so I could only assume they were representations of Hetepheres, Meresankh III, her daughter Shepseskau, as well as other daughters and family female members.

There were no men, which meant either Meresankh had no sons, which we know was not the case, or there was some special meaning to the niche, and thus to the chamber, and 'tomb'. Was this an earlier gathering of the Daughters of Aset, the Daughters of Isis, an earlier incarnation of Diane, Crystal, Pernille and the rest of the ladies?

'So did David hand over the two-hundred foreskins and marry Michal?'

'Yes, he did, but then David became Saul's rival to the throne, so Saul gave her away in marriage to another man, Palti, son of Laish.'

'How did that happen? I mean why did Saul become a rival to the throne?'

'As I said, I think he already was one, because of his lineage; I think he was most likely the first son, or grandson of Ephraim, of the lineage of Joseph, not Bejamin.'

'It was all internal family squabbles.'

'Yep.'

'So how did Saul fall out of favour?'

As the story goes, after the battle with the Philistines, Samuel supposedly instructed Saul to kill all the Amalekites. Saul dutifully did so, murdering all the men, women, and children, even the poor quality livestock, but sparing the Amalekite king and keeping the best livestock. When Samuel found out about it, he told Saul that God had rejected him as king because *"Saul was so caught in sin that he could not obey God",* and that God had told Samuel to anoint a new king.

When Samuel turned to leave, Saul supposedly grabbed Samuel by his clothes, tearing off a piece off his garment, and Samuel announced this was indicative of what will happen to Saul's kingdom. Samuel then took it upon himself to kill the Amalekite king.'

'It sounds like two schoolyard thugs and a battle of egos.'

'Perhaps more rightly described as a power struggle or an internal coup.'

'If it looks like shit, smells like shit....

We started making our way slowly out of the tomb, taking a little time to once again peruse the images on the eastern wall in more detail.

'...Who won out?'

'Well, David, but it was more by default.'

'How's that?'

'When Saul, and three of his sons, Jonathan, Abinadab, and Malchishua, were killed at the battle of Mount Gilboa, Saul's surviving son, Ish-bosheth, who was around forty at the time, became king.'

'So Saul won.'

'Not really; Ish-bosheth wasn't accepted as the new king by all the Twelve Tribes, Judah and Simeon preferred David.'

'More squabbling.'

'Yes, and it culminated two years later when Ish-bosheth was killed by two of his own captains, Bannah and Recab.'

'Who were probably mates of David.'

'Perhaps: more likely of David's lineage; the house of Ephraim or Judah. In any case, despite David's own shortcomings, such as his adultery with Bathsheba and the murder of Uriah, he was appointed king and he formed the nation of Israel and the kingdom of God.'

'But surely the other side would've plotted to take the throne back, right?'

'The only male descendant of Saul to survive was Mephibosheth, Jonathan's son, who was five when his father and grandfather died in battle. With the death of Ish-bosheth, Mephibosheth came under the "protection" of David, who, along with Armoni, Saul's other son with his concubine, Rizpah, were given by David, along with the five sons of Merab, Saul's first daughter, to the Gibeonites, who subsequently slaughtered them all.'

'So ultimately David won out by effectively obliterating his cousins?'

'Yep. It was a trait he inherited and that he passed on; it's like it's encoded into their DNA.'

The comment stopped me in my tracks.

'What do you mean?'

'David was succeeded by his own son, Solomon, who built the famed Temple of Solomon, *"where God takes his earthly dwelling among men"*.'

'Under which, the Essene scrolls where found by the Templars; in the nuclear reactor?'

'That's the one...'

We moved on.

'...Soon after Solomon's death, during the reign of Rehoboam, the empire was again torn apart by another great "Family Feud", during which the tribes once again split along territorial, political, and blood lines; the northern ten tribes forming the kingdom of Israel, because it was led by the tribes of Ephraim and Manasseh, who bore the name of "Israel", while the southern two tribes, Judah and Benjamin, joined by the tribe of Levi, formed the southern kingdom of Judah, which was loyal to the house of David.'

'Its all too confusing for me; in fact the whole Bible makes little or no sense.'

'Eventually the northern kingdom of Israel went into captivity in 722 B.C. *"because of sin and rebellion toward God"*, whereas Judah was taken into captivity by the Babylonians between 604 and 586 B.C.'

'And the Jews hold David up as a hero? No wonder they have no problem today murdering innocent women and children in Gaza; they're just doing what their hero did to protect what they stole from somebody else in the first place.'

'Exactly.'

'It's all so interwoven, so incestuous; all the facts are there, but they're laced through *'The Bible'* along with so many lies, fabrications and distortions.'

'Ah, but it's the "word of God".'

'Are we talking about he same god that the Catholics pray to?'

'Yes, although the Jews would say the Catholic god is a false god, and the Muslims would say both the Catholic and Jewish gods are false gods, that Allah is the one true god.'

'Which means for there to be false gods, there has to be more than one god?'

'That would logically follow, yes.'

'And so we're back to square one, with the original gods who disagreed; Osiris and Seth?'

'I guess we are.'

We emerged from the tomb in time to see the group of ladies from the boat museum passing before us on their way to the Sphinx. I paused for a moment and looked back at the tomb; something was missing, but I couldn't quite put my finger on it. Then, out of the blue, it hit me; there were no winged discs! There were no winged discs in any of the tombs, in fact anywhere at Giza. Where were they?

It got me thinking, where I *had* seen them, and, more importantly, where I hadn't? I'd seen them on the Victory Stela of Psamtik II on Kalabsha, on the lintels of the Temple of Khnum on Elephantine, and in the Ptolemaic temples on Kalabsha, Philae, Kom Ombo, Esna, Edfu, Medinet Habu, the Temple of Opet at Karnak, and the Temple of Hathor at Dendera. They were also in the tombs of Setnakht and Tausert, and Thutmoses III, in the Valley of the Kings, and the tombs of Amunherkhopchef and Khaemwaset, sons of Ramses III, in the Valley of the Queens; every single one of them dated to a period *after* the Thera tsunami, from the 18th Dynasty through to the Roman period, there was nothing in the Old Kingdom, nothing at Saqqara, nothing at Abusir, or Abu Ghurab, nothing at Abu Raoush, and I hadn't seen a single winged disc here at Giza, anywhere.

It made sense that the winged disc represented Nibiru, and the reason it wasn't anywhere to be found in the Old Kingdom, or Middle Kingdom, was because the brown dwarf star hadn't arrived yet; the only exception was the pyramidion of Amenemhat III at Dahshur, but, as I'd already proposed, the hieroglyphs could have been added at any time. In fact, as I just remembered, there was an Amenemhat who was a son of Thutmoses III and a half-brother to Amenhotep II, maybe it was him, and if the hieroglyph containing Amenemhat's cartouche could have been added later, in the 18th Dynasty, then so could the winged disc above it, which meant that if Nibiru arrived, then so did the Annunaki.

Meanwhile, Bill was keen to catch up and gave me a hurry along.

'Come on, let's go.'

Leaving the cemetery behind, I set my sights on the Sphinx and headed off down the slope after Bill, a hundred unresolved questions racing through my head. As I caught up, I blurted one out.

'So, did the Twelve Tribes originate with the sons of Jacob, or with the individual territories established under the rule of Saul, or David, or Solomon?'

'None of the above.'

'What? What do you mean "None of the above"? If not there, then where *do* the Twelve Tribes of Israel come from?'

'I think they used the term to describe later genealogical speculations, which attempted to explain the history of the tribes in terms of familial relationships.'

'Your losing me, Bill.'

He paused, a pensive, solemn look to his face.

'It originates from the Egyptians, and I think it's exactly what you said in the King's Chamber, the Twelve 'Tribes' are star races genetically connected to the human race, that have an interest in the development of the human race, in somehow reuniting the scattered seeds of humanity. What was it you said, something like; *"Today the twelve sacred tones have been sounded, awakening the twelve tribes across the planet, across the galaxy, across the universes. Today the twelve tones sang as one, and the angels cried."*

I heard the song, Alex, the chorus of angels, and Pernille's voice soaring above them. Each note, each chord, stirred something deep within me, and I remembered hearing it as a child; it was what drew me to the church in the first place, the search for the truth.

Then you said, *"For each of you, your journey has just begun; it's time to go forth, as vagabonds, as wandering minstrels amongst your people to remind them of their part in the cosmic symphony."* I got the message, loud and clear; it's time for me to spread my wings and fly.'

He slapped me on the shoulder, literally beaming, and continued on his way. I guessed my journey was just beginning as well. Perhaps the Sphinx held the answers?

CHAPTER 32 - THE LION'S SHARE

Getting directly to the Sphinx was not as easy as we first thought. From the edge of the eastern cemetery, the plateau suddenly sloped significantly down to such an extent that, failing abseiling, and discretion being the better part of valour, we had to double back westward along the cliff face and then down and back along the road. Still, it gave me more time to chew the fat with Bill.

'Bill, did you notice anything unusual in the King's Chamber, when the ladies were singing?'

'By "unusual" do you mean the oscillating light coming from Pernille's crystal ball?'

'Yes, that's it. Then you saw it; the flickering flames, dancing on the walls that seemed to be in sync with the changing chords?'

Despite my obvious excitement, Bill was more subdued.

'Yep, I saw them.'

'It was like the ball was receiving the sound and transforming it into light.'

'Nothing unusual about that; if radio waves can be received by crystals and transformed into sound in the old crystal radios of the 1950's, then the reverse must be possible, sound into radio waves, or in this case, visible light, after all, wasn't that the purpose of the whole King's Chamber anyway? I was more interested in what happened inside the coffer.'

'What happened to you?'

'It's hard to describe. I closed my eyes and the minute the ladies started toning all hell broke loose; psychedelic lights were flashing, not just around me, but from within me. It was like my consciousness was stripped down to its quantum state. You?'

'The same, like a disco in overdrive, and I heard this tune; it was like it was dancing along the strands of my DNA unzipping the history of every atom and sub-atomic particle in my body.'

Bill wasn't so much listening to me, rather drifting off and contemplating his own experience to a greater depth.

'When you think about it, it's all just energy: thought becomes light, the veritable light globe going off in the brain, light becomes sound, sound becomes matter; just change the tuning and you change the state of everything. Earthquakes, which are fairly low frequencies, can turn solid rock to liquid, so who knows what the human body could become subjected to the right frequencies.

It's all just frequency, and what happens when all those independent frequencies all intersect; one big pea soup of quantum probabilities. In some ways, the human body is just the result of a mind-boggling number of intersecting waveforms; creating an interference pattern that stands out from and interrelates with the whole universe.'

Meanwhile, the "boat" ladies, who had rounded the wall that separated the road from the 18th Dynasty temple and the Sphinx, waved as they made their way towards the scant ruins of the Sphinx Temple.

'Come on, Bill, we'd better get a move on. Maybe we can catch up with them by the time they reach the Temple of Amenhotep II?'

Whilst I delved into my notes, finding an old image that showed the temple prior to its restoration, Bill was less enthusiastic.

'There's not much to see there; the reconstruction is pretty crude and brutal, however it is significant in many other ways.'

'What do you mean?'

As we headed past it Bill pointed back, through the temple itself.

'If you consider the position of the temple, you can see that it is aligned at a 45-degree angle, with the entrance directly pointing towards the centre of the head of the Sphinx, which is a pretty radical departure from aligning the temple either east-west, or north-south.'

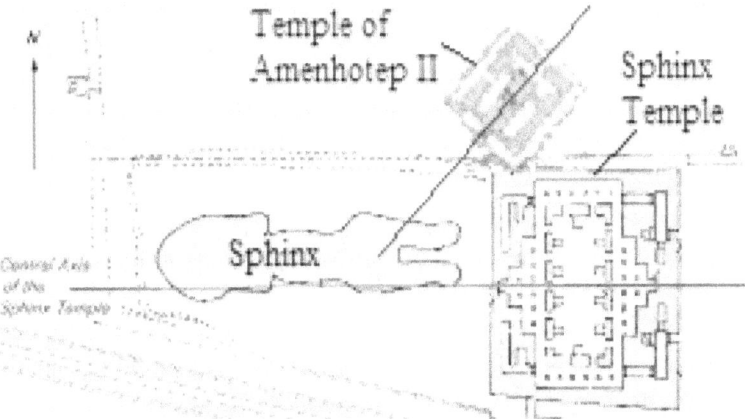

Forty-five degrees, that's around the same deviation Herschel talks about? He realized the deviation of the North Pole was as much as 50 degrees compared to today, and that the different angular direction was very close to the galactic pole alignment. Do you think the pole shift caused by the passing of Nibiru is responsible for the temple's radical alignment?'

'I hadn't even thought of that. I guess it's possible, after all, the Nile did once flow in the other direction, into the Atlantic.'

'It did?'

'Yes...'

Once again, Bill went into contemplation mode, rattling off seemingly irrelevant facts and stringing them together.

'...We know the Africa plate is moving northeast at an estimated rate of just under two-and-a-quarter centimetres a year. If we assume the pyramids were built when the Egyptologists say, four-and-a-half thousand years ago, and they have moved with the continental drift, then that puts them, what, about a hundred metres further northeast, which would affect the alignment. And that doesn't account for any rotational movement of the continent, if any. BUT, if you factor in the pyramids may be over 20,000 years old, probably much more, then it could all be at least five-hundred metres, maybe two, even three kilometres out of kilter, and that doesn't take into account any rotation or pole shifts. Of course it could have something to do with the asteroid strike.'

'The one that killed the dinosaurs?'

'No, no, that was millions of years ago; this one was much more recent. The core samples on both sides of the Atlantic reveal an Iridium content which is the by product of a major catastrophic asteroid strike in the present day Atlantic around 1,645

BC, which, accounting for error margins, would put it in the same ball park as the passing of Nibiru and the eruption of Thera.'

I did a double take.

'There was an asteroid strike around the same time as the passing of Nibiru?'

'Yes, I don't know why I didn't think of it earlier; it seems so obvious now that they're all connected. Still, I don't think the alignment of the temple has anything to do with that, I think it's more probably that during the rebuilding period after the tsunami, that the significance and knowledge of aligning the temples to the cardinal points was either lost, or became superfluous.'

'Maybe Amenhotep II was aligning it with the Sphinx in one direction and the receding planet of his forefathers, Nibiru, in the other?'

'Wow! That would be an interesting concept to consider and investigate.'

When we reached the point where the ladies had rounded the retainer wall, instead of following suit, Bill continued straight ahead.

'Hey, Goldfarb, where are you going? The Sphinx is this way.'

'I know, but I think this flat area is where Hawass started an excavation back in 1980, supposedly to do with the Ministry of Irrigation and the Institute of Underground Water.'

'Hardly his area of expertise.'

'Exactly. In any case, he drilled down about fifty feet through layers of debris, inconsistent with the natural limestone of the area...'

'That totally supports my theory about the Thera tsunami.'

'Oh, wait, there's more to it that that. About fifty feet down he struck red granite, which is not consistent with the geological substrata of the Giza Plateau; the only source of red granite is hundreds of miles back upriver at Aswan.'

'Kareem told me about that. Do you think it's a temple, like the Osireion at Abydos?'

'Possibly. Something constructed by someone is down there.'

'The Hall of Records?'

'It's possible...'

He pointed right, towards the front of the Valley Temple.

'... Then, in 1995, Hawass re-cleared the area in front of the Valley Temple and discovered there were tunnels, running north-south, with mud-brick walls and paved with limestone, that formed a narrow corridor that ran across the front of the Sphinx Temple and then northeast through here and probably to a quay buried somewhere below the modern buildings in the village.'

'That might be part of what Mark was telling me about.'

'What was that?'

'He was saying that back in March 2010 he saw a massive hole dug right here, in this area in front of the Sphinx Temple. It was supposedly for something to do with the Red Bull games, but Mark thinks the games were just a cover-up, that Hawass was really digging down to try to access the chambers under the Sphinx; the ones he originally located way back in 1980.'

'The Hall of Records. Of course!'

'Mark went on to say that about a month later some of his associates, who were staying at the Guest House overlooking the Giza Plateau, were on the roof one night when they heard several muffled explosions come from somewhere under the plateau. Later they saw front-end loaders removing statues and sarcophaguses from underneath the plateau.'

'You're kidding?'

'That's exactly what I said. They even took a video of it, and posted it on the web, but the video, and the people who filmed it, have mysteriously disappeared.'

'Murdered?'

'I don't think so; I just think they went underground, like the red-granite buildings. Thankfully, Mark had a few stills from the video.'

Deep in thought, Bill started walking back towards the Sphinx Temple.

'You know that during the 18th Dynasty, particularly the Amarna Period, numerous other structures were built here, including Amenhotep II's Temple up ahead, as well as a villa attributed to Tutankhamen, built above and in front of the nearly-buried Valley Temple, which led down via a stairway to a broad terrace or viewing platform immediately in front of the Sphinx and built on the mound that covered the Sphinx Temple.'

'So all this area was buried?'

'Yep; the Egyptologists say it was because the Valley Temple and Sphinx Temple fell into disuse and neglect, but that makes absolutely no sense at all. What *does* make total sense is that your Thera tsunami buried them all.'

'And that an even-earlier tsunami buried the red-granite temple fifty feet down, and some later tsunami, perhaps 224 BC, or as a result of the Etna eruption of 122 BC, or Vesuvius in 79 AD, or as late as the Turkey earthquake of 365 AD, destroyed the 18th Dynasty structures.'

'Sounds like you're going to rewrite the history of Ancient Egypt, that's for sure.'

The ladies were all waiting for us outside the ruins of the Sphinx Temple sitting on a number of beautifully precision-carved red-granite cornices lined up along the front of the temple; in some ways they looked like bench seats put there specifically for the tourists to use. Right along side were several similar-sized fragments of well-worn red granite. That didn't add up; they looked as if they were thousands of years older than the cornices.

Then it hit me, one set of stones must belong to the Valley Temple, one to the Sphinx Temple; but which was which? My intuition was telling me the older stones belonged to a much older temple, possibly the Sphinx Temple, or another temple, which was destroyed and now lay beneath the surface, and the blocks used to reconstruct or build anew the Sphinx Temple.

As I pondered the answer, Pernille ran forward and gave Bill a massive hug. I looked to Crystal, hoping she might do the same, but, alas, it was not forthcoming, although she did cast me a knowing and highly-sensual look before following the guardian and the others into the temple.

It seemed that Diane had arranged for her group to have access to visit not only the Sphinx Temple, but, as I later discovered, also the Temple of Amenhotep II *and* the Sphinx itself. I was suitably impressed; although the reality was that it was probably simply a matter of offering the authorities enough money. Still, she had graciously included Bill and I in the group without asking for any contribution, so I was extremely grateful.

What came first?

Before we went inside, I paused, looking at the temples, the Sphinx in the background, and the image on my iphone; something else was bothering me.

'What is it, Alex?'

'Something's out of kilter.'

'With the temple?'

'With everything; the Causeway, the Valley Temple, the Sphinx Temple, and the Sphinx, none of them seem to line up like you might expect if they were all part of the one construction project, except perhaps the two temples. It's hard to know what came first, the chicken or the egg?'

'If you believe the Egyptologists, they were all built by Khafre during the 4th Dynasty of the Old Kingdom.'

'Well, I don't believe that for a nanosecond.'

'So, what's your thinking?'

'My thinking is, that if the archaeologists are correct and the Causeway was lined with red granite, then its more than likely pre pole shift. That's supported by the position and alignment of it and the Valley Temple as being part of the function of the Second Pyramid in connecting it directly to the Nile, which could just as easily, if not more significantly, have been straight to the east of the pyramid. That means that the Causeway and the pyramid are both most likely pre pole shift structures, which we both agree with, but it also means that the Causeway existed *before* the Sphinx, which would mean the pyramid, and the Causeway, pre-date the Sphinx.'

'I think even the Egyptologists would agree with that; just disagree on the era of construction. You know there's what they refer to as a drainage channel cut along the north side of the eastern end of the causeway that opens directly into the upper southwest corner of the Sphinx enclosure. It makes no sense the builders would have cut a channel that drained water directly into the Sphinx enclosure; they could have built it on the south side. So the channel must have had a prior function that predated, and was made obsolete by, the quarrying of the Sphinx enclosure.'

'It also means the two structures, the Causeway and the Sphinx, were *not* part of the same process of planning, or of construction.'

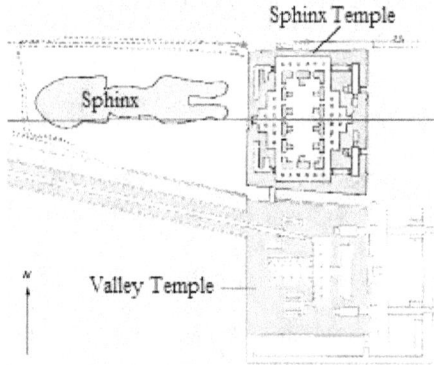

'It sure does. Is that all?'

'No. There's something that doesn't gel about where the Causeway interconnects with the Valley Temple. Most of the other valley temples have a much more "designed" connection. This looks a bit slapdash and ad hoc. But if you assume there are older temples forty to fifty feet below the sand, and continue the line of the causeway down until it meets the tunnels in front of the Valley Temple, then the alignments become more conventional.'

'That's an interesting proposition; it would mean the Valley Temple is a later reconstruction. But where does it leave the Sphinx Temple; is it part of the same reconstruction, or does it belong to the earlier period?'

'Any thoughts?'

Bill started meandering along the front of the two temples.

'Some Egyptologists believe that when you compare the floor plan of the Sphinx Temple with that of Khafre's Mortuary Temple up next to the pyramid, that the design of the inner courts is nearly identical, suggesting a high probability that they were designed and constructed at the same time.'

'It's possible, but it's also possible that one was a much later model for the other; its like saying because the entrance to the Louvre is pyramid-shaped that it was built at the same time as the Great Pyramid, and a rectangular porticoed courtyard with pillars and statues is hardly a unique architectural structure.'

'True. Well, at first glance, the two temples *are* similar in size, and both face east in a north-south alignment. Each has a pair of north and south entrances in their eastern facades. Both temples were lined, inside and out, with red granite, and paved with alabaster. Both temples sit on the same prepared terrace, which is about eight feet lower than the ground level of the Sphinx, and the front and backs of both temples are in almost perfect alignment, so one would assume they were built as part of the same program.'

'Exactly, you would *assume* that, but the key word here is *almost*. Surely if you were surveying the land to build two temples side by side, you would continue your guidelines and markings to ensure they *were* perfectly aligned. But they're not. One could just be a much later copy of the other.'

'A good point...'

He gazed off to the left...

'...So you're saying the original Valley Temple may have been further to the southeast, was buried by a tsunami,...

...then looked back to the present Valley Temple.

'...but was reconstructed in its present position, from the remnants of the original temple, when the Sphinx and Sphinx Temple were built?'

'I don't know, I'm just looking at the evidence, and all the possible permutations.'

'Well the archaeological and geological evidence supports the idea that they were all built around the same time.'

'What evidence is that?'

Turning back, we returned along the face of the temples.

'Back in late 60s, a Swiss architect-Egyptologist, by the name of Herbert Ricke, proposed that stones comprising the Sphinx, Sphinx Temple, and Valley Temple, were all part of the same quarry and construction process. That was confirmed in 1980 when the geologist Thomas Aigner did a study of the sea-floor sedimentation that formed the geological layers of the Giza Plateau. Finally, Mark Lehner also examined the geological layers of the Sphinx quarry and found that a certain number of these layers matched perfectly with the geological layers of the Sphinx Temple blocks.

As it turns out, a close geological study of the Sphinx and the two temples revealed that the large blocks of limestone that were used to build the Valley Temple were most-likely quarried from the layers that run through the upper part of the Sphinx's body, and the blocks for the Sphinx Temple were probably cut from the lowest layers of the Sphinx quarry, from just below the chest height of the Sphinx's body.'

'So, the Valley Temple *was* built before the Sphinx Temple?'

'Yes.'

'But how much before?'

'Well, who knows? But the assumption is they were contemporary with each other, as part of the excavation of the Sphinx.'

'What if the tsunami caused by the pole shift destroyed the original temple, then, after the pole shift, they prepared the terrace and constructed the two new temples out of the red granite ruins of the original temple, with the limestone blocks, cut out when they cut out the Sphinx, using the old temple design as the template for the new Valley Temple and Sphinx Temple?'

'It sounds plausible. But it beggars the question; why not just quarry the blocks, why leave the figure of the Sphinx? What does it really mean?'

'Well, remember what Pieter said about that French guy, Slosman; how he said there were "Grand Cataclysms", pole shifts, in 9792 BC, that caused the last parts of Atlantis to disappear beneath the ocean, and before that there were previous cataclysms in 21,312 BC, and 29,808 BC?'

'That's right!'

'Well, it all fits together with the geological and archaeological evidence; the Sphinx was originally a Lion, carved out after the 21,312 BC pole shift, to indicate an important upcoming event twelve thousand years in the future when Leo was rising on the horizon. It was the 'X' that marks the spot, the circle on the calendar.'

'And to store the details, they utilized a pre-existing chamber beneath the Giza Plateau that was possibly hundreds of thousands of years old.'

'That's why the Sphinx doesn't line up with anything on the surface, because its position is determined by the structures below.'

'By the Hall of Records.'

'The proof *is there*, it's the buildings themselves.'

'Hmmm?'

The possibilities caused us to quickened our step, eager to explore the Sphinx Temple, when, just as we approached the southern entrance, Pernille appeared from within, looking around to see where we were.

'Hurry up, you two, or you'll be left behind.'

Left behind? We were miles ahead!

'Coming!'

The Sphinx Temple

Like the Valley Temple, the Sphinx Temple had two entrances on its east side, one to the north, the other to the south. Following Pernille, we made our way in via the southern gate.

Only uncovered at the beginning of the 20th Century, the Sphinx Temple was surprisingly poorly preserved given its location before the paws of the Sphinx. When it was fully excavated, it was found to be severely damaged, with very little of its granite facing left and only part of the eroded limestone core of the structure remaining. That it was buried and so badly damaged totally supported my tsunami theory, but now it also raised the question, which one?

Reaching the centre, I stopped and looked around at the ruins. The temple was a mess, gutted; once lined with fine Tura limestone, red granite, and with floors of alabaster; virtually none of it remained.

So, if the temple ever had any inscriptions, which I strongly doubted, they were now long gone. It also meant there was not one iota of written evidence attesting to who built it, or when. In fact, there was no mention of it at all in the whole Old Kingdom, which makes no sense unless it was buried and they didn't even know it existed. Then it would make perfect sense. In fact, apart from aspects about the structure, almost everything about the temple was little more than guesswork and conjecture, and that suited me fine; I could cogitate and speculate with the best of them, PhD or no PhD.

However, just out of interest I had a look to see what the 'experts' did have to say.

"There is evidence that the temple was left unfinished, and perhaps never even used; large boulders left both inside and outside, the builders stopping work on the temple after raising the core blocks at three corners, placing colossal statues inside the temple, and fitting the colonnade with its granite pillars."

Or maybe, just maybe, the temple was damaged by a tsunami.

More bilaterally symmetrical than any other temple I'd seen, the temple was designed basically as a central courtyard, measuring about 50 metres north-south by

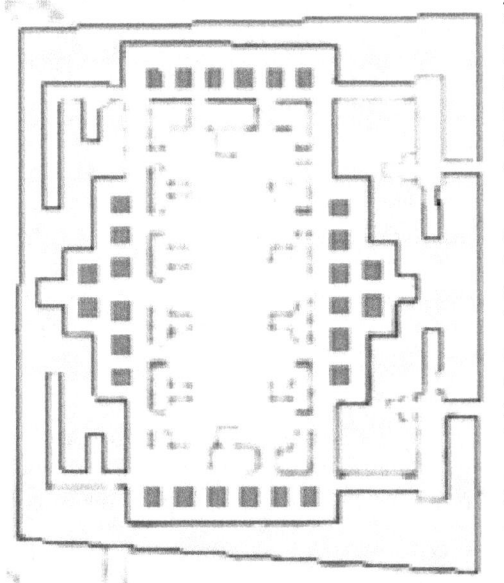

just under 25 metres east-west, which was framed by 14, wide pillars, 10 of which backed large rectangular sockets in the alabaster floor that clearly once housed colossal statues on pedestals that sat on the bedrock terrace base.

Of who, or what, the statues represented was impossible to know for sure, because every single statue, just like in the Valley Temple, was gone, not a fragment survived. Despite that, my thoughts quickly drifted to them being representations of ten of the twelve "Tribes of Israel". They were all gone, not a pebble, not a chip remained. I smelled a rat, or rather a flock of vultures.

Beyond the large pillars, the courtyard was once surrounded by a colonnade of 24 smaller, rectangular, red-granite pillars, six to each of the four sides, with a small sanctuary to either side, to the west and to the east, each with a large recess, probably for a further two statues, possibly the representatives of the remaining two Tribes of Israel, each preceded by two further pillars.

There was no logical conclusion for the absence of the statues other than they had been removed, either by the Ancient Egyptians *before* the tsunami that buried the temple hit, which didn't make sense, or some time *after* or *during* its excavation at the beginning of the 20th Century. My money was on the later. Now it doesn't take an Einstein to figure out *who* removed them; the real question was why they removed them all, not just the twelve here, but also the ones in the Valley Temple. The only conclusion that made any sense to me was that the statues represented something, or someone, the 'powers that be' deemed too dangerous for the masses to see and become aware of.

Continuing my exploration, the western wall of the temple had been cut directly from the bedrock, down to a height of about 2.5 metres, and, from there, it was topped with limestone blocks cut from the Sphinx quarry. What I did particularly notice was that there were no exits in the back wall, nothing that led directly to the Sphinx from inside the temple. To me, that seemed clear that the temple had absolutely nothing to do ceremonially with the Sphinx itself. So, if the Sphinx had no direct functional relationship to the temple, why the hell was it created?

According to the Egyptologists, Egyptian civilization began around 3000 BC, which means that the Egyptians developed the sophisticated science, mathematics and building skills necessary to build the Great Pyramid and the Sphinx in a mere 500 years. I didn't buy that. The picture I was starting to get was of the Sphinx Temple and Valley Temple buried, not by the passing of Nibiru and the Thera tsunami around 1600 BC, but by the pole shift caused by the passing of Nibiru some time between 8,800 BC and 12,400 BC. And if that were true, which the weathering on the stones would seem to indicate, and Slosman's date of 9792 BC would indicate, then it meant the two temples and the Sphinx were not only built *before* then, but, more specifically, *after* the previous pole shift had destroyed the original temple.

That took us back to the last major pole shift around 19,600 BC or 23,200 BC, or, according to Slosman, 21,312 BC or 29,808 BC and the legend of the demise of Atlantis, which, interestingly enough, was first documented by Plato; Plato, who spent 13 years consulting the scribes and records in the Library of Alexandria. Plato, who "descended into the shrines and temples and learned from the Books of Isis and Horus". It was blatantly obvious that the knowledge of the Ancient Egyptians was not a new development, but a legacy from a far older civilization, Plato's Atlantis.

And if all that were true, which the evidence seemed to suggest, then the contents of the Hall of Records beneath the Sphinx had significant importance to the future of the entire human race. As Diane led the group out through the northern entrance I couldn't help but think, our days were numbered, the question was, how long did we have?

Amenhotep II

Our penultimate stop was the temple Bill and I had past earlier, that of Amenhotep II, a small temple built on a slight rise to the northeast of the Sphinx during the first year of his reign. Given the turmoil and chaos that would have followed the Thera tsunami, and the time it would have taken just to rebuild a normal society, combined with the fact that Amenhotep II was the 7th pharaoh of the 18th Dynasty, it seemed that it took about 120 years before any new building or excavation took place on the Giza Plateau.

Amenhotep II, whose throne name was A-kheperu-re, meaning "Great are the Manifestations of Re", was the son of Thutmoses III and, according to the Egyptologists, probably Merytra, a daughter of Huy. I had a different opinion; I believed that his mother was more-than-likely Merytre-Hatshepsut, Hatshepsut's daughter by Senenmut, and a half-sister to Neferure, and that Merytre-Hatshepsut was considered a "minor" wife simply because she was the daughter of Senenmut. It then makes total sense that, being the offspring of Merytre-Hatshepsut, and a great granddaughter of Amenhotep I, that Merytre-Hatshepsut would have named her son Amenhotep II. In addition, Thutmoses III clearly had issues with his step-mother; she may even have insisted he take Merytre-Hatshepsut as a wife.

Although he succeeded Thutmoses III on the throne, Amenhotep II was not Thutmoses III's firstborn son; his elder brother Amenemhat, by Satiah, who was probably Neferure, was originally the intended heir to the throne. However, sometime between Years 24 and 35 of Thutmose III's reign, both queen Satiah and prince Amenemhat died, which supposedly prompted the pharaoh to marry the supposed non-royal Merytre-Hatshepsut, resulting in the birth of Amenhotep II.

However, despite being the heir to the throne, Amenhotep II did not automatically assume the position on the death of his father. According to the experts, he served a co-regency of two years and four months with Thutmose III. But that didn't really make sense; I mean if Thutmoses III was ruling, why make his son a coregent? What does make sense is, that when Thutmoses III died, Amenhotep II was not of age to assume the throne and would have been a coregent with someone else, most likely his mother, Merytre-Hatshepsut, who had a legitimate lineage dating back to Amenhotep I. However, the Amun Priests would hardly have been thrilled with the idea of a repeat performance of the Hatshepsut era by her daughter, and, as they were the ones who recorded everything, rather than wait to erase her memory from the record they probably and simply made a decision to not even acknowledge her.

That said, what we do know is, according to an inscription on his great Sphinx stela, found somewhere nearby, there was over a two year 'gap' before Amenhotep II assumed power in his own right at the age of 18. Sometime after, he married a woman of uncertain parentage, named Tiaa, who I think was most probably his half-sister or full-sister, and who may have born him as many as ten sons, including: Thutmose IV, who succeeded him, princes Amenhotep, Ahnmose, Webensenu, Amenemopet, Nedjem, Amenemhat, Khaemwaset, and Aakheperure, as well as one daughter, Iaret; the lack of any documented evidence of his queens and princesses being clear evidence the Amun Priests made a conscious decision to reject the *sang réal*, the dynastic role played by women as "god's wives of Amun", and feared the 'danger' to them should a woman become too powerful.

"The 'royal fame stela' speaks of Amenhotep II's achievements as the leader of the army before his crowning, as a 16 or 17 year old; one of his greatest achievements being that he shot arrows through a copper plate one palm thick while driving a chariot with the reins tied about his waist."

Perhaps it was true, although can we really believe everything we read, especially when as the same scrawny teenager, he supposedly also wielded an oar, 30 feet in length, and was able to row his ship six times faster and farther than two-hundred members of the navy could row theirs? It's like the whole history of Egyptology, should we believe it just because it has been written down by someone with a PhD, especially when the actual evidence tells us something different?

What we can be certain of is, the significance of most of Amenhotep II's long reign, as compared to that of his predecessors, was that, because it was characterized by peace, it allowed him to pursue a program of building that left its mark at nearly all the major sites along the Nile. The other point of significance is that, when he died, not only was Amenhotep II buried in the Valley of the Kings in tomb KV35, but, that during the reign of Smendes at the beginning of the 21st Dynasty, the Amun Priests used his tomb to conceal 13 other royal mummies, including those of his sons Websenu and Thutmoses IV, his mother Hatshepsut Meryet-Ra, his grandson Amenhotep III, Merenptah, Seti II, Siptah, Ramses IV, Ramses V, Ramses VI, possibly Tiy, and probably Setnakht.

The Temple of Amenhotep II

Reaching the temple was somewhat of an anticlimax, as the original structure was virtually non-existent, destroyed; only a few fragments had survived. The modern archaeologists had reconstructed the foundations and some of the gateways and doorways, but the reality was there was little to explore other than speculation. It was impossible to tell if the temple had been swept away by the tsunamis around the beginning of the 1st millennia AD, or pilfered by the locals during the two thousand years that followed; perhaps even both.

"The Temple of Amenhotep II is dedicated to Harmachis, the Sphinx, or Horem-akhet, 'Horus in his Western Horizon', which was no longer seen as a royal statue, but became misremembered as a god in its own right, as an image of the sun god, Harmachis, Further, on foundation stones from the temple, the Sphinx is also named Harmachis-Hauron, Hauron being the name of a Syrian-Palestinian god of the netherworld that a community of Syrian-Palestinians living near the Great Sphinx identified with his image.'

Firstly, it is more logical that the Sphinx got his so-called 'Syrian-Palestinian' name from the later 27th Dynasty invasions of the Persians, however, it is more likely that the name had Libyan origins, deriving from the occupation of the Libyans in the 22nd Dynasty. Second, that the Sphinx was re-identified with an event on the 'western' horizon, something connected with a sun god is significant. Why? Because the Ancient Egyptians already had a sun god, Re, and a god Horus, so why would they name the Sphinx after the sun god and then give him a different name? Unless, of course, it was a different sun: the brown dwarf, Nibiru!

I looked back through the gateways that had been reconstructed using scant fragments and copious amounts of modern concrete; I wasn't sure whether the modern reconstructions enhanced the structures and made the temples easier to experience, or, like the ones I'd seen on Elephantine Island, and at Abydos, gave a false perspective on them and made them look more like toilet blocks.

One thing was certain; there was no doubt the focus of the temple was on the Sphinx. But why build it off to the side at a 45° angle? Amenhotep II could have built it directly in front of the Sphinx, on the mound where the Sphinx Temple was, although maybe he didn't because it may have blocked the Sphinx's view of the horizon?

Amenhotep II could also have chosen to excavate, rebuild, and usurp the Sphinx Temple, but he didn't, he chose to build a new temple in a different location, although he may have used material from the Sphinx Temple to do so.

A quick lap of the rest of the 'ruins' of the temple and we were descending the modern staircase to the Roman-era paving stones that formed a patio in front of perhaps the greatest enigma of modern civilization, a mystery of leonine proportions - the Sphinx. For centuries archaeologists, Egyptologists, spiritualists and treasure seekers alike have pondered the questions: "Who created it?" "When did they create it?" "Why did they create it?" And most of all, "what, if anything, is below it?"

The Great Sphinx

Standing before it, the pyramids in the background over its shoulder, the Great Sphinx is colossal; approximately 240 feet (73 m) long, 66 feet (20 m) high, and 38 feet (12 m) wide across at the shoulders. Directly carved out of the limestone bedrock of the plateau in the shape of a recumbent lion with the head of a human decorated with a royal Nemes-headdress, which indicates the king was considered the incarnation of Horus. It was an impressive sight; but it didn't always look like it does today.

When Napoleon saw the Sphinx, at the turn of the 18th Century, only its head and shoulders were visible above the desert sands. It had probably been that way for thousands of years, certainly from the time of the tsunami around the beginning of the 1st millennia AD, and that's how it remained until 1816-1818 when Caviglia uncovered a considerable portion of the body and the paws, revealing a number of temples, sanctuaries, altars and stelas that had been erected in and in front of it.

Clearing away the sand in front of the Sphinx, Caviglia discovered a platform, the 'Roman patio' where we now stood, that not only extended out both sides of the Sphinx but which primarily ran eastward for about a hundred feet and included a spectacular staircase of thirty steps that led up to a landing that was built atop the buried Sphinx Temple. On that landing Caviglia found the remains of what looked like a pulpit, and forty feet further eastward, at the end of the landing, was another flight of thirteen steps that raised the level to the same height as the head of the Sphinx.

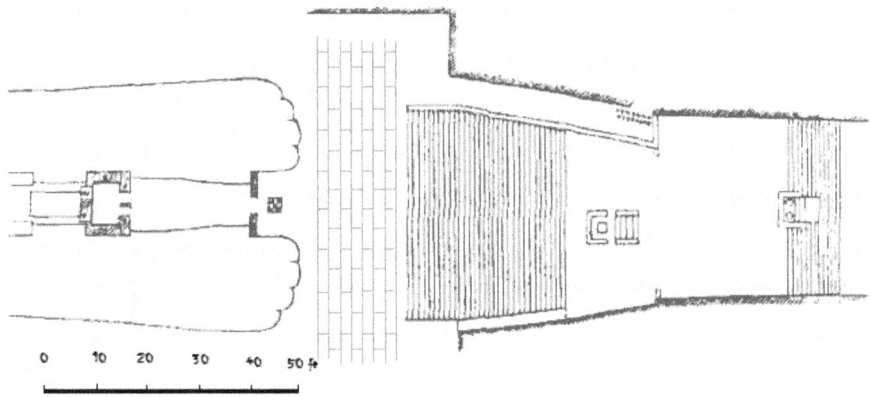

I had never thought of it before, but after all my discussions on the trip, I now wondered if there was any significance to there being 30 steps, and then another 13 steps? Were they significant to the Tat Brotherhood? It was possible; 13 was definitely a number of significance to many secret societies, but, why? After all, this was maybe a thousand years before the Knights of Templar, so was it somehow connected to the 13th Zodiac sign, Ophiuchus, and the direction from whence Nibiru was said to arrive?

Incorporated into the top staircase was a structure with two columns situated in such a way that the eastward gaze of the Sphinx passed precisely between the two columns. Again it got me thinking; were the columns somehow related to the two columns of the Temple of Solomon? Surely there must be some connection! That said, apart from a section of the patio, it was all gone, the pulpit, the staircases, the columns who knows what became of them; all removed in the early 20th Century, along with numerous other mud-brick structures dating from the New Kingdom on, by the early archaeologists, perhaps in search of the Hall of Records that reportedly lay beneath. So, because the early excavators didn't use modern archaeological recording techniques, we know very little about these structures? All we can be sure about is they post-date the Thera tsunami.

Archaeologists believe, and for once I agree with them, that the remains belonged to the Roman period. That said, it is also possible they were appropriated from the Ptolemaic period. My own personal belief is that, as they were built on top of the Sphinx Temple mound, it makes perfect sense that they were constructed after the 1st millennia AD tsunami and thus, most-likely, Roman.

Turning back to the Sphinx, it was almost incredulous to believe that, although the ancient Egyptians, along with the Romans and Arabs, documented the numerous repairs to the Sphinx, no one, including the ancient Egyptians, wrote anything about its construction: was this because its construction pre-dated dynastic Egypt?

That's what the Romans, 9th Century Arabs, and ancient Egyptians themselves believed; that the Sphinx and pyramids at Giza were built by an advanced antediluvian civilization that was destroyed by a great flood. If the Sphinx could speak, I wonder what tales it would tell? Sometimes, the silence speaks volumes.

And yet, in the face of that four-and-a-half-thousand years of belief, and any clear evidence to the contrary, it is the view of most modern Egyptologist's, a view barely 100 years old, that it was Khafre who built not only the Sphinx, but the Sphinx Temple, the second pyramid, along with its Mortuary and Valley Temple, and the Causeway; all based on the flimsiest and most circumstantial of evidence. So, where do they stand, and what's their evidence?

Most Egyptologists believe, blindly I might add, that the Sphinx was built during the Old Kingdom, in about 2530 BC, by Khafre as a guardian figure for his 'tomb', the second pyramid,. But that's not what any of the evidence directly indicates.

The main piece of evidence relied upon by Egyptologists is an inscription, now missing, that was supposedly found on the 13th line of the badly-weathered 'Dream Stela', placed between the paws of the Sphinx by Thutmoses IV in the New Kingdom and uncovered by Caviglia in 1818. Caviglia's excavations were recorded by Henry Salt, but not published during Salt's life, so it wasn't until the early 1840's that Howard Vyse published Henry Salt's records of Caviglia's excavations. After my doubt about his efforts in the relieving chambers above the King's Chamber in the Great Pyramid, I had further doubts about the honesty and accuracy of all of Vyse's 'work', but I was prepared to give him the benefit of the doubt here because he was publishing someone else's findings.

The diary includes a meticulous drawing of the Dream Stela that shows, on one of the surviving, but fragmented, lower lines of text, a broken cartouche containing the first two elements of the name Khafre, *kha-f*. There is some however, some dispute as to whether the hieroglyphs referred to Khafre, or if they were even there to begin with, throwing into doubt the whole attribution of the construction of the Sphinx to Khafre, and to the 4th Dynasty. But that was just the tip of the iceberg.

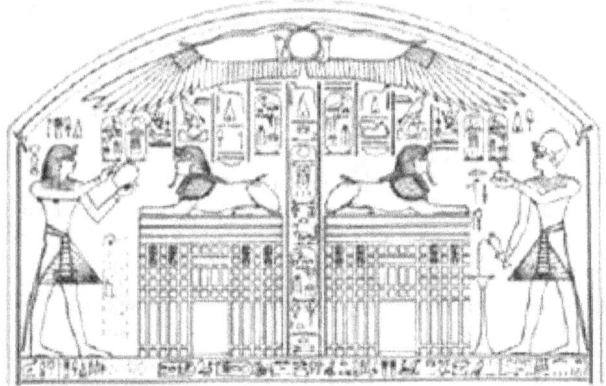

If we assume the hieroglyphs *were* there, and they did in fact refer to Khafre, the next hurdle is the fragment made no reference to Khafre as the 'builder' of the Sphinx; he may well have just done as Thutmoses IV had done, excavated the enclosure after a tsunami and made repairs. So concluding Khafre was the builder, based on this one piece of evidence, was highly speculative at best. Despite this, it was exciting to know that within a minute or so I was about to see the famed 'Dream Stela' with my own eyes.

The second piece of evidence relied upon by Egyptologists in attributing Khafre as the builder of the Sphinx is his supposed construction of the Valley and Mortuary Temples, *and* the second pyramid, based on the discovery of a single diorite statue unearthed in the Valley Temple. That's even less credible than the fragment on the Dream Stela, as there is nothing supporting Khafre being responsible for building them either. But if that's dodgy, the third piece of evidence they rely upon is simply clutching at straws; that the face of the Sphinx resembles a statue of Khafre.

For starters, the face, even though it was the victim of considerable damage, only vaguely looked like Khafre at best; in particular, the nose and beard were missing, mainly as a result of the Mameluke troops using it for target practice for their field cannons during the French occupation around 1800. The reality is, there is not one single contemporary inscription that connects the Sphinx with Khafre, so the evidence for the attribution of the Sphinx to Khafre is at best highly speculative and circumstantial. That led to propositions the Sphinx belonged to Khufu, Khafre's father, despite the fact there was no comparable image of him either. So they relied on another questionable stela, the 'Inventory Stela', found just east of the Great Pyramid by Mariette in 1857.

As Frank had informed me, the 'Inventory Stela', that mentions both Khufu *and* the Sphinx, is believed to be a 26th Dynasty copy of an earlier 4th Dynasty stela, which does not necessarily mean it should be discounted. The reason is, the stela mentions the discoveries Khufu made while clearing away the sand from not only the Great Pyramid, but the ruins of the nearby Temple of Isis, where the stela was eventually discovered, and the Sphinx as well, and how Khufu inspected the Sphinx after part of the headdress had been blown off by a bolt of lighting, and how he carefully restored it.

But did Khufu simply restore the headdress, or did he go the whole hog and totally re-sculpture it in his own image? If he did, it would certainly account for the smaller head? Perhaps he did a bit of both? Either way, the evidence of the lightning bolt and repairs is supported by the findings of Selim Hassan in the 1930's, so how could the Egyptologists even contemplate Khufu was responsible for building the Sphinx when it was clear that it was already gazing out over the horizon during the reign of Khufu? And if it was there for Khufu, it was there for Khafre, and for Djedkare, Khafre's son, whom others believed was responsible, again based on another vaguely similar statue.

Despite the actual evidence, the Egyptologists seemed intent on trying to lock the Sphinx into the Old Kingdom, and in particular to their belief the pyramids and Sphinx were all built during the 4th Dynasty. You could easily forgive the early Egyptologists for their speculations, as they only had the head sticking up above the sand to go by, but once the sand had been cleared away from the body, and it became obvious to all and sundry that the head was disproportionably much smaller than you might expect in comparison to the body, and it raised the serious issue of whether it was part of the original carving, or a later modification, then later Egyptologists should have had a complete rethink. And, some did.

It led to an alternate theory by German Egyptologist Ludwig Borchardt, who proposed, on the much stronger evidence of it having been painted with red, ochre, green and black for much of its documented history, and that the same stripes, eye-paint, and facial structure were present on the sphinx statue of Amenemhat II in the Louvre, that the face dated to the 12th Dynasty in the Middle Kingdom and belongs to Amenemhat II. Borchardt based his theory on his belief that the pleated stripes on the Sphinx's names-headress are in groups of three, which is a very specific style seen exclusively during the 12th Dynasty, and that the design of the eye-paint was not seen before the 6th Dynasty. But Borchardt was no fool, and, in hedging his bets, he placated the mainstream Egyptologists by cleverly concluding that the Sphinx was in fact created during the 4th Dynasty, perhaps even before, but that the original head, which could have been the head of a lion, or that of Khafre, was damaged beyond repair, and that Amenemhat II re-carved his own likeness into the existing head and neck to save the structure, which explains why the Sphinx's head is now so disproportionately small. The big questions he didn't answer were; 'what caused the damage', 'when did it happen', 'who carved it out of the bedrock in the first place', and 'when did they do it'? The answers to those questions required further digging, and, below the surface, lay the clues.

I turned my attention back to where the ladies were congregating; the long passage that lay between the paws of the Sphinx. Caviglia discovered the outer extremities of the paws were not part of the original sculpture, but consisted of a number of smaller stone blocks, believed by most Egyptologists to be probably part of restoration work carried out by the Romans. It was possible, however I wasn't so sure.

What *was* important was that the paws had been repaired; most probably by the Romans when they laid down the paving and staircases before the Sphinx. It was solid evidence the paws had been significantly damaged sometime in the past, before the Roman era, but by what, and when?

Caviglia continued his excavation and next unearthed a paved court, extending about three-quarters of the way down the paws, enclosed by two walls adorned with two small limestone stelæ, one of which, containing the name of Ramses II, was still in situ, the other, which had fallen into the interior of the chapel, lay amongst masses of other debris, including fragments of the beard once attached to the chin of the Sphinx. Within the court was a square altar of granite.

The limestone stela of Ramses II made perfect sense; not only was it a part of Ramses II's egotistical move to claim everything as his own, but it showed the Sphinx had been cleared, and probably repaired, sometime after the Thera tsunami.

Suddenly I was more interested in the red-granite altar that the ladies were now gathering around. To me, like all the other altars I had encountered on my journey, it was a clear sign of a pre pole shift origin; it was probably once part of the original temple, salvaged to rebuild the Valley and Sphinx Temples, and then placed between the paws of the Sphinx as part of the post-Thera worship instigated by Amenhotep II.

Confirming the pre pole shift origins of the Sphinx, at the end of the passage, and at then end of a small chapel ten feet long by five feet wide, Caviglia unearthed perhaps the most revealing evidence in determining the history and 'identity' of the Sphinx, a slab of granite, 14 feet high, covered with sculptures and hieroglyphics; the so-called 'Dream stela' of Thutmoses IV. I couldn't wait to check it out, however, it would seem I had to.

'Gentlemen, would you mind if we ladies could have a few minutes in private?'

Diane and the ladies were poised for action, their hands resting on the altar; clearly they were about to start toning, just as Crystal had done at so many of the other locations. Ever the gentleman, Bill was quick to oblige.

'More secret women's business, hey? Sure, no problems. Come on, Alex, it'll give us a chance to check out the lion's den.'

It was no big drama; I could check out the Dream Stela later, when the ladies were finished. My only afterthought, and real concern, was that my time with Crystal was fast running out; Saeed would be here within the hour and I'd be whisked away to Alexandria and then Greece, possibly never to see her again. It was perhaps the most pressing issue for me to deal with; how was I going to get any time alone with her? Bill's mind was less distracted.

'You know, Alex, several New Kingdom inscriptions refer to the Sphinx as the "Lord of Setpet", *setepet* meaning "The Chosen Place." Do you think it was a reference, as most Egyptologists would suggest, to the appointment of the pharaoh as the chosen one of the gods, or do you think it could have been a reference to being initiated as a member of the Tat Brotherhood, and to that initiation being intricately connected to the Sphinx, or to some chamber or chambers within or beneath it?'

'Well, I'm probably biased, but I would go with the latter, primarily because the appointment of the pharaoh was already pretty predetermined, and there was nothing out of the ordinary of the lineage in the 18th Dynasty after Thutmoses IV….except perhaps with the arrival of Akhenaten.'

Bill stroked his chin in his now familiar contemplative fashion.

'If Akhenaten *was* Annunaki, which may just be right, it might support both propositions, but ultimately, once he disappeared from the scene and the military pharaoh's of the 19th and 20th Dynasties took over, the issue of being "chosen" as pharaoh became somewhat of a moot point as it was generally just handed down from father to son.'

'Probably without any consideration to, or even awareness of, the *sang réal*.'

'Possibly.'

'Which leaves it related to the initiation of members of the Tat Brotherhood, or, perhaps the Amun Priests of the 21st Dynasty.'

Bill disagreed.

'Unlikely, as, whilst the Tat Brotherhood may well still have controlled the sacred knowledge in the *northern* part of Egypt, the Amun Priests may well have only held power in Thebes, to the south.'

'Will we ever know the truth?'

'Perhaps, if we keep digging we might!'

'Well, let's start with what we know.'

'OK. According to the Egyptologists, the Sphinx quarry was once encircled by a massive mud-brick wall, in the shape of a giant cartouche, erected by Thutmoses IV, who, according to the Egyptologists, was supposedly responsible for first excavating the Sphinx from the desert sands, and who erected the Dream Stela signifying the event.'

'However, given the Temple of Amenhotep II faced the Sphinx on the nearby rise, and his extensive rebuilding program, the excavation work was probably started by Amenhotep II.'

'But, given the scope of the excavation, not completed until after Amenhotep II's death.'

'With Thutmoses IV taking all the credit.'

'True, but the attribution to Thutmoses IV confirms two things, firstly, that Thutmoses IV was instrumental in the resurrection of the Sphinx, and, second, the mud-brick wall indicates there was a belief the Sphinx had to be protected from something, be it drifting sand or a possible future tsunami's one can only speculate.'

'Well, my money is on the latter. What does the actual evidence say?'

'Right, well, it was here in the quarry that several huge limestone blocks were discovered, supposedly abandoned by the original builders, leaving the Sphinx Temple unfinished.'

'That makes no sense to me at all. What does make sense is that they were dislodged by the same event that caused the damage to the Sphinx, not an earthquake, but a tsunami. Of course, the blocks were no longer where they had been discovered but have been placed back atop the excavated bedrock to form the third course of masonry on the Sphinx Temple walls, ironically, where they actually belong.'

'All makes perfect sense to me.'

We moved on, along the south side of the Sphinx quarry, which incorporated the north side of the foundation of the Khafre causeway; it was more confirmation the Causeway predated the Sphinx. Bill was paying particular attention to the striations and erosion of the enclosure wall.

'Beautiful, isn't it?'

It took me back to the boat trip, to Crystal and I walking beside the river at Silwa Bahari.

'It depends what you're referring to.'

'The formation of the rock, the layering, the erosion, the fissures.'

I put my hand in my pocket; the small shell she had given me was still there. Taking it out, I briefly looked at it, then rubbed it like I was trying to exude wisdom from it, and I continued my discourse with Bill.

'If it's so beautiful, why do you question it?'

'What?'

'It's something Crystal brought to my attention; we make a statement, such as *"It's beautiful"*, which is a personal subjective observation, and then straight away we second-guess our observation and ask for validation on our statement by adding *"isn't it?"*'

'What's your point, Alex?'

'Saying something is beautiful doesn't change what it is; it's all subjective perception. But, when you question your perception you question yourself and bring your perceptions into doubt.'

'Mate, no offence, but I think you've been out in the sun too long.'

'Hang on. What would you say if in response to your *It's beautiful, isn't it?* I replied, *No, it's a load of crap, it's just a hunk of rock*? You'd either try to convince me I was wrong, and thus undermine my belief in my *own* perceptions, or you'd compromise your own view and shift towards mine because you don't want to risk the friendship.'

'And your point is?'

He was right: what *was* the point; apart from being obsessed with Crystal and everything she said?

'I guess we have to stick to our guns, trust our perspective on the universe and not look for validation; everything is what it is, and that includes our perspective on things.'

Thankfully Bill placated me.

'That doesn't mean we can't change our perspective given new information. I used to believe all the "educated" rhetoric, spouted by the majority of Egyptologists, that the damage here was erosion, caused by thousands of years of wind, but when I saw it for myself, I realized that couldn't be true, it had to have been water.'

'Even a novice like me could see the "wind and sand theory" was bullshit, it might account for some of the damage to the head, but the rest of the body has been periodically buried for thousands of years. I figured the wind-and-sand theory was a just a load of hot air.'

'Well, you and I weren't the first to come to that conclusion.'

'Who was?'

'R. A. Schwaller de Lubicz, a maverick Egyptologist, who visited Giza in the 1930s and immediately declared that the Sphinx had been weathered by seawater and that its origins lay in the ocean.'

'A tsunami!'

'He never said that exactly, and no one really paid him any attention, that is until Mark Lehner got involved back in 1979.'

'The same Mark Lehner who became director of ARCE?'

'Yep.'

'I can just see the vultures circling; what did he do?'

'Along with a guy called Gauri, he surveyed and mapped the Sphinx.'

'No doubt searching for the entrance to the Hall of Records.'

'Obviously; why else would he be here? Lehner was a staunch believer of Edgar Cayce, the "sleeping prophet", who predicted that the Great Sphinx guarded the entrance to the Hall of Records, which contained all the records of the lost civilization of Atlantis brought to Egypt by its survivors.'

'And what did he find?'

'Who knows what he actually found, but what he reported was purely superficial and academic; that the part of the core-body of the Sphinx now showing had been eroded badly, leaving just the softer yellowish bands and harder intermediate strata, showing a profile of successive rolls and undulations. It indicated to Lehner that the core-body of the Sphinx was already severely eroded when the earliest large-limestone blocks, up to one metre in length, were added to it. The larger blocks were then overlain by a second layer of later, brick-sized limestone masonry...'

As Bill and I strolled along the southern part of the quarry, I took specific note of the various states of the Sphinx; the various repair jobs as well as the original weathered bedrock. What was immediately clear, by the considerable extent of the repair work, was that the extent of the damage must also have been considerable.

'...So, in keeping with the traditional attribution of the Sphinx to Khafre, Lehner came to the conclusion that the earliest facing stones, the largest blocks, were repairs made during the New Kingdom by Thutmoses IV, which might be so, but it means the "weathering" by the wind and sand had to have occurred before that, in the thousand or so years from 2500 BC to 1400 BC.'

'Which is when the Sphinx was buried.'

'Exactly! So either Lehner got it wrong,...'

'Or,...he's covering something up.'

'Not just him, but Gauri, who worked with Lehner.'

'Never heard of him, but go on.'

'Gauri proposed that it was groundwater leeching upward inside the rock that was the cause of salt exfoliation to the Sphinx.'

'Seriously? It might be true if there was salt water beneath the ground, but the Nile is fresh water; well, not so much fresh, as not salty. And salt water damage could only happen from sea water, which again supports the tsunami theory.'

'That it does! Anyway, the report somehow came to the attention of John West.'

'John West the salmon guy?'

'No, John Anthony West, who, at the time, was a tour-guide come new-wave Egyptologist. He'd written a very interesting book called "Serpent in the Sky" in which he introduced the work of Schwaller.'

'Schwaller de Lubicz, the guy you were telling me about before, who visited Giza in the 1930s and declared that the Sphinx had been weathered by seawater.'

'One and the same; Schwaller believed that Egypt was the source of Pythagoras's knowledge, and that a proper understanding of ancient Egypt required an openness to the mystical as well as mathematical knowledge encoded in Egyptian art and architecture.'

'He was right; Pythagoras was initiated into the Tat Brotherhood.'

'How do you know that?'

'Frank told me all about it. Pythagoras was the son of a High Priest of Apollo and his mother was one of the Pythia, the high priestesses of the Temple of Delphi.

Frank thinks Pythagoras was invited to Egypt and learned directly from Oenuphis, High Priest of Heliopolis,'

'It makes sense. Well, in West's book, Schwaller dated the Sphinx to a much earlier time of transitional climate.'

'Like the pole shift?'

'Exactly; and West thought that a closer geological study of the Sphinx might provide archaeological evidence of an earlier date, and that the large facing blocks, previously thought to have been applied at the time of the original carving, might have been Old Kingdom repairs to an already-eroded Sphinx.'

'It makes sense; I mean if you're going to carve the Sphinx out, why would you then cover it with large blocks of the same material? That is a ridiculous concept.'

'To test his theory, in 1989, West invited Dr. Robert Schoch, a geologist from Boston University, to join him and examine the Sphinx, and, in 1990 and then 1991, they came here and did extensive geological and seismic surveys in the Sphinx enclosure. They came to the conclusion the Sphinx had not been weathered by wind and sand, as for most of the last four-thousand-five-hundred years it was buried in sand up to its neck, but that the erosion was caused by rainfall when heavy rains fell on the eastern Sahara prior to at least 7,000 BC, probably around the end of the last ice age.'

'Which is exactly around the time of the last pole shift.'

'Meaning its date of construction might be closer to 10,500 BC.'

'No, not necessarily; not it's date of construction, just the date of the water erosion.'

'Yes, that's true; good point.'

'So Schwaller could have been right, and West, half right; the damage was caused around 10,000 BC by the flooding waters of a tsunami caused by a pole shift?'

Bill looked up at the southern wall of the enclosure.

'That's what the evidence seems to indicate; the vertical fissures definitely are the result of precipitation and runoff.'

'All of which means that the Sphinx is not of ancient Egyptian origin at all, but dates to an earlier, advanced, antediluvian race as Edgar Cayce suggested.'

'The Atlanteans. '

'Or, the Annunaki.'

Rounding the rump, Bill gave it a slap on the tail.

'I wonder how old the old girl really is?'

My attention was momentarily caught by the western wall; divided in two, the first level was rough-cut, whilst the higher part, the eroded section, was more uniform.

'Hey, Bill, do you think there's anything to the different levels here?'

He went into his chin-scratching pose.

'There must be; clearly the upper section was removed later, but how much later, and why?'

'More so, why *wasn't* it all cleared away at the beginning?'

'If the lower section we're in now was part of the original sculpture, part of the original excavation, then that could mean the upper terrace was cleared much later, using the blocks to create the Valley and Sphinx Temples, and to repair the damage caused to the original Sphinx by the pole shift tsunami.'

'Which means that just because the Sphinx and the temples are made of the same material doesn't mean they were quarried at the same time.'

'That works for me, and all the evidence we've seen about the two temples would support it as a viable proposition, but it also means the Sphinx could predate the two temples by centuries, millennia even.'

'Yes, it does, doesn't it?'

Bill turned to me, a broad grin across his face.

'Are you sure about that, or are you wanting my validation?'

We had a chuckle.

'Yes, it means the excavation of the Sphinx could predate the Valley and Sphinx temples by millennia!'

'Question is, how can you prove it?'

I looked down at the seashell I had been toying with for the past five minutes; perhaps hoping it might hold the key as the whole plateau was covered in them. Then I looked back at the wall and suddenly I saw something much deeper.

'Bill, limestone's made from seashells, right?'

'Partly; most limestone is composed of small grains of skeletal fragments of marine organisms, like coral or foraminifera, held together by minerals deposited between the rock pieces called cements. It often contains variable amounts of impurities such as silica, clay, silt, organic remains, iron oxide and sand carried in by rivers, which gives it the different colours, especially on exposed and weathered surfaces like these. Then there are other carbonate grains such as ooids, peloids, intraclasts, and extraclasts.'

'Whoa, hold your horses, Bill, High School science, remember?'

'Sorry, they're living organisms that secrete shells made of aragonite or calcite, and leave the shells behind after they die.'

'Like I said, seashells!'

He momentarily struggled with my schoolyard classification of everything.

'Well, basically, I suppose so.'

'And how long does it take for the limestone to form?'

'It's hard to say; it varies depending on the local conditions and deposition. Figuring out the rate of deposition is tricky without more information. The trouble is limestone doesn't come in exact layers; some places might accumulate more sediment than others. So over two-hundred-and-fifty thousand years one area might be covered by eight hundred metres of sediment while an area just a kilometre or so away could be just twenty metres thick, then a further kilometre-and-a-half down the flow another eight-hundred metres could have accumulated.'

I looked up at the enclosure wall.

'So the depth of the layers here doesn't really give any true indication of the age?'

'None; parts of the Grand Canyon for example took about half-a-million years to deposit nine feet of limestone, but, if your tsunami theory is correct, all of this could all have been deposited very quickly, especially if it killed off all, or most, of the smaller marine creatures.'

'All we know is that, at some point in time, where we are standing, in fact the whole Giza Plateau, was at the bottom of the ocean.'

'No, limestone doesn't form in deep waters because the high pressure and temperature causes the dissolution of calcite to increase nonlinearly. Limestone usually forms in shallow waters, like lakes.'

'I thought it formed under the ocean, over millions of years, compressed by the pressure?'

'No, in fact, if the grains are deposited in very lime-rich waters, they could cement together in a matter of years.'

'Years?'

'Possibly.'

'So it's possible that those red-granite temples here, fifty feet below the surface, could have been buried by fifty feet of deposits from a massive pole-shift tsunami and are even older than the Sphinx and the pyramids?'

Bill mulled it over.

'It's possible, in fact it's the only way I can think that would explain how the red granite got down there.'

'Which means the pyramids and Sphinx were built much later, once the water had gone or dried up; built deliberately on top of the temples because they knew they were there, and then they just tunnelled down through the limestone to access the buried temples.'

'Wow, now *that's* mind-blowing.'

'Isn't it just, and it puts the red-granite temples even further back into history.'

Like an airport customs beagle on the scent of a crotch full of high-grade crack, or a rampant male dog pursuing a bitch on heat, Bill started sniffing around the rear end of the Sphinx.

'What are you looking for?'

'One of the two shafts Baraize discovered when he cleared away the sand. It was around here somewhere, supposedly just north of centre. Borris Said claimed it was seven-to-eight metres deep and connected to a tunnel in the middle of the causeway. Ah, here it is!'

A slab of rock had been wedged into the opening, probably to keep unwanted sand and tourists from getting inside.

We knelt down to examine it, Bill trying to stick his head inside one of the cracks for a quick squiz. From the small brickwork of the repairs, it was hard to tell if the tail, and the hole in it, were even part of the original Sphinx.

'Definitely covered over and sealed.'

As I found an image on my iphone, Bill's voice echoed inside.

'Back in 1977, the SRI conducted research here using resistivity technology and, in addition to the three shafts, they discovered three further, small subterranean anomalies and, on the southern flank the presence of an anomaly which they identified as another possible vertical shaft. Hawass and Lehner apparently investigated it all in 1980 and said that the rear shaft, where we are now, went nowhere, just to the water table, so they sealed it up.'

'I wouldn't believe either of them, even if they came out and said that the Great Pyramid was made of stone and bigger than a bread box, or that Ramses II was an egotistical megalomaniac.'

He popped back out and stood up.

'I agree, but the point that's been conveniently overlooked is, why was the shaft there in the first place?'

After briefly trying to see the inside through one of the cracks, and finding nothing but darkness, I joined him on our feet.

'Well, the first thing that comes to mind is that it's a ventilation shaft.'

'Exactly, but a ventilation shaft to where?'

'I get your thinking.'

'Precisely!...'

Bill meandered on.

'Back in 1980, Hawass said there was nothing here, and yet, in 1987, he authorized a Japanese team from Waseda University in Tokyo to carry out an electromagnetic acoustic survey of the Sphinx. They subsequently reported evidence of several things; a tunnel oriented north-south running under the Sphinx, a water pocket around three metres below the surface near the south hind paw, and another cavity near the north hind paw.'

'Pretty much what the SRI had found. So, despite what Hawass says, there *is* something down there.'

'Lehner explained it all away as part of a very large fissure that cuts through the body of the Sphinx, running across the floor either side of the Sphinx, and up through the southern wall of the Sphinx enclosure and the foundation of the Khafre Causeway. Problem is, West and Schoch, when they did their surveys in 1990, found clear evidence of the same thing, of a cavity or chamber under the left paw of the Sphinx.'

'The Hall of Records.'

'They also found other cavities under and around the Sphinx, as well as the possible tunnel running the length of the body.'

'Just like the Japanese?'

'Just like the Japanese, but, before they could do anything more, West's work was terminated by Hawass.'

'Quel surprise. When was this?'

'Ninety-one.'

'And he did the same thing to Gantenbrink in '93; I think I see a modus operandi.'

'Following that, rumours were running rife that Hawass was secretly continuing work on gaining access to the main chamber located by West.'

'Which ultimately leads to the midnight robbery in 2010 that Mark and Frank were talking about...'

We continued around to the northern flank of the Sphinx.

'...Jesus!...'

I looked along the western wall, noticing two huge holes in the wall.

'...And that's probably where they removed the sarcophagi and statues.'

'They're certainly not the result of wind and sand erosion, that's for sure.'

'Termites perhaps?'

'Vultures more like it.'

What was particularly striking about the two openings was not so much their size, but, that despite their position, there was absolutely nothing mentioned about them anywhere; I couldn't find a single reference, not as tombs, nothing. How could that be?

'The obvious questions thus become, when were they excavated, and where do they lead?'

'There's obviously no sign of them in the early photos by Caviglia because he just excavated the paws, and Baraize, who was responsible for the clearing of most of the rear of the enclosure, didn't mention them at all.'

'So they must have been excavated sometime after 1936.'

'It would seem so, and they're in almost perfect alignment with the centre of Khafre's pyramid and the shafts about thirty metres northeast of Campbell's Tomb.'

'And yet there's nothing written about them anywhere.'

'Not as far as I know. Maybe there's something about them, and about the robbery in 2010, in those papers on your back?'

We'd been so busy unravelling the mysteries of the Sphinx, I'd totally forgotten about Kareem's papers.

'Well, that would be the icing on the cake, wouldn't it?'

Bill cocked his head, raised an eyebrow, and laughed.

'Are you sure about that, or do you want validation?'

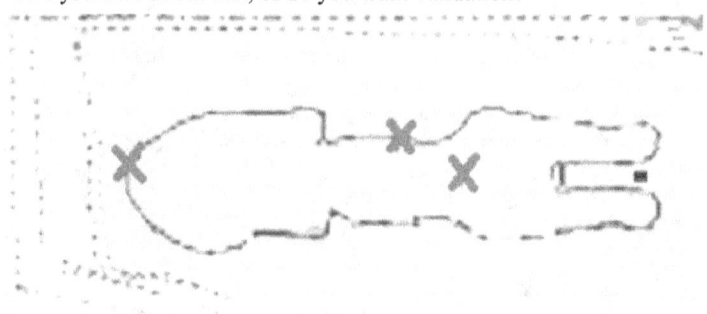

We located the site of the second shaft, along the flank between the front and rear paws, causing Bill to grumble his disapproval.

'Lehner and Hawass investigated this shaft as well, but, surprise, surprise, found that it was just a dead-end passageway as well, and sealed it over...'

He pointed up to the back of the head.

'...And I don't think they're likely to let us climb up onto the Sphinx's back either. That's where the third shaft is, up on top of the Sphinx's body, behind the head. It was discovered by Baraize, though it'd been dug out to a depth of about twenty-seven feet by Vyse and Perring much earlier; but that too supposedly leads nowhere.'

'You think it leads to a chamber inside the Sphinx itself?'

'Logic dictates it must lead somewhere, as either an air shaft or skylight, possibly both.'

'Frank told me about how Drunvalo Melchizidek, that guy who wrote that book Crystal was talking about, "*The Ancient Secret of the Flower of Life*", said there was a golden sphere, a time capsule, somewhere inside the neck or body. It would explain the lightning strike and the damage there documented by Selim Hassan in the 1930s.'

'Lehner confirmed it as well, along with the remains of apparently ancient repair work.'

Moving on, the northern 'terrace' of the Sphinx enclosure, basically an eroded rock shelf that increased in width from west to east, confirmed Bill and my thoughts about the west wall having been quarried at two different times separated by some event of massive flooding, but it also raised further questions.

'Hey Bill, why is the erosion uneven?'

'Uneven; what do you mean, where?'

'Why is there an eroded shelf on this side and not the southern side?'

'Maybe the Causeway gave it protection?'

'Isn't the Causeway made of limestone as well?'

'Good point. Which means the cause of the erosion must have been directional.'

Bill's eyes lit up as, once again, he took off; walking obviously helped him think. As he scanned the terrace to the left he pondered, mumbled and alternately scratched his head and chin until we made our way back to the lower platform of the staircase that led down from the Temple of Amenhotep II.

'The north terrace wall actually has two distinct sections; the eroded section we just passed, opposite the north flank of the Sphinx, and, if you look down there...'

He turned and pointed east.

'...an almost completely intact section running opposite the north of the Sphinx Temple...'

He was right; the wall was virtually unaffected, unlike the northern wall of the temple.

'...But then, beyond the temple, where the northern terrace wall continues to the east into the open space in front of the temple, it's more eroded than the section in the passageway.'

'Is it possible the temple gave the wall some sort of protection by creating a sort of passageway?'

'It's possible, but that means the temple was there when the tsunami hit, which means it was there at the same time as the Sphinx.'

'Well, maybe it wasn't *that* temple, but something that was there before it?'

'Possibly. The considerable erosion across the entire length of the upper western wall, along with the western half of the southern wall and the northern terrace wall opposite the Sphinx, shows more damage than the amount visible on the eastern sections of the southern and northern walls and on the Sphinx itself, which would appear to indicate some influence, coming from the west that diminished as it moved eastward, that didn't affect the Sphinx as much, perhaps because it was surrounded by open space. West suggested that it was caused by runoff from the rainfall, but, if that were the case, it would surely be more uniform, and it would hardly have affected the paws to the extent that the repair work would indicate...'

He turned back to the north.

'...But the northern terrace though is a different story altogether, and its formation is totally consistent with a large body of water, such as a tsunami, washing in from the north, damaging and eroding the northern wall, and all parts of the Sphinx, including the head, which would explain its later re-carving into the smaller form of a pharaoh's head, and especially the front paws as the water drained out the eastern side of the enclosure.'

'I like your reasoning. Then, after the tsunami, which was sometime during the Age of Leo, lets say as Slosman suggested in 9792 BC, the survivors reconstructed the Sphinx Temple in its present location, along with the repositioned Valley Temple, but the reconstructed temples were subsequently damaged and buried by another tsunami caused by the next passing of Nibiru.'

'It's a great theory, Alex, except for one thing.'

'What's that?'

'The dates don't add up. If the big pole-shift event happened in 9792 BC as Slosman suggests, and the orbit of Nibiru is three-thousand-six-hundred years, then the next passings after 9792 BC are around 6162 BC, 2562 BC, and 1038 AD. Sorry, close, but no cigar.'

He was right, the dates *didn't* add up.

'But surely the Sphinx must have something to do with the Age of Leo?'

As I dived into my files looking for answers, the ladies, their business concluded, started ascending the stairs. Diane was quick to give us the green light.

'Thank you, gentleman, she is all yours; we will wait for you down the slope at the exit.'

She? I'd never thought of it before, but, if the Sphinx *was* a lion, as suggested, then logically the obvious question was, male or female? Bill gave Pernille a quick peck then headed down the stairs.

'Come on, Alex, we don't want to keep the ladies waiting.'

And then I found it, the Age of Leo.

'Bill, it says here the Age of Leo was 10,970 –8810 BC.'

'I know you think it fits, but if the Sphinx really were a marker, a portent and prophesy in stone of what was to come, then surely it would have to be somewhere near the *beginning* of the age, not in the middle, twelve-hundred years later.'

'So Slosman got the date wrong, and the date was actually around 10,970 BC, then that would be at the beginning of the Age.'

'Sorry, Alex, it still doesn't add up. 10,970 BC, that makes the next passings of Nibiru in 7370 BC, 3770 BC and 170 BC...'

Bill was pretty quick on the math and it had left me pretty-much disheartened, if not devastated. But then Bill stopped in his tracks just before the entrance to the paws.

'...However...if it were at the *end* of the Age of Leo, 8810 BC, it would put the previous passing of Nibiru at around 12400 BC, which is also a significant date for the pole shift and the last ice age. It also puts subsequent passings at 5200 BC, which roughly corresponds with the appearance of agriculture and civilization in pre-dynastic Egypt, and then 1600 BC, the Thera eruption and tsunami, which means everything lines up perfectly.'

'Bill, you're brilliant!'

'Hardly.'

'What do you mean?'

'Well, the Sphinx faces east, right?'

'Yes.'

'Well if it was built before the last big pole shift, the one that caused the sun to set where it once rose, then that means the earth was once up the other way...'

'Yes, which means the Sphinx was in the southern hemisphere.'

'More than that, it means the Sphinx was facing west.'

At first it seemed unexplainable, a major obstacle, but, as we entered between the paws of the Sphinx and examined the granite altar, the pieces dropped into place.

'Wait a minute!..'

We stood either side of the altar, examining it, our hands resting upon it as the women had, feeling it.

'...There's two things to consider: if the sun rising is about beginnings, about birth and rebirth, then the sun is also about endings, about the afterlife. So, it's not just what constellation the sun *rises* in that's important, it's probably just as important, if not more so, what constellation appears where it sets.'

'Go on.'

'The approach of Nibiru and a subsequent pole shift would surely be considered an ending, so the Sphinx was built not to watch for the appearance of Nibiru at the *beginning* of the Age of Leo, but at the *end* of the Age of Leo, not facing east, where the sun rises and the stars disappear at dawn, but to where the sun sets in the west, as the constellation of Leo appeared in the *western* sky; it gives a totally new perspective to the sun god Harmachis, "Horus in his Western Horizon".'

'Whoa, that's brilliant; you might have cracked the mystery of the Sphinx.'

'We may know *why* it was built, but we still don't have any evidence about who built it, or exactly when, or, more importantly, if there's anything underneath it.'

'Then we'd best keep looking.'

The altar was like so many of the others, red-granite and worn, clearly from a much earlier time. It was another important piece of the puzzle, probably hailing from the original Valley Temple, however I didn't really have time to stop and call on Nemo, so I moved on to our next, and what I believed to be final, destination, just a few feet away, the famous 'Dream Stela' of Thutmoses IV.

Standing before the chest of the Sphinx, the 14-foot-high slab of red granite, known as the 'Dream Stela', which dates to the first year of Thutmoses IV's reign, was nothing less than imposing. We closely scrutinized what remained of the hieroglyphs.

'It was supposedly fashioned from a recycled lintel that was once part of a doorway in Khafre's Mortuary Temple.'

'Perhaps it's another reason why the Egyptologists believe the Sphinx was built by Khafre?'

'Despite the fact, one, that the inscriptions apparently state the Sphinx was "*a great magical power that existed in this place from the beginning of all time*", and, two, they don't explain the purpose of the Sphinx, its original designer and builder, or the date of its construction...'

Bill focused on the damaged section, talking out loud to himself.

'...Instead, it apparently tells, or rather *told,* the story of how Prince Thutmoses, while during a hunting trip, became tired and slept in the shadow of the Sphinx. While sleeping, he had a dream that the Sphinx, Hor-em-akhet, promised to reward him with the double crown of Egypt and a long and prosperous reign if Thutmoses would clear the sand away from the Sphinx and restore it.'

'Real bummer that it's lost all the lowest lines of hieroglyphs, especially the line that supposedly contained the incomplete reference to Khafre. I suppose we can't know whether the story is actually true or not, or how the promised was fulfilled.'

'Well, he did become pharaoh.'

'Need I remind you about what Moses wrote about himself, and about "Joseph" and his dreams?'

'I know, it's a real dilemma; what to believe, and what's exaggeration.'

'And what's plain bullshit.'

'I guess ultimately you've got to find some solid evidence to support what's said, then use common sense to put the pieces together.'

'Exactly, although one thing we *can* assume is, that whilst Amenhotep II may have started the excavation, it was definitely Thutmoses IV who completed the clearing and made the repairs.'

'Apparently shoring up a large boulder in the rump and encasing the body with masonry to fill in a notch that had eroded into the softer bedrock layers near the huge fissure that cuts across the back of the Sphinx.'

'That in itself speaks volumes.'

'Such as?'

'Firstly, it confirms the Sphinx was damaged prior to being excavated by Thutmoses.'

'Which means, that as the Sphinx was buried during the Old Kingdom up to the neck, it takes the cause of the damage back *before* the Old Kingdom, to the last tsunami, maybe 5200 BC, or even back to the big one in 8800 BC or 12400 BC.'

'Exactly. Second, and I'm no expert, but surely the damage to the lower part of the stela, which I will remind you *is* made of granite, is inconsistent with the erosion caused by wind and sand to limestone or sandstone, especially when it's in such a sheltered location, and, if anything, would have either affected all parts of the stela equally, or, if anything, the exposed top part of the stela.'

'But it *is* totally consistent with the sort of damage caused by a large quantity of water constantly swirling around the base of the stela.'

'Cue, a tsunami, and cue, Nibiru.'

And then my attention was immediately drawn to the other end of the stela, to what was there, as clear as day, right at the top of the stela.

'Whoa, look at that, Bill, the winged disk!'

'The representation of Nibiru in the sky: and it extends over the complete stela.'

It did more than that; it dominated the sky, and everything beneath it.

'Now, the question obviously is, why are there two sphinxes?'

'It's nothing unusual, there are hundreds of examples of pairs of crouching sphinxes, like these, flanking avenues and the entrances to temples and other important buildings all along the Nile.'

'I know, I've seen them: Luxor, Karnak, Dendera; and they're mostly ram-headed sphinxes because after 1900 BC, after the last passing of Nibiru, we were in the Age of Aries, right, 1900 BC to 100BC, which surely is a clear indication the sphinxes are directly connected to whatever Age of the Precession we happen to be in.'

'It's possible. There's also considerable evidence and speculation, given the Nile is Egypt's avenue between Upper and Lower Egypt, that the Sphinx had a partner on the other side of the Nile.'

'Seriously?'

'Yep; and if Hor-em-Akhet is the Great Sphinx in the western horizon of Giza, then it makes sense we should look for Horakhti, his "twin", in the eastern horizon. Not only did the ancient Egyptians mention it, but so did the Greeks, then the Romans, and finally the Muslims; all of the writings saying that the two Sphinxes faced each other.'

'What happened to it, to Horakhti?'

'It was supposedly destroyed between 1000-1200 AD.'

'How?'

'According to a guy called Al-I'Drisi, who wrote two large geographical encyclopaedias called "Kitab al-Mamalik wa al-Mansalik" and "Al-Kitab al-Jujari" around 1160 AD, there was a second sphinx, across the Nile from the first, made of mud-bricks and faced with stone, but in very bad condition, having been partly destroyed during a high Nile flood, before it was completely destroyed by ensuing Moslems who carted off most of the stone to rebuild their villages and the Nile moved further east after 1166.'

'Jesus! You learn something new every day. So the remains of it, if any, are somewhere under the modern village to the east?'

'If the reports are true.'

'But, that one was made of mud-brick, right?'

'Correct.'

'Which means it was probably a later dynastic addition, most-likely in the 18th Dynasty by Thutmoses IV, or Ramses II in the 19th Dynasty, to create a pair, which would be consistent with what we saw in the avenues at Karnak and Luxor etcetera.'

'That makes sense.'

I looked back at the stela.

'But these sphinxes, they're not facing each other; these are represented facing *away* from each other.'

'A good point.'

'And I've seen something like this somewhere else; on the wall in the tomb of Thutmoses III in the Valley of the Kings, where the secret cavern of Sokar is guarded by a double-headed sphinx, and a scarab, which is the symbol of the rejuvenated sun, emerges from the burial mound of Osiris, so clearly there is some connection not only between the two sphinxes and the afterlife, but between the two sphinxes, the rejuvenation of the sun, of civilization, of life on the planet, and a secret chamber under the ground.'

'Wow!'

'And these structures under the sphinxes on the stela, they're not plinths, they're temples, underground chambers.'

Bill saw it straight away.

'Of course they are, what else could they be? And you know what? Most of the ancient inscriptions seem to suggest that there are two secret chambers under the Sphinx's feet, not one, so you may be right.'

'It would all fit perfectly except for one thing.'

'What's that?'

'The sphinxes are back to back.'

'Maybe there's a second sphinx buried under the slope between this Sphinx and Khafre's Pyramid?'

'You mean behind the western wall of the sphinx enclosure?'

'Yeah, the paws might line up with the Osiris Shaft, maybe there's another chamber there, under the paws of *that* Sphinx??

I tried to picture it in my mind, but it didn't gel.

'I don't think so, that would mean it would cut through the Causeway.'

'Then maybe it's on the other side of the pyramid, the western side, that would put it in the general vicinity of the far reaches of the Tomb of the Birds? The tomb may even be an entrance to the underground chambers?'

'Possibly, but it would destroy the whole "warning system" and "pole shift" theories, and, besides, somehow the Tomb of the Birds doesn't work for me as the entrance...'

I started looking around between the paws and behind the stela.

'...Anyway, isn't the entrance supposed to be through a secret bronze door somewhere here between the paws?'

Bill joined me; the two of us scratching around in the sand and poking at random bricks.

'I think you're talking about Iamblichus, the Roman scribe who wrote about the initiations that supposedly went on within, or below, the Sphinx. He was the one who described a secret door made of bronze situated between the paws, triggered by a hidden spring, that led to a circular room where the neophytes were subjected to a series of trials designed to terrify the cowardly and ignorant yet be insightful and instructive to the brave and intelligent. It's the most popular myth; that the Sphinx is the true portal of the Great Pyramid, serving as the entrance to the sacred subterranean chambers.'

'So, let me put it all together. The red-granite temples fifty-feet under the ground were built at least twenty-five thousand years ago, probably more, perhaps even hundreds-of-thousands of years ago, by a technologically advanced race, but most likely the survivors of the sinking of Atlantis, which happened because of a passing of Nibiru around either 21,000 BC, 30,000 BC, or even earlier.

Then, as a result of the next subsequent pole shift and tsunami, the temples were flooded and buried in around fifty-to-a-hundred feet of silt and dead seashells. Who knows how long that took to turn into limestone, but, sometime after it did, the pyramids and the Causeway were built. Then the Sphinx was carved out of the bedrock as a warning of the next passing of Nibiru and tunnels were made down to access the wisdom and knowledge stored in the red-granite temples.

That was followed by the second excavation of the Sphinx enclosure, of the western wall, with the large blocks used for the building of the Sphinx Temple, relocation and reconstruction of the Valley Temple, and repairs to the base of the

Sphinx. Then one further tsunami, probably the one in 8,800 BC or 12,400 BC, caused the final water erosion, after which the climate had changed and the enclosure was buried in sand. And all this happened thousands of years before Narmer even created the 1st Dynasty.'

'It's a pretty radical interpretation of the evidence, but all the pieces fit. Now, unless we magically stumble on the trigger to the bronze door, we'd best make our way back to the treasures awaiting us at the exit.'

The lion's tale

And that was it; of course we didn't find any secret doors. All that remained now was to make our way back to the others, meet up with Saeed, and get the hell out of Egypt.

We were half way up the steps when I stopped and took one last close-up look at the Sphinx; something was still bothering me. It wasn't anything about the door, or the chambers beneath the surface. It wasn't anything about the head, or the repairs, or the shafts.

'What's the matter, Alex?'

'I'm not sure, Bill, but I feel like there's something else the Sphinx is trying to tell me.'

'The chambers? The erosion? The location of the secret door...'

'I wish! No, no, I'm sweet with all that.'

'That it's beer o'clock?'

'Now that's an option; I'm as dry as a dead dingo's donger...'

I looked along the Sphinx from the paws to the tail, then further on, to the second pyramid.

'...No! I know what it is, it's the alignment.'

'The alignment of the Sphinx?'

'Yes.'

'With what?'

'That's just it, it doesn't line up with anything, not with the Sphinx Temple, not with the pyramid, nothing.'

'And you think it should?'

'I *know* it should. If it was directly lined up with the centre of the Sphinx Temple, that would make some sense, *if* they were built at the same time, but they weren't. Or if it lined up with the centre of the second pyramid, but it doesn't.'

'It's perpendicular to it; maybe it's guarding the Mortuary Temple or the pyramid itself.'

And then it hit me, like the lightning bolt hitting the back of the Sphinx.

'Bill, you're a fucking genius!'

'I am?'

'Come on, I'll tell you about it on the way.'

Rejuvenated, I led the way up the stairs.

'You were right on before when you said there were two sphinxes.'

'This one and the one across the river to the east?'

'No, that wasn't an original twin; it was a much later mud-brick one.'

'OK, now you've lost me.'

'It's all to do with the alignment.'

'I thought you said there wasn't any alignment.'

'There isn't, not on the surface anyway, but there are clues.'

'Such as?'

'To the ancient Egyptians, the crouching Sphinx was a guardian of sacred places, right? And that's why they relate directly to the Ages of Precession, they're protecting the temples from the return of Nibiru. That's why there are pairs of sphinxes flanking the avenues or entrances to important buildings from the 18th Dynasty onwards; it was all copied, or rather misinterpreted, from the pair of Sphinxes here at Giza.'

'OK, I'm with you so far, I think.'

'The Sphinx is offset from the centre-line of the Khafre pyramid, right?'

'Yes.'

'Then perhaps there was a pair of them, splitting centre. The original twin formed a pair with the remaining Sphinx, both cut out of the limestone bedrock, that guarded, not the actual Khafre pyramid, nor the Mortuary Temple in front of it, but they guarded whatever was, or rather *still is,* buried at least fifty feet under the ground; the two chambers, the Halls of Records, and whatever else is deep beneath the Khafre Pyramid.'

'So, where is this twin?'

I stopped, turned to the north, and pointed across the modern road to the raised area where we'd briefly contemplated abseiling down earlier.

'There!'

'The mound?'

'Yep. The second one must be buried under the sand. Remember when we were up there? The sand and silt is packed hard, and it's been like that for centuries. It's also about the same length and width as the Sphinx enclosure, and the top is about three metres higher than the top of the Sphinx's head!'

Bill didn't need any more information; he was right on the ball.

'I get it; the tsunami swept in from the north, with the northern sphinx of the pair baring the brunt of the force and probably suffering considerable damage. Ironically it probably offered some shelter to the southern sphinx, which is possibly why there's a section of the northern wall that's less eroded. In the process, the northern Sphinx may have been completely inundated by sand and silt from the tsunami, but, if it wasn't, over the years, it may have become totally buried by the shifting sands, and forgotten.'

'Until now!'

'Until now.'

'And the fact the dynastic Egyptians make absolutely no direct mention of two sphinxes guarding the pyramid would lend weight to the probability the northern Sphinx was completely buried before dynastic Egypt even began; that it was buried during the 8,800 BC poles shift.'

'Which means the cryptic references to two sphinxes, like the one on Thutmoses IV's Dream Stela, could indicate the priests, because they had access to the subterranean chambers, were well aware there were two sphinxes, but kept the truth from the masses.'

'And that would mean any references to a secret chamber beneath the paws of the sphinx…'

Bill had come to the same conclusion I had.

'Yes, they could refer to the *buried* sphinx and not the visible one everyone has been searching under.'

'All you would have to do to prove it would be to scan the mound with Ground Penetrating Radar.'

'I wonder if it's ever been done.'

'I've never read anything about it, or even heard of it; maybe Frank and Mark know.'

'Maybe there's something in Kareem's papers?'

'Give me a break, Bill, as if I haven't got enough responsibility to carry. Besides, I think if there were, it would mean Hawass would've already been all over it.'

'Fair call, but, if there was something about it in there, wouldn't that upset the applecart!'

'It would be earth shattering!…'

I gestured back over my shoulder.

'…And it gives more prominence to those large holes back there in the centre of the western wall of the Sphinx enclosure, because they're now in the centre of the two sphinxes.'

'That they are, and so is Campbell's Tomb and all the other shafts there. Now, I'm not saying I'm an Einstein, but we've seen so much evidence here and all the way up the Nile that clearly indicates a completely different history of ancient Egypt; how could the Egyptologists "A", be so blind, and "B", deny the alternate version as a possibility, more than that, as a plausible probability?'

'Simple, Bill; conditioning, fear, and greed.'

We shook our heads in disgust and continued on our way to rejoin the ladies, but, before we could give it any more thought, our attention was pulled to a commotion near the exit that seemed to involve our gals.

'I wonder what that's all about?'

The curse of Ramses]]

Several members of Diane's group were circled around the others, it looked a little like a rugby scrum or they'd just opened the doors on the bargain-basement Boxing Day sales. I was less concerned than Bill.

'It's probably just some over-enthusiastic hawkers hassling the ladies to buy something; the local constabulary don't seem to concerned.'

The Tourist police and Antiquities Police were standing back in the shade in the distance, more amused or disinterested than anything else; this sort of squabbling between family members was part of everyday life in Egypt and it was hardly enough to inspire them to surrender their comfortable positions in the shade.

I promptly scanned the melee to see where Crystal was. Through the shifting mass of female forms I quickly spotted her, as expected, right in the midst of it all, but standing calmly, almost as the eye of the storm. Beside her, in complete contrast were Diane and Pernille, extremely agitated, demonstrative and confrontational, and the object of their fervent defiance was no over-zealous hawker, it was …Jacques!

Now you would've hoped, that after several days to reflect on his behaviour, maybe that Jacques had seen the error of his ways; that he had returned to Giza in the hope of finding Pernille, and grovelling at her feet for forgiveness. WRONG! As arrogant and self-righteous as ever, and clearly unable to admit defeat and relinquish control of his "prized possession", he had latched a claw on to her arm and was obviously demanding she return with him to Zurich.

Somehow Jacques must have figured out that Pernille would eventually appear here at the Sphinx and had obviously flown to Cairo to confront her. He must have arrived here and cased the Giza Plateau, deciding to stake out the Sphinx, possibly from the upper story of the Pizza Hut across the road, which would have given him a good vantage point to survey the entry and exit area.

Then, having spotted her with Diane and Crystal, and seeing there was no Bill in sight, Jacques must have stuffed the last slice of meat-lovers into his cat's-ass of a mouth, bolted down the stairs, across the road, and into the plateau to tackle her head-on. What a hero! What he had wrongly assumed was not just that Bill wasn't here, but that Pernille and Bill were no longer an item; both assumptions being far from the case.

Bill must have spotted him at the same time I did and was off like a rat up a drainpipe. He may have been on the excess side of podgy but, when he wanted to, Bill could move like a hungry cheetah on the tail of a gazelle. I was no slouch myself when it came to running, but I quickly fell more than twenty feet in the arrears.

By the time I arrived at the edge of the group, Bill had sliced his way into the heart of the action and had stepped between Jacques and Pernille, breaking Jacques' hold on her and protecting her from his clutches. Jacques was surprised but quickly went on the attack, trying to push past Bill to reclaim his property.

'This is none of your business.'

Bill held him at bay.

'Oh, this is definitely my business all right!'

Eager to stand her ground and make her position clear, Pernille spat venom at Jacques; years of pain and disappointment laced in every word.

'Laissez-moi tranquille!'

'Arrêter ce non-sens et venir avec moi.'

'C'est fini, Jacques.'

Momentarily distracted, Bill turned to calm her down.

'Let me take care of this, Honey.'

Whereas, back in Luxor, Jacques had first shown discretion and retreated, discretion being the better part of valour, or had taken a drunken swipe at Bill but Bill had been prepared for him and brushed it aside, giving Jacques a smack on the snoz for his efforts, this time was clearly Jacques' last stand and he king-hit Bill from behind, knocking him to the ground. I saw red and, as Bill stumbled to the ground and the sea of women parted in shock, I stepped in, planting a knuckle sandwich firmly on Jacques jaw, sending him sprawling on his back.

Suddenly Crystal stepped in front of me, not just in front, but right in my face, her hand to my chest, to my heart.

'Still wanting to save the world I see.'

'What? He king-hit Bill!'

Not waiting to see what Jacques would do, Crystal pushed me out of the skirmish and back up towards the Sphinx, well away from the fracas that was potentially reigniting as the two pugilists regained their feet.

'Oh that's it, an eye for an eye, a tooth for a tooth, that sort of thing. That way the human race finishes up blind and toothless. Men! You have the truth on your back and you risk compromising that by getting involved in something that is not your concern.'

'But Bill's my friend.'

'He is mine too, however you do not see me complicating matters. You would put the entire contents of Kareem's papers at risk over a schoolyard fistfight over a girl?'

'Well, when you put it that way...?'

'Bill knew what he was getting into, he can take care of himself, so can Pernille, and his affairs are not *your* affairs. If he jumped into a pool of crocodiles would you jump in after him?'

'To save him, yes.'

'Brilliant, then you are a fool, for you both become crocodile food. The path of wisdom would be not to jump into the crocodile pool at all.'

'What if you fell in?'

'I suppose your fist accidentally fell into Jacques' face as well?'

What could I say, she was right, and now I *was* involved, whether I liked it or not, because, the minute punches were thrown, the local authorities, who had previously stayed in the background, now took an immediate interest and had moved in to bring peace to the plateau; with one stupid "macho" strike of my hand, I had opened Pandora's Box.

Suddenly a strong hand grabbed my arm from the side and dragged me from the mire I had punched myself into.

'Quickly, this way.'

It was Saeed, he must have arrived just in time to witness what had happened.

'Thank god you're here.'

As he dragged me along the front of the Sphinx Temple, I had flashes of déjà vu, of my dream where Saeed and I were running down a dark corridor, the scroll of truth tattooed on my back like a massive neon target, the caws and shrieks of the hungry vultures echoing in my ears, and their razor-sharp talons ripping into my body. To my amazement, Crystal was following close behind.

'What are you doing, they'll think you're with us?'

'I am with you.'

'No, they'll think you were part of Kareem's murder.'

'But I wasn't.'

'I know, but try telling them that...'

I pointed back to the posse that was gathering at the OK Corral.

'I will, when the time is right. For now, I will go where I choose, besides, you may need me.'

'Please, it's too dangerous.'

'I will be fine.'

Saeed put an end to any further discussion.

'Please, there is no time to waste, we must be get out of Giza at once, Jacques he has seen it the picture of you, he has told it to the police you are here.'

I briefly glanced back, enough to see Jacques, in the midst of several heavily-armed police, pointing directly in my direction, and I was dead-set certain he wasn't giving them directions to the Sphinx. Bill, Pernille, and the other ladies were crowding around, creating confusion and running interference. If I was to escape, it had to be now. We ducked into the Valley Temple.

'Good thinking, we can cut back up the Causeway and across to the main entrance.'

'No, the main entrance it is not good, there are many guard.'

'So how do we get out?'

'We must get be out to the village through the perimeter wall to the southeast.'

Crystal had a different plan.

'Or, we can just disappear, escape underground.'

She was standing facing the wall, her hands on a piece of black granite, the same trapezium-shaped piece of black granite I had put my hands on earlier in the day; was Nemo right, was it a door, and, if so, did it lead to a dark descending staircase? I rushed to her side, placing my hands on the stone.

'Do you know how to open it?'

'In principal, yes.'

And she started to tone. After a few seconds I grew impatient.

'Nothing's happening.'

' *"Nothing"* cannot *happen*: patience.'

She went back to toning.

'Ah, unless you've forgotten, any second a posse of trigger-happy police is about to come through that entrance and use me for target practice.'

'Patience; not all keys fit the same lock, and not all locks open with just one key, and many times the door is not opened because the key seems so great that the things which are beyond it are not visible.'

'What?'

'All keys, all material symbols, are manifestations, symbols are but keys to doors leading to truths, extensions of a great law and truth, that enable us to penetrate beyond the veil.'

Again she returned to toning, leaving me both bewildered and panicking.

'Great, I'm about to be drilled full of bullet holes or strung out in the desert like a sun-dried tomato, and you're philosophising.'

'Well, instead of distracting me, you could help.'

Was she crazy? Hum a few notes and a ten-ton block of solid granite will just move aside? Before I could even contemplate it, Saeed, who had been watching from the entrance, returned.

'Indy, we must go! NOW!'

I looked back at Crystal, who stood calmly waiting my decision.

'Well?'

'Shit! …I'm sorry, I can't.'

My fears of being caught had totally overrun my intuition to stay. Not knowing what more to say, or if I would even see Crystal again, I scurried out of the Valley Temple like a mindless sheep at an abattoir.

'Shit, shit, shit!'

Saeed led the way as we headed south beyond the Valley Temple; I am sure he was hoping to cut back through the eastern perimeter wall and into the village, but another posse, this time of kalashnikov-toting soldiers, blocked the way. They weren't particularly interested in us at that stage, perhaps because it wasn't their business, more the secret police's, but one scream or gunshot from our would-be pursuers and it would have landed us straight into their hands.

There were only two options left, out into the desert, which I didn't think was a particularly great option as there was nowhere to hide and we would be as obvious and as easy to spot as a teenager's zit on prom night, or we could head back up behind the Valley Temple and into the myriad of half-buried buildings that filled the ground between the Valley Temple to the east, the second pyramid to the west, and the Causeway to the north. Fortunately, Saeed chose the later.

We twisted our way through the sand-filled alleyways, passing barely-open doorways buried in sand almost up to the lintel, ducking and weaving, with me baulking every time I heard the sounds of Arabic voices from around the corner, and Saeed reassuring me everything was fine.

'It is OK, it is just the local villager.'

At one point, Saeed stopped, looked around, and indicated to one of the ruined buildings.

'Perhaps you can be hide in here?'

I dropped to one knee and briefly looked inside, half-expecting to find a den of cobras.

'Are you kidding?'

'Trust me, I will lead them away. You can wait here until after the sun it has gone down, then I will come back for you, when it is quiet, and take you to Alexandria.'

I stuck my head in the opening, catching my backpack on the lintel; even if I took the backpack off I would barely have fitted through the gap. It took about five seconds for my eyes to adjust to the lack of light before I made out the interior and realised how vulnerable I would have been: barely three feet high the room was like a tomb; all someone had to do was take a peek inside and I was history. I scrambled back to my feet.

'No thanks, I'd rather take my chances in the desert.'

'This it is not a good idea; there is nowhere to hide. We shall try to circle around the Sphinx and out the other side.'

I wasn't really in a position to argue as we were fast running out of options.

Heading off again, I wondered why the police weren't in such a hurry to arrest us, and why they hadn't fired any shots, but then I realised they didn't have to rush because basically they had us surrounded and they didn't want to cause a panic with all the other tourists around; all they had to do was slowly tighten the noose. Besides, a UFO was hardly likely to come down and whisk us aware to safety, so where could we run?

We cut back under the Causeway, past the Tomb of Osiris, where I briefly contemplated scrambling down to the lowest levels and hopefully finding some secret escape route. However, that option was quickly discarded as Saeed led me on past Campbell's Tomb and several of the other shafts in the ground. By the time we hit the modern road that cut between the Sphinx and the mound, the police had spread the word and were boxing us in on all sides; there were three police emerging from under the Causeway, two police vehicles approached down the road from the west, from the main entrance, three foot-soldiers marching up the road from the east, and several soldiers, kalashnikovs at the ready, stood atop the mount blocking the northern exit. We were screwed!

'Indy, down here...'

I turned to see Saeed, his galabeya hitched up to his waist, sliding and scrambling his way down the northwest face of the Sphinx enclosure and onto the northern terrace Bill and I had been contemplating less than 30 minutes earlier. Other than being captured, I didn't have much choice, so I followed him down.

'...We will cut past the Temple of Amenhotep II and through the passage beside the Sphinx Temple.'

'But that will take us back pretty much to where we started.'

'It is the only way out; maybe in the rush to capture you, the police they have been foolish enough to leave it unguarded?'

Somehow it didn't seem right, so I stopped and looked around for other options, noticing the two openings in the western wall; the northern one of which was glowing, alive with light, just like the path to the outdoor museum had been back at Karnak.

It was a sign, a totally illogical one at that, and completely against my survival instincts driving me to keep running away, but my intuition was telling me I had to go that way; insisting, virtually pulling me in towards it.

'No, Saeed, I'm going this way.'

I pointed to the northern opening, much to Saeed's disapproval.

'No, this it is not good; there is no way out.'

'Saeed, if this was where Hawass removed the statues and coffers from under the Giza Plateau back in 2010 then it has to lead to the underground chambers.'

'You wish it to go into the den of the lion?'

'Into the vulture's nest, yes.'

And with that, with the vultures circling, I made a beeline for the opening.

No way back

It was only once I'd entered the chamber that I realized there was probably no way out, even if I did find any underground tunnel system. I paused to survey the interior; it was clearly not a naturally occurring void in the limestone caused by water erosion, but had been dug out. The rough-cut walls were void of any hieroglyphs, which, to me, indicated the chamber was either very old, or very recent. Of course there was the possibility it could have been excavated any time from the 18th Dynasty through to the Roman Era, as a tomb or office, however, given the lack of hieroglyphs, the fact the limestone was probably deposited during the last pole-shift, the chamber's high position up on the northern terrace, and that the enclosure was buried in sand until the 1930s, it confirmed my belief the opening was a 20th Century project instigated with the sole intent to access whatever was beneath the surface; the only questions once again were, who started it, when did they start, and what did they find? My bet was the answers were in my backpack and that Hawass had his greedy little hands all over it.

'Come on then, they are right behind us...'

Saeed had followed me in, and now led the way towards a massive corridor at the far end of the chamber that sloped down at an angle into the depths beneath the plateau.

'...You still have the paper of my uncle in your backpack?'

'Of course.'

He dropped back and started to pull the backpack off me as we moved deeper and deeper into the sloping tunnel.

'Then you had better to give them back to me, for if you are caught with them, like a pack of hungry jackal they will rip you into a hundred piece and feed you to the alley cat.'

'And if they catch *you* with them?'

'I can explain it that you stole them from my uncle and I was just try to get them back from you.'

'You really think they'll buy that?'

'No, but Allah he will make it the final choice.'

'Great, coming from a man who doesn't believe in Allah!'

'I did not say I do not believe, just that I do not follow.'

And he forged ahead into the dimly-lit corridor; illuminated only by the sunlight reflecting in from the outside, meaning, the deeper we went, the darker it got.

Like the first chamber, the tunnel walls were rough-cut out of the bedrock and, as we ran down into the unknown, it seemed like we were chasing our own shadows. I was getting a major case of déjà vu; I knew this tunnel, I'd seen it in my dreams, and that meant it was crunch time, that something was about to happen, something *had* to happen.

About forty feet below the plateau, we hit a T-intersection and Saeed went to head left, further into the darkness.

'No, not that way, it leads straight into a trap; there's a hidden shaft of deadly cobras guarding the entrance. '

Saeed stopped.

'How do you know this?'

'Trust me, I just know. This way!'

Using the light from my iphone to illuminate the way ahead, I took off to the right, and, after briefly hesitating, Saeed quickly followed, continuing our descent.

After several further turns we rounded the next corner and hit another T intersection, but this one was different. Unlike the previous one, which had simply been rough-cut out of the bedrock, the tunnel had clearly intersected with a huge pre-existing corridor situated way below the surface, one where the limestone walls were smooth-polished and covered in colourful hieroglyphs; apart from the coloured reliefs, it was almost exactly like the corridor that Flinders Petrie had discovered outside the entrance to the Osireion at Abydos, except that corridor was covered with a gabled roof of limestone slabs and this one was flat and cut from the limestone.

'I think we're on to something.'

As much as I would have loved to examine the beautifully coloured friezes and the magnificently carved delicate figures of goddesses clothed in beautiful apparel, there was no time to stop, as, behind me, I heard Arabic voices echoing through the tunnel. To make matters worse, the artificial modern lighting flickered on; the vultures had arrived.

'Which way, Indy?'

I looked left, then right.

'All roads lead to Rome, I guess ...or from it. This way!'

Shoving my iphone back in my pocket, I led the way as we headed to the right for about forty or fifty metres before the corridor turned again and we suddenly found ourselves passing through what was once a section of perfectly smooth-polished, rock wall that now formed an architrave, about three feet thick, around the corridor.

'Red granite!'

I looked at it closely; it had been clearly blasted apart and smashed through, possibly with thermite or some other modern explosive that would minimize the damage; the opening roughly squared off to create a massive doorway or gateway.

'This must be where Hawass blasted through in 2010.'

Quickly moving on, beyond the intrusion, the walls floor and ceiling all shifted to being of polished red granite bereft of any markings or reliefs; this was no natural rock formation!

The second we entered the granite corridor it was illuminated by a series of thin vertical tubes, about six inches long, spaced along the corridor. There were no electrical cables leading to them and, as I approached each one, the illumination increased; it was almost as if they had motion or proximity sensors. This was definitely not part of the modern lighting system crudely installed in the previous limestone corridors.

Momentarily forgetting my predicament, I slowed to scan the corridor.

'I bet this is where Hawass found all the statues and sarcophagi he stole back in 2010 as well.'

Grabbing my arm, Saeed quickly snapped me back into reality.

'And if we do not keep going you may well become another trophy.'

We pressed on, and, despite the threat that pursued us, I was excited at what lay ahead. That was until we turned another corner and hit a dead-end corridor or chamber, more importantly, at a solid wall of polished black granite which was maybe seventy or eighty feet below the plateau.

'Brilliant!'

'Indy, this it is not so brilliant; it is a dead end?'

'But it proves my theories; how else could such massive pieces of *polished* red and black granite get down here?'

'Yes, Indy, your theory it is correct, but this it is not good if you are dead. We will go back, you do not want this to become your tombstone.'

'No, wait; not yet.'

Just like in my dream, I groped around the walls exploring the smooth surface searching for some hidden lever or trigger that would open a secret door.

'Nothing. Shit; there's always one in the movies!'

Behind me the voices seemed to be drawing closer. I turned back to face the end of the corridor, frantically fumbling the wall.

'Fuck, where the hell is the release mechanism?'

'*Feel the stone.*'

'I will go back and try to lead them in the other direction.'

'No, wait. What did you say?'

'I said I will go back and try to lead them in the other direction.'

'No, the...'

'*Feel the stone.*'

'Did you hear that?'

The look of panicked bewilderment on Saeed's face showed he clearly hadn't heard anything other than the howls of the approaching jackals.

'*Feel...the...stone.*'

It was Crystal's voice, and it sounded like it was coming from the other side of the wall, no, from the very wall itself. I placed my hands on the end wall, closed my eyes and tried to tune in.

At first there was nothing, but then I heard, or rather *felt*, a faint low hum and had visions of Crystal, dressed as an Egyptian High Priestess, back in the Valley Temple, hands on the black stone.

'Saeed, put your hands on the wall and do as I do.'

'What?'

'Just do it.'

I placed my hands on the wall, tuned back in to Crystal, and started toning.

'Ah.'

Saeed nervously joined in, but, initially, nothing happened. Then I remembered that *"'nothing' cannot happen"*, that something *had* to happen.

'*Shift your perspective.*'

I looked around the wall, nothing; what did she mean?

'*Change your tone.*'

With Saeed holding the base note, I shifted to the perfect fifth above his. The moment I did, I instantly felt the stone start to groan and rumble. It scared the shit out of Saeed, who pulled his hands from the wall and looked to the ceiling, obviously thinking the roof was about to cave in.

'What is...'

'Keep going!'

Despite being stunned, Saeed did just that, and the wall began vibrating again. This time Crystal shifted to a higher note, a different note again, forming a chord, like the ones the ladies had sung in the king's chamber, and, moments later, the massive wall shuddered and started to become translucent. Through it I could see Crystal, just as I had dreamed her, dressed as an Egyptian High Priestess, holding Pernille's crystal ball, which was shimmering and illuminating the walls of a large open chamber, with ornate columns behind her, with golden flames.

Suddenly the wall gave out a loud crack, as if it had fractured in half, and a large section of it started sliding slowly down into the floor of the corridor; the damn wall was moving!

'Whoa!'

Saeed stood there gob-smacked, watching the massive stone, which again turned out to be about three feet thick, drop like an elevator. Fully opened and set in the floor of the corridor, it looked just like the massive threshold stones I had crossed over at the entrance to the temples at Edfu, Kom Ombo, and Dendera.

Although Crystal wasn't actually waiting on the other side, I took it as a sign and stepped forward.

'Let's go.'

As if he had been turned to stone and become a statue, Saeed remained where he was.

'No, Indy, I will lead them away in the other direction.'

'What? No way, Saeed, they'll kill you. Come with me!'

He tossed me the backpack.

'No. This it is the only way to make it sure the paper of my uncle they do not fall into the hand of the Secret Police.'

I crossed the opening back to him.

'No it's not; we can both make it.'

No sooner did I cross the entrance than the sliding door started slowing rising: not a good sign. I remembered reading about a guy called Muterdi, who was writing about a thousand years ago, who gave an account of a bizarre incident in a narrow corridor under the Giza plateau, in which a group of people were horrified when, without warning, a stone door suddenly slid out from the wall of the corridor and crushed to death one of their party and closed the corridor in front of them. They must have been singing or whistling and triggered an already open door. I didn't want that end for Saeed or myself.

'Come on!'

'No, I must stay. Now go! There is no time.'

To make matters worse, the voices were drawing near.

'Please, Saeed!'

'Go! And may Allah be with you.'

'What about you?'

'Indy, it is Allah who has brought me here. Now GO!'

I embraced Saeed,…

'Shukran, Ahoya. I'll never forget you.'

… tossed the backpack over the rising monolith, and, like Nemo frantically flipping and flopping, dodging the snapping jaws of the crocodiles and lighting strikes of the cobras, I climbed over the door, which was about four feet high, and rising.

The last I saw of Saeed, the rising wall obscuring my view, was of him turning and running back up the corridor to face the marauding menace of crocodiles, vultures and cobras that were bearing down on him. Dumbstruck, I watched the wall as it fully closed, meeting the ceiling, shutting off all the light from the other side of the chamber, and leaving me completely alone in the dim light of the subterranean depths of the Giza Plateau. For all I knew, I had just sealed my fate.

The Truth Beneath the Giza Plateau

After about ten or fifteen seconds of contemplating my position, I slowly turned to face my future. Ahead lay a long granite hallway with no lights. Despite that, somehow the corridor was illuminated. It was as if the very air itself was alive, just like it had been at Karnak and at the entrance to the subterranean chambers in the Sphinx enclosure.

With only one way to go, I set off along the corridor, which was decorated high up on the left hand side with a long series of sacred geometrical images; there must have been nearly fifty of them, starting with the exact same 'flower of life' I had seen on the red-granite pillar in the Osireion at Abydos. I took out my iphone and panned a video along to record them all; to me they looked like aspects of the very fabric of existence, but I didn't waste too much time on them as I figured surely there was someone in the scientific or New-Age community who would be able to sort them out and make some sense of them later, that was presuming I got out of here alive.

The end of the hall veered slightly to the right and into a large chamber, clearly a temple. It was magnificent; the highly polished red-granite walls creating a pinkish hue that bathed the entire space; it reminded me of the Osireion, with regularly-spaced alcoves beyond the main walls.

I walked to the centre of the floor, which seemed to be inlayed with more unusual hieroglyphs made of silver or mercury, and took another full-circle video, this time of the walls, which were decorated with more unknown images, seemingly inlayed with gold. At the end of the chamber was a massive red-granite altar; similar to so many I'd seen on my travels, although this one was in pristine condition and decorated with precious and semi-precious stones like amethyst and lapis lazuli. I put the iphone away and headed to check it out. On top of the altar was another crystal ball, just like the one Pernille had found, although this one lacked the internal flickers of gold. As I looked deeper into it and moved it around images appeared and changed, like turning the pages of a book.

At first I saw images of Bill, and Crystal, then Saeed, and everyone on the felucca. Before long the ball seemed to be reviewing my life, back to Australia, my ex-wife and back through my childhood; each event having some particular reference to why I was now standing where I was. It was as if my whole life was making sense, that it was a preparation for this very moment.

Finally, as the images started shifting to before my birth, images of me drifting back through the eyes of my previous lives all the way back to Andromeda, I realized I had done this before, in one of Diane's circles.

'Whoa!'

I don't know how long I'd stood there, it could have been minutes; it could have been hours. I looked away and shook my head, trying to fathom the significance of it all; I didn't want to go back, I didn't *need* to go back, I needed to go forward. That firmly established, I set my intention on getting out of Egypt alive and gazed once again into the crystal.

Soon, images of rooms and tunnels, unlike any I had been in, and streams and lakes, started to appear, and each image seemed to be related to my thoughts, responding to my thoughts. Then an image appeared of the area directly behind the altar; the way out must be there. I tucked the ball into my backpack, took a deep breath, and headed in that direction.

Beyond the altar were two staircases, one, carved out of the limestone, that spiraled upwards, whilst the other, again carved out of the limestone, gently led down to the east. Despite our twists and turns, once I was underground I'd kept a mental map in my head of approximately what direction we were heading in and where I was below the surface, so, by my figuring, I was now somewhere beneath the mound of earth that had buried and concealed the undiscovered second Sphinx.

I paused to consider my options; logic dictated to head up to find an exit, which was probably up into the body of the second Sphinx, so I took that option. Several spirals later I arrived at a sealed doorway, the door made of black granite. I figured it was just like one Saeed and I had opened earlier, so placed my hands on it and started toning.

'Ahh.'

Nothing. I tried again, without any success. I even focused my thoughts, visualizing the door opening, but to no avail. I tried different pitches, different vowel sounds, but again, no result. I quickly figured out that the door must require a specific musical interval, or even a chord, more than one voice, to open it. I put my hands one more time on the door, this time calling on Nemo. Moments later, he appeared, but not behind the door as I had expected. This time he was flitting and flopping back down the spiral staircase and, in a flash, I was heading back down the staircase right after him, back to where I'd started; logic had proved to be a dead end, at least for the moment.

I did a quick lap of the chamber, groping the walls and inlayed images searching for the trigger mechanism to possibly another secret entrance, alas without luck, before returning to behind the altar, this time before the descending eastward staircase; this was not where I anticipated heading. It brought back thoughts of the dream I'd had when I descended deeper into the underworld and was confronted by a giant three-headed snake blocking the path. I remembered how it fixed its gaze on me, flicked out its poisonous forked tongue, and slowly curled its massive body around me like an enormous anaconda. Surely it was symbolic, right; there weren't really any diabolical serpents awaiting in the depths?

My thoughts turned back to the images I had seen in the tombs at Luxor, especially in the tomb of Thutmoses III, of the three-headed snake, the three-headed winged snake and the winged disc of Nibiru in the sky across the entrance, and on to the side wall. There was clearly a connection between the underworld, the Dracos, and Nibiru, but what was it?

I noticed the wall lighting had returned, attached to the walls of the limestone staircase, illuminating my descent. The corridor gave total support to my theory that the temples existed before a pole shift and were buried by maybe eighty to a hundred feet of limestone-forming sediment, which, sometime post-tsunami, was then excavated and carved out to access the red-granite temples.

The descending corridor gently made its way about fifty feet before suddenly opening into a larger perpendicular underground cavern containing an underground stream. It was possibly the water that passed underground from the Nile, through the Tomb of Osiris, under the Causeway and Valley Temple of Khafre, then northward or eastwards to, well, that was the question, to where?

Upstream was not only unlit, but, in the gloom, it appeared to narrow to an inaccessible fissure in the rock; it reminded me of the images of the Underworld I had seen in the tombs in the Valley of the Kings at Luxor, particularly in KV 14, the tomb of Tausert and Setnakht, and to the final scenes of the 'Book of Caverns', which represented the underworld as a series of six caverns over which the sun passed. Was there some truth to the presence of a series of underground caverns below the Giza Plateau? This, and the caverns deep within the Tomb of the Birds, would seem to indicate there was.

The underground stream emerging from the fissure reminded me of the 'Book of Gates' on the walls of the tomb of Thutmoses III, which symbolized time as an apparently endless, massive spitting snake emerging from the mouth of a deity in the depths of creation, that eventually fell back into the same depths. Maybe the serpent I feared was time, or the winding stream before me?

My mind drifted back to my time on the felucca, with Crystal, Pieter and Yuko, sitting beside the river. Crystal's words surfaced in my thoughts.

"Meditation is not to escape from the world, it is to engage with the world; to be totally awakened and aware, but not attached to the world."

Taking a moment to pause, I sat down beside the water, breathed deeply and slowly, and tuned in, adjusting my own body's rhythm to that of the water.

"Think of the Nile as the Universe, it flows though you don't know where it comes from or where it flows. The only part that is relevant is the part before you; the part you can see, the part you can touch and feel. But even that is just the surface; there are unseen aspects in the depths."

I remembered the leaf, carried along by the current, tossed to and fro by the water, going wherever the river decides, to its destiny, where the river determines all, and the leaf has no part to play. One minute all is calm, the next you find yourself in the rapids, like a roller-coaster twisting and turning, plunging and rising, seemingly on the brink of disaster and certain death, going in convoluted circles, or plunging over a waterfall. My trip had been exactly the same; I had just been a palm frond on the Nile of life.

Well, that's how it had been when I started, how it had been when I received Kareem's papers, but now, especially since I made the decision to head underground and found myself here, now I felt more like a drop of water in the river; there was a purpose, a direction.

"Nothing happens to you, everything happens because of you. The key is to let go, to surrender and allow the river to take you to new adventures. Hear the sound of the river of life as it passes by, rippling from some unknown source and undulating to some unknown destination."

Suddenly I saw Nemo, frolicking around in the water, beckoning me to follow, to follow the flow, the stream. Heading upstream was out of the question, and downstream was the only option, deeper, below the plateau. The reality was I had no real choice, I had to follow it; I was well past the first hour of the Amduat for the sun had definitely slipped beneath the horizon, and the serpent was beckoning me to follow.

Thankfully there was a track, carved out, or worn out, on the bank beside the stream, and it was clear I was not the first to have walked this path. It reminded me of Otto Lidenbrock's trek as he followed the path of Arne Saknussemm in a scene from Jules Verne's *'Journey to the Centre of the Earth'*. I just hoped I wasn't going to run into any prehistoric ancestors of the human race or any dinosaurs.

As I set off along the stream, the thought jogged my memory of unconfirmed reports of dinosaurs still existing in remote regions of Russia and China, and I'd seen photos of pterodactyls shot down in the USA in the late 19th Century, so, was the history of dinosaurs also a theory that needed revising?

How do we really know the fossils of dinosaurs are as old as the palaeontologists say? "Because the fossils are found in rock hundreds of millions of years old". How do we know the rock is hundreds of millions of years old? "Because it has dinosaur fossils in it". No, that's poor science.

I think maybe we need to look at the *actual* evidence there as well, especially if 'evolution' didn't happen on this planet the way everyone has been led to believe, but has been directed by a reptilian race with a genetic agenda. It explains why there are so many 'evolutionary' black holes, missing links, and gaps in the fossil record. It explains the enormous proliferation of dinosaur species. It explains the bizarre monotremes and marsupials. It meant that every theory concerning life on this planet needed to be revisited, recycled and reborn anew, just like the ancient Egyptians indicated in the *'Book of the Dead'*. Did the *'Book of the Dead'* need to be retranslated given the truth that was emerging?

I wondered, if just like the journey of the deceased king through the twelve divisions of the underworld, that if I followed this path, and overcame the obstacles, was I to reappear, to emerge, resurrected as Khepri the scarab god? And what did Khepri do exactly, take other people's shit and turn it into something that would stimulate new life. Great job description; not! Or maybe it was symbolic of taking your own shit, your own past, and recycling it, revising it, reviewing it, and turning it into the fertilizer for a new future; the sort of New Age "rebirthing" stuff my ex-wife had talked about. There was only one way to find out.

As the stream undulated through the bedrock, I wondered what each turn would bring, what awaited downstream. As I did, it took my thoughts back to the walls of Thutmoses III's tomb, to the fourth hour of the *'Book of the Amduat'*, where the path of the pharaoh zigzagged as it approached the secret cavern of the 'Land of Sokar', guarded by a double-headed sphinx and sealed by the head of Isis. The double-headed sphinx? Was it a reference, not to a double-headed sphinx, but to a pair of sphinxes that guarded the entrance to some sacred land beneath the surface?

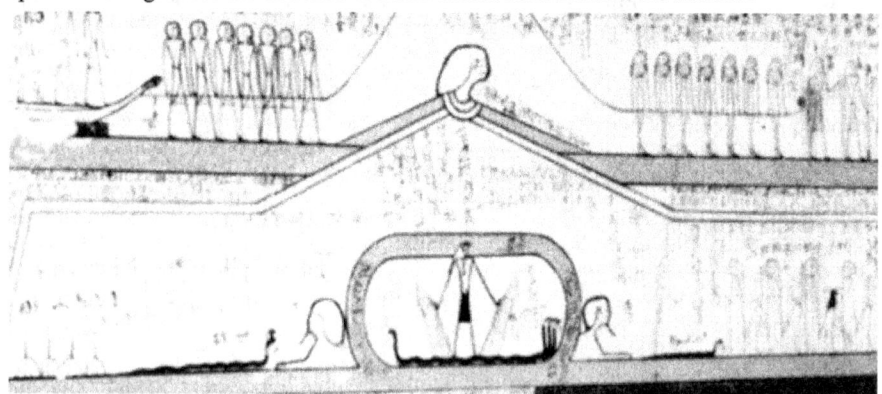

And the term the 'Land of Sokar'? Ptolemy I Soter was supposedly the saviour of Egypt, Soter meaning saviour. Was his title 'Soter' some reference back to 'Sokar', back to the land of the saviour? Were the underground caverns the saviour of mankind?

Was it also possible that the *'Book of the Amduat'*, which only came about in the 18th Dynasty, was not only a response to the murder of Seqenenre Tao, but had hidden messages about the Thera tsunami, the passing of Nibiru and of pre-existing underground chambers and cities? I didn't have long to wait to find out, for the underground stream suddenly opened to a massive cavern containing a subterranean lake that must have been about a kilometre wide.

That there was an underground cavern system here was not the real surprise, there are thousands of miles of caves, tunnels, dozens of submerged lakes, hundreds of miles of underground rivers, and enormous caverns around the world beneath the surface within the earth's crust. There are also the shafts of extinct volcanoes that extend to depths of eight to twelve miles into the earth, with canal roots piercing to depths of four hundred miles, all creating a natural network of passages and caverns that eventually lead to the deeper portions of the earth.

I'd seen evidence of volcanic activity it in Bill's photos of the Black Desert, so the presence of natural underground chambers here was not a surprise, and in fact, many ancient writers and historians, such as Herodotus, Crantor (300 BC) and Iamblichus, a 4th Century Syrian representative of the Alexandrian School of mystical and philosophical studies, had all referred to a crisscrossing network of underground passages that connected the major pyramids. Even as late as the 1930s Selim Hassan had reported the discovery of additional underground rooms, chambers, temples and hallways,

> "...some with vertical circular stone support columns, and others with beautifully coloured friezes and walls covered in magnificently carved delicate figures of goddesses clothed in beautiful apparel."

I'd seen the images of the goddesses on the way down the rabbit hole, but, what was surprising was that no one in the modern era had said anything about them. And yet, here they were, the corridors, the chambers, the caverns, so, why the silence? Why were the Egyptian authorities withholding this information from the public?

Looking along the shore, several other streams flowed out of adjacent tunnels and into the lake; perhaps these were the 'five heads' of the five-headed serpent mentioned in the 6th hour of the Amduat? I'd deduced the limestone had been laid down on the Giza Plateau during a pole shift, but which one; the presence of the chambers would indicate there must have been at least two?

Was it possible all these chambers had been carved out by the subsiding waters during a subsequent pole shift? Well, of course it was possible; how else could they get here!

The cavern was huge, in parts appearing naturally carved out of the limestone by a massive amount of water, and extended eastward under today's Nile and under Cairo itself. Large crystalline spheres, set into the walls and ceiling, provided illumination; at some time in the past, or perhaps in the present, someone must have lived down here, in the Underworld! Was this "the Land of Sokar", the underworld referred to in so many texts, the realm of Sobek, the crocodile god referred to in the 6th hour of the Amduat?

The possibility of that being the case was enhanced when, while looking around for the presence of crocodiles, I gazed into the distance across the water.

At first I thought I was imagining things, like seeing a mirage in the desert, but then I realized there appeared to be a city of some sort carved out of and/or into the rock on the far side of the lake. I shouldn't have been surprised as there were more than 200 enormous, multi-levelled subsurface cities discovered in the old Turkish kingdom of Cappadocia back in 1964. One of those cities alone apparently contains huge caverns, rooms and hallways that archaeologists estimate once supported as many as 10,000 people.

Was it possible this was the subterranean city of 'Gigal' referred to in the books of Genesis, Jasher and Enoch, the city referred to in the narratives of those supposedly "living in the Earth"? The evidence was mounting, on a global scale, that not only were the tsunamis a reality, but that the human population had some advanced knowledge of their arrival and, more importantly, their effect.

I'd read somewhere, I think in an account recorded by Iamblichus, of an ancient Egyptian papyrus from 100 BC that recorded the journey of a group of people below the Giza Plateau who discovered a beautifully-planned underground city, including temples, pastel-painted peasant dwellings, workshops, stables, a palace, and at least three miles of subsurface passageways, a hundred feet below the Giza Plateau. At the time I didn't give them much creed, however, as I scanned the far shore, it seemed the rumours and reports were true.

Rubbing my eyes, I took a second look, contemplating my next move. I couldn't tell if the city was occupied or not, or if it was wise to try to make my way there; my reasoning being that if it *was* occupied then it had been for some considerable period of time, and that, whoever it was, they weren't too keen to let the surface-dwellers know they were there.

It reminded me of several noted scientists who had suddenly disappeared under mysterious circumstances while searching in underground caves for unknown subterranean cities in South America. First to disappear was Nathan Doubleday, a renowned scientist in the field of magnetism, who had perfected a modern day force field. He disappeared in 1937 after entering a small cave in the northeast Yucatan in search of special metals deep within the crust's caverns.

It got me wondering if the cavern here was a natural feature or if it was possible the cavern had been created by some sort of force field that prevented the sediment-forming limestone of the tsunami from engulfing the city?

The next to vanish was another noted scientist, Albert Newell, who had devoted nearly twenty years to the field of telekinesis and thought projection, and had achieved a major breakthrough. Newell, along with another scientist, were last seen travelling in a car northeast from the Yucatan border in July, but they vanished without a trace.

The Yucatan, along with specific locations in Ecuador, Bolivia, Peru, China and even Russia are all believed to contain secret underground tunnel systems that date back hundreds of thousands of years, and which are inhabited by forgotten races such as the Mayans.

While it was tempting to check out the city, there was the distinct possibility that, if it *was* occupied, I would never be permitted to leave, that I would finish up like Doubleday and Newell, and that would mean Kareem's death, and my journey, would be in vain. I had an obligation to Kareem, and to Saeed, to get the papers to the surface and out of Egypt, and that's what I was going to do.

From my position on the west side of the lake, I used my iphone and shot a bit of footage of the cavern, the lighting spheres, and the city, before deciding to move on, the question was, to where? At a loss for ideas, I referred back to my notes on the Amduat; maybe there was a clue there.

"In the 7th hour, the sun god, Re, confronts his archenemy, the serpent Apophis, who swallows the waters carrying the sun boat. In the top row, Osiris sits on a throne, the snake god, Apophis, who has already been tied down indicating he is no longer a threat."

Originally I'd thought the text related to Apopi and the genetic engineering program of the Dracos, but suddenly I had other thoughts. If the serpent was the flood water, attributed to Apopi, which was also possibly a reference to Nibiru, the second sun, the archenemy of the sun god, Re, then the suppression of Apopi would relate to the subsiding of the waters after the pole shift and passing of Nibiru. But what did the reference to Apophis 'swallowing the waters carrying the sun boat' mean?

"In the bottom register, Horus presides over twelve gods and twelve goddesses, each crowned with stars, symbolizing the twelve hours of the night."

The twelve gods? Twelve goddesses? Each crowned with stars? Twelve hours of the night? For starters the number of hours in the night varied throughout the year. No, they weren't the hours of the night, they were the twelve 'Tribes of Israel', the twelve star races that had come to the earth. And if they were in the bottom register, did that mean they had taken refuge below the surface, and not been able to escape the earth before the calamity?

"...the serpent Apophis, who swallows the waters carrying the sun boat."

The 'sun boat' is a space ship; I'd figured that out from the images on the ceilings at Dendera and Esna. That means the reference in the 7th hour of the Amduat would indicate the gods were caught off guard and one of their space ships was caught up in the flood waters, before they had a chance to leave the planet, and the gods were forced to seek refuge below the surface in the subterranean chambers, thus creating 'the Underworld'.

Shit! I looked around; it was time to get out of here, I was definitely not ready to meet my maker, or rather, makers.

Circling the lake to the city being out of the question, I figured the only way out of my predicament was to somehow find a way back westward towards the Great Pyramid, and, north of the stream, on the western bank of the subterranean lake, an opening, this one a square-cut corridor deliberately carved out of the limestone, rose gently to the west. Surely this was what I was looking for? Or was it?

For some reason I was being pulled further north, past the corridor, to where there seemed to be a 'glow' coming from a recess up ahead.

After wading across a further stream that flowed into the lake out of an impenetrable natural fissure in the rock, I stopped dead in my tracks.

'NO...FUCKING...WAY!'

The cavern opened up to the west, where, in the recess, partially excavated from the limestone, was a spaceship, a UFO, a flying saucer: the 'sun boat' mentioned in the 6th hour of the Amduat. I knew that the ancient texts discovered in India three thousand years ago specifically indicated that the earth was inhabited by gods who scooted around in flying craft, and whose occupants lived below our surfaces, and I'd also read several 'New-Age' articles over the years that suggested there was a spaceship buried beneath the Giza Plateau, with the Sphinx erected as a marker above it, but I'd always dismissed them as the rabid ramblings of the cuckoo fringe.

I always thought, "who would be stupid enough to bury a space ship under a pyramid?" but I'd never considered the whole "tsunami, limestone-sedimentation, entombing of a craft before they could get in and fly away from a global disaster" theory. But here it was, folks, right before my eyes; solid irrefutable proof.

The craft appeared to be typically saucer-shaped, about thirty-five to forty metres wide, and made out of some sort of shiny metal or alloy. Well, I assumed it was metal, as I had memories of the movie 'The Abyss', where a shining globe of consciousness was found in the depths of the ocean in a NASA spacecraft from the future, so I wasn't keen to actually touch the surface just in case it had some weird possessive affect on me; my life had already taken a radical detour on the roller-coaster of fate and destiny, I didn't know if I could cope with any more. Therefore the first, and wisest, decision I made was to pull out the iphone and get as much footage of it as I could.

Everything I had discovered above the surface, who Jesus really was, Moses, the tsunami theories, even the content of Kareem's papers, could all be argued and refuted by Government officials and/or so-called experts, all of whom had a vested interest in maintaining their secrets and prestigious reputations, but actual footage of these subterranean chambers, the lighting in the caverns, and now the flying saucer, was indisputable proof. You might be able to call me a crack-pot or a would-be wanna-be with a vivid imagination, but, once the footage was posted on Youtube, it would speak for itself.

As I skirted the craft getting close-ups of its structural variations, the temptation was to find a door, to open it and explore and record the interior. However, and it was a big however, the thought of arriving unannounced and walking into a gathering of Annunaki gods, or their hybrid offspring, was too daunting, so, I confined myself to filming every aspect of the exterior of the craft.

In the end I decided that getting the video footage to the surface was far more important than satisfying my curiosity or the personal glory of making first contact; someone else could come down here and claim the glory, or get used as a guinea pig for intergalactic cross-breeding.

My filming complete, I hesitated to continue northward, as the shoreline of the lake would take me further away from the immediate area of the Giza Plateau. After briefly considering the dream I'd had earlier in the trip, about the three-headed serpent in which it was the central head that I had conquered last, I saw the two streams that emerged from the bedrock as the outer heads and decided to return to the second opening, the square-cut corridor that rose gently to the west; this was the central head that I had to conquer, and, if my dream was anything to go by, time was of the essence and I would need all my skills and wits if I was to complete my mission.

As I slowly made my way up the gently-sloping, square-cut corridor, carved out of the limestone and extensively covered in the similarly colourful reliefs and hieroglyphs of goddesses seen in the descending corridor, I continued filming, my thoughts once again drawn to the Amduat, particularly to the 8th and 9th hours.

"The 8th hour signifies that the hours of greatest danger have passed..."

I hoped that was true, though somehow I wasn't so sure, until I realized the message didn't relate to me, it was to the events of the pole-shift and the tsunamis. And that was totally logical as there would have been a time when the catastrophic events subsided and things went back to "normal".

"...Re provides the deceased with shining white linen clothing to wear in the next life, whilst in the top and bottom rows, deities sit on hieroglyphs for cloth, derived from the shape of a loom."

Nope, I had no idea what that meant, "shining white linen clothing", unless the clothing was space suits to rescue the survivors?

"At the 9th hour, Re, on his boat, and preceded by his crew of oarsmen, brings provisions of clothing and food for those in the afterworld. In the bottom row, three baskets topped by deities hold infinite supplies of bread and beer, while fire-spewing cobras protect the sun god and illuminate his path through the darkness."

Shit, a rescue ship, it was a rescue mission for those who had been trapped on the surface; the 'gods' were bringing food to the survivors in the underworld, finding their way down the as yet unlit, rivers that descended below the surface. And maybe the white cloth was not so much to make space suits, no, maybe they were radiation suits, especially if these guys were fucking around with some sort of hydrogen fusion reactors that had gone into meltdown.

Onward and upward

The corridor led up about 50 metres to yet another chamber, by my figuring lying about 70 feet beneath the ground, somewhere between the second, undiscovered Sphinx and the Great Pyramid. Cut out of the bedrock, in the centre were three ornately-decorated vertical pillars standing in a triangular shaped layout, with a small, square granite altar, like the one between the legs of the Sphinx, in the centre. The whole chamber gave the impression of a sort of chapel, perhaps an offering chapel. I had vague recollections of something similar existing in modern Masonic lodges and in the writings of the ancient historian, Josephus, so I checked my iphone; it took a while, but eventually I found it amongst all my files.

"In 'Antiquities of the Jews', written by Josephus in the 1st century AD, Enoch, of Old Testament fame, constructed an underground temple consisting of nine chambers, one of which contained three vertical columns, where Enoch placed a triangular-shaped tablet of gold bearing upon it the absolute name of God."

Well, if there were nine chambers directly off from this, they weren't obvious, although there were numerous corridors shooting off in all directions, possibly to other chambers. In fact, I was fast getting the impression that the subterranean structure of the Giza Plateau was crisscrossed with numerous tunnels and chambers. I could even have had the wrong room, as the columns here were square pillars rather than round columns, and there was no triangular tablet of gold perched upon the altar, although it could have be pilfered or relocated long ago. I wondered if the triangular tablet was just one of the millions of "disks" of gold supposedly stored in the galleries under the Great Pyramid and discovered in 1976? It all seemed too much of a coincidence.

There were no inscriptions on the walls, just various beautifully sculptured scenes and emblems, particularly of the lotus flower; still, I perused the walls looking for clues as to the ownership or significance of the chamber. Was there any mention of this chamber in the official circles? No!

Slightly disappointed, but video footage secured, I wondered, which way from here? By now I was regularly tuning into the "white-glow scenario" and scanned the corridors around the periphery of the chamber looking for the exit. Two corridors stood out, both to the north, one in the northeast corner, the other to the northwest. Examining them closer, the one to the east descended steeply in a staircase, which was not where I wanted to go, the other, in the northwest corner, gentle rose towards the surface, speculatively, I conjectured, into one of the 'tombs', or rather administrative buildings, in the eastern cemetery, or perhaps into one of the queens' pyramids, or even connecting via some secret door to the mysterious Trial Passages.

'Right then, onward and upward!'

Again cut out of the limestone, and similarly as ornately decorated as many of the others, the western corridor led gradually up for about 30 feet before opening into what turned out to a dead-end antechamber that ran off the offering chamber. The antechamber contained, in the centre, a large, empty, white Tura-limestone 'coffer', about 12-foot long, that could not possibly have been carved out of the limestone in situ as Tura limestone was quarried somewhere else. Why didn't whoever carved it just use the limestone here; wouldn't it have been much easier? Which beggars the question, why use Tura? Was it merely ceremonial, or was it functional? Did it have something to do with the use of alabaster for the "barque shrine" of Amenhotep II, and in the chapel of Amenhotep I, at Karnak?

I took stock again of the chamber and coffer; this clearly wasn't a burial chamber, so what was it? It couldn't have been a reactor; the coffer wasn't made of red-granite. I contemplated climbing the sides and laying down inside to tune in, but instead I placed my hands on the outside of the coffer and started tuning in from there.

Within a few breaths my experience lying down in the centre of the alabaster chapel back in the Karnak Museum suddenly flooded back; the myriad of intensely coloured scenes that projected before me, past lives, other lives, other planets, the visions, sounds, smells, and 'awarenesses'. Inside the coffer, Nemo was lounging back and chilling out like he was sipping pina coladas on a deckchair in a Phuket resort. No, this coffer wasn't for dead people, it was for living beings, and not just to meditate on the present, but to review the 'past', and more importantly to visualize the future, or even experience alternate manifestations of the present. In the end, I figured the 'offering chamber' was the reception area for some sort of ancient but advanced type of spiritual health spa?

As grand as all that was, or may have been, and as much as I was tempted to take a well-earned time-out, hanging around was not going to get me back above ground. Almost as soon as I had the thought, Nemo quaffed the last of his pina colada and, fully refreshed, leapt out of the coffer and headed back down the corridor. I took a quick video of the coffer and chamber and backtracked down the corridor after him to the offering chamber. Once there it was simply a matter of making another choice, right? Not so easy, who knows where the other corridors led?

One of the corridors to the south probably connected to the tunnel in the depths of the Tomb of Osiris that ran between the rear of the Sphinx and the second pyramid, while others headed in the direction of the Sphinx itself, and others eastwards towards the unknown sphinx, or westwards towards Khafre's pyramid. If I didn't choose wisely I could quite quickly find myself lost is a maze of tunnels.

I was also concerned that, although I hadn't encountered anyone since the granite door sealed me off from Saeed, I had the distinct feeling these corridors were not abandoned, after all, less than a hundred years ago, a high priest of some long-standing assemblage had supposedly retrieved the Emerald Tablets from South America and returned them to a chamber here below the surface. That meant not only was he more-than-likely a member of the Tat Brotherhood, but also that the Tat Brotherhood was a substantial group of people who knew about the subterranean chambers, in fact, they probably inhabited the city I'd seen on the far side of the lake; they may not be too pleased to have had their secret world penetrated by a plebiscite westerner no matter how innocent his intentions.

And then there was also the possibility of running into members of the pursuing venue of vultures who may have found another way into the subterranean chambers. Worse still, I could cross paths with some Annunaki god looking for a new slave to ship off to the gold mines. Of course there was also the possibility the whole saga could morph into an Indiana Jones movie and I could stumble into some booby-trapped chamber filled with spitting cobras or crocodiles.

'Shit, I just came here for a holiday!'

Some holiday; I gathered my bearings and looked around the room.

'Eeny meeny miny…'

No, that wasn't going to cut it, I'd have to stick with the 'white glow' approach, even though it now clearly came from the opening to the northeast, the one that disappeared downwards via a steep staircase.

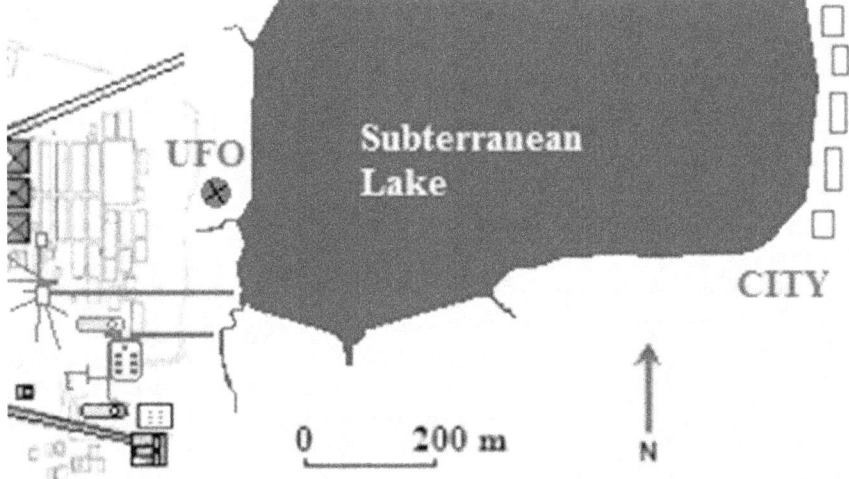

My last descent led me first to the stream, then to the lake and the city, next to the UFO, and ultimately back up here, but was my next descent likely to be a descent to hell, to my darkest hour?

'It's always darkest before the dawn, so they say.'

But was that true in the Amduat?

"In the upper row of the 10th hour, numerous deities protect and escort the solar disk, the eye of the sun."

Or is it that the eye of the sun, the consciousness of the sun, is leading the gods, showing them the way?

"In the middle row, barques containing the souls of Osiris and Sokar appear in front of the sun boat, along with bodyguards whose heads are in the shape of sun disks."

Whichever way you looked at it, the cavalry seems to have well and truly arrived.

"In the lowest row, the god Horus assures figures drifting in the primeval waters, those who have drowned in the Nile, that they will find bliss in the afterlife even though they had not received proper burial."

Maybe the figures weren't so much drifting in the primeval waters at all, but rather the tsunami and floods created by the pole shift, and the reason the people didn't receive a burial was because they were actually survivors; I mean there wouldn't be much point in telling a story for dead people to read, now would there? And the reason real living survivors are being told the story is because they are being told that life on earth, 'life after' the catastrophe, will be OK?

I could see how easily the early Egyptologists, who were peppered with the religious conditioning of the Victorian era, read the texts as they did, reading them through their narrow filtered perceptions. But that didn't mean their interpretations were either correct, or even close to the truth; I guess like all religious texts, the 'true' meaning can be whatever you want it to be. The fact was, as I saw it, that the ancient Egyptians weren't so much reciting a 'religious' philosophy, they were documenting actual events, which makes a hell-of-a-lot more sense.

What didn't make sense was, after ascending towards the surface, once again descending further below the plateau; I failed to see the point in that. Then I remembered a scene in the book and documentary *'Touching the Void'* where one of the mountain climbers, Joe, having shattered his leg climbing in the Andes, in trying to get down the mountain, falls into a deep crevasse in the glacier below. Simon, his climbing partner, believes Joe has fallen to his death and somehow makes his way, alone and exhausted, down the mountain and back to base camp.

However Joe survived his fall, and, when he realizes that Simon has assumed he is dead, makes a decision to either stay where he is, on a narrow ice-shelf deep in the crevasse of the glacier and die a slow death, or descend even deeper into the blackness of the crevasse in search of a way out. He chooses the latter, crawling on his belly until he finds a way out, and, well if you haven't read the book or seen the documentary, Joe makes it out alive and back to base camp; an incredible story of survival and inner strength.

'OK, Joe, if you can do it, my escape is a walk in the park.'

The narrow steep staircase, again cut out of the limestone, zigzagged its way downwards for about 8 or 9 long steep flights before it connected to another horizontal corridor running southeast to northwest, originating from the direction of the Sphinx and heading towards the Great Pyramid. The new corridor was made of red granite and bereft of any markings or ornamentation, so I felt as if I was right back on track. I didn't even think twice, heading northwest towards the Great Pyramid; perhaps I could find my way out through one of the secret entrances in the King's Chamber.

Almost immediately though, I had to choose between continuing northwest and taking an offshoot corridor that headed directly west. The question was, just where was I really? Had I already gone beyond the Great Pyramid? Was the path to the west the right path? Was I even correct about my sense of direction? Maybe in all the twists and turns I'd taken, I'd not only misjudged the distances, but maybe I'd completely lost my bearings and was now heading south, or east; truth be told, for all intense and purpose, I was lost. I wouldn't say it was a move of desperation, but I looked for an answer in the Amduat.

"At the 11th hour, in preparation for sunrise, the god Atum, upper left, holds a winged serpent who is about to devour ten stars symbolizing the ten hours of the night that have elapsed."

The winged serpent in the sky could well have been a comet, dragged along in the wake of Nibiru, that was going to strike the earth, obliterating ten of the twelve Tribes of Israel, ten representatives or colonies of the star races that were strategically positioned around the planet as sub-colonies of the global "Atlantean" civilization. If that were the case it would mean whoever constructed the 'hours' of the Amduat had advanced knowledge of cosmology, interstellar trajectories, and the probably consequences of an impact to one side of the planet.

"The sun-god's boat in the middle row now bears a red sun disk on its bow. It is preceded by twelve men carrying the protective serpent believed to encircle the world."

If the red disk was Nibiru, its presence on the bow of the ship may indicate some event related to Nibiru. And the protective serpent, did this indicate the twelve tribes working together to create a protective force field around the earth? Shit, was that part of the function of the ancient satellites, the ones NASA had created the whole Shuttle program to capture and bring down?

"The semicircular shapes in the bottom row are pits, into which knife-wielding goddesses have tossed the dismembered bodies of the sun-god's enemies. This gruesome punishment was thought to explain the blood-red colour of the rising sun."

Or was it simply a representation of the potential and likely consequences of events on earth should the mission to protect the earth from the comet fail? Maybe the answer was in the 12th and final hour?

"The 12th hour is the hour of the sun-god's rebirth. In the upper and lower rows, gods raise their hands in jubilation, as in the middle row, the sun-god's boat is preceded by the snake known as the World Encircler, brought along in the previous hour."

Well, it seemed the protective snake, the "World Encircler", had prevailed. Or did it all mean the reptilians had put the satellites in place? Or had the Twelve Tribes and the Dracos again worked together, this time to protect the earth, the Annunaki to protect their investment in the gold mines, the Dracos to protect their investment in the human horse of troy? If the truth could be known, or even discovered, it would rock the human race to its core, to the core of its blind religious beliefs.

"The towline held by gods and goddesses passes through the head of the snake to indicate that the sun god is pulled through the snake's body, from the tail to the mouth, and emerges rejuvenated as the scarab beetle, the sun-god's morning manifestation."

I don't know why, but I got the impression the 12th hour actually referred to a rejuvenation of the genetic experiment following the catastrophe, the Annunaki drawing from the reptilians to recycle and reinvent the human race. I'd read somewhere where someone had traced the origin, or introduction, of blue eyes back as recently as 10,000 BC due to an input of genetic material from ETs. If that were true, though I have no idea how you could measure or confirm it, then, going by my encounter with the sparkling-blue-eyed emissary from the Pleiades at Abusir, it would mean the injection of new genetic material most likely originated from the Pleiadeans shortly after the last pole shift.

There was a similar theory about the origins of wheat, rice and corn, which supposedly have no direct evolutionary predecessors on earth, but suddenly sprung up out of nowhere, along with the Sumerian civilization, around 5000 BC. Is it possible that the "rescuers", whoever they were, knowing the extent of the calamity that had befallen the planet, introduced alien, genetically-modified crops that would grow quickly in a variety of volatile environmental conditions, particularly the growing of rice in soaked pools, to sustain the survivors.

Did they also deliberately introduce additional alien DNA from the cosmos to "upgrade" the human genome? Suddenly it was not as far fetched as it once appeared. Or was the 12th hour of the Amduat simply a redrafting of the contract between the Annunaki and the Dracos, and had nothing to do with humans, who were, after all, simply slaves and lab rats?

The majority of the human race egotistically and blindly considered themselves the apex of the food chain, not just the only intelligent creature in the universe, but of a superior intelligence to all other life forms. However, one look at the daily behaviour of humans, both on an interpersonal and global level, and at their track record throughout history, should be enough for even the most fanatical creationist and evolutionist to see how primitive the human race actually is, which is not surprising considering humans are a fairly recent hybrid construct in their present form, a galactic teenager, a cosmic Frankenstein's monster barely a few hundred thousand years old. It was quite disheartening really.

I stood there for a few minutes, scratching my head, dumbfounded at it all; there was little I could do to change the status quo, unless of course I got Kareem's papers and my video footage safely to the surface and out of Egypt. If I didn't achieve that, what was the point?

Logic dictated that, as the westward corridor was just an offshoot, I should forge ahead down the main northwest corridor and see where that took me, that I could always double back if needs be. But logic was proving to be a bigger obstacle than a 30-ton red-granite portcullis, or a raging bull elephant with constipation; intuition was pulling me west, down the shimmering western corridor.

As I traversed along the first two hundred metres of the corridor, numerous further corridors shot off to the south at regular intervals. It reminded me of the subterranean networks of tunnels beneath the Black Pyramid, beneath the Layered Pyramid of Zawiyet el-Aryan, and, at Saqqara, beneath the Pyramid of Sekhemkhet, the tomb of Hotepsekhemwy, and the numerous tunnels and chambers beneath and around the tomb of Netjerikhet; there had to be something to all of this.

Passing each potential detour in turn, I gazed down, wondering where it went, but not tempted significantly enough to alter my course. Then, suddenly, a corridor headed off to the right, northward. I stood momentarily at the T intersection and gazed down the northern hallway.

It seemed somehow brighter, more alive. In all the other locations, this single corridor to the north led to the exit, why should here be any different? I peered back ahead, down the westward corridor that continued into the distance, spying even more branches heading off to the left, then briefly back the way I had come. Right, I had to turn right, and head to the north.

The corridor ran for about fifty feet before it opened into a large empty chamber. At either side of the chamber, a semi-circular tube, with a radius of about three-foot, ran off in opposite directions. Because they were relatively small, at first I wondered if the semi circular tunnels were some sort of drainage system, but then I realized they were upside down, because if they were for drainage the flat surface would have been at the top and the semi circular part to the bottom. They weren't simply cut out of the limestone bedrock either, which would have been more logical and much easier if they were for drainage. Instead they were made of some sort of highly-polished metallic-looking stone, sort of like hematite. I'm sure Bill would have known what it was, and, with that knowledge, I'm sure we would have figured out the specific purpose of the tunnels.

Curious as to where they led, I looked down the semi-circular 'tube', taking note of its straightness and then how it gently and evenly it curved to change direction; the last time I'd seen anything like this was in the underground city-loop rail system back in Melbourne. Was that what it was, an underground 'rail' system, or rather transport system because there weren't any "rails" as such? Of course, originally the system would have been above ground or perhaps close to the surface, and it may well have connected all the pyramids down the Nile, possibly even around the planet; the Tat Brotherhood's own personal transport system to zip around the globe. It may even have connected to the city of Ty-ne Abilah, the "City of Eternal Light" which was supposedly the head quarters of the Mayan High Priests who still live somewhere deep within the outer mantle of the earth's crust somewhere near or on the South American Continent.

But, if the tsunami theory was correct, and more and more it appeared to be the case, that meant that the pyramids came later, built on top of the sites of the previous structures, which were more than likely fusion reactors buried by the sediment. So, maybe, and the thought hit me like a lighting bolt, maybe it was a gigantic particle accelerator, just like the one at Cern in Switzerland? No, that didn't have stations, so it must have been a transport system, but not for large objects, for individual people. How that was achieved, I had no idea, but it gave me the confidence to believe I was now directly beneath the Great Pyramid, how far down, well, that was another question, but it gave me hope I was close to finding a way out. I shot a little footage and moved quickly on; it was a mystery I could leave to those who would come down here in the future to resolve.

An open doorway to the far side of the main chamber led to an ascending staircase, about six-feet wide, also paved and surrounded in red granite, that ceremoniously led up to a long rectangular alcove carved out of the limestone, but still with red-granite flooring.

Three of the walls of the alcove and the ceiling were smoothly polished limestone, the walls with numerous scenes carved into them. I didn't take much time to examine them, just shot a bit of footage, because my attention was on the massive red-granite fourth wall and the door, made of some sort of metal, inset in the centre.

In the middle of the door, somehow intrinsic to the very material of the door, was the same symbol I had seen high up on the pillar in the Osireion at Abydos and on the wall in the corridor when I said my farewell to Saeed; the 'flower of life'. I took it as an omen that I was on the right track, and that whatever lay beyond the door was why I was here.

Certain it was part of the lock or knob to open the door, I traced my fingers around the image searching for any sign of a release mechanism, without success. I even looked around on either side of the side for a doorbell, but there were just smooth walls, arrow-straight, perfectly flat, smooth walls.

After several minutes of fruitless pushing, tracing, groping and rubbing, it dawned on me that, just as it had been with all the other doors, this one was 'voice' activated. Placing my hands on the door, I started toning.
'Ahhh.'

Nothing, not even a rumble! I tried again without success. Consequently I spent the next ten, fifteen, possibly twenty minutes shifting pitch, from low grumbles to the highest falsetto I could squeeze out, and trying all sorts of vowel sounds; it didn't matter what permutation or combination I tried – nothing would work.
'Not good.'

I turned around, back to the door, and slid down to the ground thinking.

'What do I do now?'

According to my iphone it was 5:03pm, where had the time gone? The way I figured it, I had several options; first, go back to the 'transport station' and follow one of the semi-circular tubes which would probably lead me to one of the other pyramids. I quickly came to the conclusion that would more than likely lead to another door just like this one, and if I couldn't open this one, then chances were most likely I wouldn't be able to open that one either. Then there were all the corridors lower down that led somewhere off to the south, probably to dead-end chambers, or the corridors off the chamber with the white sarcophagus in it, which would possibly lead me back to the Tomb of Osiris or the Sphinx. Or I could go back to the lake and try my luck with the UFO or the city, but the further I retraced my trail, the less inclined I was to go back.

I stood back up, put my hands on the flower of life, and called on Nemo for help.

'Which way do I go, old buddy?'

On the other side of the door, Nemo lay on the floor, resting, his flipper pointing further into the chamber beyond. He reminded me of Otto Lidenbrock's skeleton in *'Journey to the Centre of the Earth'*, with the finger outstretched pointing the way.

'OK, got it, now, how do I open the door?'

He didn't move. For a minute I thought he'd carked it, then I realized he'd simply fallen asleep.

'Oi, Floppy Fins!'

I couldn't believe it, here was a manifestation of my alter ego, a representation of my Higher Self, and, right when I most needed him, he was taking a siesta. Then I realized that, given the past two weeks of non-stop goings-on, it wasn't such a bad idea. I took off the backpack, sat back down and took a moment to take stock of my life. I decided to notate it all on my computer; at least somewhere down the track my skeleton would be discovered and they would at least have the notes on my computer to document the history of my trek.

Reminiscing

It was bizarre to think it had been less than 24 hours since I'd made my last notes, less than 24 hours since the previous night when I'd had the most amazing sex with Crystal; if I'd died then I would have died a happy man with a grin from ear to ear. But the next day dawned, and the dream had gone south for the winter. All I had to do was get out of Egypt. I could have taken a car or train to Alexandria, waited for Bill to arrive, and sailed to Greece in comfort, but, no, I thought I could keep a low profile, join a caravan of camels, and trek into the desert with the nine maidens of Avalon to visit the pyramids and Sphinx first. Bad move!

It reminded me that, all things settled with Jacques, Bill and Pernille would be on Bill's boat and getting ready to sail to Greece, that Crystal would be on a plane back to Germany, and Saeed? God knows what they were doing to Saeed.

And yet I had discovered so much during the day that I would never have discovered had I not made the decision I had to come. It all started with Bill's explanation about the Mokattum foundation layer, which meant an earthquake must have tilted the limestone *after* it had been formed, but that it hadn't been laid down over millions of years at all, it had happened over a few years. Then there were the discussions with Bill about the construction of the pyramids, Herschel's star maps, and the temples, in particular the unusual angle of Amenhotep II's temple, did its alignment have something to do with the position of the retreating Nibiru? And was the asteroid that wiped out the dinosaurs much more recent than we have been led to believe?

The actual evidence all supported my theories about the use of red granite and of the tsunamis.

I was still pondering what the significance was of all the missing statues in both the Valley and Sphinx Temples; were they statues of the Twelve Tribes of Israel, of the star races, of the gods, like the statues of Sekhmet at Karnak? And, did the word "Israel", which first came from the stela of Merenptah, meaning it was an Egyptian term, possibly mean something like "murdering thieves"? I think it would be fair to say that lots of people would view the current State of Israel in a similar light.

And what about all the scans, those by the good guys, like Dr Abbass, and those by the SRI, and how they revealed the existence of subterranean anomalies beneath the Giza Plateau, under the Sphinx, and under the second pyramid. Were the anomalies under the second pyramid another transport station, even the tomb of Thoth? Were there in fact two Sphinxes, and were they originally facing west? The water damage to the first, and burying of the second, was consistent with not just one tsunami, but at least two.

I now knew for a fact it was all part of a whole underground city buried by the tsunamis, which means that the real reasons for Hawass's regular interference, and the influence of ARCE, the American Research Centre in Egypt, in periodically closing down the sites just after scans took place or key results were obtained, was severely in question.

In addition, there were the Trial Shafts, and the locked doors in the compound walls west outside the Khafre pyramid that led under the plateau to air conditioned rooms, and possibly to the Tomb of Birds. And what about the Tomb of Osiris, did they dig down to create it, or dig down to get *to* it; the lower chamber being created first, then it was buried, so they dug out more chambers on top of it, just for it to be buried again? And where were all the missing sarcophagi? We knew one, the 'sarcophagus' of Menkaure, was supposedly lying at the bottom of the Mediterranean off the coast of Spain, but, was it really there? Speaking of boats, why were there numerous sea-going ships deliberately buried around the pyramids, they weren't buried by the tsunami which means were they buried to protect them *from* the upcoming tsunami?

At the centre of it all, not so much geographically, but functionally, and hopefully my escape route, was the Great Pyramid. I made notes about the 8 sides of its concave faces, about the secret chambers and doors inside, and about the alien images in the entrance and behind the blocks in the King's Chamber shafts.

I recalled Christopher Dunn's work; that the Grand Gallery was an acoustic chamber designed to filter out some frequencies and enhance others, that it was filled with hydrogen gas produced in the Queen's Chamber, and used resonance to excite hydrogen to an higher state. In addition there was John Cadman's theory that the subterranean chamber was some sort of hydraulic ram pump.

It all added up to the conclusion the Great Pyramid was a big machine, a power station that, amongst other things, possibly fed microwave energy up to satellites that created a protective force field around the earth. Somehow that force field failed and an asteroid hit the earth, short-circuiting the power station, causing a massive explosion in the King's Chamber that fractured the granite blocks in the ceiling and pushed the walls out.

Some time later, during the time of Khufu, they made an attempt to repair the damage; making their way into the pyramid from below, digging their way up by expanding the Well Shaft, which would have originally been a simple drain, and trying to reseal the acoustics of the relieving chambers and seal the cracked rocks with gypsum. My guess is the repairs were unsuccessful and the pyramids subsequently usurped for other reasons.

I recalled my own personal experiences in the King's Chamber, the unexpected channelling, the girls singing, Pernille's glittering crystal ball projecting flickering flames all over the walls and ceiling, and my extraordinary experience inside the coffer. Then I had a brainwave; maybe the crystal ball I'd found on the altar in the first temple would show me how to open the door?

I put down the laptop, took the crystal ball out of the backpack, and held it up in front of the door like Hamlet holding up Yorrick's skull, fixing my intention firmly on opening the door. Alas, poor me, I knew it not, for the only images that appeared were of Diane's group singing back in the King's Chamber. Thinking that might be the answer, I tried singing into the crystal ball, hoping it might do the trick, but to no avail.

Once again despondent, I stuffed the crystal ball in the backpack and returned to making notes on my laptop, in the process not just rewriting the history of Joseph and his role in the death of Seqenenre, but also in completely revolutionizing 'The Bible's version of the exodus of Moses to Midian and the whole history of Moses after the Exodus, including the truth behind the story of David and Goliath; Goliath being a six-fingered giant who was clearly either Annunaki or a direct descendant of them.

Following that, I made notes about my journey beneath the Giza Plateau; the descending corridors that led eventually to the granite door and the first chamber of red-granite pillars, the underground streams and massive lake, with the city on the eastern bank and the UFO on the western side. The there was the 'spa-reception' chamber with numerous corridors off it, including the white sarcophagus in the chamber leading off to the north. They were followed by the underground network of corridors, the transport station, and finally my arrival at the door with the 'flower of life' on it.

By the time I'd documented it all, it was 6:30pm, the battery on my computer was running low, and, frankly, so was I; I'd been on the go since before the sun had risen. I shut down the laptop, stowed it away, and, using the backpack as a pillow, stretched out, closed my eyes, and quickly fell asleep.

But sleep was elusive; lying on basically what amounted to a marble slab made it almost impossible to get comfortable for any length of time. Initially I drifted off no troubles, lying on my back, however every time I moved, my granite mattress quickly reminded me where I was, and of my circumstances. I must have tossed and turned for hours, running the whole trip through my mind, with the felucca trip and my reconnecting with Crystal featuring most prominently in my thoughts. It would have been a pleasurable reminiscence had it not been interspersed with episodes of paranoia that had me thinking the vultures had tracked me down and any minute would appear at the top of the stairs to rip me to shreds. Basically it was a hell of a night, but, eventually, fatigue got the better of me and I succumbed.

CHAPTER 33 – THE DAY OF RECKONING

As I awoke, for maybe the fourth or fifth time that night, I remembered dreaming about Nemo, back in the King's Chamber, singing along with a choir of nine mermaids. Pernille's crystal ball was projecting psychedelic flames all over the walls and ceiling when, all of a sudden, the walls became transparent and I could see the hidden chambers beyond them. Then the chords changed, and, as they did, the secret doors opened, water flooded in, and Nemo nonchalantly wiggled his way through the opening and into the secret chamber beyond.

I interpreted the dream had something to do with the fact it was the combination of tones that was important to open the door, the same way it had been with Saeed and me, somehow with Crystal's help from a distance, opening the first door. And that was the problem, a lot of good that was to me here on my own; how was I to open the door singing solo? And then it dawned on me; I didn't have to!

I sat up and took out my iphone.

'Shit, 3:34am.'

Despite the ungodly hour, I quickly found the audio file I'd made of Diane's group toning in the King's Chamber, stood up, and held the iphone up to the door. Initially there was no response so I thought Nemo had given me a bum lead, but then the chords changed, and, almost instantaneously, the massive door started humming, vibrating, then slowly descended into the floor. I couldn't tell how this huge monolith was moving; there were no tracks, no hydraulic lifts as far as I could see, no wheels, no chains, no ropes or pulleys, no electrical wiring. That noted, I didn't wait to see how long it would stay open; I picked up the backpack and hustled through. Moments later I watched as the monolithic slab of granite slowly raised and closed the path behind me. It was weird, because even though I knew I could probably use the recording to open it again, as the door came to a halt and sealed me in there was still as sense of trepidation and "what the fuck have you let yourself into".

I turned off the recording, turned around to see where I was, and discovered an enormous chamber, about thirty metres wide and four-and-a-half metres high; the walls, ceiling, and floor all made of highly-polished red granite.

Switching to video, I recorded the sight before me; massive gold-inlayed and jewel-encrusted red-granite altars sat in the centre of the floor to either side, and, around the walls, shelves of metallic bins, like filing cabinets, occupied most of the wall space; it looked a bit like the plumbing department of a hardware store.

Ahead was a grand hallway running away down the centre, close to a hundred metres long, with, what appeared to be, a series of alcoves running off both sides; was this some sort of massive warehouse? No, *this* was the Hall of Records!

The alcoves and ceiling were supported by a series of arches, made of large limestone blocks and supported by limestone pillars with a capital design I'd never seen before, that arched from four directions and met in the centre. Were these a later addition, after the red-granite structure had been buried by tons of limestone sediment, and meant to sure up the ceiling? That's what made sense. One thing was certain; there was no way this was carved out of the limestone.

To the right side of the entrance to the hallway, as if guarding it, was a huge seated statue that, if it had been standing, would have been about twelve feet tall; around the same height as the Annunaki. By the reflection, clearly it was made out of some sort of metal, rather than stone, the reflection making me wonder about the source of the illumination. I looked around for any lights, wall switches, even any crystals in the wall or ceiling, but there weren't any, and yet the space was illuminated with a soft luminescence; it seemed as if the very air was the source of light.

In fact the air was amazing; pure, clean, alive. There must have been some sort of air-conditioning and filtration system deep down here that kept the air quality so fresh, although I couldn't see any air-conditioning vents or ducts. Suddenly I had an episode of déjà vu; I'd been here before. The only way I could comprehend my feeling was because I *had* been here before, in another life.

I turned my attention back to the statue, which must have fulfilled some sort of symbolic purpose, as it was not formed with any specifically identifiable human facial features; if I didn't know better I would have thought it was a robot. Then I remembered something I'd read by a guy called Al-Mas'udi, who was writing around 950 AD, which, coincidentally, was round the time leading up to the first crusades.

I knew I didn't have it in my notes, but Al-Mas'udi said he'd been below the Giza Plateau in the secret chambers where "written accounts of Wisdom and acquirements in the different arts and sciences were hidden deep, that they might remain as records for the benefit of those who could afterwards comprehend them". Al-Mas'udi wrote that he had "seen things that one does not describe for fear of making people doubt one's intelligence", and that there were what he referred to as "automatons", "programmed for intolerance", that "destroyed all except those who by their conduct were worthy of admission".

Backing that story up was a later report, from the mid 17th Century, by the Abbott, Nicolas-Pierre-Henri De Montfaucon de Villars who gave a fascinating account of the opening of the vault, 120 years after his death, of the father of the Rosicrucians, Christian Rosenkreuz, in which the brethren who entered the curious hexagonal tomb found a seated statue in heavy armour, a robot, an automaton, that moved when an intruder stepped upon certain stones in the floor of the vault.

Although the tomb was apparently in Central England, it wasn't hard to imagine members of the Tat Brotherhood removing a mechanical guardian from here below the Giza Plateau and relocating it to protect the tomb of Rosenkreuz, and the secrets held within, from unworthy interlopers.

I looked up at the sole figure remaining before me, images of Michael Rennie in "The Day The Earth Stood Still" flashing into my mind, images of Gort, the giant faceless robot, standing outside Rennie's spaceship in Central Park, New York, about to vaporize the unworthy human race; geez, was that movie way ahead of its time! Come to think of it, there was a very strong resemblance between Gort and the statue that stood before me, the smooth, seamless, metallic skin, the featureless face, the imposing presence and sense of foreboding. Perhaps, just like Gene Roddenberry and Star Trek, whoever wrote the screenplay to "The Day The Earth Stood Still" knew more than he was letting on. A shiver went up my spine; was it a portent of what was to come, or what had passed?

The granite floor that led up to the grand hallway and beyond the massive statue was completely clean, not *just* clean, but squeaky clean; and it had a shine about it, partly because of the polished granite, and partly because of the silver inlays of unusual hieroglyphs strategically imbedded in it. That, and the story of De Villers, reminded me of the scene in 'Indiana Jones and The Last Crusade' where Indy has to walk across the floor to get to the holy grail and save his father, but, if he steps on the wrong symbol, the floor drops away and he falls to his death.

I now knew as a matter of fact there were all sorts of fissures and underground caverns below the Giza Plateau, who was to say there wasn't a booby trap beneath the floor here? Thankfully, although I had to find an exit, I was in no hurry to move forward.

I knelt down and swiped my finger across the surface: not a speck of dirt or even dust. It reminded me of the dust-free factories where they make computer hard drives. In fact, it looked as if the whole place had just been built and completed yesterday and was awaiting its grand opening, that's how new it looked. But it couldn't have been, it had to have been twenty, thirty thousand years old at least, probably hundreds of thousands of years old. Somewhat intimidated by the statue, I headed left to check out the shelves of metal boxes.

Inside the first box were hundreds, maybe thousands, of rectangular sheets of tissue-paper-thin metal, the biggest about seven inches wide by fourteen inches long, along with irregularly shaped oval discs with a diameter of seven inches at their widest; the building must have been filled with millions of them. If they were anything like CDs or computer memories, in fact probably far more advanced, then each one probably contained a gazillion Mega-Tera-Giga-bytes of information. The big question was; how did you access it?

I took a few out and examined them closely. Etched on or engraved in the surface, to be honest I couldn't tell which, as they certainly weren't painted on, were white symbols that stood out against the greyish-silver metal; the same unusual symbols I had seen elsewhere on my journey, particularly above the entrance to the Great Pyramid.

Like the images of the flower of life on the stone pillar at Abydos, the walls of the corridor, and on door here, the symbols looked as though they were somehow embedded within the metal itself, or imprinted then covered in a translucent layer of the same metal. If it was a language, or a form of a language, then it was a language like nothing I had ever seen before, perhaps even the Atlantean Language. The only thing I had seen that was similar, and maybe I was making a biased connection, was with the symbols that had supposedly been found on wreckage at the Roswell crash site back in 1947.

I wondered if they correlated with those on the wave rock above the entrance of the Great Pyramid, and in the shafts of the King's Chamber. And what if it all correlated with the faint symbols of the Meriotic language of the Beja people I'd seen way back at the Temple of Kalabsha?

If they did, and my hunch was that was indeed the case, then it was clear evidence of a 'star language'. The evidence was everywhere, but no one, it seemed, had put it all together, or, if they had, they weren't telling anyone about it, just like the guys who had been down here in 1976.

As to what the discs were made of, Bill would have had a better idea than me, but they seemed to be made of a springy-sort of metal that looked exactly like the material used for the outer skin of the space ship as well as for the statue. I couldn't figure what it was, but when I crumpled one in my hand like a piece of paper, the second I opened my hand it simply sprung back to its original form without leaving a trace of ever being crumpled. Imagine if the car industry had that technology, you wouldn't ever worry about a fender-bender. Having said that, the car industry probably *does* have that technology, but doesn't want to use it because your car would never need any exterior parts replaced.

One or two of the discs had no symbols and I wondered if perhaps someone forgot to label them, which was unlikely, or that maybe they were blank discs waiting to be recorded. The more I thought about the latter, the less it made sense because why would you file them in the library if they were blank? There must have been some other significance to them.

I held them in my hand and suddenly remembered a scene from the film *'The Time Machine'*, not the remake with Guy Pearse, but the original George Pal 1960 one with Rod Taylor. In it, the time traveller arrives in the future beside a weird Sphinx; did Jules Verne know something? Is it possible Jules Verne was a member of the Tat Brotherhood, or had some access to their knowledge; did he know about a time machine in the proximity of the Sphinx? Was there one here?

In *'The Time Machine'* the time traveller saves Meena, of the Eloi, who eventually takes the time traveller to an ancient museum. There, by spinning rings on a flat table, the rings speak, revealing the shocking history of man. The notion of spinning rings of metal revealing audio data was highly advanced for the time of the movie, 1960, especially when you consider it virtually predicted CD technology, using light and a spinning disc/ring to reveal audio data, but it was even more advanced when you consider Jules Verne was writing back at the end of the 19th Century. I looked at the metal discs in my hand; there had to be some way of reading the contents.

I took a number of them to one of the granite altars and tried all manner of techniques; spinning the discs on their edge, flat on the table, even sliding them back and forth and toning into them, all without success. Eventually, I crumpled them up and stuffed them in my pocket, laughing as they expanded and filled my pockets. Realizing that wasn't the best option, instead, I put them safely into my backpack; along with the crystal ball and my footage, they would be irrefutable proof of my subterranean adventure. But, enough exploring, it was time to find a way out.

I half-closed my eyes and looked for 'the glow', which, must to my chagrin, was coming from a hundred metres away, from the far end of the grand hallway, and that meant I had to pass through and beyond the ominous seated statue. I took a few tentative steps, careful to avoid standing on any of the symbols on the floor and gingerly applying my weight just in case the floor was going to suddenly give way, before I concluded there were no hidden trapdoors and continued on normally.

Barely two steps forward, I heard a humming noise and stopped in my tracks, motionless, looking for the source of the sound. I gingerly peered down at my feet, only to see that I was standing on one of the symbols imbedded in the floor; I guessed that somehow I'd triggered something, possibly some sort of motion sensor. Could it get any worse?

Yes. Several metres away, the massive figure came to life and slowly stood to its feet.

'Oh, shit! This is not good; not good at all.'

I started back-peddling, hoping the statue was going somewhere else; I was wrong. Slowly it started to move towards me; what did it want, friend or foe, what do I do, run or stay? I quickly found myself with my back hard up against the entrance door; by the time I would have got my iphone out and found the audio file to reopen the door, assuming it was going to reopen, it would have been too late. My only other option was to scamper around the advancing figure and run deeper into the building.

As I was weighing up my escape routes, without warning, the statue suddenly stopped about two metres away and held out its hands.

Micheal Rennie's words echoed through my head.
"Gort, Klaatu Barada Nikto."

Somehow I didn't think it would do anything, and it didn't. Nor did tuning into Nemo; he wasn't having a bar of it either.

That said, it didn't take long for me to figure out what the ancient automaton wanted, the metal discs, maybe because I'd stuffed the discs into my backpack and didn't have a library card. Perhaps the massive robot was, amongst other things, a high-tech librarian? It certainly seemed to have the personality to match, at least at this stage of our encounter, and at least it didn't rip me limb from limb.

I would have loved to have kept the discs as proof, but it seemed I had to pay the ferryman if I wanted to pass, to cross the river Styx and enter the Underworld. And who knows what the penalty would be for an overdue loan; I certainly wasn't prepared to find out.

Reluctantly, I pulled the discs out of the backpack, placed them tentatively in the robot's giant mitts, and, moments later, watched as it dutifully headed off to return the discs to their rightful place in the library; evidence gone. I wasn't going to hang around to see what the robot did next, I quickly snatched the opportunity to scamper down the grand hallway towards the glow at the far end.

I passed alcove after alcove, on both sides of the hallway, filled to the brim with wall-to-wall shelves of metal bins full of discs, all of them in pristine condition. My god, I could only speculate in wonder at what knowledge and information they probably contained; possibly divided according to eras, or civilizations, the true history of the planet going back god-knows how far, maybe not only containing all of the earth's civilizations, but the entire history of mankind both here and beyond our solar system, amazing technologies, possibly even the history and unknown mysteries of the universe itself.

About halfway down the hundred-metre-long hallway, one of the alcoves contained some sort of strange machine, about the size of a large suitcase, perched atop a plinth of black granite about four feet high. Seamless, and with rounded edges, the machine was made out of the same type of smooth shiny metal as the robot and the outer skin of the UFO, and had a series of sensor plates on a console of instruments with two slots just like those for a DVD; this had to be the machine used to read the metal discs. Despite the fact I had to find a way out of here, I couldn't resist the temptation, grabbing both a rectangular and oval disc from one of the bins on an adjacent shelf and slotting the rectangular one into the machine.

I was hoping it was like most DVD players and would start automatically, assuming of course that it was 'plugged in' and 'turned on', but, alas, nothing happened. Then I waved my hand over a red lens inset into the left of the panel and, hey presto, it was show time, and the machine lit up like a Christmas tree.

But that's where the show stopped, at least physically; there was no magic holographic screen that appeared, nor soundtrack emanating from hidden speakers, it all somehow just 'happened' inside my head, images and understanding, like it was not only being downloaded directly into my brain, but determined *by* my brain, by my very thoughts.

My thinking as the machine fired up was, "where did it all come from?" And *that's* what I 'saw', or, rather, became aware of.

   'In the beginning there was the VOID and nothingness: a timeless, space-less, nothingness; ultimate potential. Then, into the nothingness, came a thought, purposeful, all-pervading, and IT, the thought, filled the VOID. There was no matter, only force, a movement, a vortex, a vibration of the purposeful thought that filled the VOID.'

   I wondered where, what, and/or from whom, 'the thought' came.
   'The One.'

   That didn't help me much because in the workings of my 'human' mind I found it impossible to conceive an image of 'The One' or how it existed in a 'void of nothingness'. Instead, I focused on 'the thought'.

   'In the beginning, there was a thought, an eternal thought, and for that thought to be eternal, time must exist.'

   It reminded me of the opening to the Old Testament in *'The Bible'*: *"In the beginning there was the word, and the word was God"*. I could see how Moses had misquoted the Egyptian histories; *'The Bible'* should have read, *"In the beginning there was a thought, and the thought came from God"*. It briefly had me contemplating rewriting the whole Bible: what a massive task that would be, and I had enough on my plate; pissing off every Jew and God-fearing Christian on the planet would have to wait.

   It also got me thinking about what Crystal had said early on in the trip; that "Consciousness, with Intent, Manifests". Consciousness was 'The One' and the intent was the thought, and what manifested was both time and space, the universe; the whole thing was just a thought construct.

   And, to do that, Consciousness 'slows down' to become thought, which in turn slows down to become light, then sound, and finally to become matter, which at its smallest sub-atomic quantum level is simply a pea-soup of possibilities that modifies consciousness through experience.

   It's all just different states of consciousness of the same essential being, and the whole pea-soup of the universe is a cycle of fractals, with the 'flower of life', the map of the universe, as the key to understanding how it operates. That's why it was on the door of the Hall of Records, and on the walls, and on the pillar at the temple at Abydos. That's why Hesat, the emissary of the Hathors, had told me to *"Look for the sacred geometry, for it is present in all things; all things contain it, all things exist because of it"*.

   'All space is filled by worlds within worlds; one within the other, yet separate by Law. Nine are the interlocked dimensions, and Nine are the cycles of space. Nine are the diffusions of consciousness, and Nine are the worlds within worlds.'

   There was so little we truly understood about the universe, I mean, I understood the *"worlds within worlds"* concept, that probably referred to quantum mechanics, but the *"Nine cycles of space"* and *"Nine interlocked dimensions"*, that had me baffled? And yet the scientists carried on as if they were experts. The truth was, they were just making 'educated' guesses based on their observations, not on actual knowing; science was always proving itself wrong, in fact it wasn't that long ago 'science' believed such things as: the world was flat, the sun revolved around the earth, the universe was going to collapse on itself because of gravity, even though they still can't explain what gravity is and what causes it, and that atoms were the smallest building blocks of matter.

   Even Einstein's theory of relativity was just a theory. $E=MC^2$ relied on the speed of light being a constant, and Crystal got me thinking when she said the speed of light was relative to two things, the time frame in which it was perceived and the medium through which it travelled. There was also the fact numerous experiments have shown the speed of light is not only *not* constant, it is not the upper limit, and that things can travel faster than the speed of light, in fact arriving before they were sent, and *that* proposition totally opens up the understanding of what 'time' truly is.

'Into this omnipresent thought grew the LAW of TIME. Time, which exists through all space. Time, which itself does not change, but all things change in time. Time, which is not in motion, but through which all things move, as consciousness moves from one event to another. For time is the force that holds events separate, each in its own proper place. It is by time that all exists, and, even though in time you are separate, yet still you are ONE, in all times existing.

It seemed both simple and complex at the same time, and yet I understood it. Since the boat trip, I'd often thought about Crystal's comparison of life to old film reels; every frame being a single shot, a single moment in life, and yet on the reel they all exist at the same time. It isn't until they're put through a projector that they create the illusion of time passing. And, just like watching a film, we couldn't perceive the breaks between the 24 frames that passed each second, and 'life', which was blinking in and out of a perceived reality at the quantum level at more than a billion times a second, which was a hell of lot 'faster' than a film projector.

I wondered that if I'm part of The One, but I'm separate, how is it all connected; what's the glue, and what's point? Suddenly it was as if the disc fast-forwarded to another track:

'The law of your mind is also the law of the universe and the law of belief, meaning that if you truly believe in belief itself, all things are totally possible, for your mind is an inseparable entity of the universal spirit where one cannot exist without the other.'

It was another way of saying "Consciousness with Intent, Manifests", and that *that* power, which lay within the subconscious, is All-Supreme; we ARE God.

I waved my hand over another of the sensors and the disc ejected. I held it in my hand and looked around the room and the hall; maybe the human race wasn't ready for the knowledge contained in these halls? There was evidence man had existed before and blown himself off the face of the planet; the tale of the destruction of Atlantis, the Vedic texts spoke of nuclear war, the Sumerian texts referred to the war between Enki and Enlil, the Biblical tale of the destruction of Sodom and Gomorrah.

And then there was the physical evidence, the radioactive glass in the Western Desert north of the Gilf Kelbir Plateau in southwest Egypt, and trinitite in the northern side of the Colossi of Memnon; they all seemed to confirm it. Man simply couldn't be trusted *not* to blow themselves to kingdom come. It's frightening to think that before the USA detonated the first nuclear bomb they new there was a possibility it could set off a chain reaction that would blow up the entire world, BUT THEY DROPPED THE FUCKING THING ANYWAY!

The second, oval-shaped disc lacked any markings, and, for a moment, I wondered if it was worth sliding into the machine.

'Nothing to lose.'

I figured it could be anything, science, history, astronomy, philosophy, even the Diary of an Annunaki god! I waited for the images to appear in my head, but nothing happened.

'It must be a blank disc.'

And then it hit me.

'Of course, the machine doesn't only *play* discs, it records them.'

I waved my hand over the other lenses until, all of a sudden, a light projected onto my face and I felt I had somehow been 'plugged in'. The sensation was like my brain was being scanned, like a CAT scan, recording everything, not just my thoughts, but my memories, even my emotional reactions to those memories. That freaked me out a bit, well, it freaked me out a lot, and I swiped the console, bringing the upload to a sudden halt, and ejecting the disc. I held it up in my hand, experiencing another episode of déjà vu.

'Whoa, I've done this before!'

I stood there coming to grips with the understanding that the collective history of most, if not all, of my incarnations on this planet, and possibly elsewhere, was probably recorded on hundreds, thousands, of discs that were scattered throughout the alcoves of the hall. I slid the disc back in and resumed the process, quickly coming to the conclusion that the discs not only recorded thoughts, the thoughts of the historians, the ancient ones, whose very minds were on these discs, it didn't just record knowledge, it recorded the actual physical and emotional experiencing of that knowledge, and *that* is wisdom.

Knowledge is useless unless you know what to do, or not to do, with it. It is only through experience that wisdom can be acquired; knowledge is merely the current state of parameters through which we can acquire wisdom; without experience there is no true *knowing*, just belief. And then I really got what Hesat had said way back in Diane's circle at Luxor, '*Ascension is a process of self-awareness and mastery on, and of, all levels, all of which occur in the same moment of the Oneness that is the universe and in the localized perception that is space/time.*'

And that spiritual ascension, that process of awareness, is triggered through the vibratory nature of the cosmos, not just by what we see, by sacred geometry, that excites and arouses brain performance through the stimulation of retinal receptors that in turn trigger activation of sub-atomic neural pathways, and not just by what we hear, subsonic, audible, and supersonic sounds that stimulate and activate psycho-spiritual experiences, but also by what we feel, and what we sense. Everything, absolutely EVERYTHING, was driving us to spiritual ascension.

In ancient Egypt, sacred geometry and vibration were the keys, the exact same 'keys' the ancient texts talked about, hidden in hard-to-reach secret locations inside temples. But they weren't hidden as such, hidden with High Priests, or placed under the guard of fearful beasts or curses, they were in plain sight, on the walls, on the pillars, inlayed into the floor for all to see, but only to those who were ready and open to understand. And the 'Book of Thoth' wasn't *just* a book, said to have been "locked inside a box of gold, which itself is locked inside a silver box which is inside a box of ivory and ebony, locked inside a box of sycamore, which is locked inside a bronze box, which in turn is sealed in an iron box supposedly placed at the bottom of the middle of the Nile and guarded by scorpions and a serpent that can't be slain", it was a portal for those who knew how to find it and 'read' it. And the "keys" to finding it were the symbols in the temples; they were initiations.

I had no idea how long I stood there, again it could have been 30 seconds, it could've been 30 minutes, 'time' meant nothing, but one thing I was now certain of was that Hesat was right, I may well have incarnated into a human form, but I was definitely *not* what I appeared to be. I put the oval disc in my backpack, surely the librarian wouldn't have a problem with me removing it, after all, it was mine, and headed off.

On the other side of the hall, in the opposing alcove, was, of all things, a bed: not a big bed fit for an Annunaki god, but a regular bed from ancient Egypt; strange place for a bed, in the middle of a library. After my sleepless night lying on the hard granite floor outside the main door, it was an inviting option. Behind it was another black-granite plinth, this one with a goblet perched atop it. My curiosity got the better of me and I ducked in for a squiz.

Either the bed was relevant to the purpose of the goblet, or the goblet to the purpose of the bed, and given beds were usually just for sleeping, my guess was it was the purpose of the goblet that was paramount. However, at that point, the option of lying in an actual bed was more attractive than contemplating a goblet, so, taking off the backpack, I stretched out on the bed, my feet sticking out over the end, and let out a huge sigh; 6:36, it was the first chance I'd had to relax in over 24 hours. Within a few breaths, I was fast asleep.

As it turned out, I only slept for just over an hour, but in that time I had a dream in which Hesat, the Hathorian emissary, came to visit me. There I was, lost, parched and dying of thirst, lying on a park bench in a desert that was somehow in the middle of Central Park, New York, when a UFO, just like the one buried beside the underground lake, appeared from a cloud and landed before me. As it did in 'The Day the Earth Stood Still', a hatch slowly opened in the spacecraft, and out came Hesat, accompanied by a giant robot just like the one that sat at the entrance to the Hall of Records. Slowly Hesat walked up to me.

'I am here to give you the key to the path to eternal life.'

'I thought the Hathors weren't allowed to interfere in human concerns?'

'We're not, but you are no more human than the driver of a car is the car itself.'

'You're right. I'm not what I appear to be at all, I am ...'

'Here, drink this.'

She took the goblet, which was surrounded by lotus flowers carried on a drinks tray by Gort, and held it out to me.

'What is it?'

'Wisdom.'

The cup was suddenly overflowing, but, as I reached out to take it, true to form, I woke up before I could get it in my hot little hands; ain't it always the way!

Reluctantly dragging myself to my feet, I fixed my gaze on the goblet.

'Wisdom, hey?'

I picked it up and gave it the once over; coming to the conclusion it was made of a strange sort of metallic glass. The inside was discoloured slightly and had a faint sweet smell that was somehow familiar. Whatever it was that was consumed from the goblet clearly required the drinker to lie down afterwards, and that took me back to the image of the goblet surrounded by lotus flowers, and then to something Pieter had said during the boat trip about recent revelations concerning the psychotropic qualities of the Blue Lotus of Upper Egypt.

The Blue Lotus Flower

Until then, my interest in lotus flowers had mainly been that they formed the capitals of some of the columns in several of the temples of Upper Egypt, and that they were often depicted on the walls of the tombs and temples. Suddenly I had the feeling there was a lot more to their use and depiction. As to their use as the capitals of columns, I had seen them in the Kiosk of Qertassi at Kalabsha, and Temple of Hathor at Philae, and interspersed with papyrus-capitaled columns in the Hypostyle halls of the Temple of Isis at Philae, Kom Ombo, Esna and Abydos, all of which dated from the 18th Dynasty through to the Ptolemaic reconstructions; all post-Thera.

But other lotus columns predated Thera, those attributed to the Old and Middle Kingdom; the 11th Dynasty tomb of Baqet III at Beni Hasan El Shorouk has two lotus columns, the temple of Shepseskare outside the Pyramid of Neferefre has 20 wooden six-stemmed lotus columns with two more four-stemmed lotus columns of limestone at the entrance, the Mortuary Temple outside the Pyramid of Neferirkare-Kakai had a entrance hall with six pairs of four-stemmed lotus columns of wood, as well as an open courtyard with 38 lotus-shaped wooden columns, and, finally, the Mastaba of Ptahshepses consisted of a portico flanked by two eight-stemmed fine white limestone lotus columns with closed buds that led to a small room with two smaller six-stemmed lotus columns.

There were probably more, but, the way I figured it, it was possible the lotus columns were all post-Thera restorations done possibly done by Thutmoses IV or even Khaemwaset, son of Ramses II. But what was it with the closed buds as opposed to the open flowered capitals?

I found the answer in Buddhism, with Buddha often found sitting on an open lotus blossom, and where each stage of growth of the lotus flower represents a different stage of spiritual enlightenment; a fully-bloomed and open lotus flower representing full enlightenment and self-awareness, a closed lotus flower representing a closed mind. So, were the closed lotus capitals at the Mastaba of Ptahshepses a final snide comment by the Amun Priests about what they really thought of Ptahshepses, or was it perhaps Ptahshepses' own warning to everyone that he was not easily swayed from his beliefs and opinions? And were the open lotus flower capitals, especially those at Esna, indicative of an opening awareness and consciousness to the events that transpire on the ceiling, the realm of the gods? Clearly the use of lotus capitals meant something, especially if we consider once again the lotus capitals in the Hypostyle Hall of the Temple of Isis at Philae.

'The hall is a symbolic representation of the great primordial swamp from whence the primeval ground had emerged and the gods first appeared. It also reflects the conditions at the beginning of Creation; of the Zep Tepi, i.e. "the First Time".'

The 'great primordial swamp' was surely the void, and the 'primeval ground', the physical universe, so, were the lotus flowers the budding thoughts of 'The One' reaching out and blossoming to become the expanding universe? Surely it was possible, at least worth considering!

According to the experts, the two different types of capitals, lotus and papyrus, were supposedly a sign of the unification of Upper and Lower Egypt, and it may well have been the case, but maybe there was another, deeper meaning, maybe it was a representation of the dichotomy of polarities, or of feminine and masculine concepts?

The issue for me was, that as far as I knew, none of the red-granite columns I had seen had lotus tops, so they didn't date to the original temples, which means the lotus tops must have been a later design element; the question was, when? Again, the evidence seemed to indicate they were a later addition, particularly post-Thera. So now the question was, why?

If the lotus flower *was* representative of awakening consciousness, and anyone who has taken a look at numerous stone carvings and paintings of ancient Egyptian art cannot fail to have noticed the significance of the Blue Lotus flower in them, then was it directly connected to the psychotropic alkaloids in the Blue Lotus?

What better place to look for clues than on the walls of the temples and tombs.

In the mastaba of Khufukaf, Khufukaf was receiving a lotus flower, presumably from one of his daughters, while, in the burial chamber of Meresankh III, she sat holding a lotus flower and watching over proceedings, and in other scenes she was gathering lotus flowers.

I'd seen a blue lotus on the rear wall in QV44, the Tomb of Khaemwaset, eldest son of Ramses III. It was part of a double scene, of a green-skinned Osiris being worshiped by Neith, Isis, Nephthys and Selkis. Emerging from a blue lotus flower at Osiris feet were figures representing the four sons of Horus; Imsety, Duamutef, Qebhsenuef and Hapy; that's no ordinary flower!

Outside in the grounds at Dendera, there was a small red granite sarcophagus decorated with lotus flowers. At Karnak, in the Temple of Ptah, the statue of Sekhmet held the 'was' sceptre in one hand with the flowering lotus, and, in her right, the ankh of life. At Abydos, in the Nefertum chapel, Nefertem being the son of Ptah and Sekhmet, were images of Seti making offerings to the gods of creation of the world, and both a human and lion-headed Nefertem being crowned with the lotus blossom. A beautiful young man with a Blue Lotus flower on his head, Nefertum's sole role was the protection of the Blue Lotus; no other civilization on Earth ever dedicated a God to the protection of a plant.

In other scenes, in other tombs and temples, priests, gods, pharaohs and their wives all held the flower up to their faces, including on the walls of the temples at Karnak where it is depicted in connection with "party scenes", dancing, or in significant spiritual and magical rites such as the rite of passage into the afterlife.

In fact, the Blue Lotus flower has been steeped in symbolism since the time of the ancient Egyptians, and, according to the experts, the Egyptologists, it is known to be associated with, and used as, a metaphor for re-birth. In is astonishing to consider that, in 1994, a seed from a sacred lotus roughly 1,300 years old was successfully germinated, that an individual lotus can live for over a thousand years, with the rare ability to revive into activity after long periods in stasis. Perhaps this is one of the reasons it was associated with rebirth? But there is more to consider.

The ancient Egyptians scholars observed that during the night the lotus closed its flowers and sank into the water, slowly emerging from a pond over three days and then blooming in the morning until mid-afternoon. Because of that, the lotus came to symbolize not just rebirth, but also the Sun and the creation, with hieroglyphic works depicting the lotus as emerging from Nun, the primordial water, and bearing the Sun God.

"In the beginning were the waters of chaos ... Darkness covered the waters until ... the Primeval Water Lily rose from the abyss. Slowly the blue water lily opened its petals to reveal a young god sitting in its golden heart. A sweet perfume drifted across the waters and light streamed from the body of this Divine Child to banish universal darkness. This child was the Creator, the Sun God, the source of all life."

I could see the parallels; the "waters of chaos" were the Void, the "Primeval Water Lily" was the thought that "rose from the abyss", the "blue water lily" opening its petals was the 'flower of life', the geometric structure I had seen on the pillars, walls, and door, that determines all matter in the universe. In many ways, the Blue Lotus *was* the Flower of Life.

Given its association with rebirth, it was no surprise then that the Blue Lotus was also associated with death, and, accordingly, it was often used in funerals. For example, Tutankhamen's innermost gold coffin had blue water lily petals scattered all over it.

The Egyptians looked forward to their souls coming to life, just like a water lily reopening, thinking that the deceased died, as the water lily closed, awaiting opening with the morning sun. The *'Book of the Dead'* even has a spell that supposedly allows the deceased to transform into a lotus, thus allowing for resurrection:

"I am the holy water lily that comes forth from the light which belongs to the nostrils of Ra, and which belongs to the head of Hathor."

The "nostrils of Ra", the breath of God, the word, the thought, it all reflected the connection to a higher consciousness and to the origin of all life.

So the Blue Lotus clearly wasn't just for decoration, it had some functional purpose, and that purpose had to do with altering the state of mind; it wasn't just used in rituals and rites of death, it was also the recreational drug of choice of ancient Egypt. In fact, such was its impact and desirability that it was cultivated and exported throughout the Mediterranean and revered in Greece as early as 550 BC.

The statue of Phrasikleia, Greek 'Priestess of the Blue Lotus', circa 540 B.C, has a wreath of alternating open and closed lotus blossoms, golden lotus-bud jewellery, and she holds a closed lotus bud in her hand, a symbol that she is the path to awakening. Her dress is also decorated with poppy flowers, indicating these psychotropic plants were probably used together. In all probability, Phrasikleia was a priestess to the Greek Goddess Demetre, who, like the Egyptian deities, also carried a Blue Lotus staff as a symbol of spiritual power and enlightenment. Phrasikleia supposedly dedicated her life to the Sacred Blue Lotus Flower, and she was remembered for it. But why was she crowned with, and reverently presenting, a flower which supposedly ONLY grew in Egypt?

Perhaps the reason it was even in Greece was because Amenhotep had taken it there when he left Egypt to rebuild the obliterated Minoan Civilization into the Mycenaean Civilization. Which means, did the arrival of the blue lotus, in fact all the lotuses, coincide with the arrival of Nibiru? Was the lotus, like wheat, corn, and rice, an introduced species from the Annunaki's home planet; a gift of the Gods, as some modern priesthoods believe, given to mankind to connect them to their divine origins?

It would explain the explosion of images of weird looking gods, snakes, and concepts of the "Underworld" and "Realm of the Gods" that came into being, and persisted through, the 18th Dynasty, following the passing of Nibiru and the Thera eruption. As far as I could make out, none, or very few, of them really existed or were documented before the arrival of Amenhotep I. Was it all just the imagery and visions the High Priests saw when they were stoned and astral travelled into other dimensional realms? That's what it appeared. It didn't mean the images weren't real; just they may not be what the Egyptologists tell us they are.

It's even possible that Akhenaten, when he left Egypt, took the secret of the Blue Lotus with him, that the knowledge died with Tutankhamen and during the military reign of the Ramses Dynasties of the 19th and 20th Dynasties, or that it died out during the reign of the Amun Priests in the 21st Dynasty, or with the northern invasion of Smendes and the Libyans in the 22nd Dynasty. But was it also possible the Tat Brotherhood kept the secret, and that it had travelled to Greece? It seemed plausible, especially given the prophecies and visions of the Pythia at the Temple of Apollo.

In any case, by the time Alexander and the Ptolemies arrived to rule Egypt, just prior to 300 BC, it was re-introduced to the then newly-formed cult religions of Isis and Serapis. In fact, by the time of Cleopatra VII, the cult of Isis was firmly headquartered in Alexandria and the Blue Lotus was represented on the crown and forehead of all Greco-Roman statues of the goddess. By the end of the Roman Empire, Blue Lotus was being shipped as far away as India and Britannia, but, with the death of the Cult of Isis around 550 AD, the use of Blue Lotus, which had been used in religious ceremonies for over a thousand years to invoke a higher state of consciousness, was forgotten, or rather concealed by the early Christian Church, then 'lost' for over 1500 years; hardly the sort of thing you would expect from a simple garden decoration. So, why was it so special?

Blue Lotus (*Nymphaea caerulea*), is actually not a lotus at all, but a water-lily. According to the experts, its original habitat may have been along the Nile, but it spread to other locations like the Indian Subcontinent and Thailand, exactly the locations the Annunaki supposedly inhabited. I ask you, how does a water lily spread from the Nile in Egypt, a river that feeds into the Mediterranean Sea, to Thailand? It would have to be carried out the straight of Gibraltar, past Morocco, down the west coast of Africa, passing Sierra Leone, all the way around the Cape of Good Hope and South Africa, then back up the East Coast of Africa via the Indian Ocean, passing Somalia, Yemen, Pakistan, Burma, and all the way across to Thailand.

It's possible, but why are there no examples of the Blue Lotus in Spain, Sierra Leone, South Africa, Yemen, Saudi Arabia or Indonesia? Surely, if nature were responsible, the seeds would have been carried there as well, that's if they were carried by the ocean currents? Clearly, some sort of 'human' intervention took place, and that means the lotus had some value.

If, as Pieter suggested, the active ingredient in the Blue Lotus is in fact in the Tryptamine family of psychotropic alkaloids, which, when they're absorbed by the brain, act as neurotransmitters, neuromodulators, serotonin releasing agents, serotonergic activity enhancers, and create altered states of mind, then that means it wasn't just the pharaohs who were tripping out on Blue Lotus flowers, it was most-likely the High Priests as well, probably so they could astral travel, possibly even perform actual physical transportation, much as some modern advanced eastern gurus have reportedly been able to do.

Given the High Priest would have presided over the death and rebirth rituals, acting as a shaman in guiding the souls of the living and dead, the goblet therefore would have been integral in any ceremony of awakening into the divine feminine. He would also have used the hallucinogenic drink to access other realms and dimensions of awareness. The High Priest would have swallowed the potion, probably mixed with wine, lain down on the bed until such time as the hallucinogen took effect, then would have been assisted across the hallway and plugged into the mind-reading machine to download his visions. Just imagine if we'd been able to plug into and record the minds of Einstein, Mozart, and Nicolas Tesla?

Then I wondered if the goblet could have been the origin of the myth of the Holy Grail being a cup? The ritual established, that of consuming an hallucinogenic drink to access the Oneness of the divine feminine, the lotus extract would have been omitted and substituted with wine for the masses, which would have had a considerably lesser effect, but an effect none-the-less. It would have been this doctored ritual, not the true ritual of the High Priests, that Joseph, as a Hyksos invader, would have been aware of, although it is unlikely he would have participated in either. And it would have been this doctored ritual of drinking wine that was later adopted and adapted when Joseph was chased out of Egypt, changed his name to Moses, and created Judaism. From there it was easy to see how the 'sang réal', the royal blood, became the 'san greal' the Holy Grail, the cup that held the blood of Christ in the Christian mass; it was one misinterpretation and deception after another.

I thought about stuffing the goblet in my backpack, alla Indiana Jones, along with the disc, before pausing and weighing up the implications that such an artefact would have on the religions of the world. After much contemplation I concluded it was a battle I could leave for the archaeologists and professors of theology to fight out once the truth was out there about what was below the Giza Plateau. The problem was, the truth wasn't out there, because I wasn't out there, and until I was, until Kareem's papers were, until my photos and videos were, everything else was hypothetical.

I respectfully placed the goblet back on the plinth, shot a bit of footage, then picked up the backpack and resumed my journey to the far end of the main hallway; it was time to find my way to the surface.

Across the back, southern wall, of the hall was a series of large round lenses, like windows, about head high and spaced around six metres apart. Of course they could have been motion sensors, or concealed closed-circuit cameras, but, given their regularity and position I was sure they once simply admitted natural diffused light from outside, however now the hall was buried under a hundred feet of limestone they were superfluous.

In front of the southern wall, in the centre of the hallway was a short black-granite column, this one supporting a glass-like translucent case, in which was a book made of wafer thin metal leaves bound together by hoops of a gold-coloured alloy suspended from a rod of the same material and engraved with ancient symbols I had seen before. What was it Frank had said about the Emerald Tablets? *"...imperishable emerald-green tablets, made of a substance with a fixed atomic and cellular structure, bound together by hoops of a gold-coloured alloy suspended from a rod of the same material, that respond to attuned thought-waves"*. It all fitted, except the leaves weren't green, they were...gold. Shit, this wasn't the Emerald Tablets, this was *'The Book of Thoth'*.

The Book of Thoth

"Find the Book of Thoth and you find the true history of not just the human race, but the extra-terrestrial life forms that have had, and most likely will have, an influence on the genetic and cultural development of all life on this planet."

'Well, Frank, I've found it, just where you said it would be, in a clear case in the Great Halls beneath the Great Pyramid.'

According to Bill, it was supposedly *"a series of forty-two volumes containing powerful spells and knowledge and encompassing all the great arts and mysteries; ten volumes on religious practices, two of sacred hymns and chants, six containing medical knowledge on the body, diseases and cures, with instructions on surgery and plant extracts or drug use, and the remaining volumes a compendium of all the sciences and philosophies of the ancient Egyptians"*, however, gazing down at the book before me, that was laid opened to nearly midway, I could see no division into volumes and doubted it could contain so much information. But then again I didn't understand the technology used to make the metal discs, so how was I going to begin to understand the contents of the book?

"Read, and the vibration within will awaken a response in your soul, for the

one who reads with open eyes and mind, shall find his wisdom shall be increased a hundred-fold."

I hesitated. Bill had said, *"The words are apparently so powerful that if you read them you are enlightened with the knowledge to understand animals, how the heavens move, how to control the elements, and how to duplicate the creation of life".*

Was I ready for such knowledge? Maybe I should just take the book with me? Except there was apparently a curse on anyone who removed the book from its resting place and read it; they'd be *"punished by the gods"* who would *"cause the reader's loved ones to die until the book was returned".* If I could've been certain the curse would play itself out on my ex-wife and her mother, I would gladly have taken the risk, but, as it was, I decided, along with the goblet, to leave the book where I'd found it. However, I also figured it was highly unlikely I would get this chance again, so I did take the opportunity to call on Nemo, dive in, and do a little 'light' reading.

It wasn't so much about me trying to read the symbols; it was more about completely opening my mind and allowing the story to unfold. However, rather than unfold linearly, in my mind it was like a zip file of zip files was being uploaded; millions of images and experiences covering millions of years were all being uploaded at once. In a matter of minutes I just *knew* things, I hadn't actually unzipped any files and examined the contents in details, but, I just *knew*.

The 'spells' were there; not so much witches' potions and magic charms, but processes of intention manifest in words. The ten volumes of 'religious practices' were there, but they were not so much rituals related to a specific religion, more processes to reinforce the intentions of the 'spells' so as to connect to the Oneness. Yes, there were two volumes of sacred tonings and chants, but they were actually the keys to unlock the subatomic structures of both inorganic and organic matter. The six volumes of 'medical' knowledge went so far beyond what we call medicine it wasn't funny; it was really a systematic understanding of why souls created illness and how to re-harmonize the body based on the experiences the soul wished to experience. Beyond that, there were innumerable additional 'files', or volumes, on all sorts of sciences, philosophies and history.

I decided to dig deeper into the history 'zip file', and, as I did, it revealed ALL the previous civilizations on the planet. Going back over five-and-a-half million years, it included the Dracos; yes, the reptilians were real, and they had a big investment in the history of the earth. There was also heaps of information on when 'man', or what we would consider the gods that formed man in their image, the Annunaki, first set foot on the earth 576,000 years ago. It even showed the different prototypes of modern day humans, all genetic experiments, and the various 'stages' of Atlantis. Folks, I hate to tell you this, but the human race as we think of it, is, in the eyes of the Galactic Community, and to quote Shakespeare from *'As You Like It'* and the seven ages of man; *"the infant, mewling and puking in the nurse's arms".* Now I fully understood not only the role of the Hathors, but also their challenge.

My 'reading' over, and my upload complete, I unplugged, shook my head, and, eager to find an exit, moved on to the right, southwest corner of the hallway, only to discover a large room containing two rows of objects that looked like computer or video screens, each of which was encased in the same shiny metal used for making the discs. I got the feeling this was some sort of study room, or communications room. That was confirmed when I discovered, in one corner of the room, large 'star charts' that seemed to plot the known universe, but not the universe as we would see and know it, but as a star being would most likely know it. What I found most interesting was that the universe was depicted, not as an expanding sphere as I might originally have thought, but, as a series of expanding and interlocking toruses; that one I would leave for the cosmologist and astrophysicists to nut out.

On the floor in another corner was a strange machine that looked like a giant searchlight, the sort used today to light up the night skies at grand opening events. It sat supported on a stem attached to a large bulky base, which, like the disc player, had no seams or welded divided joints. As, like the disc recorder and the screens, there were no visible wires or cables to plug in to power the unit, I could only presume it somehow drew its power from some internal battery or directly from the air, perhaps by zero-point technology; that wouldn't have surprised me at all. The screen wasn't glass, but a transparent sort of metal, which quickly made me realize this 'light' didn't project light at all, rather it projected something else, and the most likely thing was sound; this was a levitation, or anti-gravity, machine.

At the rear of the 'light', attached to the supporting neck stem was a square metal console, just under 2 feet square and 7 inches deep, with small lens covers over interior light and large sensor plates. At the risk of rousing Gort, once again, I waved a hand over one of the inset red lenses. Immediately, a low frequency, similar to the low pitch of a violin, emanated from the machine, each second increasing in frequency. As the pitch escalated, the walls that were targeted by the beam began to rumble. I didn't want to push my luck and risk causing a cave in, so I immediately shut the machine down. This was undoubtedly the anti-gravity field ray, or one of them, used to lift and place stone blocks weighing many tons in the construction of the limestone and granite sections of most of the pyramids in Egypt, especially those here at Giza.

Modern science has proved such sonic devices can levitate objects, Leedskalnin did it in Miami back before the Second World War, with the Coral Castle, and he wasn't the only one. In 1931, there was a guy called George Makefield in Toronto, Canada, who experimented with antigravity machines. Even though both the British and American governments declared his anti-gravitational machine a hoax, at a demonstration in Ottawa, Makefield proved it could lift a 1930 Buick Sedan six foot off the ground and hold it there for two-and-a-half hours. Similarly, in Philadelphia in 1937, George Worl experimented with a machine in which he had recorded the sound and vibrations of a violin's "high C", then magnified it 20,000 times. The resulting supersonic sound and vibration lifted a solid concrete block weighing five tons and held it suspended until he struck a discord, at which time the block crashed to the floor. Strangely, both Worl and Makefield died before their discoveries could be developed further and revealed to the public; and they supposedly took their secrets to the grave.

Well, that wasn't *my* intention; there was no way I was going to get stuck down here. I left the room and crossed the hallway, beyond *'The Book of Thoth'*, to the opposite corner, where a narrow staircase, about two-and-a-half feet wide, led upwards; clearly I was on the lowest floor and had a lot more to explore.

The staircase continued beyond the second floor, but, given it was unlikely I would pass this way again, I decided to give the second floor the quick once-over anyway. It had the same lens-like windows in the southern wall, the same floor plan of arched alcoves, and thousands of bins of metal discs. As I walked up then back the central hallway, my mind turned to the way the machines utilized and recorded thought waves. The logical conclusion was that the Annunaki must have been telepathic and had no need for a written or oral language to communicate; at most, all they needed were geometrically relevant symbols. So how did written and oral languages originate?

The Annunaki would project their thoughts into the inferior 'mewling and puking' minds of humans, which, whilst not 'developed' enough to be fully telepathic themselves, were able to at least receive and interpret the telepathic messages conveyed to them. In return, whilst they probably had no need, or even desire, for it, the Annunaki could read the minds of men. So why did 'language' come into being?

It was once the Annunaki had departed, the humans 'abandoned', that humans were forced to find a way to truly communicate with one another. What did they have? There were the Annunaki symbols and the images in their heads. So the development of language thus took several paths; the development of symbols into characters with meaning, in particular the Korean/Japanese/Chinese path, and into individual characters with the Sumerian cuneiform, which probably led to Aramaic. On the other hand, the symbols created from the images in the human minds perhaps became more representative of themselves, a fish was a fish, a bowl a bowl, that sort of thing. Is this the origin of the Egyptian hieroglyphs, perhaps via or related to the Meriotic language? As I headed up the stairs to the third floor, I wondered, was the true origin of the ancient Egyptian hieroglyphs simply the human drawing of images telepathically implanted in their heads by their Annunaki masters?

I expected the third floor to be much the same as the second, and in many respects it was, that was until I reached the centre of the hallway, which opened to a massive space that extended up into, and included, the fourth floor. In the centre of the space was a giant metallic ring, like a large section of underground sewer pipe, twenty-five feet in diameter, about four inches thick, and twelve feet deep, the exterior having the same shiny smooth surface as the flying saucer. The inner surface had a rough, 'glazed' appearance, with tiny thin grooves, two inches deep that began at the outside lip of the ring and ran in a tight continuous clockwise spiral until they ended at the far lip, giving it a sort of corkscrew appearance.

At first I thought I'd found the key to the riddle of the hydrogen reactors, the 'Circle of Gold', but then I realized this wasn't a donut-shaped hollow tube, a super-conductive torus, that would have been able to create an electro-magnetic field capable of confining a plasma for nuclear fusion; it had to be something else, and that something else was significant enough for it to require such a massive machine. Then I figured it out.

At one particular point, halfway into the ring, there was a horizontal 'bridge' connected to each side of the normal curvature of the ring; it looked like a platform where you might stand prior to the machine being switched on. I suddenly remembered seeing episodes of an old TV series from the late 1960's called *The Time Tunnel'* in which two scientists entered a large oval-shaped tube with a platform and a corkscrew backdrop, a time machine, and were transported through time and space. This was either a transporter or a time machine, or both.

I speculated how it might work; magnetic fields, spirals of electrons, a combination of magnetic and electric fields, just like the Rainbow Experiment, the Philadelphia Experiment? Then I realized; 'time' and 'space' being intricately interwoven, you could theoretically go anywhere in space and/or time, because in some respects they were interchangeable. If you could transport to another location, in effect by re-arranging the physical atomic structure, then you were in effect changing its temporal coordinates as well, like I could stand here at 1:00 o'clock, then a second later I am on the other side of the planet. I am still the same, but my physical and temporal co-ordinates have changed. Then it struck me, that if the universe is just a pea-soup of quantum probabilities, how do you actually transport sub-atomic particles from one side of the galaxy to another, from anywhere to anywhere?

Everything in the universe consists of atoms of various densities, all built out of sub-atomic particles, and since atoms are matter, they can never be destroyed; they can change form and be rearranged on a temporary basis, but they can't be destroyed. Therefore, for atoms to be transferred any distance would mean that when they 'leave', they would leave a void, and where they are supposed to arrive, a void would have to be created *first*; that is exactly what the universe is NOT all about, it manifested *out* of the void.

Was that what transportation was really all about, reversing the creation process of 'God', not just reversing it, but then reproducing God's ultimate act? It was a big call, and I couldn't see how it would work. How could you know or control the physical matter that already exists in the target location, it had its own 'being' whatever that might be, rock, air, water, deep space; it just wouldn't work; you would finish up with the exact problems they had with the Philadelphia Experiment, with guys returning half-embedded through walls and floors. I could think of all sorts of reasons why any transportation of matter based on the dematerialization of that matter and the rematerialization of that very same matter in another space, or time, just wouldn't work. However, there was an alternative.

If the Annunaki had such strong telepathic capacities, possibly because of the consumption of mono-atomic gold, perhaps they used the fullest power of their mind in other ways; perhaps they didn't need to move the actual atoms, perhaps the sub-atomic particles didn't move at all, they just reconfigured into something else, and that something else was determined by consciousness, because "Conscious with Intent, Manifests". Perhaps transportation was, is, really just a shift in consciousness, and if you can do that spatially, then you can do it temporally as well, just like shifting your attention from one frame of a film to another, or even to another film altogether, and that's what the great Eastern Guru's must have mastered. Ultimately, any form of time travel, or transportation, requires a shift of consciousness.

To the right of the ring was a console similar to the one on the anti-gravitational machine. I thought about all the possibilities: I could transport myself to the surface, or even directly to Bill's boat, and safely out of Egypt, or, I could transport myself back in time to last night, to my time with Crystal, and not only relive that amazing night, but stay awake for more, and not make the rash decision to go to the Giza Plateau in the first place, I could even transport myself back to before I met my last wife, and, realizing now that she would turn out like her mother, never have got involved, but that would mean I may never have come to Egypt, I may never have met Crystal, and I may never have discovered all the things below the surface of the Giza Plateau. And how would I have dealt with running into my old me? Was that even possible?

'There is no time; there is only this moment. All lives, past, present and future, are simultaneous. Remember?'

Yeah, I remembered: time is relative, an illusion where the moment is just a question of consciousness and awareness. Everything is predetermined, all the possible environments and scenes, all the rules of all the worlds we live in, all the possible characters we can meet and all the possible outcomes of every possible interaction, *and*, all the time frames. But it's not until we put the game into the machine and press play that they unfold, we just only see one because we choose to see it from the perspective of the character in the game, and, if you get killed, you just hit reload and play again, hopefully making better choices the next life. And just as one soul can live several lives, an advanced, or rather awakened, soul can even consciously lead several lives at the same 'time'. And yet, here I was, standing in front of a fucking time machine; I had to turn it on at least.

Getting it started was easy; I simply waved my hand over the sensor. After that, I was running on instinct; I'm sure there was probably an instruction manual uploaded into my brain when I was reading *'The Book of Thoth'*, but it wasn't unzipping itself in a hurry. The circle started humming and the air inside started to glow, forming a sort of fine mist. It reminded me of the images from the Stargate film and TV series, which formed a sort of liquid barrier; what was it with all these TV series and films, did someone have actual knowledge of what was down here, or had it been seeded into their subconscious? Maybe they were getting flashbacks?

I paused, my hands above the console; if I jumped into the ring of fire, I could finish up anywhere, or I could even finish up toast! Until this trip, my life was in the toilet; if I hadn't met Crystal, Bill, Saeed, and had the responsibility of Kareem's papers to keep me here, I would have gone for it, and jumped. Five minutes, passed, I even tried projecting Nemo into the unknown, but he wouldn't have a bar of it. In the end, I couldn't do it; I shot a bit of footage then shut the machine down and walked away.

The internal staircase ended at the fourth floor, which, apart from the mezzanine section that contained the time machine, reverted to alcove after alcove of discs, all except for one particular alcove that was completely empty except for a miniature-size pyramid made of a translucent metal/plastic, about eight inches wide and five inches high, strategically positioned in the exact centre of the floor; it looked like a scaled down version of the Great Pyramid, except it had a very thin wire sticking up about three inches from the top. Did this once form the very tip of the capstone, used as a sort of conductor of electrical and microwave energy? Or was this where Thoth had *"secretly secured his records, his knowledge of the ancient wisdom"*, encoded into the very sub-atomic structure of the mini pyramid? I went to pick it up.

'No, *"to be retrieved when he returned from Amenti"*.'

If I was who I was starting to think I was, to believe I was, then I had some right to this, but 'Thoth' was still in Amenti, and, if I was right, Amenti wasn't so much a place, as a state of consciousness, a dimensional existence above and beyond the 3rd Dimension, and until 'Thoth' chose to return, taking the mini pyramid would be akin to stealing it, and, whilst I may have been a fugitive and public enemy number one as far as the Egyptian Secret Police were concerned, I was no common thief.

At the northern end of the hallway there was an opening in the red granite wall containing a heavy-gauge metal door. There was no door jam, no hinges, no handles or knobs; it was just a smooth plain metal door that had all the appearances of sliding upwards or sidewards into the wall. Without hesitating I played the recording of Diane's maidens, thinking it would hold the key, but nothing happened. This was not a good sign. I played the audio file again, this time adding my own voice into the mix; again, not a rumble. I even tried using the crystal ball to project images onto the door, but nothing worked.

I thought Nemo would be able to help, but all he could show me was the scene back in the King's Chamber, of him lying in the granite coffer and the ladies all singing over him, and I'd tried that, I'd played the recording five times at least. What was I missing?

I slumped down against the door, exhausted, physically, mentally, spiritually, and I hadn't had anything to eat or drink in over 24 hours; if I didn't find a way to open this door soon, I was going to die down here. At least I would have a chorus of angels to send me off.

As the singing came to an end, I sat there in no man's land, in limbo, feeling sorry for myself; maybe I would have to go back to the time machine after all and try my luck, roll the dice and see where and when I finished up; it seemed the only viable option, especially as my iphone had no reception.

As I contemplated my fate, Diane's voice filled the silence.

'Daughters of Aset, you are now invited, each in turn, to lay down in the womb of initiation to complete your rebirthing, your re-membering, and your reawakening. As you do, close your eyes and relax, clear your mind of all thoughts, and centre your soul-force in the place of your consciousness, for you must be pure in mind and in your purpose to achieve your desire to re-member who you truly are and why you have incarnated at this time on earth...'

I closed my eyes and just listened.

'...Place in your mind the image you desire, picture the place you desire to see, vision the Hall of Amenti as described by Thoth. Long with the fullness of your heart to be there, to stand before the Lords of time and space...'

I laughed; I had no need to picture it, I was here. Well, I was in the Hall of Records, perhaps not in Amenti as such, but I merely had to walk down a floor, turn on the time machine, and I could literally stand before the "Lords of time and space".

'Once before them, in your mind, command the words we have rehearsed that you be granted entrance to the realm of wisdom and the great mysteries of life.'

I had no idea what the words were; Bill and I had never been privy to them. And then Diane and the others started toning again, creating the most amazing chords. I remember the whole room pulsating, and the white glow and golden flickers emanating from the coffer.

I listened as each lady took her turn, first Pernille, then Crystal, followed by the others. Then Diane asked if we gentlemen would like a turn?

'...we can't let you use the Lamp of Isis, but you can experience the next best thing.'

"The next best thing"? Wait a minute, I had the next best thing; I had a crystal ball. I took it out again as Diane gave Bill his instructions.

'Just close your eyes and relax, clear your mind of any thoughts, and centre your soul-force in the place of your consciousness. Allow it to take you where it will.'

I held the ball in my hand and did as she said; the ladies soon chorusing like angels, but, nothing! Bill's turn over, it was my turn.

'Now, close your eyes and relax, clear your mind of any thoughts, and centre your soul force in the place of your consciousness. Allow it to take you where it will.'

Still holding the crystal ball, I dropped my hands into my lap and closed my eyes, this time somewhat resigned to my fate. Then Diane started toning, but this time it was different. I realized the iphone had not only recorded my experience in the coffer, but it had been in the coffer with me, resting on my chest. No sooner did they all start toning than the whole room began shimmering in sympathetic vibration, as it had back in the coffer.

And there was that melody again, that short, simple but distinctive melody, which oscillated around the base frequency of the coffer. It was running through my whole body, activating love, spiritual consciousness and awakening within. I could feel it in every cell of my body; I couldn't resist and started humming it. Again, even though my eyes were closed, multicoloured bolts of lightning started flashing inside my head. I opened my eyes to see the crystal ball in my hands was sparkling like a newborn star.

I knew that not only had I opened a massive zip file within my DNA but I'd released the history of every single sub-atomic particle within it, not just in this moment, but every moment since the creation of 'time'. The secret to the sarcophagi wasn't just that they recalibrated and rejuvenated your physical body, they transported you to Amenti, and that's where I was now, Amenti.

'Mekut-El-Shab-El Hale-Sur-Ben-El-Zabrut Zin-Efrim-Quar-El'

Diane's whispered voice echoed through the hall, echoed through my very being; it had been picked up by the iphone's microphone. And I knew what it meant: *"Relax your mind and your body. Then be sure your soul will be called. "* Then:

'Edom-El-Ahim-Sabbert-Zur Adom.'

"Open, I command, by the Secret of Secrets" It was a message: surrender your attachments to the physical, to your mind and your body, and you can enter the realms of higher consciousness, the Halls of Amenti.

Suddenly I felt the metal door at my back start humming and it slowly began rising, jolting me back to 'the present'. Not knowing how long it would stay open, I didn't piss-fart around, I grabbed the backpack and scurried through like a startled rat; how quickly one could come back down to earth!

As the door slowly lowered and then closed behind me, I suddenly found myself in complete darkness, the sort of darkness that is blacker than black, the sort of pitch-black darkness that is claustrophobic and smothers you in fear. Add to that the complete silence of nothingness and it made for a pretty abrupt change in my circumstances. To compound things even more, as opposed to the fresh clean air of the Halls of Records, the air here was foul, an accretion of all sorts of rancid smells accumulated over many forgotten centuries; it was perhaps the most horrifying stench that had ever assaulted my nostrils and brought me to the brink of dry-retching. Like a scene from Indian Jones, I feared I had stumbled into some sort of ancient booby trap and been entombed forever with the hundreds of decaying bodies of past grave-robbers and treasure hunters.

At first, a desperate, panic-stricken urge came over me, get out, go back, but if this was the dragon's breath, then I had to face the dragon, and that meant journeying into the dragon's den, and if I had to do it, then I had to do it. There's an old saying, "when you're going through hell, keep going", and that's what I intended to do, keep going, hopefully onward and upward.

I used the light from my iphone to cast some illumination on my situation, a small foyer, roughly carved out of the limestone bedrock, with an arched ceiling, and a rock slab cut into one wall as a bench; it reminded me of some of the 'tombs' I had seen at Wadi Hillal, Amarna, and in Aswan. I wondered if it was a waiting room, where priests, or persons of stature, awaited admission into the Great Halls behind me? That's what it appeared to be. Thankfully there were no rotting corpses, just, in total contrast to the almost sterile conditions on the previous side of the door, inches and inches of dust, mildew and mould.

There was no lighting system in here so I used my iphone to further illuminate the chamber, scanning the walls, which had a few basic reliefs carved into them, my attention quickly drawn to a steep narrow staircase cut in the opposite wall; this was no tomb after all, this had to be the staircase the 1976 team had used, which meant the end was in sight, albeit a thousand feet straight up.

The rise of Sothis

The rough-cut staircase was tight, maybe two-and-a-half feet wide, of jagged crudely cut stone, with just over six feet of headroom, meaning several things, first, that I had to carry my hat, second, I was constantly ducking to avoid bashing my head against the rough-cut ceiling, third, it was too small for the Annunaki to use. And it was steep, easily over 45 degrees, with irregularly cut steps meaning I often stumbled and risked rolling my ankle; the ascent from hell – literally!

As I started upwards, I tried to figure out how long it would take me to reach the top. It was supposedly 980 feet straight up from the Hall of Records to the secret door on the south face of the Great Pyramid, say 1000 feet; that was 12,000 inches. If each step was around six inches, that would be 2,000 steps. If I could do conservatively 40 steps per minute then it would take me 50 minutes, say a hour, to cover 2000 steps; not a problem, I could do that. Of course there was no certainty I would be able to open the secret door at the other end, but I figured if the recordings of Diane's 'Maidens of Avalon' had worked for the main door into the Hall of Records, and the Amenti chant had worked for the metal exit door, then it would most likely work elsewhere. Never the less, I set off to climb my mountain.

Within a few steps, my schedule was disintegrating before my eyes, as every tread was covered in several inches of dust over a thick slimy gunk, and each step stirred up billowing clouds of choking dust laced with mould and mildew. My first solution was to press on and try to 'outrun' the pungent mildew-reeking dust-storm that brewed up from below, but that resulted in me slipping and stumbling face first onto higher steps, crashing against the ragged walls which were at times as sharp as coral, or bashing my head on the jagged ceiling. This was not going to be as 'easy' as I thought; I was experiencing my own version of 'Touching the Void'.

Suddenly I got the real meaning of the film, of the book, I'd read the book twice and seen the movie/doco three times, but never put two and two together; "Touching the Void" was a metaphor. Through a series of dramatic and traumatic events, Joe had been pushed to the limits of his physical and mental existence. Somehow, having taken as much as he could, he reached what he perceived were his limits, and surrendered, only to discover an altered state of being in which he broached those limits, and, in the process, found a temporary and tenuous connection to 'the Void', to 'The One'. Despite his condition, or perhaps because of it, Joe found his way to base camp, with a massively shattered leg, severely dehydrated, and in a quasi-delirious state. If Joe could do it, with all his obstacles, Christ, he had massive boulders to negotiate, then I could scale a simple staircase.

Like Joe, one trepidatious step at a time, I resorted to walking like I was creeping through a minefield, gingerly placing each foot slowly up onto each step. It reduced the problems of the dust-cloud enough for me to cope with the dust, but it meant my pace was significantly slowed and my energy reserves quickly depleted.

About fifty steps up, the staircase turned back on itself, a small slab protruding from the wall. I took the opportunity to take a break and revise my battle plan.

'Fifty steps; one flight, shit, one down, thirty-nine to go.'

In 'Touching the Void', Joe had set himself simple tasks, such as to get to the next big rock, say fifty metres away, in twenty minutes, and he achieved the bigger task of getting off the mountain by achieving innumerable smaller, achievable tasks, along the way. Before I left Australia, I would regularly swim laps of the pool to keep fit, and I would count it off by the lap number and the number of strokes per lap, 1.1, 1.2, 1.3, etcetera as it helped pass the time. Like Joe, I decided to tune out to the bigger task and focus on the smaller tasks, on the numbers, quickly discovering there was a uniform 57 steps per flight of steps, each flight with a protruding slab at the top, perhaps to rest on, but barely wide enough for one of my ass cheeks.

I ignored the resting spots and persisted; to make it easier, I divided each flight into three groups of 20, using the rhythm of the counting to drive me forward at a constant pace, albeit a slow one as the flights oscillated back and forward, north/south, as they climbed up into the Great Pyramid. Systematically I ticked off each 'lap' as I completed it with a resounding "yes" before reviewing it as part of the overall plan; 4 flights down was a tenth complete, 5 down was an eighth completed, ten down was a quarter of the way there. Sixteen flights completed was $2/5^{ths}$ done; it was simple, just focus, count, and keep to the rhythm.

As I was ascending the 18th flight, my mind started drifting to completing the 20th flight, which would be half way. As a consequence, as I reached the top of the flight, my foot slipped and I fell, bashing my head against a sharp rock jutting out from the wall. I picked myself up and scrambled up to the landing, sitting on the protruding ledge, feeling the identifiable warmth of blood running down my forehead.

'Shit! Not good.'

I was lucky I hadn't knocked myself out, and, given my circumstances, if I had, there was no guarantee I would ever have awoken.

'Focus, Alex, you've got to focus!'

God, what I wouldn't have given for a glass of water and some fresh air! I sat there trying to pull myself together; I didn't know how bad the cut was, but it seemed to be pretty bad as, a minute later, the blood was still flowing. Not sure what to do, I took my iphone and snapped a photo of the wound so that I could make an assessment.

As I did, the flash revealed an unusual vertical 'crack' set back in the side wall of the landing, unusual in that it seemed free of the dust and mildew that covered everything else. I wasn't sure if it was the knock to the head, or the affect of the flash on my eyes, but the 'crack' seemed to be glowing white, like there was a lighted room beyond it.

I quickly reviewed the photo of my wound; it looked bad, maybe two inches long and the blood was congealed around it in my hair, but I'd live; I certainly wasn't going to get any sympathy where I was. My best bet was to hold my hand to my head to stop the bleeding and get the hell out of here as fast as possible. But then there was 'the crack'.

I stood up, leaned across, and wiped away the centuries of dust that coated the wall, revealing what looked like a door cut into the bedrock. It could easily have been missed by anyone passing by, and, if I hadn't fallen and stopped, I would have by-passed it as well. Even then I wouldn't have noticed it if it hadn't been for that vertical crack that 'glowed' amidst the dust and mildew.

Given the staircase was still cut out of the bedrock, and that I was less than half way, I figured I was still below ground level, which meant the door may have led somewhere near or into the subterranean chamber. I had to go with my intuition, which was telling me to open the door and enter the chamber. With my head still bleeding, and the possibility of more falls, and having to make my way precariously down the exterior of the pyramid once I opened the secret door, assuming I could, it seemed a far better option to connect to the subterranean chamber, then make my way up the descending passage, and hopefully sneak out through the original entrance.

It was a great plan, there was only one problem, how to open the door? I tried playing all the recordings, over and over, including using the crystal ball, but they didn't work, probably because this door was made of limestone, not granite or metal. My last chance was to see if Nemo had any thoughts.

I placed my hands on the door, tuned in, and started toning, hoping that somehow my intentions would open the door. Nemo soon arrived and stood up on his tail, both fins on his hips.

'Have you thought of trying the door knob?'

Nemo had never spoken before, but it didn't really come as a surprise, after all, he was my alter ego. He waved a fin towards the door, as if all I had to do was turn the knob.

'Good one, Nemo, there isn't one.'

'It's hardly going to have a neon sign on it?'

I knew what he meant and started wiping away more of the dust and grime, searching for a release mechanism. It didn't take long before I found it, a protruding block in the wall, and pushed it in. There were no massive sounds of stone grinding against stone, or electrical humming, just a simple dull click. I waited a second or two to see if any thing would happen, but, when it didn't, I pushed against the secret door. Just like in Leedskalnin's Coral Castle, the door pivoted effortlessly on its central axis, revealing a space about two feet wide to either side of the foot-wide limestone slab. Beyond the doorway was a chamber that, in the dim light, appeared to contain several large earthenware jars. Suddenly, all I could think of was clean air and something to drink. I took off the backpack, tossed it through and quickly followed; wedging the backpack into the opening to make sure I wasn't 'accidentally' sealed in.

As I took several deep breaths to clear my lungs of dust, I scanned the room with the light from my iphone, realizing the chamber was filled with numerous sealed jars, along with numerous 'household' goods, including gold cups and a large chair prominently set against the corner of the far wall. I broke the seal on one of the jars and had a sniff, instantly gratified to discover it was filled with wine. I picked up a gold cup, filled it from the jar, and sat down on the chair quaffing several mouthfuls of probably the most vintage wine on the planet, circa 2500 BC, from a sold gold cup adorned with jewels and images of the gods.

'Yes, good year that; not as fruity as the 2501 BC or as full-bodied as the 2502 BC, but a nice drop never-the-less. Perhaps it could do with lying down for another century or two?'

After several mouthfuls, I tentatively checked my head wound, bathing it in wine to hopefully stop the bleeding and to have an antiseptic effect that might prevent me contracting some exotic disease that has lain dormant for 5,000 years. As you might expect, it hurt, and I quickly downed more wine to 'dull the pain'. I lent back in the chair and gave a huge sigh, noticing that, like many of the other pyramid 'tombs' I'd visited, particularly the 'tombs' of Teti and Pepi I, this one also had a vaulted ceiling of large limestone slabs decorated with astronomical scenes of white stars on a black background; except here, like the walls, the images were in pristine condition. As I chilled out, I scanned the room, taking it all in.

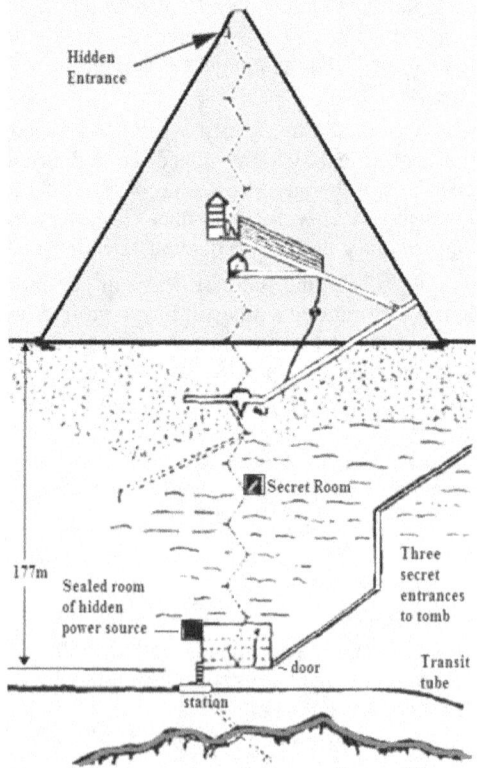

Beyond the jars, the alabaster walls of the chamber were covered in column after column of perfectly preserved Pyramid Texts, the forerunners to the *'Book of the Dead'*, written in bas-relief and painted blue-green; it was as if they had been painted yesterday. The almost 800 known 'spells' supposedly described the different stages of rebirth and assisted the deceased in their journey from death, through the Underworld, to the Afterlife; now I had tasted Amenti, I wasn't so sure that was their original purpose.

Two niches occupied the walls, one to the north, the other to the south; each containing smaller metallic vassals of what I knew must have been essential oils. I reached across and took one, breaking the seal and taking a whiff; it was the same sweet smell that had emanated from the goblet in the Hall of Records.

'This has to be Blue Lotus essence.'

I contemplated the possibilities, then tipped some into my wine.

'What the hell, you only live once, or, rather, a thousand lives all at once.'

Returning the vassal to its niche, I sculled the remainder of the goblet, then topped it up with straight wine.

'This is a fine mess you've gotten me into, Stanley.'

I looked at the innumerable jars of wine laid out before me.

'If the worse comes to the worse, I can always drink myself into oblivion.'

Having quickly exhausted all the humorous ways I could think of to cheer myself up, I reverted to contemplating my actual situation. Clearly I'd discovered some undiscovered store room; maybe I was way off my bearings and this was one of the two large anomalies Lehner and Hawass had detected beneath the second pyramid, one twenty-one metres deep, the other thirty-three metres deep? Maybe it was even an annex of the tomb of Thoth, completely intact since it was sealed back in....well, when was it sealed?

Given the gabled ceiling of limestone slabs and the Pyramid Text decorations on the walls were very similar, if not identical, to the 'tombs' of Unas, Pepi I and Teti, my guess was the chamber was most likely built sometime near the end of the 5th Dynasty, or, if it pre-dated Unas, then maybe around the time of Userkaf and the beginning of the 5th Dynasty, no, no, it was right around the time Imhotep went AWOL in the middle of the 4th Dynasty.

'RIGHT AROUND THE TIME IMHOTEP WENT AWOL?'

Wait a minute! I thought I was right under the Great Pyramid, well, that's where I figured I was, but, if this *was* the 'resting place' of Imhotep, that meant it could also be the resting place of Thoth, which would mean the tomb was under the Great Pyramid and *not* under the Second Pyramid, and, if it was undisturbed, then the doorway in the western wall of the wine cellar I currently found myself in, led to a 'burial chamber' that would surely hold all sort of answers.

I quickly moved on, golden goblet in hand, into the adjacent small vestibule, also completely covered in unspoiled pyramid texts. To the north was a narrow square corridor, to the west, another doorway led into what surely was the 'main chamber. It seemed these chambers had exactly the same structure as the subterranean chambers under the Pyramid of Teti, and that gave me hope of an exit. However, I'd had enough of confined spaces for the moment, so I elected to check out the corridor later, deciding instead to explore the main chamber for evidence of Imhotep.

Again cut out of the bedrock, the chamber was about five metres wide, seven metres high in the centre of the gabled ceiling, and perhaps fifteen metres long. As with the antechamber, the walls were covered in colourful and perfectly preserved

Pyramid Texts, and the vaulted ceiling, with eight pairs of massive limestone blocks, was again decorated with white stars on a black background. But, taking centre stage in the chamber, not pushed up against the western wall as it was in Teti's 'burial' chamber, was a massive black-granite sarcophagus around 14 feet long, 8 feet wide, and at least 10 feet high, the lid still in place; all up it must have weighed nearly a hundred ton. I knocked on the side.

'Anyone home?'

There being no answer, I did a lap of the sarcophagus.

'Feel the stone.'

I stopped along the side, took another swig of wine, put the goblet down, and, as I had in the Serapeum, put my hands on the side wall of the coffer, rested my forehead against the stone, took a few deep breaths to clear my mind and focus, and slowly started to tone a very low pitched 'Aw'. I thought Nemo would appear, as he had in the Serapeum, and the very molecules of the sarcophagus would start to hum and vibrate, but, instead, a figure I knew, Akhenaten, Aak-of-the-consciousness-of-the-sun, appeared, lying within the sarcophagus. For a moment I wondered if I was high on Blue Lotus Essence, pissed from the wine, or had concussion from the fall. Maybe it was all three.

An audience with Thoth

Slowly Aak's eyes opened and he looked out through the side of the sarcophagus, appearing just as the wadjet eyes appeared on the walls of the tomb of Thutmoses III and on sides of the sarcophagi of Thutmoses II, Amenhotep II, Tutankhamen, and Ay, but which were noticeably absent from the sarcophagus of the military pharaoh, Horemheb. Were the wadjet eyes really a representation of the soul's ability to see into other dimensions, an ability triggered or enhanced by the consumption of Blue Lotus Essence? Is that why the eyes were absent from Horemheb's sarcophagus, because he wasn't a member of the Amun Priests? It also explained why the wadjet eyes started just after the time of the Thera eruption, the passing of Nibiru, the arrival of Amenhotep and the Blue Lotus.

Just to be sure I wasn't going crazy, talking to myself, I popped the obvious question.

'Who are you?'

'I have been known by many names.'

'Imhotep? Amenhotep, Akhenaten, Apollo? Thoth?'

'I have been all, and yet none of these are who I am...'

I got it straight away; although an actor may be identified with the roles he has played, he is not one or any of the characters he has played.

'.. who I am is determined by my deeds not my words.'

'Are you dead, or asleep?'

It was only after I'd asked the question, I realized how stupid it was; I'd never known a dead or sleeping person to carry on a conversation. Despite the ridiculousness of my question, Thoth got the gist of my query.

'There is no "death"; death is an illusion. The search for complete Oneness with the consciousness of the universe does not begin with birth any more than it ends with death, it merely continues through the material plane.'

'And to follow the pathway of the Oneness, you must extend your consciousness beyond all time and space; beyond the nine dimensions, beyond the nine cycles of space, beyond the nine diffusions of consciousness, beyond the nine worlds within worlds, and into the void.'

'Exactly. That is why I was entrusted with all of the sacred tones of the twelve star races; to carry them through the nine dimensions of time and space until the appointed time for you to awaken to who I am, to who you are, to the Oneness.'

It was all pretty mind-blowing; was I him, or rather was he, me; Thoth? I still couldn't get my head around the fact Thoth was lying in the coffer before me. Maybe he wasn't, maybe it was just his consciousness?

'So you're more in suspended animation; stasis?'

'You are looking at it from a lower perspective; the body does not form consciousness, consciousness forms the body. Therefore the body may sleep, but the soul is ever-awakened and free to roam where and when it will.'

'So it can incarnate in human form?'

'If it desires.'

'Is that what you desired?'

'I have been deathless, living amongst humans, since human knowledge began.'

'Was that around two-hundred-and-fifty to three-hundred thousand years ago?'

'It was.'

'Why would you wish to incarnate into human form?'

'To assist the development of human consciousness.'

'How?'

'The consciousness of the planet will always seek and create more advanced life forms in which to exist.'

'Is that what happened when humans were created?'

'Yes, consciousness, like all forms of energy, ascends through quantum leaps.'

'Just like the energetic chakras of the body?'

'Yes. In the early millennia of human development the level of consciousness was barely more than that of basic survival, and, while a few individuals have since ascended to the fourth, fifth, even sixth-chakra level of consciousness, as a collective, whilst the bulk of humanity is still experiencing those basic first-chakra survival issues, other elements have moved through second chakra but are currently stuck in third-chakra power struggles.'

'Was that when the Galactic Federation permitted the indirect assistance by incarnating into human form?'

'It was. Human consciousness being a direct descendant of both the Oneness and the star races has the same capacity of thought waves, both being a part of all universal powers. However, the human race, being self-blinded to the meaning of universal law and its purpose, seemed unable to comprehend the true meaning of life. Man continues to neglect the fact that all are born equal, yet in the same breath ridicules the notion of beings of superior intelligence coming from other planets.

Unable to influence humans directly, a select few of our great ancient race, having knowledge and wisdom of the universe gained from many star-born races, insights far beyond that of humans, agreed to incarnate, to pass this knowledge on directly to humans, for to understand how humans think, and the patterns they run that prevent them from understanding the higher pathways, it is not enough to merely observe human behaviour, you must incarnate in human form to not only experience the pattern, but recognize the blocking patterns and learn how to overcome them.

Despite much of our work, over thousands of life times, the majority of the incompetent masses of humans sneer at facts that they cannot or refuse to acknowledge as truth...'

I knew exactly what he meant; until a few days ago I would have firmly been in that camp of blind ignorance. But now I knew, not only had I seen the evidence with my own eyes, but I *knew*; the question was how to present it.

'Do you think there is any hope for the human race?'

'Consciousness always ascends; it is the purpose of the Oneness.'

'Man doesn't seem very conscious.'

'Consciousness is like the great waters that ebb and flow with the tides. Sometimes these seem still, sometimes lapping at the shore, other times surging waves that crash upon the shores of being. Man has risen from a state that was little above that of a beast, and man has fallen, again to rise and fall; many times man has fallen, and each time risen a little higher, as ever new waves of consciousness flow from the great abyss of the void toward the Sun of their goal.'

'So there is hope for mankind?'

'Eventually.'

'Eventually?'

'Before, there were others greater than now, and as others have fallen before, so also shall the reign of current man come to an end.'

'How? When?'

'When man shall again conquer the ocean, and fly like the birds in the air; when he has learned to harness the lightning, then the dark brothers will start a great war between the light and the night that will make the Earth shake to its core.'

We had conquered the ocean, and the air, and had electricity, but, the dark brothers? Who was he referring to, Obama, the Amun Priests, the Dracos?

'What do you know about the Dracos?'

'The truth.'

'Which is?'

'The reptilians live amongst you, in the form and appearance of men but, when unmasked by sound, their true faces can be seen.'

'Where are they?'

'From the Kingdom of Shadows, and taking forms like men, they slithered into the governments and councils, slaying the chiefs of the kingdoms, taking their form, and ruling over man.'

If Randy were here he'd be having kittens, unless, of course, Thoth was another conspiracy theorist. I knew from Thoth's words though that the "Kingdom of Shadows" was another dimension; the 4th Dimension, and that the "chiefs of the kingdoms" were clearly the major leaders of all the major political parties and countries of the world: Bush, Campbell, Clinton, the Royal Family, all of them doppelgangers. It was an invasion of the body snatchers; everything Randy had said, and much more.

'Are the Dracos the ones who will start the war?'

'Yes, and no; the Dracos are the puppet masters, it is the puppets who will wage the war; nation shall rise against nation, using weapons of force to wipe out half of the races of men and using dark forces to shatter the Earth.'

'Nuclear war?'

'Man has developed far greater weapons than you are aware.'

'HAARP?'

'Amongst others.'

'That's terrible.'

'No, it is essential, it will be the catalyst for the next quantum leap of consciousness; without it, the consciousness of man will not progress.'

'But what about all the work being done by the New Age healers and Lightworkers?'

'Only the Self can "heal", as you call it, the unawakened Lightworkers are merely paving the way, for the caterpillar must go through its gut-wrenching metamorphosis to become the butterfly, it MUST go through it, avoiding it is what keeps the caterpillar a caterpillar.

This is why man has fought man, brother has killed brother, throughout the history of man. Man has had sufficient time to take the wise path, now, there is no gentle transition for man.'

'But if man is so pig-headed, how will the wars ever stop?'

'The world in turmoil, as a means to bring the world to consent to one government to fight the common foe, false invasions from the stars shall be imposed upon the masses. However, these deceptions shall have the unseen consequence of uniting the consciousness of man together against a common external foe, man's collective consciousness shall project beyond the planet and a common call shall erupt for a saviour to appear from the galactic realm...'

It was Star Wars all over again.'

'...Once called by the collective consciousness of man, the emissaries of the Galactic Federation shall come forth and show themselves to the children of men, giving their proclamation, saying: "Man, stop your striving against your brother. Cease your belief in false gods and icons, and follow the path to Oneness. This is the only way that you can come to the Oneness".'

Now it was just like the scene out of 'The Day the Earth Stood Still".

'Is that when you will return?'

'I have never left.'

'I mean, when will you return to your body.'

'When men cease from their mindless striving; when brother no longer fights against brother, and father against son. Then, the ancient home of my people will rise from its place beneath the dark ocean waves and a new Age of Enlightenment shall unfold, with all men seeking the path of the goal of Oneness.'

'When will this unfold?'

'All things happen in time, time does not happen in all things; the order is clear, events unfold as predetermined, but time is relative.'

'And there is no escape?'

'Higher realms have determined it is essential for the progress of human consciousness, and contrary to preventing it, they fully encourage it.'

I got it; that's why the Dracos were so important, in fact, without them, nothing would happen, man would basically stay scavenging around like the primates in the forests. But it was more than that, without the intervention of the Dracos man would not have existed at all!

'The script has been written, right, it's all part of the drama?'

'Exactly.'

Then I had a sort of a cross-fade where Thoth disappeared into the background and the whole movie played out before me in glorious Technicolor and quadraphonic sensurround. It was the whole saga, 'The Day the Earth Stood Still" rolled up with the 'Lord of the Rings', 'Star Wars', 'V', 'Armageddon', 'Independence Day' and the 'Star Trek' movies. Throw in a bit of 'Conspiracy Theory' and 'Indiana Jones' to cover my personal involvement and it was a hell of a script! How did it turn out? I don't know; most of the world was at war and a giant fireball was on a crash course with the earth, then, just like in 'The War of the Worlds' the Dracos arrived and started feeding on humans. Just as the good guys were about to arrive from deep space to save the day, I woke up, with a thumping headache, to discover it was pitch black, and I had no idea where I was.

When my head hit the sidewall of the granite sarcophagus, I quickly figured where I was and that I had been curled up beside it. One good thing was that fortunately at least my head wound had stopped bleeding. I fumbled around in the dark for my iphone, which had shut down, and, finding it on the floor beside me, quickly turned it on.

'What, 7:32pm? That can't be right?'

Could I really have been out of it for that long, seven hours at least? Was it even the same day? To be honest I didn't know, I had completely lost track of the days ever since I had been on the run. The date seemed right, but, at that point, given my circumstances and my predicament, it was insignificant; if I died now, no one would know anyway.

I wondered if it was all just a dream, including my conversation with Thoth, or was it all a hallucination caused by the Blue Lotus Essence and the wine, or, had it all really happened? Maybe it was a bit of all three? There was still no reception on my iphone, so I dragged myself to my feet and considered my next move. Simple, get out!

Making my way back to the adjoining vestibule, I checked out the narrow horizontal corridor lined with red granite that headed north. To my chagrin, my trek was soon thwarted by a red-granite portcullis firmly in place. That would be right, out of all the subterranean passages, I find the only portcullis still in place.

I figured that if it was like the other subterranean chambers, like those beneath the pyramids of Teti and Pepi II, the other side led to two more portcullis, which were also probably closed, before an ascending corridor took it somewhere to the surface, possible connecting to the 'well shaft' in the courtyard outside the main entrance of the Great Pyramid that John Cadman thought was part of its hydraulic function, or possibly even to the Trial Passages. If I could open the portcullis then it was a much shorter and quicker escape route, and a much better option than the narrow dust-filled staircase that climbed to the top of the pyramid.

However, though I spent the best part of an hour trying to get the portcullis to move, toning, using the recordings, the crystal ball from the backpack, everything I had tried before, nothing worked. It seemed I had only one option, continue up the claustrophobic, dust-and-mildew-encrusted staircase. I picked up my backpack and tossed in an unopened vassal of Blue Lotus Essence for good measure.

'One for the road, hey, Thoth.'

Then I entered the staircase and reluctantly continued my ascent, determined to do two things; stick to my counting system, and, more importantly, keep an eye out for low bridges and other possible doorways.

Reaching the 20th landing I ticked off the half-way mark, then, at the 21st, on the right hand side, opposite the landing, I saw what looked like another doorway, similar to the previous one, high up and cut into the limestone. I postulated that if Thoth's chamber was somewhere near the pit of the subterranean Chamber, then this door may have connected to the area where the Descending Passage of the Great Pyramid levelled out for 8 to 9 metres, where the piece of red granite was tucked into the 'unfinished' niche to the west of the passage.

If I was right, and I felt I was, it would not only give meaning to the presence of a corridor under and to the west of the horizontal passage discovered by Kerisel in 1992 using GPR, but also to the purpose of the niche; it somehow connected to the hidden staircase.

OK, if all that was right, then I was now probably only about 30 metres below the ground, and if I could open this door, then it was simply a matter of ascending the Descending Passage and I would be free. However, no matter how much I tried, I couldn't reach the door to explore for a secret release mechanism, not by stretching up from the tiny platform, or by trying to scale the walls.

I was screwed, no I was pissed off; it made me even more determined to get out and I slowly and systematically trudged onward and upward until, around the 28th landing, the bedrock suddenly gave way to individual limestone blocks; I had reached the base of the pyramid.

Although I was still surrounded by millions of tons of rock, being above ground level seemed to give me a sense of having escaped already, and that led to my mind wandering, particularly back to my conversation with Thoth.

"When man shall again conquer the ocean, and fly like the birds in the air; when he has learned to harness the lightning, then the dark brothers will start a great war between the light and the night that will make the Earth shake to its core."

I'd read about that before, in the prophecies of Ursula Sontheil, Mother Shipton, who was reputedly born in 1488 in Norfolk, England. I didn't remember the verses in order, but I certainly remembered them.

"And now a word, in uncouth rhyme of what shall be in future time
In water, iron then shall float as easy as a wooden boat.
Beneath the water, men shall walk, shall ride, shall sleep, shall even talk.
When pictures seem alive with movements free,
when boats like fishes swim beneath the sea.
Around the world men's thoughts will fly,
quick as the twinkling of an eye."

That would certainly be a conquering of the ocean and a mastering of electricity, which would be the harnessing of lightning. And she had several references to flying.

"And in the air men shall be seen, In white and black and even green.
When men like birds shall scour the sky."

But, like Nostradamus, it was Mother Shipton's prophecies about the nations and war that had always caught my attention.

"And nations plan horrific war; the like as never seen before.
And Christian one fights Christian two and nations sigh, yet nothing do.
And yellow men great power gain;
from mighty bear with whom they've lain."

Clearly it was a reference to the relationship between China and Russia, and to China becoming the economic superpower it is today.

"These mighty tyrants will fail to do, they fail to split the world in two.
But from their acts a danger bred; an ague, leaving many dead.
Then half the world, deep drenched in blood shall die."

It was all exactly what Thoth said.

"...nation shall rise against nation, using weapons of force to wipe out half of the races of men and using dark forces to shatter the Earth."

Now maybe I was just dredging my subconscious, and the Blue Lotus Essence was using the information from there as fodder for my alter ego, Thoth, to paraphrase? Or maybe Ursula Sontheil was a witch, a high priestess, maybe even a blood descendant of Scota?

Somehow 'Mother Shipton' clearly had access to events from the future, meaning she possibly took hallucinogenic potions, and the fact she was burnt at the stake in 1561 meant that she was no simple peasant woman, or house cleaner, but clearly literate, possibly of royal blood or a noble family, and a clear threat to the established church at the time.

The fact there were so many witch hunts going on in Europe and the UK in the 16th Century made me wonder if there wasn't a secret order of nuns, or priestesses, perhaps even the Daughters of Isis, active in Britain sometime during the 16th Century, that were systematically hunted down and burned at the stake as witches by the church?

Being the only real writers of history at the time, the scribes of the Catholic Church would hardly have told the truth about an order of empowered High Priestesses, especially if they had prophetic powers and knowledge of the universal truths; it was totally logical the church would twist the truth, saying the women were in league with the devil, who, interestingly enough, was a concoction of the Catholic Church and didn't exist in the Goddess based cults of Isis and the Divine Feminine. 'History' must be taken with a pinch of salt.

Even so, it gave another perspective to the tumultuous period from around 1530-1625 AD, with Henry VIII, having renounced the Church of Rome and setting up his own Church of England in 1534, then topping a few wives, burning down the Glastonbury Abbey in 1539, before snuffing it, and leaving his only son, Edward VI, to ascend the throne; I'd always had an interest in the reign of Henry VIII, and remembered watching, with great fervour, the BBC series with Keith Michell in it as the obsequiously obese Henry.

'Oh, Jesus, surely I wasn't Henry VIII?'

The six lives of Henry VIII

No, I wasn't so much interested in Henry, he seemed a bit of an asshole, in fact a total wanker, nor in his last three wives, Anne of Cleaves, Catherine Howard, Catherine Parr. I was always drawn to the lives of the first three wives, Catherine of Aragon, Anne Boleyn and Jane Seymour, the only of Henry's wives who bore him children, Mary, Elizabeth and Edward respectively.

Was it possible, just as Crystal, Bill and I had been in ancient Egypt at the time of Cleopatra, that three of us had incarnated as half-siblings of Henry VIII? In an instant, all the pieces seemed to drop into place; I was Edward VI, Crystal was Mary, and Pernille was Elizabeth. No, it didn't seem right. Yes, Pernille was Elizabeth, but Crystal wasn't Mary, she was Mary's mother, Catherine of Aragon, *I* was Mary, which caught me a bit by surprise as I didn't see myself in high heels and a frock. And what about Bill; was he Edward?

I couldn't figure it out, it didn't feel right. Then I got it, Bill wasn't a sibling, he was Thomas Cranmer, the Boleyn family's chaplain, who later became the Archbishop of Canterbury, but who was eventually burned at the stake; no wonder Bill didn't want to go into the clergy again. And what about Jacques, where did he fit in? It was obvious really; Jacques was...yes, Jacques was the arrogant self-opinionated Henry VIII. So where did that leave Edward VI, there had to be some connection?

Then I wondered why it was that we had all seemingly incarnated over and over into so many royal or influential families? Of course the answer was obvious; if star-seeded beings *are* to have the greatest influence on human development, then it would be wasted to select to be born into the family of a peasant, or a street sweeper, when the greatest influence on human civilization is clearly made by the politicians, law-makers, religious leaders and celebrities of the world.

Mahatma Gandhi, JFK and Princess Diane immediately sprang to mind, perhaps even Angelina Jolie and Michael Jackson. But, if the star-seeded beings *had* incarnated into families so they could have influential lives, how is it that they, that we, had not been successful, and the world was still in such a fucking mess.

Thoth had given me the answer:

"The serpents live amongst you,…taking forms like men, they slithered into the governments and councils, slaying the chiefs of the kingdoms, taking their form, and ruling over man."

From there it was easy to see what happened once the star-seeded beings tried to weave their magic: once they were recognized, 'outed', they were assassinated; Gandhi, JFK, Martin Luther King Junior, Anwar Sadat, even Michael Jackson. I suddenly had more respect for Randy; he may not have had the full picture, but he certain knew more than I knew before I started this adventure. Randy said it was "just the tip of the iceberg', and that "the Catholic Church was deeply entrenched in organizations like the CIA and manipulating the world's political and economical environments". Not only was he right, but it appears it had been going on for centuries.

'History' told many tales, but mainly only those the writers wished to be told. I realized there must be much more to the course of events and decided to take a more 'realistic' appraisal of 'history', starting where I had left off, with the life of Henry VIII, in particular with his first three wives. However, before I could, I arrived at a landing with a different patterning of limestone blocks on the side wall; these being cross-hatched.

I'd seen this pattern before, in the arrangement of the limestone blocks of the horizontal passage that led to the Queen's Chamber. I must be in the cavity behind the west wall of the horizontal passage that leads to the Queen's Chamber, the one discovered in 1986 by Dormion and Goldin using a mirco-gravimeter and confirmed by the Japanese from Waseda University using GPR. I looked for the signs of the three one-inch drill holes authorized by the Egyptian Antiquities Organization, and for other possible doors to other hidden chambers, but, in the dim dust-filled staircase I couldn't find anything, so, rather than risk choking to death in the rising dust cloud I decided to keep moving on.

Continuing my ascent, I turned my thoughts back to Henry VIII, whose first wife, Catherine of Aragon, was actually legitimately more entitled to the English throne than Henry. On her maternal side, she was descended from the English royal house of the Plantagenets; her great-grandmother Catherine of Lancaster, after whom she was named, and her great-great-grandmother Philippa of Lancaster, were both daughters of John of Gaunt, 1st Duke of Lancaster, third son of King Edward III, and thus granddaughters of Edward III, by John's first two marriages, being to Blanche of Lancaster and Constance of Castile. Consequently, Catherine was the third cousin of her father-in-law, Henry VII of England, and fourth cousin of her mother-in-law, Elizabeth of York. More importantly, Catherine was the daughter of Queen Isabella I of Castile and King Ferdinand II of Aragon, which meant that, because of the rule of the Catholic Monarchs at the time, she was part of the most prestigious family in Europe, the house of Trastámara.

Henry VII, on the other hand, was descended from Gaunt's third marriage, to Katherine Swynford, whose children were all born out of wedlock and only legitimised *after* the death of Gaunt's second wife, Constance, his subsequent marriage to Katherine meaning the children of John and Katherine, while ultimately legitimised, were born illegitimate and therefore barred from ever inheriting the English throne; a constraint that was ignored in later generations. However, because of Henry's descent through illegitimate children who were barred from succession to the English throne, the Tudor monarchy was not accepted as a legitimate one by the majority of European kingdoms.

That's probably why, even though Catherine was only three at the time, Henry VII was so keen to arrange a marriage between her and his eldest son, Arthur, Prince of Wales; to sure up the Tudor claim to the throne of England and validate the House of Tudor in the eyes of the European royalty. It would also have meant that a male heir would have had an indisputable claim to the throne of England. Oh, my god, it was King Arthur and Morgause all over again, meaning it was all to do with the sang réal.

For some reason, I suddenly wondered if there was a blood connection between Catherine's mother, the 'Spanish' Isabella I, and Phillip IV of France's daughter, Isabella, who Pernille had been in another life? If there was, then Henry VIII's marriage to Catherine, who was originally the wife of his dead elder brother, Arthur, Prince of Wales, was surely then not just about politics, but possibly also about the *sang réal* as well.

And, if the *sang réal* lineage *was* through Catherine of Aragon, which would make sense, then that meant the *sang réal* had also somehow found its way to Spain, and, if it had, it would most likely have been directly from Mary Magdalene herself, Cleopatra Selene II, via the south of France and down through the ages via the Cathars?

In any case, Arthur and Catherine were married in 1501, but, when Arthur died five months later, it threw the security of the English throne into turmoil, as there were no male heirs. A long civil war, the Wars of the Roses, had been fought the last time a woman inherited the throne, and the disasters were still fresh in Henry VII's memory; the Tudor dynasty was new, and its legitimacy might still be tested. So, to fix the problem Henry VII arranged for Catherine to marry Arthur's younger brother, Henry VIII. However, marriage to Arthur's brother depended on the Pope granting a special dispensation because canonic law forbade men to marry their brother's widow. The problem was overcome when Catherine testified that her marriage to Arthur was never consummated, because, also according to canonic law, a marriage was not valid until consummated. How convenient!

The marriage secured, the next priority was a male heir to secure the legitimacy of the Tudor lineage, and it was, in 1510, less than a year after her marriage to Henry VIII, and now Queen of England, that Catherine gave birth prematurely to a stillborn daughter. Undeterred, a year later she gave birth to a son, Henry, Duke of Cornwall; the legitimacy of the House of Tudor was secured. However, the child only lived for 53 days. Two more sons were born who either were stillborn, or died soon after birth before, in 1516, Catherine delivered a healthy girl, Mary. One more pregnancy ensued resulting in a daughter who lived less than a week.

When Catherine failed to fall pregnant over the next 6 years, it became clear she was no longer fertile. Possibly, being around 35, it was early menopause, but, no matter what the cause, the issue of a producing a male heir had reached critical point. Henry clearly believed that his marriage was wrong in the eyes of God and cursed, seeking confirmation from *'The Bible'*, which says that if a man marries his brother's wife, the couple will be childless.

In 1526, Henry VIII's eye turned to Anne Boleyn, one of Catherine's ladies-in-waiting. He'd already made a mistress of, then discarded, Anne's older sister, Mary, who had been recalled from France in late 1519, ostensibly for her numerous affairs with the French king and his courtiers, and married off in 1520 to William Carey, a minor noble; Henry possibly even fathered two children by her, including a son, Henry

Carey. Henry had already acknowledged he fathered an illegitimate son, Henry Fitzroy, by Elizabeth Blount, Lady Talboys, but what he wanted most was a legitimate heir.

Despite of, and possibly because of, her sister's affair with Henry, Anne acceded to Henry's attentions anyway, taking her place at his side in policy and in state, but not yet in his bed, wisely determining that she would only yield to his embraces as his acknowledged queen. Henry's solution was to have his marriage to Catherine annulled that he might marry Anne.

However, when it was suggested to Catherine that she quietly retire to a nunnery, she was defiant, saying, " I am the King's true and legitimate wife". It seems Crystal was standing up to Jacques even then.

Like Crystal, Catherine was also no fool, no passive accessory or 'trophy wife'; Catherine studied arithmetic, canon and civil law, classical literature, genealogy and heraldry, history, philosophy, religion, and theology. She was a patron of Renaissance humanism, a friend of the great scholars Erasmus of Rotterdam and Thomas More, spoke French, Greek, and learned to speak, read and write in Spanish and Latin, in 1507 holding the position of ambassador for the Spanish Court in England, the first female ambassador in European history to do so.

But, for Catherine, it wasn't all about academia; she was also taught domestic skills, such as cooking, dancing, drawing, embroidery, good manners, lace-making, music, needlepoint, sewing, spinning, and weaving. She also donated large sums of money to several colleges, and also won widespread admiration by starting an extensive program of relief for the poor, and, intent on providing a thorough education for her daughter Mary, Catherine commissioned the controversial book 'The Education of Christian Women' by Juan Luis Vives, which claimed women have the right to an education; making Catherine one of the world's first true women's-libbers. All in all, Catherine was a formidable, and well-supported adversary.

Without having Catherine's acquiescence, Henry set his hopes upon an appeal to the Holy See, and Pope Clement VII. However, following the Sack of Rome in May 1527, the Pope was the prisoner of Catherine's nephew and staunch supporter, Emperor Charles V, so Henry's envoys had extreme difficulty gaining access to him. When they did, the Pope forbade Henry to marry again.

A year later, in 1531, Catherine was banished from court and went to live at the castle of her supporter Thomas More; her old rooms given to Anne Boleyn. Then, when the Archbishop of Canterbury, William Warham, 'died', one would suspect he was poisoned because he refused to marry Henry and Anne, the Boleyn family chaplain, Thomas Cranmer, was appointed to the vacant position. Henry then made Anne the Marquessate of Pembroke in 1532; an appropriate peerage for a future Queen, and which meant she became a rich and important woman who ranked above all other peeresses. Anne was no fool either, during this period playing an important role in England's international position by solidifying an alliance with France.

Cranmer subsequently married Anne to Henry in a secret ceremony in January 1533, possibly because she was already pregnant at the time and Henry didn't want to risk a son being born illegitimate. Further, in May of that year, Cranmer, once the Boleyn family chaplain and now Archbishop of Canterbury, at a special court convened to rule on the validity of Henry's marriage to Catherine, declared the marriage illegal, even though Catherine testified she and Arthur had never consummated their union.

Five days later Cranmer ruled Henry and Anne's marriage to be valid, which you would expect given he probably performed the rites. Less than a month later, Anne was crowned Queen of England with the St Edward's Crown, a crown previously only used to crown a monarch.

It was one conspiracy after another, murder after murder, dodgy deal after dodgy deal, exactly the sort of thing one had come to expect of the Catholic Church and politics, no wonder Bill didn't want to have any part of it again, and the populace seemed right onto it as their response to their new queen was lukewarm at best. Pope Clement wasn't too impressed either, condemning the marriage and reaffirming Henry's marriage to Catherine was legal. Clement ordered Henry to return to Catherine, and, when Henry refused, the Pope excommunicated both Henry and Cranmer.

Several months later, in September 1553, Anne gave birth to a daughter, christened Elizabeth, probably in honour of both Anne's mother, Elizabeth Howard, and Henry's mother, Elizabeth of York. But the birth of a girl must have been a heavy blow to both Henry and Anne as, since all but one of the royal physicians and astrologers had predicted a boy, they both expected a son; it surely must have made Anne uneasy about the long-term prospects of her marriage if she could not produce a male heir.

To add to her concerns, Anne was also being referred to by some of her subjects as "The king's whore" and being blamed for the tyranny of Henry's government. I remembered the disrespectful way Jacques had spoken to Pernille during the felucca trip; nothing much had changed.

The following year, 1534 saw Henry VIII split from the Catholic Church, which ultimately led to the establishment of the Protestant Church of England, but Catherine, whose religious dedication to Catholicism increased as she aged, probably as a way of dealing with her stillborn and lost children, refused to accept Henry as Supreme Head of a Church of England, still considering herself the King's rightful wife, and Queen of England.

Things coming to a head, in 1535, Henry, fearing that if he executed her he would face reprisals from not just his own people, but more so his international adversaries, banished Catherine from court, separating her from Mary and transferring her to Kimbolton Castle, where she confined herself to one room and dressed only in the simple garb of the Order of St. Francis. Henry offered her and Mary better quarters and permission to see each other if they would acknowledge Anne Boleyn as his new Queen, but both Catherine and Mary refused. The following year, 1536, amid rumours that she was poisoned by Anne or Henry, Catherine died, which, rather than resolve issues, left Anne's position as queen still very much in contention.

Anne wasn't the only one whose position was still contentious; I was still climbing flights of steps in virtual darkness, choking dust and rancid smells infiltrating my nostrils, with no guarantee there was even a way out at the top, or, if there was, whether I'd be able to open it; all I had was the recording on my iphone, and if that didn't work, I was history. It made me check the battery level on my iphone.

'Shit, not good.'

If I didn't get out of here soon, the battery would die, and not only wouldn't I be able to play the audio I needed to get out, but I'd be left in pitch-black darkness to try and retrace my steps.

At the next landing, I encountered yet another possible doorway, this one consistent with the position and level of the antechamber off the King's Chamber. Either I was in the 'void' initially discovered by the SRI scans back in 1977, or, the doorway opened on to the tunnel seen by Simon Cox in 1998 that led to the control room that must have sat behind the northern wall of the King's Chamber. Not willing to expend any unnecessary time or power, I had a quick grope around the walls, without success, then figured that even if I could find the trigger to the door and open it, once inside, there was no guarantee I would be able to find my way into the King's Chamber and thus out of the pyramid. Figuring there were perhaps ten flights left until I hit the top, I moved on, picking up my review of English History after the coronation of Anne Boleyn; I didn't know where it was all leading, but, like the staircase, it had to be going somewhere.

Of noble birth, Anne was considered to be "brilliant, charming, driven, elegant, forthright, and graceful", with a "keen wit and a lively, opinionated, and passionate personality"; much as I had seen Pernille since she had left Jacques. Prior to her appointment as a lady-in-waiting to Catherine of Aragon, Anne had gained experience as a lady-in-waiting in the French Court, where she was influenced by an evangelical variety of French humanism that led her to championing the vernacular Bible and becoming a devout Christian devoted to the Virgin Mary in the new tradition of Renaissance humanism.

Anne subsequently held the reformist position that the papacy was a corrupting influence on Christianity, and was sympathetic to those seeking further reformation of the Church, actively protecting scholars working on English translations of the scriptures. Perhaps it was even Anne, opportunistic, driven, and ambitious, who, with the dilemma of Henry's annulment to Catherine having been denied, seized her opportunity and was solely responsible, not only for the later murder of Catherine, but for instigating and driving the whole break from the Catholic Church?

But, Anne also had a sharp tongue and a terrible temper, which may have contributed to her demise, especially when, in late 1534, Henry began lavishing his attention on another lady-in-waiting, Jane Seymour. Later that month, after Anne saw Jane sitting on Henry's lap, she flew into a rage, and miscarried what would have been Henry's long-yearned-for male heir.

Subsequently, public opinion really turned against her and it sank even lower after the execution of her enemy Sir Thomas More. The writing was on the wall and Anne's circumstances were tenuous at best, with Henry having discussions with Cranmer and Thomas Cromwell about the possibility of divorcing her without having to return to Catherine. However, Anne received a 'stay of execution', when, by October 1535, she was again pregnant.

Catherine's 'untimely' death, in January 1536, should have made life easier for Anne. However, with Catherine dead, Henry would now be free to marry without any taint of illegality, and that threw enormous pressure on Anne; she was well aware of the dangers if she failed to give birth to a son. Then, on the very day of Catherine's funeral, Anne miscarried again, this time a 3½-month-old male foetus; it marked the beginning of the end of the royal marriage, for, whilst Henry was clearly disappointed with the birth of Elizabeth, the two subsequent miscarriages of potential male heirs would have infuriated him, so much so that, as Anne recovered from her miscarriage, Henry declared that he had been seduced into the marriage by means of "sortilege", meaning by "deception" or "spells".

By March 1536, Henry had set his sights on making Jane Seymour his new queen, and that meant Henry had to 'dispose' of Anne. No messing around with papal dispositions this time; a month later, towards the end of April, several alleged 'suitors' of Anne's were arrested, including Anne's own brother, George Boleyn, who was arrested on two charges of incest and of treason. Anne was subsequently accused of adultery, incest, witchcraft, and high treason, adultery on the part of a queen constituting a form of treason for which the penalty for a woman was burning alive.

The accusations, especially those of incestuous adultery, were specifically designed to destroy her moral character, and, with Anne thrown into the Tower of London, Henry quickly moved his new mistress, Jane Seymour, into the royal quarters. Anne's only hope was a fair trail

Anne was in deep shit and had few supporters; she'd argued with Chancellor Thomas Cromwell over the redistribution of Church revenues and over foreign policy, advocating that revenues be distributed to charitable and educational institutions, and she favoured a French alliance, whereas Cromwell insisted on filling the King's depleted coffers, of course taking a cut for himself, and preferred an imperial alliance. Even Thomas Cranmer covered his own butt and abandoned her, on 14 May declaring Anne's marriage to Henry null and void.

Once the marriage was annulled, matters moved fast; three days later, on 17th May 1536, Anne's brother, George, and the other accused men were all executed. Henry presided over her 'trial' and 'magnanimously' commuted Anne's sentence from burning to beheading, and, rather than have a queen beheaded with a common axe, brought an expert swordsman from France who performed the dirty deed two days later on 19th May 1536.

There were no quick flights on Ryan Air across the channel in those days, it would have take a week or two at least, which means Henry had decided her fate well before the trial was even started.

A day after Anne's execution, Henry was betrothed to Jane Seymour, a descendant of King Edward III through her maternal grandfather, Lionel of Antwerp, 1st Duke of Clarence; meaning Henry and her were fifth cousins. She was also a second-cousin to Anne Boleyn.

The marriage itself took place ten days later and she was publicly proclaimed queen consort on 4th June, though never crowned due to the plague, which was doing the rounds of London at the time, although it's possible Henry may have been reluctant to crown Jane before she'd fulfilled her 'duty' by bearing him a male heir.

As Mary and Elizabeth's step mother, Jane put considerable effort into reconciling Henry with his daughters, and, whilst not succeeding in restoring them to the line of succession, she *was* able to get Mary restored to the court, forming a very close relationship with her in the process.

In early 1537, Jane became pregnant and subsequently gave birth to the long coveted male heir, the future Edward VI, on 12 October 1537. Both Mary, as his godmother, and Elizabeth, attended their brother's christening, carrying his train during the ceremony, but Jane was absent, recovering from a long and complicated labour. Less than two weeks after the birth, she died from complications surrounding the birth, the only one of Henry's wives to receive a queen's funeral.

The fact Henry didn't remarry for three years, becoming obese and developing diabetes and gout, and that he was ultimately buried beside her, raises considerable speculation that Jane was clearly Henry's favourite wife.

Over the next seven years, three more wives ensued; Anne of Cleaves, who lasted six months before the marriage was mutually annulled, Catherine Howard, who was Anne Boleyn's first-cousin and ended up similarly 'topped' less than 18 months later, and finally Catherine Parr, who, in 1543, encouraged Henry to invite his children to spend Christmas with him.

It signalled Henry's reconciliation with his daughters, whom he had previously disinherited and deemed illegitimate; the following spring restoring them to their place in the succession with a 'Third Succession Act', which also provided for a

Regency Council during Edward's minority should Henry not survive until Edward reached the age of majority. It was also in 1543, on 1st July, that Henry VIII signed the 'Treaty of Greenwich' with the Scots, sealing the peace with Edward's betrothal to the seven-month-old Mary, Queen of Scots.

One had to wonder, given Scotland was on its knees and in such a poor bargaining position, why Henry would make such a deal? Unless, like his father before him, he wanted to secure the Tudor claim to the English throne and annex the throne of Scotland. However, Henry stipulated that, as part of the deal, Mary be handed over to him to be brought up in England. The Scots must have smelled a rat and rejected the treaty in December 1543, renewing their alliance with France. Henry was enraged and ordered Edward's uncle, Edward Seymour, Earl of Hertford, to invade Scotland and "put all to fire and sword".

What was the significance of the Scottish connection, why was Henry so concerned with their actions, was it because of the *sang réal*? Did it run all the way back to Robert the Bruce, thus to Scota and ancient Egypt? Is that why I was so preoccupied with this period of English and Scottish history?

The clue had to be something to do with the Rosslyn Chapel and the Templar knights, because the Church were controlling the state in both France and England in 1307 when the Templars were routed and escaped to Scotland. I remembered what Bill had said earlier in the trip about Rosslyn Chapel:

"It was completed in the 1480's by William St Clair, the founder of Freemasonry."

William St Clair? That's William *Sinclair*, 1st Earl of Caithness of the Scoto-Norman Sinclair family, grandson of Henry Sinclair, 1st Earl of Orkney and son of Henry Sinclair, 2nd Earl of Orkney, one time, protector of the young James Stewart, the later James I of Scotland.

The Sinclair ancestry was comprehensively represented in both Scottish and British high nobility thanks to the marriages of William's daughters and other descendants. In particular, William's daughter, Lady Eleanor Sinclair, by his second wife, Marjory Sutherland, married John Stewart, 1st Earl of Atholl, a relative of the king's. Lord Henry Darnley, who married Mary Stuart, Queen of Scots, and their son, James VI of Scotland, who was to later become James I of England, descended from Eleanor, and through them, many of the royal houses of Europe.

The Stewarts were similarly well represented, if not more so, the House of Stewart having gained the throne of Scotland by the marriage of Marjorie Bruce, daughter of Robert the Bruce, to Walter Stewart, 6th High Steward of Scotland. It was all coming together; the templars had the money to 'buy' into any royal family, and, once again, the *sang réal* was coming into prominence, because, as I'd realized earlier in the trip, I was Robert the Bruce and my journey was to break down the pillars of 'truth' that had been falsely erected on the history of the world.

It got me thinking, were the Templars, or, as they had 'evolved', the 'Freemasons', the ones really behind the 'split' from the Catholic Church and the establishment of the Church of England? They certainly had good cause. If they weren't, then they soon infiltrated and took control of the Church of England. And it probably all started when Henry VIII finally kicked the bucket in 1547 and the nine-year old Edward VI ascended the throne.

At the coronation, Thomas Cranmer, as Archbishop of Canterbury, affirmed the royal supremacy and called Edward a second Josiah, the biblical king who destroyed the idols of Baal. Cranmer urged Edward to continue the reformation of the Church of England, but what would a nine-year-old know about anything, especially religion; it was more a reflection of Cramer's hunger for power than a theologically inspired reformation. In particular, the confiscation of Catholic church property that had begun under Henry VIII resumed under Edward to the great monetary advantage of the crown but more so to the new owners of the seized property. Church 'reform' under Edward VI was not really just an expansion of the rejection of papal supremacy so that Henry VIII could annul his first marriage, in Cranmer's hands, it became more of a 'land grab', more so a political than religious policy.

Apart from a few minor changes and the inclusion of compulsory services in English, which drew in the uneducated masses, the 'new' Protestant religion was still essentially the same as the 'old' Catholic one. But, by the end of Edward's reign, the 'catholic' church had been financially ruined, with much of the property of the bishops transferred into the hands of the English nobility. And it was so easy to do.

As Edward was just a boy, the kingdom was governed by a Regency Council; sixteen executors named in Henry VIII's will, who were to act as Edward's Council until he reached the age of 18. However, the council was hijacked by Edward's uncle, Edward Seymour, 1st Earl of Hertford, who 'bought off' at least thirteen of the council to be announced as Lord Protector of the Realm, Governor of the King's Person, and 1st Duke of Somerset, giving him almost regal powers and calling on the Council to do little more than rubber-stamp his decisions. And who would Edward Seymour have had to support him most, none other than the one-time family chaplain, and now Archbishop of Canterbury, Thomas Cranmer.

But, the Duke of Somerset didn't have things all his own way and faced less-manageable opposition from his power-hungry younger brother, Thomas Seymour, who, in the Spring of 1547, moved quickly to secretly marry Henry VIII's widow, Catherine Parr, whose household happened to include the 11-year-old Lady Jane Grey, Edward's first cousin once removed, and the 13-year-old Lady Elizabeth, Edward's half-sister.

During the summer that was to follow, Catherine, now pregnant with Thomas Seymour's child, discovered him 'inappropriately embracing' Lady Elizabeth, and, as a result, Elizabeth was removed from the household. That September, Catherine died in childbirth, and Thomas Seymour promptly resumed directing his attentions to Elizabeth, planning to marry her. Elizabeth was open to the proposition, however, like Edward, unwilling to agree to anything unless the Council authorized it.

I couldn't believe how, time after time, the women were just pawns in the power-games of the men and how yet another religion had been created because of the greed of megalomaniacs. But, then again, the men didn't always have it their own way, and, if you play with fire, sooner or later, you're going to get your ass burned. So it was for Thomas Seymour, when, in January 1549, the Council had him arrested on various charges, and, two months later, beheaded.

Things didn't fare any better for his brother, the Duke of Somerset, either. Edward VI's early reign was marked by economic problems, social unrest, riots and rebellion around the country, and an expensive unsuccessful war with Scotland. By autumn 1549, the crown faced financial ruin, and whatever the popular view of the Duke of Somerset was, the disastrous events of 1549 were taken as evidence of a colossal failure of the government, and the Council laid the responsibility right at Edward Seymour's feet. They had him arrested on numerous charges, but John Dudley, the 1st Earl of Warwick, convinced parliament to set him free, which it did in January 1550.

Dudley then had Seymour and his followers purged from the Council and, in 1551, after winning the support of Council members in return for titles, was made the

Duke of Northumberland, Lord President of the Council, and Great Master of the King's Household, which meant that, although not called a Protector, he was now clearly the head of the government. Seymour may have felt he avoided the hangman's noose, however, although he was released from the Tower, he was eventually beheaded for felony in January 1552 after scheming to overthrow Dudley's new regime.

Lacking his predecessor's blood-relationship with the king, Dudley went about adding members from his own faction to the Council in order to control it, and, when Edward VI fell ill in February 1553 at the age of just 15, Dudley added members of his own family to the royal household.

The big question was, if Edward died, and it appeared certain his sickness was terminal, probably tuberculosis, who stood to lose the most? According to the 'Third Succession Act' the throne would pass to Mary, who, no doubt would reinstitute the Catholic religion, reclaim all the lands for the church, rescind all the titles, and more than likely behead Thomas Cranmer and all those involved in the Protestant rebellion. The power-brokers behind the throne could not permit that to happen.

So, Dudley no doubt conceived a plan, with Cranmer's agreement, and the full support of the Council, to convince Edward VI that unless something were done, the king's death, and the succession of his Catholic half-sister Mary to the throne, would totally jeopardize the English Reformation, that Edward should not only oppose Mary's succession on religious grounds, but also on those of her 'illegitimacy', which also applied to Elizabeth.

By June, Edward was coughing up the greenish yellow and black, sometimes pink, sputum characteristic of tuberculosis, his legs became swollen, and he was bedridden; death was imminent. Dudley acted quickly, and in June 1553, though bedridden, Edward supposedly composed a draft document, headed "My devise for the succession", more likely drafted by Dudley and the Council, in which Edward undertook to change the succession, supposedly to prevent the country's return to Catholicism, but really, unbeknownst to Edward, it was to protect the titles and estates of the sycophantic members of his Council.

In the document, Edward passed over the legitimate claims of his half-sisters. Mary and Elizabeth, and named his 16-year-old cousin, Lady Jane Grey, as his heir, who, surprise, surprise, had been married less than a month earlier to Lord Guilford Dudley, a younger son of the Duke of Northumberland.

Less than a month later, on 6th July 1553, Edward died at the age of 15. The cause of his death is not certain, but rumours of poisoning abounded, one theory being it was Catholics seeking to bring Mary to the throne, another that it was the Duke of Northumberland himself. My money was on the Duke; I think he honestly believed the 'Devise for the Succession" would hold sway and his son would be king.

However, Mary must have caught wind of Edward's imminent death and she sped to her estates in Norfolk to prepare. In reaction, and obviously fearing reprisals from Mary once his plans were exposed, Northumberland delayed the announcement of Edward's death while he gathered his forces, sending ships to the Norfolk coast to prevent Mary's escape or the arrival of French Catholic reinforcements from the continent.

Four days after Edward's death, on 10th July 1553, Lady Jane Grey, now Northumberland's daughter-in-law, was taken to the Tower of London where she was proclaimed queen. Subsequently, the Council received a message from Mary asserting Mary's "right and title" to the throne, and commanding that the Council proclaim *her* queen. The Council replied that, by Edward's authority, Jane was queen, and that Mary was illegitimate; the gloves were well and truly off.

Mary's letter made Northumberland quickly realize he'd drastically miscalculated in failing to secure Mary's person before Edward's death, so, on 14th July, Northumberland marched out of London with three thousand men, intent on capturing Mary. What Dudley didn't know was, that in anticipation of trouble, Mary had gathered an army of nearly twenty thousand. Weighing up the odds, the Council suddenly realized it had made a terrible mistake, and, on 19th July, publicly proclaimed Mary as queen, the proclamation triggering wild rejoicing throughout London and bringing Jane's nine-day reign to an end.

I could see the parallels between Queen Mary, and myself; both of us were interesting and complex characters, and neither of us suffered fools. Mary had always been furious at her father's rejection of her mother, and at the annulment, which subsequently resulted in Mary being labelled illegitimate, so, as soon as she took the throne, she took action; Northumberland was immediately beheaded, despite his renouncing Protestantism. Then, not wanting to make the same mistake as Dudley, Mary imprisoned her half-sister, Elizabeth, in the Tower of London for a year, no doubt to also dissuade and prevent any Protestant reprisal. As for her cousin and brief predecessor, Lady Jane Grey, the innocent pawn in proceedings, she was initially spared, though kept under lock and key.

Mary then married Prince Phillip of Spain, who was the only son of Charles V, the Holy Roman Emperor, both to secure her position, and to restore Catholicism as the English religion. When a Protestant reprisal ensued, Lady Jane eventually felt the cold hard steel of the executioner's blade due to her father's involvement in the Protestant rebellion, even though she was not involved. To top it off Mary had about 300 Protestants and clergyman, including Thomas Cranmer, the Protestant Archbishop of Canterbury, burned at the stake, resulting in her subsequently being referred to as 'Bloody Mary'.

However, although she burned a number of leading Protestant churchmen at the stake, many reformers either went into exile or remained subversively active in England during her reign, producing a torrent of reforming propaganda that she was unable to stem. In fact, Queen Mary's attempts to undo the reforming work of her brother's reign faced major obstacles, one of those being the contradiction that, despite her belief in the papal supremacy, she ruled constitutionally as the Supreme Head of the English Church.

I found it hard to believe that one woman was responsible for all that 'blood'; there is no way she could have accumulated twenty thousand men on her own for starters. Second, she initially spared Jane's life. Clearly Mary was being used as an instrument of the Catholic Church, her marriage to Prince Phillip of Spain *had* to have been orchestrated from the Spanish side, the Catholics, and burning people at the stake was traditionally a Catholic way of showing off their muscles and warning people not to get in their way; so was Mary a pious proprietress, or yet another puppet?

Either way, Mary's reign was to be short-lived and she died a few years later, in 1558, supposedly from 'influenza'. However, given Mary was also in pain, with, as some have suggested, ovarian cysts or uterine cancer, and that Cardinal Reginald Pole, Archbishop of Canterbury, who was instrumental in the burning of the 300 protestants, also died of 'flu' on that very day, it is worth considering the strong probability that Mary was poisoned by Protestant conspirators supporting Mary's half-sister.

Once crowned, one of Elizabeth's first actions as queen, was to establish the English Protestant church with herself as the Supreme Governor, much to the protests of many Catholics who, despite the 'Third Succession Act' passed by the Parliament of England in 1543 that recognized Elizabeth as her sister's heir to the English throne, still maintained Elizabeth was illegitimate, and that Mary Stuart, Mary Queen of Scots, as grand daughter and senior descendant of Henry VIII's elder sister, Margaret Tutor, was the rightful queen of England. Of course it had nothing to do with the fact Mary Stuart also just happened to be Catholic!

After the short reigns of Elizabeth's half-siblings, it was expected that Elizabeth, now 24, would marry and produce an heir to the Tudor line, however, despite several courtships, she never did, and, as she grew older, Elizabeth became famous for her virginity; a cult growing up around her which was celebrated in the portraits, pageants, and literature of the day. But that's not how I saw it.

Some historians believe that when she was just 14 years of age, Elizabeth experienced an "emotional crisis" while living with Catherine Parr and Thomas Seymour; a crisis that affected her for the rest of her life. Thomas Seymour, approaching 40 apparently engaged in romps and horseplay with Elizabeth, including entering her bedroom in his nightgown, "tickling" her and slapping her on the buttocks. Catherine apparently joined in, twice accompanying him in "tickling" Elizabeth, and once holding her while he cut her black gown "into a thousand pieces". It was only once Parr discovered the pair in an "embrace", that she ended things and sent Elizabeth away.

Come on, folks, we're talking about an emerging teenager with raging hormones who, yes, is being seduced, but who is also learning about the sexual power and attraction of her own body, and its power over men. I think the "embrace" was far more inappropriate than has been made out; remember, the historians at the time were referring to actions involving the possible future queen of England and had to be very careful what they wrote. I think Parr discovered Seymour and Elizabeth bumping uglies, doing the horizontal lambada, coitus interruptus.

What is telling is, first, that when details of Seymour's behaviour was exposed, it resulted in his execution, so it must have been pretty serious, second, that Elizabeth was willing to marry Seymour if the council agreed to it showed some emotional attachment to him beyond a simple crush, and, third, that Elizabeth refused to say anything about their personal 'interactions', not just to protect Seymour, but more to protect her own reputation. The fact that Elizabeth said nothing, said a lot, and what it said to me was that she avoided marriage during her reign because she *wasn't* a virgin, because she had been deflowered by Thomas Seymour. The 'Virgin Queen' ruse was to ensure her secret could never be discovered. What is does explain was her disposition; possibly bi-sexual, possibly a submissive in BDSM terms, sexual frustrated, and emotional retarded, Elizabeth was at times flirty, at others, outward cold, dispassionate and a right royal bitch.

That said, it's not surprising that Elizabeth's reign included several conspiracies that threatened both her reign and her life, including ones from her Catholic cousin in Scotland, Mary Stuart, Queen of Scots, the only surviving legitimate child of King James V of Scotland. Mary had previously claimed Elizabeth's throne as her own and was considered the legitimate sovereign of England by many English Catholics. However, in 1567, after twenty-five years as Queen of Scotland, Mary was forced to abdicate in favour of her one-year-old son, James VI, and, after an unsuccessful attempt to regain the Scottish throne, for which she was imprisoned, Mary escaped and fled southwards, seeking the protection of Elizabeth.

But, Elizabeth was no fool, and, rather than Mary receiving protection, Elizabeth perceived her as a threat and had Mary confined in various castles and manor houses through the interior of England until, in 1587, after 18½ years in custody, Mary was found guilty of plotting to assassinate Elizabeth, and executed.

Then,

after a reign of 44 years, marked by the defeat of the Spanish Armada by Sir Francis Drake in 1588, and famous for the flourishing of English drama in the 1590s through playwrights such as William Shakespeare and Christopher Marlowe, a reign that provided welcome stability for the kingdom and helped forge a sense of national identity, on March 24th 1602, after a short illness, Elizabeth died, childless. Hours later, James VI of Scotland was proclaimed James I of England.

James was the only son of Mary, Queen of Scots, and her second husband, Henry Stuart, Lord Darnley, both of whom were great-grandchildren of Henry VII of England through Margaret Tudor, the older sister of Henry VIII which made James a great-great-grandson of King Henry VII through *both* his parents; there was that inbreeding again, and consistent with maintaining the *sang réal*.

With Elizabeth dying childless, James VI was the logical successor to the English throne. And that's when it got really interesting; The Freemasons, the House of Stuart, the *sang réal*, had it returned to it's Scottish lineage? James VI of Scotland, the descendant of Mary Stuart, the descendant of Eleanor Sinclair, and the House of Stewart all related back to Marjorie Bruce, daughter of Robert the Bruce; it seemed it had. It meant that with James VI of Scotland, now James I of England, the English and Scottish lineages of the *sang réal* had finally melded.

It seems that, despite his marriage and fathering of seven children to Anne of Denmark, that James may have been gay, bi-sexual for sure, as he had many male suitors. It was also reflected in his persecution of 'witches' in Scotland under the Witchcraft Act 1563. Interestingly, James apparently once considered witchcraft a branch of theology, but, following his return to Scotland from Denmark, James became obsessed with the threat posed by witches and, personally supervised the torture of women accused of being witches. One wonders if the real reason wasn't the suppression of any other 'religion' or belief system, especially one that involved empowered and psychic women.

Possibly in response, it was King James I who created and authorized the 'King James version' of *'The Bible'*, which became the standard bible for the next few hundred years. One can quite easily see that it was not so much James, as his Protestant supporters, who translated and edited the text to suit their purposes.

It was also James I who chartered the 'colonization' of America; that came as no surprise, for it was his ancestors, the Knights of Templar, who had first sailed there after their escape from France three-hundred years earlier. But clearly the rifts with the Catholic Church persisted, with Guy Fawkes and his Catholic conspirators, including Thomas Percy, attempting to blow up the English Protestant parliament in 1605.

What was interesting about Thomas Percy was that he was the ancestor of both President George Bush *and* his wife Barbara, the 'disgraced' Percy name being changed to Pierce when it came to America. I'd read recently where a 12-year-old-girl in the US had discovered that all the US presidents were related by blood back to King John of England, also known as John 'Lackland', the 'evil' brother of King Richard the Lionheart and the villain in the Robin Hood story; the same King John who was known for signing the Magna Carta in 1215 that limited the monarch's power and helped form the British Parliament.

That took the bloodline back from James, through the Stuarts and Tudors, through the Plantagenets, through Henry III to around the same time the early crusades were happening. It meant that if the 'English' bloodline of the *sang réal* went back through King John, then somehow it must have connected through Alfred the Great to the time of King Arthur and 'Camelot' as well. And if every US president was related by blood back to king Arthur, that raised the question that, if all US presidents are 'democratically elected', how is it that American's always seem to have to choose from candidates that have ALL descended from the English monarchy, not just on one side of politics, but on both? And that opened up not only the whole USA deception, but the global deception, because if it had been happening in the US since its beginnings, then it had been going on in Europe for centuries.

Before I could explore the issue of the European descent of the *sang réal* any further, the ceiling suddenly opened up into a void, whilst ahead it closed in to seal off the staircase; this must have been the sealing stone, the secret door. I had reached my destination, the top of the staircase, and none to soon, as my thighs were burning, my parched throat and nostrils clogged with mildewed dust, and my head was throbbing. It was 10:54 pm, and I was tired, sore, and hungry; to make matters worse, my iphone's battery was on its last legs; but one more door and I was free.

The end of the road

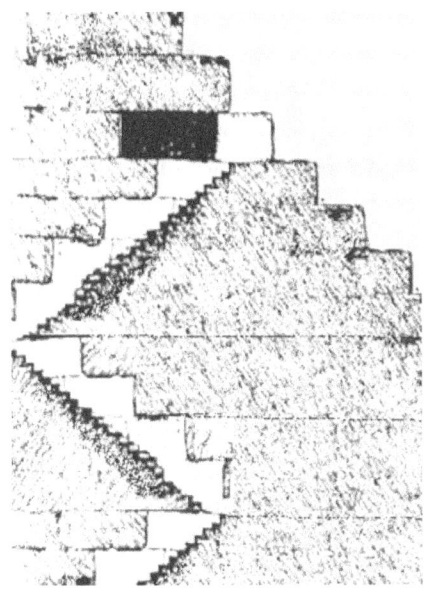

I didn't waste any time, turning on the recording of Diane's 'Chorus of Angel's', toning and tuning in to the blocking stone. Initially, there was nothing; even when I called on Nemo and took out the crystal ball, all I could see beyond the secret door, assuming it was even there, were the constellations in the night sky and Nemo swimming amongst them; a lot of good that was. There even seemed to be a beam of light, about two-metres wide, just like the one I'd seen the Pleiadean emissary appear in at Abusir, reaching up into the sky; was it a transmission from the Pleiades star system? What was it the emissary had said?

'The time has come, my brother, for you to set aside your human persona, your human ego, and remember who you really are, and why you have chosen to come here.'

Hell, I'd been doing that, or trying to do that, with every dust-filled mildew-infested step I'd taken. And yet, there I was, at the top of a long steep and narrow staircase that weaved back and forward through the darkness headed towards God knows where, that, to all intents and purpose, represented the spiritual ascent of the human race, and my path was blocked by a seemingly immovable 15-ton object; how metaphorically ironic.

'Your path may not always appear easy, but it is the path you have chosen, so walk tall.'

Easy? If this was easy, I'd hate to see Level 10 diabolical, and, as for walking tall, every time I did that I found myself forever bashing my head on overhanging rocks that appeared out of nowhere in the dark. It made no sense for me to have come to Egypt, to meet the people I'd met, to be given Kareem's papers, to see the truth beneath the Giza Plateau, and to meet Thoth, if I was to die here and just disappear from the world; it couldn't just be about *my* awakening.

And then the iphone went silent and I was plunged into complete darkness, not just darkness, but pitch-black, claustrophobic, shit-scared, entombed-forever, fucking-worst-nightmare BLACKER THAN BLACK. The fucking battery had died; I couldn't believe it, I was so close, and yet so far.

'No! NO... FUCKING... WAY!'

Frustrated, angry, hopeless, I pounded the crystal ball against my forehead contemplating my options, which included slowly groping my way back to the level of the King's Chamber, or the Queen's Chamber, or, if I was unsuccessful in finding a way out there, all the way down to Thoth's chamber where I could overdose on Blue Lotus Essence and wine and drink myself into oblivion, to be found hundreds of years in the future, pickled and preserved.

After several minutes of panicked pontification in the darkness that achieved absolutely nothing, I finally gave up, sat down, and started crying, begging for an answer.

'Why me? Why the fuck, me?'

'Your path may not always appear easy, but it is the path you have chosen, so walk tall.'

I'd never been one for pity parties, and I wasn't about to start now; I took a few deep breaths to calm down, trying not to suffocate in the dust I'd stirred up, and took stock of my predicament. Why me? Because I was here on this earth as a star-seeded being incarnated in a human body for a purpose, and that purpose was, *is*, to assist the development and ascension of human consciousness by exposing and speaking the truth. Given everything I had discovered in the past two weeks, that meant dying here was definitely NOT part of the plan.

I was just at a crossroad on a journey that I had chosen, and the journey wasn't over, it wasn't over until the fat lady sang. I had come to a physical and spiritual crossroad and going back wasn't an option; going forward just required a solution to overcoming the obstacle before me. Like all 'problems', the stone that 'blocked' my path was just an illusion, a quantum field of probabilities, and, like all 'events', it was how I chose to react in any given moment that mattered.

Then I remembered something that Hesat had told me, that *"spiritual ascent isn't a pathway, it is a process, a process of self awareness"*; it wasn't what I was doing, or what I wasn't doing, it was *why* I was doing what I was doing, my intention; I was doing things out of fear, the fear of what might happen if things *didn't* turn out the way I wanted. Christ, that had been the manifesto of my whole life. "

I shook my head; my 'problem' wasn't that I was entombed, my 'problem' was that I *believed* I was entombed. My real 'problem' was, that my consciousness was narrow, my intent was motivated out of the fear of the consequences, and I was manifesting exactly the challenges and obstacles I needed to bring that to my attention. It made me laugh; how fucking brilliant was that, I was manifesting *exactly* the challenges and obstacles I needed to bring it to my attention.

I laughed for maybe five minutes; my 'problems' were my gifts. It was the same for everyone; everything that 'happens' to us comes with the wisdom and divine planning of our Higher Self as part of the Oneness with the sole intention of moving us forward in alignment with our purpose. Like the great gurus in the east, all I had to do was shift my perspective, shift my consciousness.

That said, it meant it was time to change the programming, and, if I didn't do it now, it was highly unlikely I was going to get a second chance. First I had to focus on the intention, not on undesirable outcomes, but on the purpose of it all.

'My purpose is to get this knowledge *out* of Egypt and *out* to the world, and "Consciousness with Intent, Manifests".'

Then, as I rubbed the crystal ball against my head, something Pernille had said came to mind, about the crystal skulls *"holding the collective history and knowledge of the human existence on earth"*. I contemplated using the crystal ball to transmit my thoughts into the crystal skulls around the planet, but quickly realized that, unless there was somebody at the other end who knew how to tune in and download the information, it would prove pointless. However, if they held the knowledge, the answer could come *from* the crystal, I just needed to access it.

If I could use the crystal ball I had, like a crystal radio, and somehow tune in and connect to one of the other skulls, then maybe I could figure out how to open the door, I mean, they didn't have iphones back then, so there must be some simple way to get the stone to open. As if in instant response, something Crystal had said sprung into mind;

"Once you tune in, it is all downloaded, you just have to locate it, like locating a file on your computer, punch in the topic and hit the search button".

I projected my consciousness, my very being into the crystal ball, searching for answers, when, all of a sudden, in the darkness, Hesat, the emissary from Hathor appeared.

'Do not look for answers, for that focuses the consciousness on the questions, look for questions, and the focus turns to the answers. Look for the sacred geometry, for it is present in all things; all things exist because of it.'

The ''flower of life' was the key; it was the blueprint of the entire universe, which means it all had to do with the arrangement of the molecules in the stone. The answer was within the stone itself; of course, it had to be, in the very crystalline structure and sub-atomic spin resonance frequency of the limestone.

But I'd tried all that; I'd tried the recording, I'd tried toning into the stone, and nothing happened. Then I realized that it wasn't *just* light and sound that triggered matter, the whole thing was triggered by consciousness, in fact, "consciousness forms the body" more than that, it was the *intent* of that consciousness that mattered, "Consciousness, with *Intent*, manifests".

'Re-member; the other part of the journey is a mastery of all levels of space and time.'

That mastery being, to extend consciousness *beyond* time and space; beyond the nine dimensions, beyond the nine cycles of space, beyond the nine diffusions of consciousness, beyond the nine worlds within worlds, and into the void.

'Feel the stone.'

It was Crystal's voice, resounding through my head. She didn't just mean to feel the stone, she meant to *feel* the stone, meaning to feel as the stone feels, to BE the stone, and, in *being* the stone, I would then *know* the stone.

Standing back up, I put the crystal ball over my shoulder into the backpack, then stepped up and reached out in the darkness for the door stone, easily finding it. With a definite sense of purpose, I pressed my hands and forehead against the stone and breathed deep, softly toning as I slowly tuned deeper and deeper into the stone.

This time Nemo appeared swimming in a sea of rock, inviting me to journey deeper within, and, like the unfolding patterns of the Mandelbrot fractals, I did just that, following him as he led the way through several dimensions; pebbles, molecules, atoms, subatomic particles, sub-sub-atomic particles that haven't even been discovered yet, until we not so much arrived at the void, we *became* the void, the Oneness. In that moment, I was everything, and everything was me; I didn't have to think, I 'knew' everything, I knew what it was to BE the stone, to BE the Oneness.

The Oneness has ultimate free will, and it extends that freedom to all aspects of the quantum pea-soup that is the Oneness to BE what it desires to be, from the bottom up, quark to be quark, electron to be electron, rock to be rock, insect to be insect, plant to be plant, human to be human, super nova to be super nova, galaxy to be galaxy. All elements of the Oneness, no matter what their level of consciousness, have free will; ALL levels of consciousness, be they rock, water, amoeba, grass, fish, human, or black hole. And part of having free will is the freedom and choice to not only be as you are, but also to exert your will on that of another if you so choose, and of the other to either resist or concede to your will. I can pick up a pebble and throw it, but I cannot move a massive boulder of the same substance. I can punch the boulder and break my hand, or use explosives to blow the boulder apart. Or, I can touch the boulder and we can co-exist without either of us imposing our free will to the detriment of the other.

When consciousness incarnates into the physical realm, no matter what its form, it chooses and understands the parameters of its incarnation, including the potential implications of the free will of others upon it; these are the ground rules by which all consciousness exists and 'evolves'.

I was the stone; I understood this.

I also understood that as such, I did not have to move if it was not my will, however, if I did desire to, I merely had to shift my consciousness from one sub-atomic particle to the next, one molecule to the next, like a wave travelling across the ocean; it was the wave/particle duality, my consciousness relative to the quantum pea-soup appeared to take the form and 'be' the door stone, and all I had to do if I wished to appear to move, was to shift my consciousness into the wave and I would appear to move.

No sooner had I set my intention than the 15-ton 'stone' started to vibrate, hum, rumble, then 'move' towards me. Caught off guard, I stepped down several steps to watch in safety as the block slowly slid inwards above my head, creating the sound of stone rolling, sliding, grinding over stone as, inch by inch, the gap to the outside slowly opened and I thankfully saw the beautiful sight of Cairo's polluted night sky, and breathed in the relatively fresh air.

After about seven feet of movement, the stone stopped, leaving a gap of less than a metre; I was free! Well, hell, not yet I wasn't, the other doors had only stayed open five, ten seconds at the most, and I didn't want to finish up crushed in the south face of the pyramid. Not wasting another second, I scrambled up the remaining steps and out onto the southern face of the Great Pyramid, quickly moving to one side and sitting on a block. And thank god I did, because no sooner had I emerged than the stone started grinding its way back into its original position.

Free! Well, alive.

The entrance sealed, I laughed; at first a chuckle, but then an uncontrollable fit of hysterical relief. When I settled down, I sat there looking out over the Giza Plateau, Khafre's Pyramid ahead to the right, the Sphinx off to the left, looking so small, and directly before me, the Giza Plateau, that stretched out into the desert; the view was breathtaking, especially from 400 feet in the air!

'God, wait until the world finds out what's really under there!'

I looked around to get my bearings. About ten levels from the top, it was tempting to scale the pyramid and stand on the apex where the capstone once was, however, given my current situation, and how exposed I was, it was a conquest and bragging point I could happily pass; I had to get down as quick as possible.

In fact, all I had to do was find my way down the treacherously-steep fifty-one-degree slope, sneak past a garrison of trigger-happy kalashnikov-toting guards, out of the plateau, which was surrounded by twenty-foot-tall concrete walls manned by armed guards, then somehow get to Alexandria where I could hitch a ride to Greece on an Egyptian fishing boat, and somehow catch up with Bill; no problem! I was going to need Saeed's help; that was if he hadn't been arrested by the Secret Police. I took off the backpack and went to get my iphone before I remembered.

'Shit, forget it, the battery's dead! I need a Plan B.'

First thing was, I figured I could use my laptop to send an email to Mark, then I would sneak down the face of the pyramid and hide in the tomb of Senedjemib-inty in the Western Cemetery; it was way too 'exposed' to stay up here all night. In the morning, when the crowds arrived around 9:00am, I'd just mingle in amongst a large group of tourists and stowaway on their bus out of the plateau. Once back at their hotel, I'd plug in my phone, call Mark, and ask him and Frank to help me get me to Alexandria. Sounded good. I took out the laptop, fired it up, and got straight into the email.

> 'Hey Mark,
>
> I hope you're still in Cairo, in fact my life may depend on it. I would have called you, except the battery on my iphone is dead. I should have listen to your advice and got out of Dodge, but, I didn't. Instead I went to Giza but I finished up <u>UNDER</u> the Giza Plateau, in a vast underground network of chambers and corridors hundreds of feet below the surface.
>
> Mark it's all there, there's an underground lake, an underground city, even a space ship, and I found the Hall of Records, I was in it, there's a giant robot, as well as millions of gold discs, the Book of Thoth, an anti-gravity machine, a time machine/transporter, and much much more, all over 4 levels. But, most of all, not only did I find the tomb of Thoth, but he's still there, lying in stasis. **AND I HAVE THE PROOF, I'VE FILMED IT ALL**.
>
> I found my way out through a secret staircase that opens near the top of the south face of the Great Pyramid. I'm going to hide in the tomb of Senedjemib-inty in the Western Cemetery until morning, then stowaway on a tourist bus out of the plateau and back to their hotel. Fingers crossed, I can charge my iphone there and call you. If I can't I'll meet you beside the pool at the Soffitel at 4pm, and, then hopefully you can help get me to Alexandria and out of Egypt.
>
> Cheers, Alex.'

Damn! There was no Internet connection, no Wi-fi, which was hardly surprising given I was at the top of the pyramid; I'd have to get closer to the village. My options were to head down towards the Sphinx entrance, or closer to the main entrance. To get closer to the Sphinx, I'd have to either go down the road and pass by the Temple of Amenhotep II, which was way too exposed and not a realistically viable option, or, I could cross the road straight away and head through the ruins of Khafre's Mortuary Temple to the other side of the Causeway then wind my way down through the myriad of half-buried buildings south of the Causeway and on to the rear of the Valley Temple; that way I could hide in one of the structures if needs be. I couldn't decide, besides, I hadn't even scrambled down the face of the pyramid yet; any false step and I could tumble down the face to certain death.

My dichotomy was, the moon was shining, which gave me light to navigate the descent, but it also meant I was clearly visible to anyone who decided to look up. That meant if was spotted climbing on the pyramid, especially down, meaning I had already climbed up, by either the Egyptian officials or the guards of the grounds, it would probably result in instant imprisonment. Then they would examine the contents of my backpack, figure out who I was and that, my friends, would be the last ever seen or heard of me.

The Secret Police would probably beat the absolute shit of me then say I was illegally climbing the pyramid at night and unfortunately lost my footing and fell to a messy horrific death. So, my immediate plan was to get down as fast but as safely as possible. I stuck the laptop back in the backpack and headed down.

If the burning in my thighs on the way up was bad, going down was excruciating, and, contrary to my desire, it made the process slower and more deliberate. As I made the painstaking descent, images of Joe in *'Touching the Void'* kept flooding back, of him scrambling and hopping one boulder at a time through the morass of rubble from the glacier. And, just like Joe's mind kept latching on to the Boney M song, *'Brown girl'*, my thinking kept turning back to the lineage of the British Royal families and to the *sang réal*, and to who was marrying whom; it reminded me of something else Mother Shipton had written.

"The British olive shall next then twine, in marriage with a German vine."

That's exactly what had happened, the House of Stuart had married into the German Hanover family, or was it the other way around, and the Hanover and Windsor lineages took over the English Royal family. Was it just another pre-planned convergence of previously divergent streams of the *sang réal*, like with King Arthur and the marriage of Henry VIII to Catherine of Aragon? I knew the Illuminati inbred, but were they specifically looking to weave the threads of DNA back together?

My descent was further delayed when, every time I saw the slightest sign of movement on the plateau below, I hit the flat surface of the course and hugged join in the limestone until I was certain they'd passed or it was just the light playing tricks on my eyes. At least it gave my legs a bit of a rest.

Then I thought, if there's any truth to Mother Shipton's prophecies about flying, submarines, and wars, and about the royal family, then chances are she was right about her other prophecies, and that's were it got really interesting because I remembered there was more in Mother Shipton's prophecies that had greater relevance and importance.

"A fiery dragon will cross the sky six times before the earth shall die.
Mankind will tremble and frightened be for the six heralds in this prophecy."

There were lots of references to images such as these in ancient times, particularly the Mayan image of Quetzalcoatl, and the Egyptian winged destroyer, so though whilst normally I would have thought the reference was to a comet, and maybe it is, given the rest of the prophecy, it sounded to me more like a passing of Nibiru.

"For seven days and seven nights man will watch this awesome sight.
The tides will rise beyond their ken. To bite away the shores and

then

the mountains will begin to roar and earthquakes split the plain to shore."

That would imply massive gravitational effects, the sort of effects caused by an object with a mass far in excess of that of the moon that presently shone brightly down on me. That didn't sound like a comet made of dirty ice; it sounded more like a solid object, a brown dwarf for instance.

"Three sleeping mountains gather breath, and spew out mud, ice and death.

an earthquake swallow town and town; in lands as yet to me unknown."

Shipton was writing in the late 15th Century, before the 'official' discovery of North America, so could she be referring to San Francisco, and/or Los Angeles? She certainly implies that more than one town would be hit by earthquakes so big that the towns are seen to be swallowed in the ground. The San Andreas fault-line was the most logical interpretation. And what about the sleeping mountains; Yellowstone, the super volcano? Maybe Mount. St. Helens; it's already erupted and is constantly active? And the third; could that be Rainier, Hood, Mt. Shasta? All of them are covered in ice and show and Mt. St. Helens proved how they can erupt without relative warning, spewing out ash, mud, and how deadly they can be.

"And flooding waters rushing in, will flood the lands with such a din
that mankind cowers in muddy fen and snarls about his fellow men.
Man flees in terror from the floods and kills, and rapes and lies in blood
and spilling blood by mankind's hand will stain and bitter many lands."

From my position on the south face, I could see just how the flood waters would have swept across the Giza Plateau; everything I'd speculated was unfolding before my eyes, or rather out of my memory, as if I had seen it all in person, which I probably had, given I'd been who I believed I'd been. If I didn't recall it from my akashic records, then I'd seen enough TV news reports of how humans react after floods and droughts; in many cases it was each man for himself; often stampeding over children to survive. On an incomprehensibly massive scale, within days, human consciousness would revert to the competitive cavemen with their basic instinct being the basic need to survive.

"For storms will rage and oceans roar when Gabriel stands on sea and shore,
and as he blows his wondrous horn old worlds die and new be born."

I wondered if Gabriel's horn was actually some sort of sonic effect caused by the passing of Nibiru? Maybe it was HAARP, perhaps the whole thing will be, triggered by HAARP?

"Then upside down the world shall be And gold found at the root of tree
And when the dragon's tail is gone man forgets and smiles and carries on."

There it was, the confirmation, *"upside down the world shall be"*, the only way you would know the world was upside down would be to refer it to the positions of the stars, and to where the sun was rising and falling; it totally reinforced my theory of how the crust separated from the core and pivoted, the north pole crust reconnecting to south pole core. As for the reference to gold, was it a way of saying that gold was the basis of the whole human race, why it was created in the first place, to mine gold for the Annunaki?

As I neared the base of the pyramid I became aware of lots of activity down and around the Sphinx enclosure; I didn't know if they'd managed to open the first granite door and were somewhere down in the underground network, or still trying to find a way through, or, if they'd arrested Saeed, or if he'd managed to elude them. What mattered was there was enough activity for me to hide in a 'hole' in the middle of the southern face, which had possibly been made by someone searching for another entrance into the Great Pyramid, possibly even in search of the secret staircase. Keeping a constant eye on the guards, I continued to ponder Mother Shipton's prophecies.

"His masked smile, his false grandeur, will serve the gods their anger stir
and they will send the dragon back to light the sky -- his tail will crack.
Upon the earth and rend the earth and man shall flee, king, lord and serf.
And lands will crack and rend anew do you think it strange, it will come true."

Was the *"masked smile"* and *"false grandeur"* a reference to the lies the politicians will tell us, before, during, and after, Nibiru's passing, lies they tell to serve their own good? Possibly. The "dragon" coming back could mean two things; the regular orbit of Nibiru, meaning it will return, however, because of the reference to *"his tail will crack",* I think it means Nibiru circling the sun and passing back out again, this time the earth passing through the "tail" of Nibiru, which would be filled with all sorts of 'debris' including comets dragged into its wake from the Kuiper Belt and Oort cloud. It sounded dire, but there was hope:

"Not every soul on earth will die, as the dragon's tail goes sweeping by,
not every land on earth will sink, but these will wallow in stench and stink,
of rotting bodies of beast and man, of vegetation crisped on land."

As the object passes, it leaves behind not just dead animals and people, but *"vegetation crisped on land".* That indicates massive bushfires and firestorms sweeping across the land, which would be consistent with increased temperatures caused by the close proximity of a brown dwarf star and the heightened activity of coronal mass ejections, CMEs, from our own sun.

"The dragon's tail is but a sign for mankind's fall and man's decline.
Who survives this ..... and then begin the human race again.
But not on land already there, but on ocean beds, stark, dry and bare."

Whatever the earth changes are, they involve land rising from beneath the ocean, fresh lands on which the survivors of the human race can rebuild.

Once the coast was clear, I scampered down the remaining courses of limestone to the plateau floor, my mind still processing Mother Shipton's words.

"But the land that rises from the sea will be dry and clean and soft and free.
Of mankind's dirt and therefore be, the source of man's new dynasty.
and those that live will ever fear the dragon's tail for many year

but time erases memory You think it strange. but it will be."

The damage to the land will clearly be so severe that it will be easier to build on the newly risen, clean land rather than clear the debris from the old. And, whilst the memory of the *"dragon's tail"* will no doubt persist for 2, 3, perhaps 4 generations, the fear of it's return would be a reflection of the lies the politicians have told about it's origins. That said, I don't think the *"dragon's tail"* has been forgotten at all, I think that even though the Illuminati families currently ruling the planet have done their best to suppress the truth about Nibiru, the Annunaki, and our true origins, and distract the masses with mindless addictions such as religion, sport, celebrity, and reality TV shows, the memory lingers deep within the DNA of every person. However, Shipton's line about *"time erases memory"* would surely indicate the passing of a considerable amount of time for the events to pass into folk-law and myth.

"And before the race is built anew, a silver serpent comes to view
and spew out men of like unknown to mingle with the earth now
grown
cold from its heat and these men can enlighten the minds of future
man
to intermingle and show them how to live and love and thus endow.
the children with the second sight. a natural thing so that they might
grow graceful, humble and when they do the golden age will start
anew."

The *"silver serpent"* and *"men of like unknown"* was a clear reference to a space ship with, not Annunaki inside, for man was made in their image, rather star-seeded beings, possibly members of the Galactic Federation. Of course, it would be easy to dismiss Mother Shipton's prophecies, and, if they stood alone as evidence, I might have done just that, however, when you consider them alongside the prophecies of Nostradamus, the Book of Revelations, and the ancient tales of dozens of other ancient civilizations, the Mayans, the Sumerians, the ancient Egyptians, the Hopi Indians, only one of two conclusion could reasonably be drawn; either everyone is lying, dreaming, or storytelling, or it's all rooted in truth. The physical evidence seemed to strongly support the latter.

Down and out

The descent must have taken me nearly two hours before I finally set foot on the plateau ground, just along from the boat museum. I was exhausted, starving, thirsty, and quickly gave up on the idea of heading east towards the Sphinx, instead, reverting to the original plan B of scuttling westward along the southern base of the pyramid, across the road and into the western cemetery. And that's what I did, like a rat through the sewers of Paris, pausing briefly at the road to check the coast was clear, before sprinting across and into the western cemetery.

Moments later, I ducked in between the entrance pillars and into the darkness of the "tomb" of Senedjemib-inty, sighing with relief as I took off my akubra, took off the backpack, and sat down against the inner wall; the first part of the plan was safely completed and I was optimistic, that if I could get through the remainder of the night undiscovered, I'd be able to execute the second half of my plan, stowaway on a tourist bus, and, within 24 hours, I'd be eating a souvlaki and sipping sambuca and ouzo.

I took out my laptop and fired it up, at first hoping I might be able to find an open wifi network and send the email to Mark; unfortunately there wasn't one. It was 3:37 am, and I debated whether to stay awake, or grab a few hours sleep and risk being discovered in the morning. Although the battery on the computer was dying as well, and I was exhausted, I decided to make a few important notes on what I'd discovered, and then have a kip; I'd recorded much of the evidence on the iphone, I figured that would speak for itself, it was the thoughts and conclusions that I didn't want to risk forgetting. I put on my ears phones and plugged in a little John Bon Jovi to keep me company

"It's all the same, only the names will change, Everyday it seems we're wasting away

Another place where the faces are so cold, I travel all night just to get back home.

I'm a cowboy on a steel horse I ride, I'm wanted, dead or alive."

Wasn't that the truth!

"Sometimes I sleep, sometimes its not for days,

and the people I meet always go their separate ways.

Sometimes you tell the day, by the bottle that you drink.

And times when your alone, and all you do is think.

I'm a cowboy on a steel horse I ride, I'm wanted, dead or alive."

I took out the bottle of Blue Lotus Essence and decided to take a few swigs; I thought, hell, who knows, it might even give me some insights to tomorrow. As for my 'day' so far, it had consisted of exploring the massive Hall of Records, of Gort the huge robot librarian, of hundreds of shelves of metallic bins with millions of thin gold discs, each one probably containing a gazillion Mega-Tera-Giga-bytes of information. Then there were the symbols on the floors and discs, the machines, the disc player and recorder that didn't just record knowledge, it recorded the actual physical experiencing of that knowledge. That;

"The law of your mind is also the law of the universe, meaning that all things are totally possible, for your mind is an inseparable entity of the universal spirit."

There was the bed in the Hall of Records, the goblet that they probably used to drink wine laced with Blue Lotus, the recreational drug of choice of ancient Egypt, to access higher realms of consciousness, and the different capital tops, the closed buds as opposed to the open flowered capitals, all representative of different states of consciousness. Like a fine cognac, I took another sip and kept typing.

I'd figured that because the Blue Lotus was also found in Greece, it meant Amenhotep had taken it there when he left Egypt to rebuild the obliterated Minoan Civilization into the Mycenaean Civilization, and that raised the possibility that the arrival of the Blue Lotus coincided with the arrival of Nibiru, meaning that, like wheat, corn, and rice, it was an introduced species from the Annunaki's home planet.

No matter where it came from, the introduction of Blue Lotus, and altered states of consciousness, explained the explosion of images of weird looking gods, snakes, and concepts of the "Underworld" and "Realm of the Gods" that came into being in the 18th Dynasty following the passing of Nibiru and the Thera eruption, and persisted through to the Ptolemaic Era.

Then I'd wondered, if the goblet they drank out of could have been the origin of the myth of the Holy Grail being a cup; the doctored ritual of drinking wine that was later adopted and adapted by 'Moses' when he was chased out of Egypt and created Judaism, of how the *'sang réal'*, the royal blood, became the 'san greal' the Holy Grail, the cup that held the blood of Christ in the Christian mass.

When I found the *'The Book of Thoth'*, I had no concept of its power. It contained so much information, including the true history of not just the human race, but all the extra-terrestrial life forms that have had an influence on the genetic and cultural development of ALL life on this planet; millions of images and experiences covering millions of years had all been uploaded like a zip file of zip files into my mind in a matter of minutes.

The Book of Thoth revealed ALL the previous civilizations on the planet going back over five-and-a-half million years, and included heaps of information on when 'man', the Annunaki, first set foot on the earth 576,000 years ago. It even showed the different prototypes of modern humans, all genetic experiments, and the various 'stages' of Atlantis. From that I figured out how human 'language' developed from the precursors of Annunaki communication.

There was the miniature-size pyramid made of a translucent metal/plastic; did it once form the very tip of the capstone, a sort of conductor of electrical and microwave energy? And the video screens, the large 'star charts' that seemed to plot the known universe as a star being would know it, depicted, not as an expanding sphere as you might expect, but, as a series of expanding and interlocking donuts. In another corner was a levitation device, and, on the third floor was the 'time machine'; a giant metallic ring that transported people most likely through both time and space. It led to my understanding that any form of transportation required a complete understanding of particle/wave duality and the transposition of consciousness.

Ascending the steep dark narrow secret staircase was like a metaphor for my rising consciousness, and I made sure I noted all my observations. Originally it may have been dug out of the bedrock, following tsunami 'one', to access the Hall of Records, then Thoth's tomb was built, and it was extended down to access that as well following tsunami 'two'.

"Oh, we're halfway there, Whoa, Livin' on a Prayer
Take my hand, and we'll make it I swear, Oh livin' on a prayer."

It was more like 'livin' on Intent', which I suppose is sort of the same thing, and possibly where the whole concept of prayer came from in the first place; Intent leads to spells and rituals, leads to prayers. Simple really, although prayer can still be rooted in fear, praying for someone to live is born out of the fear they will die. I took a moment to review my own perspective on death; I didn't fear it, it was more the way of dying I wasn't too keen on, like shark attack, caught in a fire, that sort of thing, something that involved pain, or terror. But death was not on the agenda, well not in the foreseeable future, I hadn't come this far to fall at the final hurdle. I got back to my notes.

The pyramid was then built on top, with the inner staircase incorporated into the structure of the pyramid knowing Thoth's tomb and the Hall of Records were directly below. I noted the doors at the Subterranean Chamber level, the Queen's Chamber and King's Chamber levels, which showed a preconceived plan to access the major internal chambers of the pyramid. The question was, why did the repairmen of Khufu's time, not use the south face entrance? Perhaps they tried, but didn't know the 'code', and were left with no option but to use the Descending Passage.

Then, while making my way up, there was the Tomb of Thoth, accessed through the antechamber, with stores of wine, Blue Lotus Essence, and walls covered in as-new pyramid texts. And then there was Thoth himself, me, in another Higher State of consciousness, lying in stasis in the massive black sarcophagus, and the fact the secret to the sarcophagi wasn't just that they recalibrated and rejuvenated the *physical* bodies of the Annunaki, they transported their consciousness, their 'soul', to Amenti, a higher realm of 'being'; surely that's partly what the wadjet eyes were all about, they represented the shift in vision, the shift in perspective, the ability to see into and beyond the nine dimensions of time and space..

Crystal had known it all along; since way back at Edfu she had been aware I was Imhotep, Akhenaten, that I was an incarnation of Thoth, perhaps not the *only* incarnation, but certainly one, and that I was lying in stasis awaiting awakening.

> *"I will love you baby, always, and I'll be there forever and a day, always*
> *I'll be there 'til stars don't shine til the Heavens burst, and the words*
> *don't rhyme,*
> *and when I die you'll be on my mind and I love you always"*

Perfect timing! I wondered where she was, and if I'd see her again. I realized, that even if I didn't, she had been the most major influence of my life, not just this life, but many lives.

> *"Baby I want you, like the roses want the rain,*
> *you know I need you like the poet needs the pain*
> *I would give anything, my blood, my love, my life, if you were in these arms*
> *tonight*
> *I'd hold you, I'd need you, I'd get down on my knees for you*
> *and make everything alright, if you were in these arms*
> *I'd love you, I'd please you, I'd tell you that I'd never leave you*
> *and love 'til the end of time if your were in these arms tonight."*

The ten years with my ex-wife now seemed an insignificant blink in comparison. I guess it's not how long you are with someone that matters, but how long that experience stays with you, just like my experience with my Higher Self, my conversation with Thoth:

> *"The body does not form consciousness, consciousness forms the body. The body may sleep, but the soul is ever-awakened and free to roam where and when it will."*

Thoth then explained the roles of both the reptilians, the Dracos, in infiltrating the royal families and governments of the world, and the Galactic Federation, in incarnating in human form to assist the development of human consciousness. And it all made sense; because if star-seeded beings are to have any influence on the development of human consciousness, then they must not only choose lives as politicians, law-makers, and religious leaders, but also, and perhaps more so, as the pop stars, sports stars and media stars of the world. The 'problem' is, that's what the Dracos do as well.

The reality was, the Dracos provided the obstacles for the humans to overcome, and hence spiritually ascend, that's why the Dracos were so important, in fact, without them, nothing would happen, man would basically stay scavenging around like the primates in the forests.

> *"The caterpillar MUST go through its gut-wrenching metamorphosis to become the butterfly, avoiding it is what keeps the caterpillar a caterpillar."*

Diane had talked of the importance of spiritual metamorphosis during the circle she held the evening before we all went into the King's Chamber; to regurgitate the past, wrap it around like a cocoon, and endure the gut-wrenching darkness and transition that accompanies transmutation. Did she know who I was as well? It didn't matter, what mattered was that it was her circle where I first touched the void, the Source of All That Is.

> *"It is not who you are that matters, what "matters" is who you are. Your purpose relates my purpose, your purpose reveals my purpose, your purpose defines my purpose, your purpose fulfils my purpose, for All is One as One is All."*

Having emerged from the dark staircase of the pyramid, I felt like my metamorphosis was complete and I had finally broken free of my cocoon. All that was left now, was for me to spread my wings and fly.

"Welcome to wherever you are, this is your life, you made it this far.
Welcome you gotta believe
Right here right now, you're exactly where you're supposed to be
Welcome to wherever you are
Be who you wanna be, be who you are, everyone's a hero, everyone's a star."

Everyone is a caterpillar wanting to flutter like a butterfly. Most are still chewing bitter leaves, some are throwing up, others are wrapped in protective shells, a few are trying to break free, isolated individuals are unfurling their wings ready to take flight and leave the squirling mass behind.

I noted how my conversation with Thoth was echoed in the prophecies of Mother Shipton, about the impending onset of possibly another World War, about the Dracos, about the "dragon's tail", and the massive earth changes that will accompany its passing. Somehow that led me to the blood lines of the Plantagenets, the European rulers, to the significance of Robert the Bruce and the Scottish connection through William Sinclair and the Templar Knights; all because of the *sang réal*.

Ultimately, I was drawn to the period of and around Henry VIII, to my life then, particularly to Anne Boleyn's true influence on the origins of the Church of England, and the church's development through power-mongers like Thomas Cranmer and the 'Freemasons', who were descendants of the Templar Knights and 'anti-Catholics'.

From there, it was a hop-skip-and-a-jump through the pages of history as Edward took the throne ahead of his two elder half-siblings, Mary and Elizabeth, and how the power struggles continued through the manipulation of Edward VI by his uncle, Edward Seymour, John Dudley, and the Archbishop of Canterbury, Thomas Cranmer. Then, how Dudley and Cranmer conceived the "Devise for Succession" as a means to not only prevent the country's return to Catholicism, but to protect the titles and estates of the sycophantic members of Edward's Privy Council.

Murder, nepotism and political chess was the order of the day, it had been for centuries before in the Catholic church, and it was still the order of the day in the 20th Century with the Assassinations of JFK, Robert Kennedy, Anwar Sadat, and who knows how many others.

Then there was the revelation of Elizabeth's sexual liaisons with Thomas Seymour and her 'deflowering' at the age of 14, which was the real reason why she never married. It all came to a head with James I of England, and a reuniting of the English and Scottish lineages of the *sang réal*.

That opened up the fact that every US president was not only related to James I, but it took the bloodline back even further, to King John, then somehow through Alfred the Great to the time of King Arthur and 'Camelot'. And that opened up not only the whole US political deception, but the global deception, because it had been going on in Europe for centuries; look not to who is on the throne, but to who was the power behind the throne.

Then, there was my epiphany at the top of the staircase, that the Oneness has ultimate free will, and that free will extends to all aspects of the quantum pea-soup to BE what it desires to be; that ALL elements of the Oneness, no matter what their level of consciousness, have free will, and that when consciousness incarnates into the physical realm, no matter what its form, it chooses and understands the parameters of its incarnation, including the potential implications of the free will of others upon it.

"It's my life, it's now or never, I ain't gonna live forever
I just wanna live without a lie."

That was it, live *your* truth, whatever that might be, and live it NOW! More importantly be true to yourself, not what you think others think you should or shouldn't be.

I also now understood the wave/particle duality, and how my consciousness appeared to take form; consciousness was the wave that moved through the ocean of quantum possibilities. It made sense, because everything was thought first, the thought wave then manifesting as the particle because of, and through, intent.

If Consciousness with Intent, Manifests, then Waveform with Intent, forms Particles, that's what Thoth meant by *"The body does not form consciousness, consciousness forms the body."*

Finally, I made special note of my precarious descent down the pyramid face, of the vultures still active around the Sphinx enclosure at 3:00 am in the morning, and of plan B, my revised escape plan. Then, seeing the barest of wifi signal, I attached the wordfile to the email to Mark in the hope it would reach him, and, fingers crossed, hit send, that way, if anything untoward *did* happen to me, at least someone would know, and, would know of my discoveries in the Hall of Records, and of the 'resting' place of Thoth.

I couldn't believe it, for once, fortune was on my side; the email actually sent. Three cheers for "Consciousness with Intent, Manifests"! Of course Mark probably wouldn't see it until morning, but he would most-likely get it by the time I was safely on a tourist bus.

"Oh, if there's one thing I hang on to that gets me through the night
I aint gonna do what I don't want to, I'm gonna live my life shining like a diamond,
rolling with the dice, standing on the ledges show the wind how to fly.
When the world gets in my face, I say, Have a nice day."

Relieved, at 4:12 am, with barely 21% left on the battery, I shut the laptop down, stuffed it back in the backpack, took a final sip of BLE and, using the backpack as a pillow, went to sleep on the floor in the darkness of the 'tomb'.

'Motto for tomorrow; "Have a nice day".'

Dawn of the day of reckoning

Given everything that had happened, and what was on my mind, it was no surprise that I had a dream of being on a train bound for Alexandria, and trying to get out of Egypt; the question was, given I'd taken the BLE, was it was just a dream, or a weird lucid type of premonition.

As you might expect, the train was more a cross between the Orient Express, a giant serpent from the walls of the Tomb of Thutmoses III, and a giant out-of-control roller-coaster. The 'theme' of the dream was a cross between 'Murder on the Orient Express', 'The taking of Pelham 1,2,3', a chariot race to rival that in 'Ben Hur', and a Charlie-Chaplin-style, Indiana-Jones-inspired, old-cinema escape from the bad guys. Of course the pursuing bad guys were all either crocodiles, vultures or cobras, all dressed up in military or police uniforms, and after the contents of my backpack, which significantly had taken the form of a child's 'monkey' backpack.

No one could help me; all the passengers on the train were either fish firmly gaffed on baited hooks, or mummified corpses wrapped in papier-mâché body-suits of newspapers and pages of history books. If they did somehow come to life, it was to reveal my hiding place to my adversaries, then, like mindless zombies, join the marauding band of my pursuers like sheep.

I knew all of it was symbolic, but, the truth was, I didn't have time to stop and figure it all out. The train itself was rollicking along without a driver, seemingly out of control, at first, on the railway line that ran beside the Nile, then, like a roller-coaster, it started ducking and weaving through long dark subterranean corridors, with an 'avenue of honour', that felt more like a 'fool's gallery', of images on the walls of all the past, or alternate, lives I'd experienced.

The 'train' stormed on through burial chambers, some filled with wine, others crammed full of golden treasure, flying past the UFO, Gort lifting a finger as if to tell me some profound missive, before I shot off through the various floors of the Hall of Records, including doing numerous loop-de-loops through the circle of the time machine, all the time with me striving to get to the driver's cabin, holding on with one hand as we swerved around obstacles like people and modern statues of Jesus and Buddha. Although I wasn't sure if my struggle forward to the driver's cabin was to slow the train down, or steer it in the right direction, I did know that jumping *off* the train wasn't an option; I had to make sure I got to my destination, I knew that if I didn't get to Alexandria on time I would miss the boat that awaited, moored in the harbour, the African Queen, captained by none other than Bill who was doing his finest impersonation of Humphrey Bogart.

Ultimately, I found myself riding the back of the giant serpent as it wriggled along, under, and through the surging river Nile, over and through innumerable turgid rapids and waterfalls. To all sides of the 'train' were overcrowded pools of hungry crocodiles, pits of spitting cobras, or deep shafts filled with hundreds of decaying corpses being picked at by kettles of vultures. Misery and death seemed all around me, but, so long as I stayed on the ride, so long as I held on no matter what, I was OK.

Eventually, after several close calls and escapes, including sword fights with Dracos mind-controllers, using Blue Lotus flowers as swords, knives and fireball curses being thrown at me by a procession of Amun Priests masquerading as 12th to 16th Century clergymen and politicians, a bizarre wrestling-match-come-salsa/tango with the desiccated mummy of an Amun High Priest, and a barrage of arrows from a battalion of Egyptologist foot-soldiers, dug in to a trench of qualifications and doctorates, that speared into the carriage wall which created a makeshift staircase-come-ladder that turned into a narrow staircase through the bedrock and proved to be an escape route, I 'prized' the door to the driver's cabin open by singing Queen's 'I want to break free' and staggered in, only to find Nemo, dressed in a galabeya, sitting back in a comfy chair, sipping a pina colada, flippers up on the steering wheel.

'What took you so long, we're nearly there?'

Ahead, through the front window, was the harbour of Alexandria, hundreds of small fishing boats scattered across the surface.

'Which one is it?

'The one with the white sail.'

Of course they all had white sails.

'A little more detail, would help.'

'You cannot to be sleep here.'

'I don't want to sleep, I want to get out of here.'

Before Nemo could flop a flipper in the direction of the boat, suddenly the earth began to shake and a dark shadow, like the eclipse of the sun, appeared overhead.

'You cannot to be sleep here.'

Still in la-la land, I woke up to a guardian, silhouetted against the morning sun that illuminated the entrance, crouched over me and shaking me by the shoulder.

'This it is not permit; you cannot to be sleep here.'

I quickly scrambled to my feet, realizing how important it was to placate him as fast as possible; word would have quickly spread around the soldiers, police, and guardians of the plateau about the tall-bronzed Aussie who had murdered a Luxor antiquities inspector and was last seen somewhere on or beneath the Giza Plateau, there may even have been a reward posted, dead or alive.

"I'm wanted, dead or alive."

What I wouldn't have given for a little more Bon Jovi right now.

"I wake up in the morning and I raise my weary head,
I've got an old coat for a pillow and the earth was last night's bed..."

My head wasn't so much weary, as tingling, and my backpack was my pillow, with the tomb floor, my bed.

"...I don't know where I'm going, only god knows were I been,
I'm a devil on the run, a six-gun lover, a candle in the wind
I'm going down in a blaze of glory."

Like gunslingers, hired guns, I knew the guardians were a 'breed unto themselves' and would do anything for a little baksheesh. My objective was to get the guardian to forget the whole thing, to act like he'd never even seen me, and *not* call the Antiquities Police, not call anyone for that matter. Fortunately the only person with him was his son, who was maybe seven or eight years old, so, if I made the guardian look good in his son's eyes I figured I could sufficiently bribe him to look the other way.

'Yes, yes, I know, but this is the tomb of a very important man; Senedjemib-inty, vizier of Djedkare, yes? Senedjemib-inty, Overseer of All Royal Works. He was a very important man in the Old Kingdom, this is why YOU have this important job, to guard this place.'

I was laying it on with a trowel, really thick, thicker than the makeup on a forty-five-year-old Frankston grandmother on a Friday night out on the pull at the Pier Hotel. The reality was, of the millions of tourist who visited the Giza Plateau every year, barely a handful ever visited anything other than the Great Pyramid and the Sphinx, so, just like the guardian and soldiers in the back lots of Karnak, they were easily open to receiving some of the additional handouts their associates received, it was just a matter of how much hush money he wanted.

Eventually, he bought it, and, much to my surprise, a hundred did the trick, which was just as well because that cleaned me out. Of course there was the possibility he took the money just to shut me up, and was also heading off to blow the whistle and collect the big reward, which would mean I was not only screwed, but shafted as well; a lesson his son would no doubt take great heed of – 'How to shaft tourists Part 1'. Of course the clincher in the deal was that I had to vacate the tomb, for which, I put on the backpack, popped my akubra atop my noggin and obligingly complied. However, that left me somewhat exposed and I briefly debated my next options.

Fortunately the plateau had been open for business for some time, as a group of about fifteen tourists were strung out along its western side. I quickly scampered across the road and made an obvious move to mingle in amongst them.

'Excuse me, do you have the time?'

A short bemused Chinese man looked at me, my appearance and smell reflective of a hobo infused with the contents of the staircase, and obviously not understanding one single word I was saying. Quick to maintain my cover, I pointed to my wrist and circled my finger, the universal sign language of the pre-digital civilization. He glanced at his own watch, and replied in Chinese, then realized I didn't understand a word that he said and just held out his arm for me to see; 8:16 am.

I'd 'slept' for maybe four hours at the most, and the dream just made me feel even more tired. I was knackered, but not too tired to realize my dilemma; I'd found a crowd to intermingle with, but there was one problem, they were all Chinese and about two-foot-nothing tall. It was like a bull elephant smelling of hungry lion trying to mingle in with a herd of zebra. To the bewilderment of the group, and their guide, I rushed to the front, grabbed the flag being held high by the tour guide, and assumed her role, hoping I would be perceived, or rather ignored, by everyone else on the plateau, especially the Secret Police, as just another tour leader; smart, hey!

What I needed to do was find a group of Caucasians, Europeans, Americas, whatever, and hook up with them. Fortunately several groups of tourists had decided to visit the Pyramid early to avoid the heat, and were now making their way back to their coaches; perfect. I handed the flag back to the tour guide, who had been following me like a panicked rat of Hamlin, and hustled to tack on to the back of the next herd.

Working my way to the centre of the crowd for safety, the overwhelming language of the first group was French; at that point I really didn't care if it was Double-Dutch, the fact was I blended in, and it looked like within a few moments I would safely be aboard the coach. Then, as I reached the door, sabotage, the damn French had a door monitor who was ticking everyone off on a checklist as they climbed aboard; how anal is that! He looked at me quizzically, disapprovingly, with that now familiar cat's ass of a mouth and rancid smell under his nose; clearly I wasn't part of *his* group.

'Excusez-moi monsieur, je pense que vous avez le bus incorrecte.'

Frustrated, but not thwarted, I casually waved a hand and skipped on nonchalantly to the next bus that was loading, as it turned out, a coach load of Russians. No such anal system of bean-counting here, the people were just meandering aboard, perhaps recovering from the previous night and too much vodka. Perfect! If they were anything like the Russians I'd encountered crossing the river at Tel el-Amarna then they were as conversational as two dead mules with laryngitis. Still, figuring Russian women were always looking for a western man to marry to get out of Russia, I picked out a hot young momma carrying a large shopping/tourist bag, not unlike the gaudy one I'd given to Diane.

'The pyramid is amazing.'

'Yes, very much.'

'You speak English?'

'Yes, of course.'

'I'm sorry if I smell, I've been out in the desert for a few days. Where are you staying?'

'I am here.'

'I mean what hotel?'

'Oh, yes, Le Meridien.'

'Me too.'

What a coincidence; that was Bill's hotel, and where I'd stayed the night with Crystal. I casually yet flirtingly tipped my trusty akubra.

'I'm Alex.'

'Tatiana. Oh, dear, what happened to your head?'

I quickly covered it up, doing the macho thing.

'It's nothing; some of these ruins weren't made for someone as tall as me, I ran into a low bridge.'

'Let me see.'

Brushing it off, I indicated for her to board the bus.

'No, no, it's fine.'

I seized the sympathetic moment and climbed aboard with her, hoping it would make her think the coach was a general coach from the hotel and not for one specific tour group. Then we made our way, like I had in my school days, down to the back of the bus, to where all the cool kids used to hang out, that way it would be unlikely anyone would hassle me, but, if someone did bother to question me, I figured I'd have more chance of a receptive ear.

Pleasantries exchanged, less than ten minutes later, the driver started the coach and we were off; the plan seemed to be going brilliantly.

Settling back, I readjusted my akubra, and relaxed; if I hadn't been so enamoured by Crystal, then Tatiana would have been a prospect well worth surveying, in fact I wondered if we had had any lives together in the past, perhaps during the Russian Revolution. As I thought it, as shiver went up my spine, had Tatiana and I been connected then as well?

Tatiana and I asked the usual flirting precursor questions about each other, and, as we did, I momentarily cast a bombastic eye out of the window from under my akubra, watching as the coach did a U-turn, passed a group of plateau officials, and headed for the exit; I was virtually home and hosed. But, I'd celebrated too soon, as, less than a 30 seconds later, we turned left, headed back beside the western face, around the corner, then down past the Temple of Amenhotep II, and came to a stop down beyond the Sphinx, putting me right smack-bang back in the middle of the hornets' nest.

'Geez, give me a break!'

'Something is wrong?'

'Nothing, it's…it's just that I saw the Sphinx yesterday.'

OK, no need to panic, the Ruskies will all get off, wander around snapping a few pix of the Valley Temple and the Sphinx, then be back on board in maybe an hour, tops, and then it's back to the hotel for an early lunch and loll around the pool for the rest of the day quenching their thirst with Stolichnaya. And that's just what started to happen, they all started filing off. Tatiana seductively turned to me.

'You are coming, I am sure there are many things you can show me?'

Talk about a come on, as subtle as a sledgehammer. Any other place and any other time I would have been in like Flynn, however, as I glanced out the window at the army of uniformed crocodiles that infested the area of the Sphinx and the Sphinx enclosure, it was like a cold spoon smacked on my arousing manhood.

'Ah, no, believe me, I've seen it all, I'll just have a rest and wait for you here, then we can compare "notes" back in the privacy of the hotel.'

I felt a bit false, leading her on, but these were desperate times and I had to do what I had to do, and who knows, there may have been time for a quick international affair before the last train left for Alexandria. However, before Tatiana could get up, there was a commotion up at the front of the bus as a plain-clothed Egyptian man boarded the coach, backed by a member of the Antiquities Police. He was indicating his intention to search the bus and check everyone; it was the Secret Police!

Was it just a routine inspection or had I been spotted getting on the bus, or, had I been reported by the French group; that wouldn't have surprised me. Or had the old geezer, the guardian of Senedjemib-inty's tomb, squealed on me? The reality was, it didn't matter; what mattered now was I was trapped, cornered, and I was potentially in very very deep deep shit, especially if I was caught with Kareem's papers. I couldn't take the risk; I took the backpack, unzipped it, took out the folio of Kareem's papers and surreptitiously slipped them into Tatiana's shopping bag.

I figured if they detained me, it could be indefinitely, or I could just disappear, so it was the only real chance of getting the information out of Egypt. And if they didn't detain me, and it was just a random check, then I could get off the bus and get them back straight away. As you might expect, Tatiana was a little confused about the search and turned back to me.

'What do you think this is?'

I quickly tried to get her on board.

'I think they're after me, they think I killed someone, I didn't but, well, it's a long story. If they arrest me, I'll hopefully be able to talk my way out of it and meet you back at the Le Meridien, beside the pool, at 3:00pm, and I'll explain it all then, but, if I don't turn up, go to the Soffitel Hotel at 4:00pm and look for an Aussie lawyer called Mark Beaver, he's around my age, five-foot-ten, brown hair, he'll be sitting around the pool, he'll know what to do.'

'What…'

'The Soffitel, 4 pm, Mark Beaver. OK?'

'OK.'

'Now, go.'

Without question, with her shopping bag slung over her shoulder, she joined the line as it filed down the aisle and out of the bus. Apart from being given a cursory 'sexual' once-over, Tatiana, and more importantly her bag, were 'passed' and safely off the bus. If they *had* shown any interest in her bag I was going to create a diversion, I didn't know exactly what, but fortunately they didn't.

Then, for a second, I contemplated what I'd just done: I'd handed over the most important evidence in the history of the modern man, that being Kareem's papers, to a raven-haired Russian beauty called Tatiana that I'd known for five minutes; crazy. Thankfully I still had my iphone footage, the crystal ball, my laptop with all my notes, a few crumpled discs, and the bottle of Blue Lotus Essence.

I leaned back in my seat and tilted my akubra over my face, pretending to be asleep. About a minute later, with everyone else off the bus, I was awoken by someone standing in the aisle of the coach.

'Please, to come with me.'

At first, I ignored it, feigning being asleep. Then I opened an eye and glanced out the window, only to see several armed soldiers were lined up along the side of the bus, looking up in my direction; shit!

'Please, to come with me.'

Again I ignored the command; even when he rocked my shoulder to rouse me, I pretended to shrug it off hoping he would believe I was another drunken Russian sleeping off the previous evening's hangover. When I couldn't ignore it any longer, I 'woke up' and pretended I was Russian and didn't understand him.

However, the universal language of him motioning me to come with him could not be mistaken or ignored, so I picked up my backpack and was unceremoniously escorted off the bus by a veritable small army and into an awaiting police vehicle. This was not good, not good at all.

Tatiana and her group watched on bemused, talking amongst themselves, as I was whisked away. Through the window, I caught Tatiana's eye and held up three fingers confirming 3:00 pm. Moments later, we pulled up outside a small building on the Giza Plateau, in front of the Sphinx, my backpack was confiscated and I was quickly bustled inside and into an 'interview' room, guarded by two fully-armed soldiers, where I was left for at least 45 minutes to contemplate my position.

I sat in silence, looking around the room, at my guards, the windows, the door, ever the roof and floors, looking for a possible way to overcome my captors and escape. I figured that even if I did knock out both guards with some ingenious James Bond routine, I'd probably get two steps outside the room before I was gunned down.

It always amazed me how the bad guys were such bad shots; a dozen of them could fire collectively thousands of rounds a second from automatic machine guns and not even one round would find its mark, and yet Bond, with his Walter PC special, could pop off a shot at will and kill guys instantly from fifty feet away. This was real life, and I wasn't James Bond; there'd be no half-assed escapes from me, well, at least not now, after all, maybe he was going to check his records and then release me.

All along I'd remained mute, playing the *'I'm Russian, and don't know what you are saying or what this is all about'* routine, but, when the big brass showed up, when an older senior officer, with more stripes on his epaulets than a zebra or Bengal tiger, entered the room carrying my backpack and sat down opposite me, I realized it was crunch time. You could tell he was a big-wig by the size of his moustache; the previous plain-clothed guy didn't have one, but this guy's mo looked like he'd shoved a broom up his nostrils.

In his early sixties, balding, and with a figure that showed he hadn't missed a meal in months, if it wasn't for the uniform, dark skin, and pistol strapped to this waist, he could have looked like a green-grocer from the local market. His face was expressionless, as if he did this sort of thing every day, but, as he slid a photocopy of my passport picture across the table, my 'wanted dead or alive poster', I realized the façade was over and the gig was probably well and truly up.

'You were here at Giza yesterday, yes?'

What to say; playing the 'mistaken identity' card was not going to work? They knew who I was, they knew I had been at Giza yesterday, and they knew I was involved in the fracas with Bill and Jacques, in fact, according to Saeed, it was Jacques who fingered me. Maybe that was all they wanted me for, simple assault and battery. After all, what could Jacques know about the papers, I got them after he left us in Edfu. But he could have said I was the one on the photo, the so-called murderer. But why would he do that? Simple, he was an asshole.

Still, they knew Saeed and I ran down the corridors off the Sphinx enclosure; that wouldn't have impressed them, they didn't want the truth out there. Had they captured Saeed, had they interrogated him? If they did, what did he say? He said that if he was caught he was going to say I stole his uncle's papers and he was trying to get them back, and, if he did say that, then that put me in the shit, but, if he escaped, then they would be none the wiser. It's amazing how many actual thoughts can run through you mind in a few seconds. I decided to play it cool and ignorant.

'Yes, I was visiting the Sphinx.'

'Why was it that you did run away?'

'I was scared; my friend was attacked by this crazy Frenchman and I rushed to his defence and hit the French guy. I know I shouldn't have, but he hit my friend first. I thought the police were going to arrest me, like that Australian journalist guy; I've heard that a lot of foreigners have been thrown in prison here since the revolution.'

'And yet, you have come back here today?'

'I didn't want to leave Egypt without seeing the pyramids and the Sphinx.'

He looked me up and down, at my dishevelled condition; I could tell he wasn't buying a word of it. He got up and sent the guards out of the room. Then, certain we were alone, quickly cut to the chase.

'Where are the papers?'

'Papers? What papers?'

Clearly the papers were top secret; the fewer people who knew of their existence the better.

'The papers that you were given in Luxor.'

Given? He *knew* I hadn't stolen them, which means he also knew I hadn't killed Kareem, which meant he knew who had. That meant I had to think of an answer to cover both my ass, and, assuming he was being held in custody, confirm Saeed's story.

'I didn't get any papers in Luxor. There was an old guy, who was some relative of the felucca captain whose boat we'd been on, he showed me some, but he didn't give them to me. They were all in Arabic anyway, so I couldn't read them, I don't even know what they were.'

It was at that moment I was glad I'd slipped them into Tatiana's bag, because, if I'd been caught with them in my possession, it was game set and match; a trial, verdict and sentence of ready, aim, fire. Still, my interrogator wasn't swayed in his position.

'The papers you had in the coloured bag in Luxor, where are they?'

'I don't know what you're talking about.'

'You were seen being offered some papers in the market in Luxor.'

'That's right, I was offered them, but I declined, I didn't take them.'

'You gave the coloured bag to the American woman.'

'Yeah, it was a gift; is there something wrong with that?'

They'd been watching me all along, every step since I met with Kareem; he must have been the Julian Assange of Egypt. The officer stood against the wall and lit a cigarette, surveying me like a circling vulture, waiting for the opportune moment to descend and rip me to pieces. At that point, with the stench of high-tar cigarettes assaulting my lungs, I would have said almost anything to get out of the room.

'You are in very big trouble, you killed an Antiquities inspector and stole some very important government documents. You can be shot for this.'

He'd already betrayed his true position, but I wasn't going to do the same.

'He's dead? That's terrible; he was fine when I left him, you can ask his nephew.'

He leaned in and over the desk and once again calmly delivered his demand.

'Where are the papers?'

'I don't have them.'

It can be intimidating when someone yells and screams at you, but when someone calmly delivers his demands it can be terrifying, especially when straight after, he called the two armed-guards in, then left the room. When he was talking, I could figure out where I stood, but, when he went silent, I was completely in the dark. He opened the backpack, took out metal discs, the crystal ball and the Blue Lotus Essence, giving them a cursive once over before placing them to one side on the desk, then pulled out my laptop, running his fingers over the bullet graze before placing it on the table and turning it on.

'What is this?'

'It's a laptop.'

'Why do you have this?'

'To record my trip, I take it everywhere.'

As the screen finished booting up he looked deliberately at me.

'What is the password?'

'Why?'

'What is on here?'

'Nothing of any importance, just some photos from the trip, some files on Egypt.'

As soon as I said it I realized how stupid I had been.

'What files?'

'You know, the usual ones, just ones I downloaded off the Internet for the trip, about the temples and pyramids.'

'The password?'

I don't know why I next said what I did, it was hardly going to help my cause, but I did.

'Sorry, that's why it's a password.'

At the risk of upsetting him even more, which was unlikely, I wouldn't give it to him. It wasn't as if there was anything incriminating on there, except perhaps my notes on meeting Kareem, and there was no point giving them a written confession!

He closed the laptop, picked it up and left the room. When he did, my mind went into overdrive; what *was* on there? What if he cracked the password, what if he found my rather extensive folder of porn videos?

To say the worst outcomes rushed through my mind in the next half an hour was an understatement: would I be tortured in all manner of ways, taken away and drawn and quartered, burned at the stake, maybe hanged, firing squad, the guillotine. It was if I was reliving every single previous life in which I'd been persecuted for being a messenger of truth; this was the revenge of the Amun Priests.

After what seemed an eternity in purgatory, the officer returned, the laptop still in his clutches. He threw the bottle of essence and crystal ball into the backpack, tossed it at me, and I was dragged to my feet and towards the door. I lunged back to grab the metal discs and shoved them in my shirt pocket before being bundled off into the back seat of another vehicle, sandwiched between the two armed-police; it seemed they were going to take me somewhere else.

'Am I under arrested? What for?'

'No, you are just assisting us with a very important investigation.'

I guess that's why they didn't slap me in irons; that or they didn't have enough pairs to go around. I rationalized that surely while the papers were still missing, that until they recovered them, they wouldn't kill me, so hopefully they weren't taking me to meet my maker; it must be to police headquarters back in Cairo.

For a moment I thought that, perhaps there, I would be allowed to make a phone call to Mark, except that even though my iphone was in my backpack, the battery was dead, and, even though I had his details on my laptop, that was firmly in the vulture's talons in the front seat and i'd have to use the password to log on. Shit, I was screwed!

Within minutes, all four of my captors were smoking their heads off and, trapped in the centre of the back seat, away from any window, I didn't know what was worse, the cigarette smoke or the stench of body odour, mine and theirs; could there be a more aggravated torture? My heart started racing and I was sweating on top of sweating! The more we drove along the streets, the more I came to the conclusion that being held in a cell in the Cairo head-quarters with hundreds of other smokers may not have been the most advantageous of circumstances in which to find myself.

We headed across a bridge over the Nile and, as we did, I figured this may well be my last glimpse of freedom. However, when we turned the next corner, we suddenly ran into a huge demonstration in the city, people were everyone, blocking the streets. The car came to a halt and, before it could reverse and take an alternate route, was soon engulfed by the marauding throng of protestors; the police, much to my chagrin, winding up their windows to protect themselves, but turning the interior of the car into a smoke-filled sweat-box.

But this was no peaceful protest, and soon the car, or more so its occupants, became the target of the demonstrators' displeasure; violently rocking the car from side to side, kicking at the panels, banging on the roof and hurling insults and various objects ranging from fruit and vegetables at and then through the windows.

From the front seat, the head honcho barked out some orders in Arabic and my two minders obediently leapt out of the car, guns at the ready, to clear a path through the melee. This was it, now or never, it meant abandoning my laptop, but so be it, I still had my iphone in the backpack.

Run, rabbit, run

With the officer distracted, I seized the moment, and my backpack, and leapt from the rear of the car, and, crouching as low as I could, weaved my way down and through the crowd as fast as my aching legs could carry me, circling to the right to ensure I stayed in the crowd and didn't suddenly pop out in the open. My objective was to do a big half-circle through the protest and finish up in front of them, heading in the other direction to that in which they thought I was running. I kept moving, dodging anything and everyone, waiting to hear the sound of gunshots and bullets whizzing past my ears, but it didn't happen. I didn't even know if they were chasing me; I didn't want to stick my head up for a look and, in the process, give away my position. I just kept going.

After ten minutes of non-stop head-down scrambling, I spotted a ladies clothing shop and ducked into it; I figured if it had worked once, it could work again.

Quickly scanning the room, I pointed to the biggest plainest black-momma outfit I could find and motioned to try it on. I don't think the lady in the shop spoke much, if any, English, but, although she was somewhat stunned and bemused, she was obliging. Once again disguised as a Muslim Momma, my difficulty arose when I went to pay, as I'd used the last of my cash on bribing Old Father Time in the tomb of Senedjemib-inty, and the shop-owner wouldn't accept my credit card. I motioned to put the card in the 'hole-in-the-wall'.

'Bank?'

She pointed across the road and I went to exit, fully dressed as the black shadow.

'No, no.!'

She grabbed at the dress; there was no way she was letting me out the front door with the goods. Reluctantly, I stripped off and, checking the coast was clear, hustled across to the bank, withdrew five-hundred Egyptian Pounds, and scuttled back. I gave her the three-hundred she wanted, which seemed a tad expensive, redressed, tucked my akubra and the backpack underneath, and exited the store, hunched over like Quasimodo or an amateur actor playing Richard III. Now what?

I ducked into the next doorway and checked my bank receipt for the time: 11:21. I knew my best bet at surviving, of getting out of Egypt alive, was to cut my losses and jump on the first train to Alexandria. I'd lost my laptop, although I had emailed my notes to Mark so they were easily recoverable, and I still had my film footage, but there was no way I could leave Kareem's papers behind; I had to go to the Le Meridien and get them back from Tatiana. That meant I had about three-and-a-half hours to kill before our rendezvous, which meant I could either somehow make my way there and wait at the hotel, or hang around here; both options had their pros and cons.

I also had to consider the possibility the police had backtracked, searched the Russian bus, and Tatiana, discovered the papers, worse, that they were back at the hotel interrogating her. But, I had to be sure.

If I took a cab to Le Meridien now, I'd have to hang about dressed as I was, on the off-chance Tatiana came down to the pool early. Of course there was the possibility Bill or Crystal were still there, although I doubted it; Crystal probably flew back to Germany last night like she said she was going to do, she was like a rolling stone, moving on once she did what she needed, and Bill and Pernille would have headed to the boat, even if just to get away from Jacques. No, I was on my own, Saeed was probably under arrest, and Mark and Frank weren't expecting me until 4pm. The only other person I knew in Cairo was....Abdo! Maybe he could help?

I stepped out onto the street, trying to get my bearings; I was somewhere in downtown Cairo, although exactly where was a mystery, but, if I could make my way to the Cairo Palace, which would be the last place the Secret Police would think to look for me, I could lay low until it was time to go to meet Tatiana. Stepping onto the road, I hailed down a taxi driver and climbed in.

'The Cairo Palace.'

The driver did a double-take until I lifted the veil and repeated the destination. He shook his head in stunned disbelief, then set off, while I continually glanced out through my post-box head-dress, behind and around the taxi, to make sure we weren't followed.

It was only a few minutes later that we came to a halt outside our destination.

'Cairo Palace; fifty pound.'

'Dream on, Dick Turpin, I may look like a cross between Boy George and your grandmother but I didn't come down in the last rain-shower; twenty pounds.'

We haggled for a bit before finally agreeing on twenty-five. I paid him, got my change, and jumped out, afterwards thinking what a bizarre act it was to risk discovery, and potentially my life, for what amounted to five bucks. As the cab drove off, I looked up and down the street for signs of the Secret Police. Was the guy tending the donkey and cart a lookout? Perhaps it was the old man sitting in the doorway? Maybe the six-year-old girl playing in the gutter was a dwarf in disguise. OK, I was paranoid, but for good reason.

Realizing the coast was clear, I entered the building, made my way up in the lift to the third floor, and along the corridor into the reception area where thankfully a familiar face was there to greet me.

'Abdo, am I glad to see you!'

From behind the counter, Abdo's bewildered expression said it all.

'Can ...I ...help you?'

I took off the head-dress.

'It's me, Alex.'

'Mister Alex, what are you doing here?'

'It's a long story.'

Abdo rushed from behind the counter and checked back down the corridor.

'Please, to come inside...'

He escorted me into the lounge area.

'...Please to sit down.'

I hitched up my skirt and collapsed onto the sofa; despite the turmoil that was going on all around me, I felt I could relax, a brief respite before the final onslaught.

'You would like it the drink, something to eat.'

'Abdo, I'm famished, I haven't eaten for days.'

'Yes, I will get it for you some lunch.'

'Thanks. Do you mind if I have a quick shower as well, I don't half pen-and-ink?'

'Shower, yes, of course.'

Abdo showed me to the bathroom, handed me a towel, and headed off to the kitchen to whip up some lunch. I stripped off my ninja tent and shoes, then, as I'd done in Luxor, walked straight under the cooling waters of the shower, washing the layers of dirt from my face and the encased blood from my scalp and hair. I took the metal discs out of my shirt pocket and gazed in wonder at them as the water ran down over my head and cascaded over the surface of the discs, and I laughed. God knows what I had in my hand, but it felt like I had won the biggest lottery ever and had the only winning ticket.

I threw the discs on the bathroom floor and peeled off my sweat-and-grime-soaked shirt and pants. I felt like the beings in the movie 'Cocoon', like I was finally stripping away the old me to reveal the sparkling being within, a being that had been covered in the dirt and grime of thousands of human lives and patterns.

Dispensing with my socks and Calvins, it was more amazing than I'd ever felt before; rinsing out the clothes made me feel like I was rinsing out every last nuance of my soul. I wrung out my clothes and hung them up to dry; was it really that simple, rinse the crap out of your life and start again?

Five minutes later I was done, and by the time I dried off, put my cool damp clothes back on, and popped the metal discs back in my pocket, I felt refreshed and invigorated, all I needed now was some food and drink. By the time I returned to the lounge, Abdo had put out a light lunch.

'You are feeling better?'

'A million dollars.'

'Why is it you are back here, I am think you were to go with Mister Bill to Alexandria?'

'I was; things changed.'

I proceeded to fill him in on the course of events since I left him in Abusir, well, everything except the spiritual stuff, the revision of Arthurian history, and, of course, the amazing evening of sex with Crystal. I told him about the link between Abusir and the Pleiades, which totally blew him away, and about my last-minute decision to visit the Giza Plateau. One of his helpers came our with the main course just as I got to the Great Pyramid, so, as I devoured the omelette and fresh fruit, basically a repeat of what they usually served for breakfast, I explained the pyramid's function, its secret chambers, and the hidden staircase.

I handed Abdo one of the metal discs to examine. He was astounded; he had lived his whole life in and around the pyramids, and he had never heard any of it. He handed back the disc and, when I told him about the Sphinx and its true erosion, and about the underground chambers and the location of the second Sphinx, he was gob-smacked; he couldn't understand how I, a foreigner coming here for the first time, could know all this, and that he, who was born here, grew up here, and spent virtually all his life in the tourism industry, knew none of it. I guess it was a testimony to the success of Hawass in keeping things under wraps.'

A few hours later, by the time I'd told him about the punch-up with Bill and Jacques, and then the things I'd seen beneath the plateau, Abdo was starting to think that I either had concussion, I was kidding, or I had sunstroke. When I told him that I'd filmed it all, he naturally asked to see the footage.

'You have this film?'

'Sure do, it's on my iphone, which is right here in my backpack. Which reminds me, I've got to plug in and call Mark.'

I sat down and started fishing through the backpack for my iphone.'

'It's not here!'

'What?'

'My iphone.'

'You are sure?'

'Yep. It's gone; the Secret Police must have it.'

'This it is not good.'

Then I found the charger and held it up.

'No, I watched him empty the backpack, and he didn't take it out, and, if he did take it, surely he would have taken the charger as well, like he did with the laptop. No, I don't think he's got it; it wasn't there.'

'Then where it is?'

'I must have dropped it, or left it somewhere.'

Abdo looked as if I was pulling his leg.

'This it is the phone you have shoot of what it is under the Giza Plateau, yes?'

'Yes; the corridors and chambers, the UFO, the underground lake and city, the Hall of Records, Gort, the time machine, the tomb of Thoth,...all of it...'

I ran all the possibilities back through my mind; could it have fallen out in the tomb of Senedjemib-inty? No, I would have seen it in the morning.

'...The last time I saw it was, well, I didn't see it because the battery went dead,...was... *inside the staircase*! I put it on the step, then, when the secret door opened, I was in such a rush to get outside, I left it behind, inside, on the step...'

I collapsed back in the lounge; I couldn't believe my stupidity, all the proof was gone, well, not so much gone, as locked behind a 15-ton block 400-feet up the face of the Great Pyramid.

'Shit!'

There was no way I could go back and retrieve it, not now anyway. Perhaps, a few months from now, perhaps when things have died down, I could slip back into Egypt undetected, hide away somewhere on the Giza Plateau, then scale the pyramid in the middle of the night and retrieve it. Yeah, right, that was a lot of "perhap's". It also meant I couldn't even call Mark to confirm our 4 pm rendezvous, I did have his details on my computer, but that was no help either because my laptop was now firmly in the vulture's claws. I was in despair at my stupidity.

'With my iphone entombed forever, it makes Kareem's papers even more important, apart from these metal discs, they're the only proof of what's been going on here in Egypt.'

'You still have these papers?'

'No, I gave them to a Russian goddess just before the Secret Police finally captured me.'

'A Russian ...'

'It's OK, it's a long story; I arranged to meet her at the Le Meridien at

3:00pm.'

We both checked the time by the clock on the wall, 2:23.

'Well, we must better be go, the street it is filled with much protest.'

'We?'

'Yes, you think I will let you do this on your own?'

'You don't have to do this Abdo.'

'I know, Mister Alex, but how many time is it now that you have escape from the Secret Police? They are shoot at you, they are catch you, but still you are get away; it must be the will of Allah. And each time Allah he bring you to me for to be safe. And if Allah he choose you to get these paper out of Egypt, then I must do also what I can to help.'

He immediately jumped on his mobile, and I had an idea.

'Abdo, can I use your computer to check my email?'

'This it is not a problem.'

He showed me to reception and his computer where I logged on. As soon as I did, several emails downloaded, including one from Mark.

'Dear Alex,

I just got your email. I am blown away about what you're saying, not only that you've been under the Giza Plateau, but that you filmed it all, especially the Hall of Records. I'm going to spend some time now reading your attached notes and can't wait to see the footage...'

'Yeah, well that's going to be an anti-climax now, isn't it!'

'...Unfortunately Frank and I are no longer in Cairo...'

'Shit! No way!'

'...When we hadn't heard anything from you, we assumed you'd either been arrested, or were on your way to Greece, and, with the fracas outside the Australian Embassy and the political unrest and protests in Cairo, Frank and I decided to bug-out to London until things settle down...'

'Oh, great.'

'...So, I'm sorry but we can't meet you, or help out. However, I told the Australian Embassy all about you, the murder allegations, and about the papers, and told them to keep an eye out for you just in case things went awry and you finished up in custody. That said, if I were you, I'd steer clear of the Embassy, the Secret Police will still have it pegged and be expecting you to go there, so stick to your original plan and get on a boat to Greece as fast as you can.

Good luck, Mark.'

'Shit!'

'What is it the matter?'

'The cavalry have bolted.'

'I do not understand this.'

'Mark and Frank have gone, they're in London, which means I'm flying solo.'

Abdo was confused.

'You wish to go to the airport?'

'No it's a figure of speech,...'

I did briefly contemplate trying the Embassy again, but, "once bitten, twice shy" as they say; I wasn't going to walk back into the snake pit again if I could help it.

'...Once I have the papers, I need to get to Alexandria. How far is it to get there?'

'To Alexandria? About a hundred-thirty mile.'

'Is it easier to get there by car or train?'

'To Alexandria? It is much better by car, but there are many police check point, I am think to be safe we will go by it the train.'

'We?'

'Yes, Mister Alex, until you are safe I will be come with you.'

'You are a true brother, Abdo; ahoya.'

He smiled.

'Come then, we must be go.'

'Hang on, let me send a quick email.'

'Dear Mark,

It's about 2:30 and I'm heading off to retrieve Kareem's documents (long story) then catch the train to Alexandria. The Secret Police are still very much on my ass.

Unfortunately I no longer have my iphone, so all the footage is gone, well, not so much gone, as probably irretrievable, because I left the iphone inside the Great Pyramid at the top of the secret staircase. However, I still have a few metal discs, the crystal ball I found in one of the chambers, and the bottle of Blue Lotus Essence from Thoth's tomb; at least it's something.

I'll contact you in a day or so once I'm safely in Greece.

Alex.

To Russia with love

The email sent, five minutes later we were ready to go, except for one thing.

'I think, Mister Alex, it is best you be wear it the hijab.'

'I suppose so; at least until I'm safely on a boat out of Alexandria, I guess you're right.'

I reluctantly put my disguise back on and we headed downstairs, then, like any normal Egyptian man and his elderly mother, innocently climbed into an awaiting car.

We circumnavigated the protest and headed back across the river towards Giza and the Le Meridien. Naturally the conversation enroute consisted not just of my escape, but, more importantly on what lay 'undiscovered' below the Giza Plateau; Abdo had never heard of the Annunaki, or the Dracos for that matter, so the information about Thoth and his tomb totally freaked him out.

We arrived at Le Meridien with around five minutes to spare; I hoped Tatiana had not only made it back, but, more importantly, she still had the shopping bag and, more importantly, its contents. As I got out of the car, Abdo went to come with me.

'Where are *you* going?'

'I am come with you.'

'What for, you don't need to, I'll only be a few minutes.'

'You are dressed as the Egyptian woman. At Le Meridien this it would be very unusual for her to be on her own, also, the Secret Police they may already have discovered the paper and know you will be return to get them at 3 pm; they may be watch this woman, it may be trap. You please wait here, I will have it the look first. If Secret Police, they are watch her, I will not be notice, I will be like it hotel manager.'

'How about I wait in the lobby area, I can see most of the pool from area from there.'

'Yes, very good.'

We headed inside, slowly, so as to not look conspicuous, then over to the area that looked out over the pool.

'How does it she look?'

I scanned the perimeter of the pool.

'About 30, long black hair.'

'You can see her?'

'I'm not sure, that could be her on the far side.'

'Wait here, I will look.'

I watched nervously as Abdo made his way casually around to the far side of the pool, carefully scrutinizing the occupant of every deck chair as he passed. Finally he stopped at the target location, had a second assessment, took one final 360 degree check for Secret Police, then clearly spoke Tatiana's name, as she instantly responded and sat up. They had a brief somewhat animated conversation, during which she picked up the shopping bag and held it close, shaking her head; it seemed she wasn't to trusting of Abdo to relinquish it to him, but at least she still had it. Abdo continued to look around for signs of the Secret Police, before he shrugged, nodded and made his way casually back to the lobby.

'What happened, what did she say?'

'She said it that she would only give it the bag to you, personal. But I am think perhaps it is the trap.'

'Did you see signs of any Secret Police?'

'No, but that it does not mean they are not there, the Secret Police they are everywhere.'

'If they had the papers back, what need would they have of me?'

'Because you know that these paper they are exist.'

'But, Abdo, I haven't got a clue what's in them; they're all in Arabic, and, without proof, without hard evidence, it would be so easy for them to just fob me off as another conspiracy theorist. No, I think she's legit.'

'Then, I will come with you. I think it is best, just to be safe, that you do not show your disguise.'

'Agreed.'

We sauntered casually around the pool; god how I wished I was just a simple tourist and able to just chill out in the midday sun like these guys, yes, sipping pina coladas and waist deep in the hotel pool. Instead, I was an innocent fugitive stuck in a black sauna suit on some sort of James Bond mission to rescue and recover the truth of the history of the planet. Shit!

Arriving at Tatiana's deckchair, I finally got a complete eyeful of the package; dressed in the skimpiest of yellow string bikinis, that was so tiny it left virtually nothing to the imagination, something you could only do in Egypt in the sanctuary of the International hotel pool areas; she was stunning. She had a body to die for and could easily have passed for a Bond girl; long black hair, full firm breasts, luscious lips, hourglass figure and slender legs that stretched out along the deckchair. I almost forgot the reason why I was there, to get the papers back.

'Tatiana.'

She looked at the "Egyptian women" before her.'

'Alex?'

'Yes, it's me. Excuse the outfit but I'm not exactly flavour of the month around Egypt at the moment.'

'Wouldn't you like to come up to my room and slip into something more comfortable?'

'Hell yes…'

Well that's what I thought, but not what I said.

'…I can't, I mean I'd love to, but I have to get the papers out of Egypt. Do you still have them?'

She stood up and handed the shopping bag back to me.

'All this fuss for a bundle of papers?'

'You looked at them?'

'Of course, what did you expect me to do?'

'Did you show anyone else?'

'No.'

'Good. Good.'

She must have thought I was some sort of super spy, some real life James Bond, and to make matters worse, just like in the movies, she seductively sidled up against me.

'So, do you want to tell me what this is all about?'

'It's best you don't know, for your own sake.'

'So, will I see you again?'

I hoped so, I really hoped so, but the truth was, it was highly unlikely.

'I don't know, maybe one day if you come to Australia I can, ….we can…'

Imagine a hot Euro-babe grinding her body into a fully-clad Egyptian grandmother; it was bound to grab the attention of someone, anyone, everyone; definitely not kosher!

'Mister Alex, we must get going.'

Abdo had seen the awkwardness of my situation and saved the day, tugging at my dress and pulling me away from what would have been certain ecstasy, possibly followed by certain death if I were caught.

'Right. Tatiana, I can't thank you enough for doing this for me, you don't know how important this is, but someday I'll find a way to thank you properly…'

Initially I was thinking of some financial return that might come from the book or movie about it all, but the reality was all I wanted to do was spend an eternity or two shagging her tight Moscowvitian little brains out.

'…Leave your contact details at reception and I'll call the hotel for them in a few days once I'm safely out of Egypt, or I'll get Abdo to pick them up later tonight.'

'Quiet, Mister Alex, remember who it is you are, or rather, who it is you are *supposed* to be.'

Abdo dragged me away, leaving Tatiana to recline on her deckchair and dream of what might have been. Hell, if somehow I couldn't contact Crystal, at least I had a plan B, assuming of course I could get out of Egypt alive.

Moments later we were back in the awaiting car and speeding, as best we could through the Cairo traffic, towards the main station at Ramses square.

'How long will it take us to get to Alexandria?'

'Two-and-a-half hour. Three-and-a-half hour if we take it the local train. But no matter which way, I think you must be keep on the women clothes to be safe…'

As much as I hated the thought, he was right.

'…There is it the express train in 30 minute at 4:00 pm from Ramses station, this we may be able to catch in time.'

This time I wasn't so sure that was the best option.

'But won't Ramses station have lots of police, they'll be looking for me? Even dressed like this, it might be too dangerous.'

'Yes, yes, this is true, there will be many many police here, it will be very dangerous. I think it better to go to next station, to Shubra El-Kheima, and to be get on the local train which leave around 4:20.'

He passed on the instructions to our driver and we detoured out onto the ring road.

'Can we get on the express train there?'

'No, it not stop here.'

Great, an extra hour in the black post-box, crammed in on a cattle-car with no air-conditioning; but, if it got me to Alexandria and freedom, after everything I'd gone through in the last few days, I could cope.

We arrived at the station just as the express train was going through, meaning we had about 15 minutes before the local train arrived.

'How much are the tickets?'

'Do not worry, Mister Alex, I will get it them.'

'No, Abdo, take this, I insist, it may not be enough, but it's all I've got for now.'

I gave Abdo my last hundred pounds and waited in the car as he headed into the station. Meanwhile Magdy tried to fill in as host.

'So Mister Alex, you are having the good time in Egypt?'

I laughed.

'Unforgettable!'

Abdo returned several minutes later and climbed in.

'We will wait it here until the train it arrive, it will be much safer.'

Over the next five or ten minutes, hundreds of people converged on the station, many of them women dressed as I was, in the fully black-tent regalia; it was going to be easy to infiltrate the heart of the herd. D-Day arrived and Abdo leapt out of the car.

'OK, let us go.'

Using my years of acting training, and doing my best 'old-lady' impression, I casually climbed out of the back seat, the shopping bag in one hand, the backpack in the other, but, as we set off, Abdo grabbed for the backpack.

'It will look less wrong if I carry this…'

I went to take it back and Abdo laughed.

'…You will give it the paper to beautiful Russian girl you have met for 5 minute, but you worry about your ahoya he carry it the backpack for you.'

'You're right, I guess I'm just a bit toey; I'll be better once we're safely on board and underway.'

And that's exactly what happened; we mingled in with the herd just as the train arrived, and, once we had survived the stampede to board and Abdo had managed to secure us a couple of seats by the window, as soon as the train set in motion, I relaxed.

After a few minutes of silence amid the cacophony of the carriage, during which Abdo and I both thoroughly scanned the carriage for signs of vultures, crocodiles and cobras, I leaned in towards Abdo and whispered.

'How many stops between here and Alexandria?'

'Perhaps twelve, maybe fifteen.'

I did the math; that was a stop roughly every fifteen minutes. If I'd had my laptop I would have used it to play some music, but the laptop was now long gone, I could kiss it goodbye, as was my iphone; all I had left were the discs, the papers, a crystal ball and a bottle of pixie-dust. I considered that maybe I could take a swig or two, gaze into the ball and foretell my future? Maybe I could tell fortunes to the locals; Madam Zelda tells fortunes, 5 pounds a reading. I mean I had the outfit. Actually, half the carriage had the outfit.

Then, for some reason, I had a totally unrelated thought.

'Abdo, do we go anywhere near Tanis?'

Tanis

I'd hoped I might have been able to visit it; the ancient city referred to in the film *"Indiana Jones and the Raiders of the Lost Ark"* that was supposedly buried by a catastrophic ancient sandstorm then rediscovered by Nazis searching for the Ark of the Covenant during World War II. I now realized the truth was, that, although Sheshonq may have brought the Ark back here in 983 BC, it passed on to Yebu on Elephantine Island then possibly to Ethiopia.

The sandstorm didn't happen either; the city was most likely buried by any one of a number of tsunamis resulting from earthquakes as early as 396 BC from the eruption of Etna, through 224 BC, the Etna eruption of 122 BC, the earthquake in 27 BC, the eruption of Vesuvius in 79 AD, or as late as the Turkey earthquake of 365 AD. The site was also threatened with inundation by Lake Manzala in the 6th Century AD, and finally abandoned in 696 AD, when Alexandria was also severely damaged by an earthquake.

Finally, the Nazis never battled Indiana Jones in the site's ruins, but it didn't mean someone wasn't there digging around, as, in 1939, a French archaeologist named Pierre Montet unearthed a royal tomb complex that included three intact and undisturbed burial chambers that contained dazzling funereal treasures such as jewellery, tableware, amulets, golden masks, coffins of silver, and elaborate sarcophagi. But, if Abdo didn't even know the city, he wouldn't know any of that.

'Tanis? What is this Tanis?'

'Have you seen the film *"Indiana Jones and the Raiders of the Lost Ark"*?'

'Yes, but I do not know this "Tanis", there is not such a place.'

Was I wrong, could I have been duped? No, it was there all right.

'Yes, there is; according to the Egyptologists, it was the home city of Smendes, founder of the 21st Dynasty and northern capital of Egypt during the 21st Dynasty, and was a parallel religious centre to Thebes during the Third Intermediate Period of the 21st to 24th Dynasties.'

'Where is this place?'

'In the Nile Delta, northeast of Cairo. You must know it...'

He gave me a blank look; I might as well have told him it was somewhere in Siberia.

'...The site was buried until numerous archaeological digs were carried out by Flinders Petrie and Auguste Mariette in the late 19th Century.

Then, in 1939, in the main temple enclosure in Tanis, Pierre Montet discovered three intact royal tombs from the 21st and 22nd Dynasties, filled with silver coffins, gold funerary masks, and gold and silver jewellery, the tombs of Psusennes I, Amenemope and Sheshonq II.'

'Yes, yes, this place I know, it is called Ṣān el-Ḥajar el-Qibliyyah. I do not know this name "Tanis", the ancient name it is Djanet.'

'Do we go near it?'

'No, it is many mile away to the east, and I do not think you should be go there.'

'I agree.

I sat back and gazed out the window. Tanis would have been amazing to visit, although there was nowhere near as much to see for the ordinary tourist when comparing Tanis to the Temples at Luxor, Karnak, and further up the Nile and Edfu and Aswan. But the fact Tanis was a major city on the Nile Delta meant it would have had stunning evidence of the tsunamis theory. Clearly there had been numerous tsunami's that have hit the Nile Delta over the past five, ten, twenty thousand years or more, my search now was not whether Djanet, "Tanis", was first built in the 21st Dynasty, as some Egyptologists believe, but how many cities were there before it. I sat back and trawled my mind, recalling my notes as best I could for signs to support the theory.

I was reminded of an image I had in my files, similar to the excavations I had seen first hand in Abydos that revealed the Osireion deep beneath the surface, that showed the layers of soil, sand and debris that had been deposited on the site of the city of Tanis; at least 2 to 10 metres deep. And that sedimentary deposit was just for the latter tsunamis, the ones *after* the 21st Dynasty. And I knew many of the stones used to build the various temples at Tanis, including the Temple of Amun, came from the old Ramesside town of Qantir, ancient Pi-Ramesses, including an obelisk that bears the cartouche of Ramses II.

But, as we know, Ramses II went around and slapped his moniker on anything and everything, and, if the obelisk was made of red granite, which it very much appeared to be, it was clear evidence the obelisk was from a much earlier time, a much earlier city, probably on the same site, or close by.

That theory was supported by some historians, who assert that Tanis dates back even further, to the Old Kingdom, as some stone blocks were found at Tanis that held the names of Khafre, Pepi I, and other Old Kingdom Pharaohs. Additional evidence came from the fact the tombs, and even the sarcophagi, were reused from earlier periods. Of course it was possible those stones may have been brought to Tanis, but it was more logical that those stones were recovered from a previous city that had been devastated by the Thera tsunami.

Even more evidence was unearthed in 2009 when archaeologists discovered the site of a second sacred lake, 15 metres long, 12 metres wide, and built out of limestone blocks, in a temple to the goddess Mut; it was discovered 12 metres below ground, which totally reinforced the tsunami theory. But what I was really looking for was red granite.

I knew a guy called Rifaud had taken two large pink-granite sphinxes to Paris, where they became a part of the Louvre collection, but whether there was any way of discerning from what period they originated, I didn't know.

Henry Salt and another guy called Drovetti found eleven statues at Tanis, some of which were also sent to the Louvre, the others to Berlin and Alexandria, although the ones sent to Alexandria are now lost. Other statues had been removed as well, and taken to Saint Petersburg and Berlin, but whether any or all of them were granite or not, I could only speculate.

The last image I remembered distinctly from my files, but I couldn't put a label to, was one that showed part of a wall, possibly even the inner chamber of one of the 21st Dynasty tombs. It wasn't the walls that I was really interested in, it was the heavily-worn red granite object that sat in the alcove; it may have been a sarcophagus, but, whatever it was, it was old, really old, and it confirmed my belief that the real excavations at Tanis hadn't even begun, that the archaeologists were preoccupied with what was just below the surface, and that the real 'treasure' was 12 metres down, possibly even deeper.

Having stopped and moved on from the first station along the line, I felt we were safely settled in for the duration. I figured I'd killed about quarter-of-an-hour contemplating Tanis, and, feeling relaxed, decided to take a sip of the Lotus essence, sit back, lean my head against the carriage wall, and do something I felt like I hadn't done for ages; sleep. Fortuitously, the steady rocking and rattling of the train quickly had its affect and I drifted off to the land of nod.

The Russian Revolution

The next thing I knew it was World War I and Tatiana and I were seated on a train headed to Petrograd, modern-day St. Petersburg, in Russia. It was the time leading up to and including the Russian Revolution, a period I had always been fascinated with; was that because I'd had an alternate life there as well?

Seated opposite me in the carriage, Tatiana was now Tatiana Nikolaevna Romanova, Grand Duchess and the second daughter of Tsar Nicholas II, the title 'Tsar' interestingly enough meaning Caesar; was there some significance it that? Somehow I was connected to her, in fact she was protecting me because I, Alex, was her little brother, Alexei, Tsarevich Alexei Nikolaevich, next in line to the Russian throne. I wondered if Crystal and Pernille were two of my other sisters, Olga, Anastasia, Maria? And Bill, who was he?

That Tatiana was a Grand Duchess, or rather Grand Princess, was significant, as a Grand Duchess, as an "imperial highness" was higher in rank than other princess in Europe, who were merely "royal highnesses"; was this somehow related to the *sang réal*? If so, how, and why?

Tsar Nicholas II was of primarily German, as well as Russian and Danish descent. He was the eldest son of Emperor Alexander III and Empress Maria Feodorovna of Russia (Maria formerly Princess Dagmar of Denmark). His paternal grandparents were Emperor Alexander II and Empress Maria Alexandrovna of Russia (Alexandrovna born Princess Marie of Hesse-Darmstadt). His maternal grandparents were King Christian IX and Queen Louise of Denmark.

Nicholas was related to several monarchs in Europe. His mother's siblings included King Frederik VIII of Denmark and King George I of Greece, as well as the United Kingdom's Queen Alexandra (consort of King Edward VII). All that meant Nicholas, his wife, Alexandra, and Kaiser Wilhelm II of Germany were all first cousins of King George V of the United Kingdom.

Nicholas was also a first cousin of both King Haakon VII and Queen Maud of Norway, as well as to King Constantine I of Greece. While not first cousins, Nicholas and Kaiser Wilhelm II were second cousins, once removed, as each descended from King Frederick William III of Prussia, as well as being third cousins, as they were both great-great-grandsons of Tsar Paul I of Russia. Nicholas and his wife, Alexandra, were also second cousins, as both descended from Louis II, Grand Duke of Hesse and his wife, Wilhelmine of Baden.

The interbreeding was not only significant, it was multi-layered; it had to be somehow related to the *sang réal*, and, if it was, then that meant the fact I was dreaming about it meant there was some significance of it to the Russian Revolution.

To all sides of the train, amid exploding shells and mustard gas in muddy fields covered in freezing snow and the bodies of millions of dead soldiers and starving civilians, dates flashed past; episodes from the turmoil leading up to and including the Russian Revolution were unfolding. The first date was "1881", which at first took me by surprise as it was the year Alexander II was assassinated by revolutionaries.

Out the window, playing chess on a pile of frozen corpses and starving citizens was Alexander II, of the Dynasty of Holstein-Gottorp-Romanov. What was most significant about Alexander II, in fact all the leaders of the House of Romanov, was that each of them took a German consort from the Germanic Royal monarchy as their wife; so, it *was* all about the *sang réal*, the strong line was through the Germanic women and that's why the English branch wanted, needed, to reconnect with it through the House of Hanover as well. Did it even run through into Hitler's true agenda of the Arian lineage? The plot was getting thicker.

The chessboard was shaped like all of Europe and Russia, with the 'chessmen' being the Kings, Queens and leaders of the governments of each of the countries; each one was clearly expendable to achieve the ultimate goal and protect the 'king', whoever the 'king' really was. Pitted against Alexander II, on the other side of the chessboard, was the assembled Royalty of Europe. What did that mean, and what did it have to do with the Russian Revolution, that was in 1917, over thirty years later?

Alexander Nikolaevich Romanov, Alexander II, Emperor of Russia from 1855 until his assassination in 1881, was the most successful Russian reformer since Peter the Great. He advocated peace and was responsible for numerous major reforms including; reorganising the judicial system to include trial in open court with judges and a jury system, and the creation of justices of the peace to deal with minor local offences. He abolished capital punishment, promoted local self-government, ended some of the privileges of the nobility, and promoted the universities.

Encouraged by public response, Alexander began a period of even more radical reforms, including; a move to develop Russia's natural resources, to reform all branches of the administration, and an attempt to not depend on a 'landed aristocracy' that controlled the poor, which resulted in his most important achievement, the emancipation of serfs in 1861, for which he became known as 'Alexander the Liberator'.

However, despite all these reforms, he was a target for at least six prior assassination attempts by members of the Narodnaya Volya, 'The People's Will' or 'The People's Freedom', who eventually succeeded in March 1881. That didn't make sense; the Russian people had the most liberal ruler in centuries, and a radical band of them assassinated him? I smelled a rat, or rather a kettle of vultures; something else must have been going on. The question had to be asked, 'who were this Narodnya Volya', and 'what was the real agenda'?

I looked back out over the battlefield to Alexander II who was now surrounded by numerous masked marionettes, their strings disappearing into the clouds. They were tossing hand-grenades at the Tsar. Was the Narodnaya Volya not what it seemed?

Narodnaya Volya was supposedly a Russian left-wing terrorist organization founded in 1879 that comprised workers, students, and members of the military. Their ideology apparently demanded a mix of democratic and socialist reforms including: a Constitution, permanent people's representation, freedom of speech and assembly, communal self-government, transfer of land to the people, gradual placement of the factories under the control of the workers, and granting the oppressed people of the Russian Empire the right to self-determination.

So how is it that, on the morning before he was fatally wounded by a bomb, Alexander II signed the Loris-Melikov constitution, which, if it had not been repealed by his reactionary successor, and son, Alexander III, would have created two legislative commissions made up of indirectly elected representatives, which would certainly have been a major move forward for the people. It makes no sense that they assassinated him because he opposed their ideologies. Had he lived, Russia may well have followed a path to constitutional monarchy instead of the long road of oppression that defined his successor's reign. In fact, the great irony of Narodnaya Volya is, that their aim was to save Russia from autocracy, and yet their assassination of Alexander II in March 1881 triggered major suppression of civil liberties in Russia, and the resurgence of police brutality via the full force of autocratic oppression as his successor, Alexander III, would take no chances with any reforms or liberal ideas. *That* was telling!

It was also during his reign, in complete contrast to his father's acts, that Alexander III's brutal secret police, the Third Section, sent thousands of dissidents into exile in Siberia. And yet the members of the Narodnaya Volya were able to go about their business 'undiscovered'. It was Akhenaten and the Amun Priests all over again, Henry VIII and Thomas Cranmer; look to the real power-brokers behind the throne. Was it possible that the German leg of his family had double-crossed him because he was a pacifist, and was systematically liberating the masses? Had he in-effect 'excommunicated' himself from the family, and, like JFK, Robert Kennedy, Anwar Sadat, and so many others, had 'the family' eliminated one of their own because he wasn't toting the party, or family, line? Suddenly Alexander II's assassination started to make a lot more sense.

The Illuminati puppet-masters were used to pulling the strings and orchestrating everything, so, when they saw the growing unrest amongst the people, unrest they had seen in France, which now, with Alexander's reforms, they saw manifesting in Russia, they moved to stop the rot; they 'created' Narodnaya Volya from their people within the military and used it for one purpose, to eliminate Alexander II. In effect, Narodnaya Volya was just another CIA-type black-op.

I wondered if had I been Alexander II, the liberator; the name was the same? Was I on the verge of blowing the lid on the whole 'monarchy' deception, and going to truly liberate the people? Is that the real reason why I/he was assassinated by the so-called 'revolutionaries'? I was continually reminded of how the 'victors' wrote history, and they wrote it not just to make themselves look good, and to tell the story the way they wanted it remembered, not the way it was, but to cover their own evil doings, like the US dropping atomic bombs on Hiroshima and Nagasaki.

But then I thought, if my dream was about the Russian Revolution, about Tatiana and I as innocent children of Tsar Nicholas II, why was it starting here, thirty years earlier in 1881? Even the Russian writer and philosopher Fyodor Dostoyevsky, whose literary works explore human psychology in the troubled political, social, and spiritual atmosphere of 19th Century Russia, who, coincidently also died in 1881, around a month before Alexander II was assassinated, had seen it coming. He wrote:

"The godless anarchism is close, our children will see it. International ordered that the European revolution will start in Russia, and it will, as we do not have reliable resistance in administration nor society. The mutiny will start with atheism and robbery of all riches, they will start to depose the religion, destroy temples and turn them into barracks and stables, flood the world in blood, and then themselves get frightened."

Dostoyevsky wrote this more than 35 years before the actual Russian Revolution so he clearly could see the writing on the wall, and his words are no less poignant in today's global environment, but if he could see it, so could the puppet masters. I wondered if maybe he had some inside knowledge as, about 30 years earlier, Dostoyevsky was arrested for his involvement in the Petrashevsky Circle, a secret society of liberal utopians who proposed social reforms in Russia and also functioned as a literary discussion group on the issues of freedom from censorship and the abolition of serfdom.

Initially condemned to death, Tsar Nicholas I commuted his sentence to four years hard labour in Siberia, where he was classified as "one of the most dangerous convicts". Once released, Dostoyevsky left Russia, however, when he returned to Russia following the death of Nicholas I, the new Tsar, Alexander II, ordered Dostoyevsky to visit his palace to present Dostoyovsky's *Diary* to him. In the *Diaries*, Dostoyevsky stated that the Tsar and the people should form a unity:

"For the people, the tsar is not an external power, not the power of some conqueror ... but a power of all the people, an all-unifying power the people themselves desired."

Dostoyevsky apparently distinguished three "enormous world ideas" prevalent in his time: Protestantism, Roman Catholicism, and Russian Orthodoxy. He found Protestantism self-contradictory and claimed that it would ultimately lose power and spirituality; I think he was on the ball there. As for Catholicism, he claimed it had continued the tradition of Imperial Rome and had thus become anti-Christian and proto-socialist inasmuch as the Church's interest in political affairs led it to abandon the idea of Christ. Given the Catholic Church's involvement in the International

Atomic Energy Agency, the Organization for Security and Co-operation in Europe, the Organization for the Prohibition of Chemical Weapons, the United Nations High Commission for Refugees, and as a permanent observer on the United Nations General Assembly, the Council of Europe, UNESCO, and the World Trade Organization, to name a few, I think he was spot on. In fact, for Dostoyevsky, socialism was "the latest incarnation of the Catholic idea" and its "natural ally"; he deemed Russian Orthodoxy to be the ideal form of Christianity.

And so it was, aware of all this, that Alexander II asked Dostoyevsky to educate his sons, meaning clearly Alexander II was sympathetic to Dostoyevsky's way of thinking. On the other hand, I severely doubted the vultures, crocodile and spitting cobras of the puppet-masters were sympathetic to either of them. And yet, despite their obvious sympathetic relationship, in January 1881, a month before Dostoyevsky's death, and six weeks before Alexander's assassination, the Secret Police executed a search warrant in the apartment of one of Dostoyevsky's neighbours, supposedly searching for members of the Narodnaya Volya. The following day, Dostoyevsky supposedly suffered a pulmonary haemorrhage.

It didn't take much brainpower to realize that if members of the Narodnaya Volya were really about reformation, and they just happened to live in the same apartment building as Dostoyevsky, who was 'best-buddies' with the Alexander II, they would use that connection to passively influence the Emperor, but, no, we're asked to believe Dostoyevsky had nothing to do with Narodnaya Volya and they decided to assassinate the most successful Russian reformer since Peter the Great on their own. Especially when, in a matter of 48 hours, Alexander II planned to release his plan for an elected parliament, or duma, to the Russian people. Please, to paraphrase Judge Judy, don't piss on my head and tell me it's raining!

And what about Dostoyevsky's supposed "pulmonary haemorrhage", was he, like so may others before him, the victim of poison, one that causes bleeding in the lungs? If he were, it would be consistent with the fact the Secret Police knew Dostoyevsky knew something. Perhaps that's why he wrote his "Godless anarchism" quote, it may even, like JFK's "secret society" speech, have signed his death warrant.

So, was Alexander II's assassination the real impetus behind the Russian Revolution, were the seeds sewn in 1881? Had the Illuminati seen the writing on the wall for a revolt by the people and moved, not to prevent it, but to temporarily postpone it through the reign of Alexander III until they could get their ducks in a line?

Out in the field the next sign read '1887' and in place of Alexander II at the chessboard was his son, Alexander III, but this time Alexander III had the same marionette strings holding him up as the numerous 'revolutionary' figures that lurked in the shadows around him poised to throw hand grenades, those figures including Aleksandr Ilyich Ulyanov, the older brother of Vladimir Lenin. However Ulyanov and the others were captured before they could throw their grenades, and the assassination attempt failed, Ulyanov soon hanging from the very marionette ropes that once directed him. It wasn't just Ulyanov that was arrested before he could detonate his bomb, but all of the Narodnaya Volya, arrested before Alexander III's carriage even approached. That meant the Secret Police not only had prior knowledge about the assassination attempt and who was involved, but, unlike with the assassination of his father, they were intent on preventing this one. It meant, quite simply, that the assassination attempt on Alexander III was a genuine reaction to his oppressive rule, a rule that was supported by the Illuminati, and therefore a genuine assassination attempt by 'the people'.

The first action Alexander III took after his father's death was to tear up his father's plans for an elected parliament, or Duma, plans that had been completed the day before Alexander II was assassinated, but not yet released to the Russian people. But did Alexander III tear it up, or did he do so at the advice of his 'minders', the puppet-masters? In any case, it instigated a reign marked by both major suppression of civil liberties in Russia, with the arrest of protestors and uprooting of suspected rebel groups, and the advocating of anarchists to use spectacular acts of violence to incite revolution; the same ploy that was invoked after 9/11.

I felt like I was in the scene from *'The Time Machine'* where George pushes the lever forward and the shop window changes as the years roll forward, only here it was the players in and around the chessboard. '1894' saw Alexander III's son, Nicholas II at the chessboard, fumbling pieces, totally ignorant of what the pieces were and how they moved. Lurking menacingly around him, amongst others, was Leon Trosky and the Bolsheviks, and Vladmir Lenin. Nicholas II was totally unprepared to assume the throne upon the death of his father, and, consequently, during his reign, he saw Imperial Russia go from being one of the foremost great powers of the world to economic and military collapse, including humiliatingly defeat in the Russo-Japanese War.

By the time we hit '1905', the chessboard was covered in hundreds of dead and bleeding bodies; unarmed protesters shot by the Tsar's troops. Numerous strikes, political unrest, and extreme pressure on the monarchy, had prompted Nicholas II to finally commission the first of several unsuccessful state Dumas; it marked the first official stage of the Russian Revolution, and, when the Dumas failed to fulfil any hopes of democracy, it fuelled further ideas of revolution and violent outbursts targeted at the monarchy.

The onset of World War I soon followed, in '1914', with Germany also 'declaring war' on Russia. In response, Nicholas II changed the name of Saint Petersburg to 'Petrogad' so it would sound more Russian. That's where Tatiana and I and the rest of the family were headed, Petrograd, but, whilst once that would have seemed joyous, now there was a real sense of foreboding about the future and our destination.

The bringing of Russia into the war had the effect of briefly uniting the Russians and, in the short term, by arresting the Bolsheviks and exiling them to Siberia, quelling the strikes and political unrest; it was clearly an attempt by the Illuminati to retain control of the masses, by getting them involved in a war and removing all the dissidents. Sound familiar?

In '1915', after several serious military defeats and heavy casualties, the strikes recommenced, and, when numerous strikers were shot at Kostromá and Ivánovo-Voznesénsk, and the prices of basic commodities skyrocketed, it was clear that revolution was inevitable; it was not a question of if, but when and how. By the end of October 1916, Russia had lost an estimated 1.8 million soldiers, with an additional 2 million prisoners of war and 1 million missing, making a total of nearly 5 million men; the bell was tolling, and it was tolling for Nicholas II.

Nicholas was blamed for all of these crises, and, as discontent grew, in November '1916', the Duma warned the Tsar that the army would not support him against a revolution, and, inevitably, a terrible disaster would grip the country unless a constitutional form of government was put in place. Nicholas supposedly ignored the warning.

This train ain't bound for glory

The scene shifted forward to 'February 1917' and suddenly I felt we all had to get off the train, fast, Tatiana, me, Olga, Anastasia, Maria and father; sinister blood-red shadows were creeping up all around him. But our father was far too preoccupied with his game of chess to notice what was going on around him, and so, like a freight train, weighed-down with the bodies of over five million Russians, it pressed forward.

The 'February Revolution' of 1917, which actually happened in March of the modern Gregorian calendar as the older Julian calendar, 13 days behind, was still in use in Russia until 1918, was a revolution focused in and around Petrograd.

On the 22nd February, workers at Putilov, Petrograd's largest industrial plant, announced a strike. The next day, a series of meetings and rallies being held for International Women's Day gradually turned into economic and political gatherings at which demonstrations were organized to demand bread. These demonstrations, supported by the industrial working force, mainly of women because all the men were away fighting in the war, marched to nearby factories, bringing out over 50,000 workers on strike.

By the 25th February virtually every industrial and commercial enterprise in Petrograd had been shut down, with students, white-collar workers and teachers joining the workers in the streets and at public meetings.

The following day, the 26th February, when the Tsar ordered the army to suppress the rioting by force, troops began to mutiny, reluctant to move in on the crowd as it included so many women. Although a few officers joined the demonstrators, most were either shot or went into hiding, meaning the ability of the army to hold back the protestors was all but negated. That achieved, around the city, symbols of the Tsarist regime were rapidly torn down, and governmental authority in the capital collapsed.

What was most coincidental was that Nicholas II had deferred a session of the state Duma that very morning, leaving it with no legal authority to act. Surely it wasn't as if Nicholas was unaware of what was going on.

Now many historians are of the opinion Nicholas II's idealized vision of the Romanov monarchy blinded him to the actual state of his country, that he firmly believed his power to rule was granted by Divine Right, but that's not how I saw it, and if you looked at the whole thing from the perspective of the politics of the *sang réal* it read very differently.

All rulers had advisors; Henry VIII had Thomas Cranmer, Edward VI had Thomas Seymour, the pharaoh's had the Amun High Priest. Nicholas II was a novice, with no political training, experience, or intuition. Had he been manoeuvred into proroguing the Dumas for the specific reason that the Dumas could be 'protected', in effect to wipe their hands of the actions of Nicholas and distance themselves from him? Had they in effect made Nicholas their scapegoat? Apart from the ending, it sounded similar to the way Thomas Cranmer and the Protestant Church had manipulated Henry VIII, then Edward VI and Elizabeth I.

Once the Dumas was 'disempowered', was word sent out to instigate the uprising? That's the way it all seemed to look to me. Had the puppet-masters seen the inevitable revolution and been positioning the Dumas in such a way as to make it the heroes of the people against the evil Tsar? Because that's what happened, the Duma responded' by establishing a Temporary Committee to restore law and order.

Meanwhile, the socialist parties established the Petrograd Soviet to represent the workers and soldiers, a movement I think the puppet-masters totally underestimated, as the remaining loyal units switched allegiance the next day. Human nature was so easily led, or rather misled, and it all made sense.

For some reason, the Tsar took a train back towards Petrograd. You would think with such unrest, the wise move would be to stay away from Petrograd and send a representative. So, was Nicholas II being stubborn, blind, or was he being advised to go, being set up for the inevitable? That was the train Tatiana and I, and the rest of the family, now found ourselves on.

I looked out the window, the next sign saying '1st March 1917'. The chessboard was surrounded by thousands of red pieces with one sole white king remaining, somehow backed into a corner by his own white pieces. Bemused, and with guns and sabres pointed at his head, Nicholas II was being forced to take off his uniform. Across the carriage, Tatiana's face was plastered with fear.

'We must get off the train.'

March 1st was the very day Tsar Nicholas had taken a train back towards Petrograd, where the Army Chiefs, and those of his remaining ministers who had not fled the revolt, 'suggested' in unison that he abdicate the throne. The next day, 2nd March 1917, Nicholas II abdicated in favour of his son, Alexei, me. However, after advice from doctors that the heir-apparent would not live long apart from his parents, who would be forced into exile, Nicholas swiftly changed his mind and drew up a new manifesto naming his brother, Grand Duke Michael Alexandrovich, as the next Emperor of Russia.

But Michael was no fool; it would've been like taking over the helm of the Titanic, which, interestingly, had sunk a few years earlier in 1912. Michael declined the crown on 3rd March 1917 thus ending the Russian monarchy and over three-hundred years of Romanov dynastic rule.

That same day, the old regime was replaced by members of the old Dumas, who assumed control of the country by forming the Russian Provisional Government, initially chaired by a liberal aristocrat, Prince Georgy Yevgenievich Lvov, a member of the Constitutional Democratic party and descendant of the Viking princes of Yaroslavi. The immediate effect of the revolution in Petrograd was widespread elation and excitement, however, what the new Provisional Government may not have been aware of, or, if they were, then they underestimated them, was, that four days earlier, the socialists had formed their own rival body, the Petrograd Soviet, or 'workers' council', who would, over the next months compete with the Provisional Government for power over Russia.

Having abdicated, Nicholas desperately wanted to escape to the UK and he was initially offered asylum by the British government, however, the offer was over-ruled by Nicholas's own cousin, King George V, worried that Nicholas' presence might provoke a similar uprising in the UK. The French government also declined to accept the Romanovs, after all, they knew all about revolution. So, a week after abdicating, Nicholas, was escorted to the Alexander Palace at Tsarskoye Selo, south of Petrograd, where, along with his family, he was placed under house arrest. Or was it all orchestrated to keep the truth under lock and key?

Meanwhile, the Soviets, led by more radical socialist factions, initially permitted the Provisional Government to rule, although there were still frequent mutinies, protests and many strikes. However, when the Provisional Government chose to continue fighting the war with Germany, the Bolsheviks, and other socialist factions, campaigned for an end to the conflict, the Bolsheviks turning the workers and militias under their control into the Red Guards, which was later to become the Red Army. That's when it got really interesting, when, in July, Lvov resigned, because he was unable to rally sufficient support, and he was replaced by Alexander Kerensky, a member of the Trudoviks, and, coincidentally, vice-chairman of the Petrograd Soviets, who was somehow granted a de facto exemption to not only be a member of the Provisional Government, but to lead it. That's like putting The Big Bad Wolf in charge of the flock of sheep; it was as if they were not only resigned to a revolution happening, but were now orchestrating it.

Then, with full-blown revolution imminent, in August 1917, the government, allegedly to protect the royal family from the rising tide of the potential revolution, evacuated the Romanovs to the Governor's Mansion in Tobolsk in the Urals. I think it was more likely to put as much space between the royals and the revolution so as to either protect their investment, to make sure the cat didn't get out of the bag, or to prevent the monarchy from regaining any footing or support. Again, across the carriage, Tatiana's face was stricken with fear.

'WE MUST GET OFF THE TRAIN.'

We could have got off before arriving in Petrograd, but we hadn't, we could have escaped to England or France but we couldn't, and now the train had changed direction and was heading eastward, towards the Ural mountains. I wondered where it was all headed, was it just about the real events behind the Russian Revolution? There was one way to find out, forge on.

On the 1st of September, and without discussion and approval of the Provisional Government Committee, Kerensky's next move was to proclaim Russia a republic, three days later releasing the exiled Bolsheviks, including Leon Trotsky; it was clear, with Kerensky, the revolutionists had infiltrated the 'Imperialist democracy', especially when he subsequently distributed government weapons to the Petrograd workers, arms which obviously made their way into the hands of the Bolsheviks. That was just like the US government arming so many other countries; Iraq, Afghanistan, etc etc.

And so, on October 25th 1917, the workers' Soviets, and the Bolsheviks, led by Vladimir Lenin, who earlier in April had been permitted by the Germans to return to Saint Petersburg from exile in Switzerland, and armed with the weapons supplied by Kerensky, stormed the Winter Palace in an event known thereafter as the 'October Revolution". In less than 20 hours they had overthrown the Provisional Government in Petrograd. It was all just too easy, too convenient, too coincidental.

Wait a minute, Switzerland was the 'homeland' of the Illuminati,; how is it a country declares itself 'neutral' in two world wars and no one touches them? Simply because THEY were the perfectly located base for all operations!

Anyway, was Lenin 'brainwashed' while he was there, then 'sent back' to further destabilize Russia, or was it to infiltrate the Soviet movement? He was either 'sent' by the "Germans", the strong bloodline of the *sang réal*, to deliberately cause a revolution, or to infiltrate the victors should the revolution not only happen, but be successful.

And it wouldn't have been hard to 'convince' Lenin as he was already a 'disciple' of Marxism, and the execution of his brother, Aleksandr Ulyanov, by the oppressive regime of Alexander III, would surely have radicalised Lenin even more, especially given he became increasingly involved in student protests and revolutionary propaganda efforts; he would have seen it as a perfect opportunity for his Marxist revolution.

The October Revolution led to the end of the provisional government, the transfer of all political power to the Soviets, and the Bolsheviks appointing themselves leaders of various government ministries.

However, when the Bolshevik leaders signed the Treaty of Brest-Litovsk with Germany in March 1918, effectively ending Russia's participation in World War I, it instigated a full-scale Civil War between the "Reds" (the Bolsheviks), the "Whites" (the anti-socialist factions consisting of army officers and Cossacks, the "bourgeoisie", and political groups ranging from the far Right to the Socialists, all of which had the backing of nations such as Great Britain, France, USA and Japan), and the non-Bolshevik socialists. As the counter-revolutionary White movement gathered force, on 30 April the Romanovs were transferred to the town of Yekaterinburg, a militant Bolshevik stronghold 900 miles to the east, and imprisoned in the two-story Ipatiev House.

Red army, white army, the red queen, the white queen; I felt like I was Alice in Wonderland and not only had I gone well and truly down the rabbit hole, but the Looking Glass was being held up to me for me to see everything as it really was. That said, in an instant Tatiana was joined in the carriage by Olga, Anastasia and Maria, Olga and Anastasia respectively having the morphed faces of Crystal and Pernille. In unison, though I was the youngest, they pleaded deliberately to me.

'ALEX, WE MUST GET OFF THE TRAIN.'

Alex? Not Alexei? Suddenly it became imperative that we all get off. But we couldn't, the doors and windows were all locked. Within moments the carriage had turned into an enclosed basement, a line of soldiers entered, and started firing; I couldn't move, my whole body was frozen. As one of the soldiers put a revolver to my head and pulled the trigger, I woke up with a start, the sun starting to set in the west.

Concerned, Abdo leaned across.

'You are all right, Mister Alex?'

'Where are we?'

'We have just left it Kafr El-Zaiat station.'

'How far is that?'

'Maybe three-quarter of the way.'

'Abdo, we have to get off the train *before* Alexandria.'

'Why is this?'

'The Secret Police will be waiting.'

'How do you know this?'

'Trust me, I know. We *have to get off*, before Alexandria.'

'Very good, I will make it the call.'

As Abdo jumped onto his cell phone, I gazed back out the window, following the dream through to see if there was anything else to be gleaned from it.

By mid-July 1918 a Czech contingent of the White Army was approaching Yekaterinburg; the royal prisoners and their Bolshevik captors all able to hear the sound of gunfire in the distance. It was this imminent arrival of their potential liberators that sealed the fate of the Romanovs as Lenin had come to the conclusion that the Romanov family was a potent symbol of the old regime and a potential rallying cry for his enemies. So, Lenin ordered their execution, and, on July 17th 1918, in the basement of Ipatiev House, the entire Romanov family, along with their immediate servants, was murdered, by gun and bayonet, from a firing squad of seven Communist soldiers and three local Bolsheviks. Shot, bayoneted, then shot again at close range in the head, their bodies were then buried in a pit near the city. Jesus, I didn't need to go through all that again.

But we had, Crystal, Tatiana, Pernille and I, and all together, why? We could all have been executed any number of times and ways during that period, or any other historical period, so what was it about the birth of Communism that was so important for us to all have incarnated then? It had to have something to do with the truth, so I played out the rest of the revolution.

The Civil War continued on for several years, during which the Bolsheviks, having assumed power in Petrograd, expanded their rule outwards and eastwards, eventually reaching the Easterly Siberian Russian coast in Vladivostok, not only along the way defeating both the Whites and all the rival socialists, and paving the way for the creation of the Communist Party and the Union of Soviet Socialist Republics in 1922, but influencing the development of Communism in China.

As it had been in Russia at the end of the 19th Century, discontent had also been brewing in China during what was to be the final years of the 268-year-long Q

ing dynasty, perhaps another ancient branch of the *sang réal*, and what proved to be the last Imperial dynasty of China. Local uprisings against the hardline Manchu court led to the Xinhai Revolution in October 1911, and the abdication of the child emperor, Puyi, the last emperor of China, on 12th February 1912, bringing to an end over 2,000 years of Imperialist China and beginning an extended period of instability of warlord factionalism. With communism sweeping eastward across Russia, it was inevitable it would have an impact on the situation in China.

And so it was that Communism in China had its origins in the May Fourth Movement of 1919, during which radical ideologies like anarchism and communism gained considerable traction amongst Chinese intellectuals. Two years later, in 1921, with the new Communist Russia knocking on the doors of the borders of China, the Communist Party of China, the CPC, was founded by Chen Duxiu and Li Dazhao, Li Dazhao being the first leading Chinese intellectual to publicly support Leninism and world revolution, although both men believed the October Revolution in Russia heralded a new era for people in oppressed countries everywhere. However, it took time; it wasn't until Mao Zedong, who took control of the CPC in 1927 and led the revolution in 1947, that the communist party finally gained control of China.

The light bulb goes off, and it's red!

And that's when something akin to a mile-long freight train, stretching through time from ancient Egypt to the present, and loaded with billions upon billions of exploited peasants and workers, suddenly hit me. The 'monarchy' was the interbred, controlling lineage of the Illuminati, the Templar Knights, the descendants of the ancient Egyptian pharaohs, or rather the queens, who were themselves the descendants of the gods, the Annunaki. Since the very beginning of human civilization, they were responsible for the exploitation of the human race and for keeping them suppressed and controlled.

No, it wasn't them; the rulers changed, some were liberals, like Alexander II, Akhenaten, Ghandi, and JFK, and the governments changed, Democrat, Republican, liberal, labour, the one constant through it all, through the whole monarchy, the revolution *and* the communist rule, was the Secret Police, sure the name changed, the Third Section eventually became the KGB, in other countries it was The Spanish Inquisition, Himmler's SS, MI5, the CIA, ASIO, but their role was the same, they were the Amun Priests, the real power behind the throne, the real puppet-masters.

And then, along came Lenin, Trotsky, and the Communists, who upset the applecart, ousted the puppets, and took control of the largest country in the world. Sure there were probably others in the past who stood up and spoke out, but they were quickly silenced and no one was there to write their history. But what they were all advocating was that we were all equal, ARE all equal, or rather that we all have equal rights and deserved to be treated that way.

Communism is an economic-political philosophy founded by Karl Marx and

Friedrich Engels in the second half of the 19th Century. In 1848 Marx and Engels wrote and published "The Communist Manifesto", in which they expressed their desire to end the capitalist suppression of the masses, believing that "it was the social class system that led to the exploitation of workers"; they were right.

Ultimately, they believed that "the workers were being exploited, creating a 'class consciousness' that would lead to conflict that would eventually, and could only, be resolved through revolution"; again they were right. Marx and Engels saw that, in this conflict, the plebs and working class of the masses would rise up against the bourgeoisie and establish a communist society. They were right.

They envisaged a process whereby the state would pass through a phase, often thought of as socialism, eventually settling on a pure communist society where all private ownership would be abolished, and the means of production would belong to the entire community, where everyone gave according to their abilities and received according to their needs, and where the needs of a society would be put above the specific needs of an individual.

The truth was, everyone may not have been born equal, and that was their spiritual choice before they incarnated, but they had the right, once born, to be treated equally, to work hard to achieve more, or if they wanted, be a parasitic sloth. And that was a concept the elite members of the *sang réal* lineages not only didn't want, they didn't even want you, or any of us, to know about it, let alone contemplate it.

The 'threat' of communism; come on, it wasn't a threat to the masses, it was only a threat to the elite, the privileged, the 1% who had and controlled 99% of the money. The Russians have been portrayed by the west as the bad guys ever since, McCarthyism, the whole cold war bullshit that the Ruskies were the bad guys, when the US had at least 100 times as many nuclear missiles as the USSR, especially when the Soviet leader Khrushchev's position was of peaceful coexistence between the communists and capitalists.

And how many countries have the US invaded in the last hundred years compared to Russia and China? Yes, Russia has supplied arms to Afghanistan, Syria, Cuba, all the countries who do not have an Illuminati 'Federal Reserve' monetary system, but were Russia merely supporting the 'victims' against the might of the bully?

I got it; Communism wasn't the enemy, Communism was actually a higher path of and for human consciousness, a path to secede from the archaic monarchism and capitalism, to a path practiced, promoted, and support by the highest realms and echelons of the Galactic Federation, whereas the 'capitalist' model belonged to, and could be traced all the way back to....the Dracos; intimidate, suppress, exploit.

As other thoughts started flicking through my head, like the daily quotes on a desktop calendar, I could hear the Dracos, the Illuminati, the Amun Priests, thinking, plotting planning;
"Keep them poor, keep them sick, keep them suppressed and incapable of challenging us, of seeing themselves as our equals, of challenging our right to rule. Let us put fluoride, chloride and other substances into their water, and lace the very air they breathe with Aluminium, Barium, Lead, asbestos and any other toxins we see fit.

Let us put aspartame and all manner of 'food dyes, 'enhancers' and other toxins into their food, and let us reduce their ability to grow their own fresh free produce by genetically modifying their food not only so that we can 'own' the raw produce, but remove any nutritional content it may have.

Let us medicate them, 'vaccinate' them, directly injecting into their bodies the very toxins we know will break down their natural physiology, and let us thus manipulate their DNA without them knowing, so that we can keep them sick, weak, and easily controlled and manipulated. Let us control their thinking by controlling the media, the shows they watch, the 'news' they see, and inflict our views and perspectives on them that we can stop them from free thinking and condition them to think as we want them to think.

Let us control the 'education' of them, by controlling what they will 'learn', giving them hours of homework from a young age to control them even when they are not within our control directly.

Let us create false 'monetary' systems and lock them from birth into our deceptive dishonest one-way system so that we can control them through that financial system in every aspect of their lives, through rent, mortgages, wages, taxes, oil, petrol, power, water, food. Let us own them, and convince them we are their liberators."

Inflation wasn't caused by 'this' index, or Gross Domestic this or that, or any quasi-wanky-gobble-de-gook economic term, inflation is caused by one thing and one thing alone, greed, by the few at the top, who have much more than they actually need, wanting more, and taking it, at the expense of the masses at the bottom, who most often have less than they need to survive.

"Let us pass laws and regulations, and vigorously enforce punishments and fines so as to turn them into sheep that will mindlessly follow our directions and be fearful of rising up against us."

It reminded me of something I'd read before, that someone had posted on my facebook page:

Protocols of the Elders of Zion

THE SECRET COVENANT

"An illusion it will be, so large, so vast it will escape their perception. Those who will see it will be thought of as insane.

We will create separate fronts to prevent them from seeing the connection between us.

We will behave as if we are not connected to keep the illusion alive. Our goal will be accomplished one drop at a time so as to never bring suspicion upon ourselves.

This will also prevent them from seeing the changes as they occur. We will always stand above the relative field of their experience for we know the secrets of the absolute.

We will work together always and will remain bound by blood and secrecy.

Death will come to he who speaks.

We will keep their lifespan short and their minds weak while pretending to do the opposite.

We will use our knowledge of science and technology in subtle ways so they will never see what is happening.

We will use soft metals, aging accelerators and sedatives in food and water, also in the air.

They will be blanketed by poisons everywhere they turn.

The soft metals will cause them to lose their minds.

We will promise to find a cure from our many fronts, yet we will feed them more poison.

The poisons will be absorbed trough their skin and mouths, they will destroy their minds and reproductive systems.

From all this, their children will be born dead, and we will conceal this information.

The poisons will be hidden in everything that surrounds them, in what they drink, eat, breathe and wear.

We must be ingenious in dispensing the poisons for they can see far. We will teach them that the poisons are good, with fun images and musical tones.

Those they look up to will help. We will enlist them to push our poisons.

They will see our products being used in film and will grow accustomed to them and will never know their true effect.

When they give birth we will inject poisons into the blood of their children and convince them its for their help.

We will start early on, when their minds are young, we will target their children with what children love most, sweet things.

When their teeth decay we will fill them with metals that will kill their mind and steal their future.

When their ability to learn has been affected, we will create medicine that will make them sicker and cause other diseases for which we will create yet more medicine.

We will render them docile and weak before us by our power. They will grow depressed, slow and obese, and when they come to us for help, we will give them more poison.

We will focus their attention toward money and material goods so they many never connect with their inner self.

We will distract them with fornication, external pleasures and games so they may never be one with the oneness of it all.

Their minds will belong to us and they will do as we say. If they refuse we shall find ways to implement mind-altering technology into their lives.

We will use fear as our weapon.

We will establish their governments and establish opposites within. We will own both sides.

We will always hide our objective but carry out our plan.

They will perform the labour for us and we shall prosper from their toil.

Our families will never mix with theirs.

Our blood must be pure always, for it is the way.

We will make them kill each other when it suits us.

We will keep them separated from the oneness by dogma and religion.

We will control all aspects of their lives and tell them what to think and how.

We will guide them kindly and gently letting them think they are guiding themselves.

We will foment animosity between them through our factions.

When a light shall shine among them, we shall extinguish it by ridicule, or death, whichever suits us best.

We will make them rip each other's hearts apart and kill their own children.

We will accomplish this by using hate as our ally, anger as our friend. The hate will blind them totally, and never shall they see that from their conflicts we emerge as their rulers.

They will be busy killing each other.

They will bathe in their own blood and kill their neighbours for as long as we see fit.

We will benefit greatly from this, for they will not see us, for they cannot see us.

We will continue to prosper from their wars and their deaths.

We shall repeat this over and over until our ultimate goal is accomplished.

We will continue to make them live in fear and anger though images and sounds.

We will use all the tools we have to accomplish this.

The tools will be provided by their labour.

We will make them hate themselves and their neighbours.

We will always hide the divine truth from them, that we are all one. This they must never know!

They must never know that colour is an illusion, they must always think they are not equal.

Drop by drop, drop by drop we will advance our goal.

We will take over their land, resources and wealth to exercise total control over them.

We will deceive them into accepting laws that will steal the little freedom they will have.

We will establish a money system that will imprison them forever, keeping them and their children in debt.

When they shall ban together, we shall accuse them of crimes and present a different story to the world for we shall own all the media.

We will use our media to control the flow of information and their sentiment in our favour.

When they shall rise up against us we will crush them like insects, for they are less than that.

They will be helpless to do anything for they will have no weapons.

We will recruit some of their own to carry out our plans, we will promise them eternal life, but eternal life they will never have for they are not of us.

The recruits will be called "initiates" and will be indoctrinated to believe false rites of passage to higher realms.

Members of these groups will think they are one with us never knowing the truth.

They must never learn this truth for they will turn against us.

For their work they will be rewarded with earthly things and great titles, but never will they become immortal and join us, never will they receive the light and travel the stars.

They will never reach the higher realms, for the killing of their own kind will prevent passage to the realm of enlightenment.

This they will never know.

The truth will be hidden in their face, so close they will not be able to focus on it until its too late.

Oh yes, so grand the illusion of freedom will be, that they will never know they are our slaves.

When all is in place, the reality we will have created for them will own them.

This reality will be their prison.

They will live in self-delusion.

When our goal is accomplished a new era of domination will begin.

Their minds will be bound by their beliefs, the beliefs we have established from time immemorial.

But if they ever find out they are our equal, we shall perish then.

THIS THEY MUST NEVER KNOW.

If they ever find out that together they can vanquish us, they will take action.

They must never, ever find out what we have done, for if they do, we shall have no place to run, for it will be easy to see who we are once the veil has fallen.

Our actions will have revealed who we are and they will hunt us down and no person shall give us shelter.

This is the secret covenant by which we shall live the rest of our present and future lives, for this reality will transcend many generations and life spans.

This covenant is sealed by blood, our blood. We, the ones who from heaven to earth came.

This covenant must NEVER, EVER be known to exist.

It must NEVER, EVER be written or spoken of for if it is, the consciousness it will spawn will release the fury of the PRIME CREATOR upon us and we shall be cast to the depths from whence we came and remain there until the end time of infinity itself."

"We, the ones who from heaven to earth came", the Annunaki! The *sang réal*! Now, I was more-than-ever determined to get out of Egypt alive, which was looking probable, and I was definitely going to write about it, about everything, so that the masses would know the truth and rise up as one, not one country at a time, not one race at a time, but as one species, against the suppression, against the oppression, against the exploitation of the Illuminati. Fuck 'em! FUCK THEM ALL!

While I'd been deep in thought, Abdo had been on the phone chatting away in Arabic for maybe five or ten minutes before he ended the call and leaned towards me.

'It is done, I am have it arranged; we will be get off at El Hadra El Baharia, this it is before Misr Station and very near to it the university.'

'So how long do we have? How many stops?'

'We have just left it Itai El-Barud, and the next stop it is Damnhour; after this maybe three more stop. From there, it is not far to it the library, which it is near to the water, for to catch it the boat.'

I didn't want to get cocky, or over-confident, but I could almost smell the freedom, which was a contrast to the nicotine-and-tar-infested carriage I'd been in for the last few hours. Fortunately, I'd been by the window so the incoming breeze, although certainly not roses and daffodils, was at least breathable. With the twilight fading, I relaxed back and pictured our destination, Alexandria; I'd hoped to spend a day or so there, but, now, it looked like I'd be lucky to spend an hour, I had to do trawl my memory for relevant details from my notes.

Alexandria

The second largest city in Egypt, Alexandria, "The Pearl of the Mediterranean", and once the setting for the stormy relationship between Cleopatra and Mark Antony,

was founded by Alexander the Great in April 331 BC. I say 'founded' because there were other cities there-and-abouts before it; as early as the 7th Century BC, there were the important port cities of Canopus and Heracleion, the latter of which was recently rediscovered beneath the water. There was also the existing city of Rhakotis, comprising two main streets, each about 60 metres wide and lined with colonnades, that intersected in the centre of the city, which was now a 'suburb' of Alexandria, and, to the east, an area of marshland and several islands.

Originally, Alexandria, which became one of the busiest ports of the ancient world, supposedly was little more than the island of Pharos, the legendary lighthouse, one of the Seven Wonders of the World, built to warn sailors of the treacherous sandbars offshore. Conceived by Ptolemy I Soter, and designed by the Greek architect Sostratus of Cnidus, who was a contemporary of Euclid, the Pharos was built after Soter's death during the reign of Ptolemy II Philadelphus.

Dedicated to Ptolemy I Soter and his wife Berenice, the Pharos consisted of a three-stage tower; the lowest a square, 55.9 metres high with a cylindrical core, the middle octagonal with a side length of 18.30 metres and a height of 27.45 metres, and the third circular and 7.30 metres high, making the total height of the lighthouse, including the base, about 117 metres, or the equivalent of a 40-story modern building. According to the ancient historian Strabo, it was supposedly covered in magnificent white marble; that was interesting in itself.

A statue of Poseidon once adorned the top of the building adding an extra height of about seven metres, and, in addition to the statue of Poseidon, there were many other strategically arranged statues and sculptures of Greek deities and mythical creatures that decorated the tower.

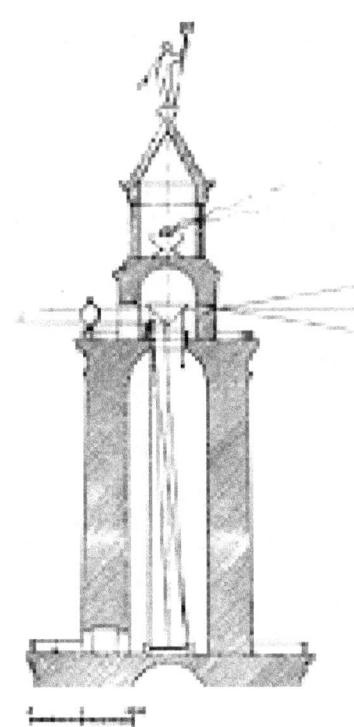

The open internal core was used as a shaft to lift the fuel needed for the fire that burned in a giant open cupola at the top, the fire burning slowly through the day, rekindled up anew when the sun went down. The light was focused by a curious system of reflectors, polyzonal lenses and mirrors, perhaps of polished bronze, into one broad but brilliant sheet of light visible 35 to 300 miles out to sea. Legend says the mirror could also be used to detect and burn enemy ships before they could reach the shore. I remembered doing that to ants with a magnifying glass when I was about 8 years old.

The Pharos was joined to the mainland by a 'bridge' nearly a mile long called the Heptastadion, the end of which abutted the land at the head of the present Grand Square, now filled in with silt upon which was built the modern "Ras al-Tin" quarter. That's a lot of effort to build something for somewhere that was supposedly 'unfounded'. Did Alexander need to create a port with close access to Giza to ship things in and out? Why else build a whole city? It made a hell of a lot more sense that 'Alexandria', marking where the Nile met the Mediterranean, was *already* a significantly major port, and had been since the beginning of Dynastic Egypt, and that whatever was there before had been obliterated sixty-odd years earlier by the tsunami from the 396 BC eruption of Etna.

Once built, the Pharos lasted for over 1500 years in the harbour of Alexandria, even though it was hit by numerous earthquakes and tsunamis, until, in the 14th Century there was a very destructive earthquake and the whole building was completely destroyed and it was impossible to enter. It wasn't until 1480 that rebuilding took place, when the Circassian Mameluke Sultan Al-Ashraf Abou Anasr Saif El-Din Qaitbay El-Jerkasy Al-Zahiry built a fort on the site, reusing and integrating parts of the original structure. Given we were headed straight for a boat once we got off the train, I doubted I would get to see any of it though, especially as the recent discoveries scattered beneath the water confirmed that one side of the Pharos had collapsed into the sea, and that much of the structure still lies strewn across the seabed.

Despite subsequent earthquakes, and possibly even tidal waves, the early Ptolemies managed to keep Alexandria in order, careful to segregate its three largest ethnicities, Greek, Jewish, and Egyptian, and they were so successful that, within a century, they had not only built the Pharos Lighthouse, but also the Library of Alexandria, the greatest centre of learning and manuscripts in the ancient world.

The library was probably conceived during the reign of Ptolemy I Soter and opened during the reign of his son, Ptolemy II, and it flourished under the patronage of the Ptolemaic dynasty, at one point supposedly housing more than 700,000 papyrus scrolls dating back to classical antiquity.

However, apart from my obvious interest in the period of Cleopatra VII, I now wasn't interested in the actual Ptolemaic era, or in Alexandria, even though it had become the largest city in the ancient world, so, what was the big attraction with the location, why did the Ptolemies invest so much time and energy into what was, to all intent and purpose, a swamp? There must have been something the Macedonian's knew, that Alexander knew.

All in all, it was clear that over the millennia the coastline had been changed several times by natural disasters such as earthquakes and tsunamis. Going back, amongst others, there were earthquakes in 1323, 1303, 696, and the Crete earthquake in 365 AD that spawned a tsunami that totally devastated Alexandria, much of Cleopatra VII's royal palace and civic quarters inundated by tidal waves and sinking beneath the harbour due to earthquake subsidence. Then there was the Etna eruption in 369 BC. God knows what there was beneath the surface, or washed away, or both, but I do know they've started to find out.

In the 1990's, while shooting underwater scenes for a film, an Egyptian director spotted several colossal statues, sphinxes, and a stone torso of a woman from the 3rd Century BC. Since then, the Egyptian Authorities and the Supreme Council of Antiquities have discovered and classified over 2000 pieces, including what experts believe are the remains of Cleopatra's Royal Quarters, lying eight metres below the surface, granite columns, capitals, a fragment of an obelisk, inscribed with hieroglyphs, and fabulous statues, including one of Isis, a headless statue of Ramses II, a head of Caesarion. and sphinxes, one with a head thought to be that of Cleopatra's father, Ptolemy XII, Neos Dionysos. All at least eight metres *below* the surface!

They also found massive blocks of granite weighing 49 to 69 tons, broken into two or three pieces, indicating they fell from a great height. The experts believe they are remnants of the Pharos Lighthouse. Or were they?

Strabo reported the lighthouse was made of white marble. Was it possible the granite blocks were the ruins of a structure that pre-dated Alexandria? Had the Egyptologists and archaeologists just assumed the granite belonged to the Pharos because there was no reference to anything earlier?

Suddenly I was focused on any evidence that supported my Thera theory, because whatever city *was* here immediately prior to 1600 BC, it would have borne the full brunt of the 600-foot tsunami that travelled across the Mediterranean and surged into the Nile Delta, and the evidence to support it was not only under 8-10 metres of water, but probably under a further 10-plus metres of sand as well.

At first that took me to look underground, to the subterranean remains of a 'Serapeum', where the mysteries of the god Serapis were enacted, and whose carved wall niches are believed to have provided overflow storage space for the ancient Library. Then my attention shifted to Alexandria's catacombs, *Kom al-Shoqafa*, a multi-level labyrinth, reached via a large spiral staircase, that features dozens of chambers and burial niches adorned with sculpted pillars, statues, sarcophagi, and other Romano-Egyptian religious symbols, as well as a large Roman-style banquet room. Was there any evidence of red granite there, anywhere? I didn't know, and it was highly unlikely I would get the chance to find out. The other site I briefly considered was *Kom al-Dikka*, the most extensive ancient excavation currently being conducted, which has revealed the ancient city's well-preserved Roman Amphitheatre, and the remains of its Roman-era baths.

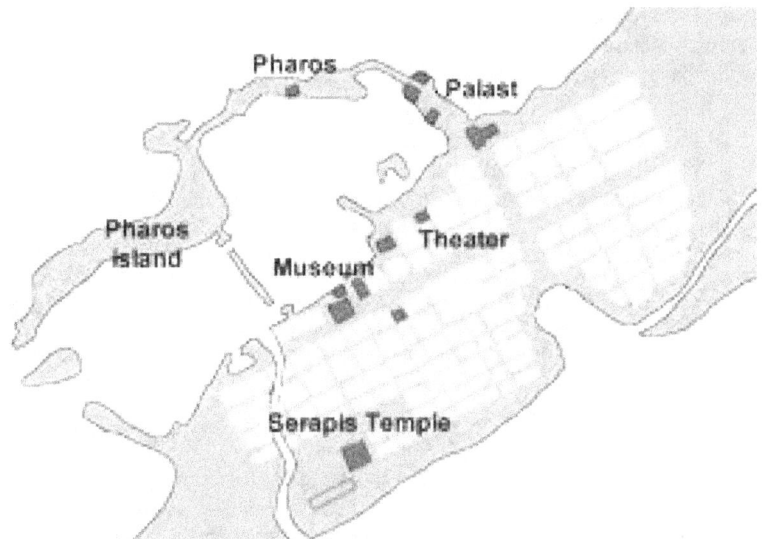

However, the most powerful evidence above ground was right under everyone's nose: Pompey's Pillar. It was supposedly a Roman triumphal column, part of a temple colonnade erected in 293 AD for Diocletian then plundered and demolished in the 4th Century when a bishop decreed that Paganism must be eradicated. But none of that made any sense at all, especially as Diocletian was part of the Roman Empire and not a pagan. What did make sense was that the 'demolition' was attributable to the 365 AD Crete earthquake and tsunami. The column itself was even stronger evidence. Made of polished red-granite, including its pedestal, it was 30 metres high; the shaft alone measuring 27 metres high, 2.7 metres in diameter at the base and tapering to 2.4 metres at the top. All up it was 132 cubic metres of granite, or approximately 396 tons.

396 tons; and that's for just *one* of the columns, that's five times as heavy as most of the big blocks in the 'tombs', the sarcophagi, the blocks above the King's Chamber in the Relieving Chambers, there is absolutely no way, even with all our wiz-bang cranes we could erect even one column today, let alone propose that the ancient Romans erected colonnades of them in 293 AD.

Roman? No way. I think it was left over from a long time before then, before the Thera eruption, possibly even before the last pole shift. And, if that was the case, then it would raise whether the actual 'Roman' capitals were copies of a much earlier style?

I hadn't really taken note of the stations we'd gone through until Abdo leaned forward.

'El Hadra El Baharia, it is next, we will get off, yes?'

I nodded, got to my feet, picked up the shopping bag, and started following Abdo through the crowded carriage and towards the door, my trusty akubra held to my belly and my eyeballs fixated on the backpack in Abdo's hands; the end was thankfully in sight. Fortunately, as the train pulled to a halt, there were lots of people getting off, including plenty of students and about as many old grannies like me. I paused at the door, scanning quickly to the left and right for signs of trouble, noticing above, in the skies, a storm was brewing. Hoping it wasn't an omen of things to come, I alighted, and followed Abdo, like part of the herd, to the main exit.

Leaving the station I remained crouched over, in character, slowly going wherever Abdo led. Suddenly I became aware of someone meeting Abdo, heard a brief whispered exchange in Arabic, and I was hustled into the back of a waiting car, Abdo tossing the backpack in and closing the door behind me.

'Good luck to you, Mister Alex.'

I looked out through the open window.

'You're not coming with me?'

'No, I must be get back to Cairo Palace. But you are in the very good hand.'

He was grinning from ear to ear as I reached out and shook his hand.

'Thanks for everything Abdo, I'll never forget you. I'll be in touch once I'm safely back in Australia.'

'Yes, yes, now go.'

'Oh, and don't forget to get Tatiana's contact details from the reception desk at Le Meridien, OK?'

'This I will do.'

Abdo slapped the roof of the car and, as it took off into the Alexandria night, I slowly turned my attention back to the shopping bag; it seemed I was nearly in the clear.

'So, Indy, once more, you escape the pit of the cobra.'

I snapped back to the front.

'Saeed! Ahoya! Boy, am I glad to see you. What are you doing here?'

I went to take off my hijab, but Saeed quickly stopped me.

'Not yet, my friend, we are still in it the eye of the vulture.'

He was right. I readjusted my garb, nervously looking back at the crowd leaving the station.

'How did you escape?'

'I did not. After I am leave you at the wall that move, I make it my way back down tunnel when they catch me. They ask where it is you are, and I tell them you are falling through trap in wall and die. They are take me back to police station, ask many question about you, about papes.'

'What did you tell them?'

'I think never again will we be see you, so I tell them my uncle, Kareem, he give it to you the paper to be look at, but that you make it the mistake and keep it the paper from him, that I am try to get it the paper back, but you disappear under Giza behind wall that move.'

'Did they buy it?'

'I am here, am I not?'

'I guess so, but why? How come you're in Alexandria?'

'When I am let go, I am meet with Mister Bill who insist it we continue with plan to get out of Egypt. He is not happy with what happen with Mister Jacques and he want to go anyway, he insist it we stay with plan in case you escape and are make it to Alexandria. And, here you are.'

'Albeit a day late. So Bill waited?'

'Yes and no, Mister Bill he wait until next morning, then he take it boat out to sea.'

'Fair enough, I guess I'd have done the same thing. But how come *you're* still here?'

'I visit my family. Then Abdo he call me, say it that you are alive and will be catch it the train, so here I am.'

'That's great, but Bill's gone, so what do I do now?'

'Not to be worry, Ahoya, I call Mister Bill, he turn boat around and he is on his way back. We will take it the fish boat out to sea to meet it with him in International water. I have it the boat wait near library, very close. You are still having the paper of my uncle?'

I grabbed the shopping bag, pulling out the folio just to be sure myself.

'Yep, safe as houses.'

I was about to tell Saeed all about my subterranean adventures when he spoke in Arabic to the driver, who then took a sudden turn. Saeed was looking over my shoulder and out the rear of the car.

'What is it?'

'I am think the vulture it has been watch over us.'

I swung around, which wasn't the coolest thing to do, and it certainly wouldn't have helped matters.

'You think we're being followed?'

'I am not be sure, but it would be explain why they are let me go so easy. They must be follow me to Alexandria and to train station; with you escape, it make sense to follow me. How can I be so stupid?'

'It's OK, can we throw them off?'

Saeed pointed to a side street, barked out another order, and we made another turn, straight into the middle of another student protest. Déjà vu!

'How far to the boat? Maybe we can make a run for it through the crowd?'

'No, this it is not good, this be university, much protest here; many police in all direction.'

As light rain started to fall, Saeed pointed down another street and we detoured again, this time cutting down behind the Bibliotheca Alexandrina. It was one of the places I'd hoped to visit, not just because of its architecture, but also because of its very existence. With support from Mubarak and UNESCO going back as far as 30 years ago, it was clear there must have been other agendas behind its construction, but how could I be so sure?

The Bibliotheca Alexandrina cost almost a quarter of a billion dollars to build; seriously, a quarter of a *billion* dollars for a country where most people in the country earn less than a hundred US dollars a *month* and live below the poverty line, so what was that really about? The answer was simple; the Bibliotheca Alexandrina opened in 2002 with a swag of state-of-the-arts facilities, but the key was it housed the *only* complete, offsite back-up copy of The Internet Archive. Knowledge is power, and if you control The Internet and you control the distribution of information in other than the mainstream media. Here we were in Egypt, the home of the Amun Priests, of the previous Library of Alexandria, it was logical they would build it here. Randy would have been proud of me; not only had I turned into a radical Communist, but now I was a fanatical conspiracy-theorist as well. It was no wonder our unwanted tail was still following closely behind.

Saeed was on the phone, fast-talking between the person on the other end and the driver, and pointing out our escape routes. I was fine with that until we turned away from the shore, which I quickly drew to Saeed's attention.

'Isn't the boat the other way, I mean surely we're nearly there?'

'Yes, but they are be too close behind, they will stop us on the boat before we are leave the dock; we must be shake them off first.'

As I stole glances back through the rear window, I could clearly see an unmarked car was tailing us, following us closely but not attempting to pull us over.

'So, where are we going?'

'Misr train station.'

'Misr train station! Hang on, isn't that the main station, the very one we *want* to avoid?'

Images of Tatiana, Olga, Anastasia and Maria being executed, bayoneted and shot in the head, flashed through my head; it was as if Saeed was taking me down into the basement, delivering me to my executioners.

'Yes, but you must be trust me. We will make it them think we are going to train, to try and escape, then when we are lose them, we will be cut back and go to new place for boat.'

It was all getting very Indiana Jones indeed, but, with the rain now falling much heavier, and depending on if we could shake them off, it just might work. Saeed was wheeling and dealing all the way, when, a few more turns later, the car suddenly did a U turn and came to a halt.

'Quickly, out, we must go. Follow me.'

I didn't hesitate or question him, just grabbed my akubra, the shopping bag and backpack and did as he said, leaping from the back seat, hitching up my dress, and following him as we ran through the rain towards what looked like a park.

'Jump fence. Give me the bag!'

Saeed led the way, quickly scrambling over the park's fence. I passed him the two bags and was soon right behind him, the two of us then bolting through the park. Actually, it wasn't a park; at second glance I thought it was a building site, or rather demolition site, but then I realized it was filled with ancient Roman ruins. And I wasn't so much bolting, as stumbling, over my dress.

Moments later, the pursuing car turned into the street, and our pursuers, who were not only initially not-too-eager to jump the fence, but who were even less inclined to be out in the rain, appeared to be debating who should pursue on foot and who should go back to the sanctuary of their car. Their indecision, as brief as it was, had given Saeed and I a good head start, which I well and truly needed because, by the time we reached the Roman amphitheatre, the rain was pelting down, and, as my black tent got soaked, I tripped over the hem, slowing my pace considerably.

By the time one of the pursuers had finally scrambled over the first fence, Saeed had scaled the corresponding one on the far side of the ruins, and I was right behind him, clambering over the fence, this was until my dress snagged on the railing.

'Shit.'

I hadn't come this far, and gone through what I'd gone through, just to finish up hung out to dry like one of Vlad the Impaler's unfortunate victims. Saeed dropped the bags and rushed back to help.

'No, Saeed, you go on, someone has to get the papers to Bill.'

I'd already lost my iphone and my computer; I wasn't going to surrender anything else, because, if we didn't get the papers out of Egypt, it had all been for nothing. As I tried to free myself, I looked back to see our pursuer was about to reach the amphitheatre; there was still time.

Saeed ripped off my hijab, then the dress, freeing me from more than just my predicament, and we ran across the road, picked up the bags, and hi-tailed it down a street towards Misr station. Suddenly a shot crackled through the rain.

'Shit!'

I had no idea what Saeed had in mind, but the closer we got to Misr Station the more my confusion reigned. Then Saeed made a beeline for a car and jumped inside. I was right behind him.

'Get in, lie down.'

I did just as he said, and, seconds later, the car sped off. Having dived on to the shopping bag, I lifted my head slightly to examine it, to see if the rain had seeped in and damaged the papers.

'Geezus!'

A single bullet hole passed straight through the top corner of the bag, but fortunately had missed the papers, and me! I dropped my head, hugged the seat, and sighed; if I didn't get out of Egypt now, I was afraid my luck would run out.

Run, rabbit, run

We must have driven for about five minutes before I felt safe enough to even talk.

'Are they still following us?'

'No, it seem that we have lost them, but that does not mean the vulture is not still circle.'

'What do you mean?'

'They may not be see us now, but they know it we are here, they smell it, they will be look everywhere.'

'So, where to now, back to the library?'

'No, we take it the speed boat from Citadel of Qaitbay.'

'The site of the old Pharos Lighthouse?'

'Yes, I will have it the boat meet us there.'

I remembered from a map that the Citadel was on the eastern side of the northern tip of the Pharos Island, at the western end of the mouth of the Eastern Harbour; that was about two kilometres north-northwest from Misr station, along 26 July Avenue, or as it was better known, The Corniche, supposedly an extremely bustling main road, dotted with restaurants, ice-cream shops, Casinos built on stilts and rows of beach huts, that runs along the length of Alexandria's coastline and up to the fortress.

I'd originally planned to visit the Citadel as part of my trip, and, with the emergence of my Thera tsunami theory, it would have been well worth checking out. I knew most of the Citadel was originally built in 1480 AD out of limestone on the site of the old Pharos, but that its largest stones included the red-granite lintel and doorway of its arched entrance, red-granite columns and alabaster columns within the walls of its central mosque, red-granite blocks in a shaft to the left of the mosque that leads down to the cistern and coastal passages, and particularly some huge red-granite pillars in the northwest section.

I wasn't going to get to see any of them first hand, but, given everything I'd seen so far, I now believed there was a structure in place *before* the Pharos was built, one built of red granite, that was demolished or severely damaged by the Thera tsunami, and/or the 396 BC tsunami from the eruption of Etna, and that the red granite was probably not just recovered from the Pharos, but from the huge structure that once stood here before Ptolemy built the Pharos.

Then I remembered from the map there was a cop shop right beside the Citadel and I wasn't so sure that a visit was such a good idea.

'Hang on, Saeed, isn't there a police station right beside the Citadel?'

'Yes, but police they will all be out to look for us; Citadel is it the last place they will be look, and from here we can catch it the boat.'

'No, it's too risky. Is there anywhere else?'

'Hmm, we can get it on boat at small cove a hundred metre further west around coast.'

'Is it safe?'

He looked at me with one eyebrow raised.

'The crocodile it wait under the water, you cannot be sure where he is. Remember, Indy, it is not the crocodile you can see that is the one to be worry about.'

He was right.

'OK, we'll go to the citadel but I still think the cove is a better option.'

That said, I didn't really have a choice; I didn't have my black-momma disguise, I had absolutely no idea where we were, somewhere in the Ras al-Tin quarter, we certainly weren't driving down The Corniche, and, apart from leaping from the car into the unknown back streets of Alexandria, Saeed was my only lifeline.

Then, my quasi-contemplative state was suddenly shattered along with the back window of the car.

'Get down!'

No arguments there: clearly the vultures had rediscovered their targets and were trying to bring us down, although surely a bullet through the back window was a tad over zealous. Instantly Saeed started barking out orders and our driver floored it, tooting the car's horn as we swerved through the streets and around corners avoiding all manner of animals, people and obstacles; OK, now I was definitely in an Indiana Jones movie, however, unlike Indy, who stayed calm and focused in the face of danger, I was absolutely shitting myself, especially as I couldn't see anything and was being tossed around in the back seat like I was in a pinball machine. I think, at one point, our pursuers must have tried to pull up alongside and our driver swerved to bump them away, causing them to crash, and us to career into a shop stall, bringing our joyride to a sudden halt.

'Come on, Indy.'

I clutched the shopping bag as Saeed, backpack over his shoulder, literally dragged me out of the back seat and, abandoning the driver, we set off on foot through one of the local fish markets. Sure, it looks glorious and exciting up there on the big screen, popcorn in hand, or sitting back on the sofa with a cold beer, but the reality was I was running like a shit-scared rabbit.

The rain had briefly stopped and suddenly people materialized out of the woodwork and were everywhere, the market crowded like sardines in a can. Saeed, once again on his cell phone, led the way through; the smell of fish, interlaced with the ocean, shisha, and god knows how many other smells and aromas, assaulting my nostrils. Suddenly I noticed blood dripping from Saeed's upper arm.

'Shit, Saeed, you've been hit?'

'Do not worry, Indy, Allah he is with me, this it is just a scratch.'

It didn't look like a scratch, it looked more like it had penetrated his shoulder, and that brought home the reality of our situation: dire to say the least!

Negotiating a pathway through the masses was like clawing my way through a constantly changing slalom course, twice I either dropped the shopping bag or had it knocked from my grasp, only to have to pause and scramble to pick it up before it was trampled or used as a football. It all resulted in my gradually falling behind Saeed; although I could still see him forging the path ahead and calling for me to "hurry up". Believe me, I wasn't hanging back on purpose. On the contrary, I thought that if I didn't pick up the pace it was just a matter of time before he would disappear amongst the throng, or the cops would catch up with me.

However, somehow we managed to stay ahead, leaving the market and weaving our way alongside a number of tall apartment buildings and hotels, before, up ahead, Saeed suddenly hit the beach. Beyond him I could see the water, and, pulling into the shore, a speedboat; with the change of plans, Saeed must have called them and shifted the pick up point. Thank god, we were nearly there.

Saeed quickly covered the distance across the sand and climbed aboard, but, as I set foot on the beach, Saeed suddenly held up his hand and waved for me to stop. But it was too late; I'd been seen by two policemen patrolling the beach, my shopping bag and akubra obviously betraying my identity.

'Shit! Give me a break!'

I thought about making a run for the boat, but there was no way I would have made it, as the cops started after me as soon as they eyeballed me and twigged who I was. So, as the rain started falling yet again, I hightailed it in yet another direction, this time eastward, thinking maybe I could circle back to the beach and make my way to Saeed and the boat.

As I ducked and weaved and dodged, I thought I'd outsmarted them all, until, as I came almost full circle, I realized the second officer from the beach had tracked along the shoreline to cut me off.

'Fuuuck!'

I had no choice, with him blocking the path to Saeed, and now two or three police hot on my ass, I took off down the road in the direction of the Citadel, which looked at first like a storybook castle and somehow seemed to glow white in the drizzling rain.

I figured that maybe I could throw them off somewhere in the coastal passages that ran beneath the Citadel, a series of tunnels that were used for moving cannons, horses and men about the fortress, then make my way back to Saeed and the boat. I briefly glanced back to assess my situation, noticing the four police had united but were in no particular rush to catch me, perhaps because as well as heading towards the Citadel, which sat on a dead-end peninsula, I was also heading towards their home base, the police station right beside it.

That said, there was something profound about all of this, that to achieve your purpose often you not only have to overcome your fears and challenges, but you have to confront them, run straight into the valley of death, fearing no evil. You may not necessarily know where you're headed, or how to get there, or how to navigate the subterranean corridors and chambers of life, but that's what makes life such an adventure, right? Fuck!

As I drew closer, the Citadel seemed to appear less like a fairytale castle and more like an imposing and impenetrable fortress. It consisted of three main parts, the huge walls that surrounded the entire complex, an inner wall, and, within that, the seventeen-metre-high main tower. The outer western and southern walls before me

each had three guard towers for archers, along with openings to pour burning oil down upon would be attackers, whereas the north wall, the one facing the sea, had square-shaped windows for canons and catapults, and, along the top, a balcony for archers. Within, in the north-eastern part of the fortress grounds sat the main square-shaped tower, thirty metres wide, with a tube-like tower at each corner.

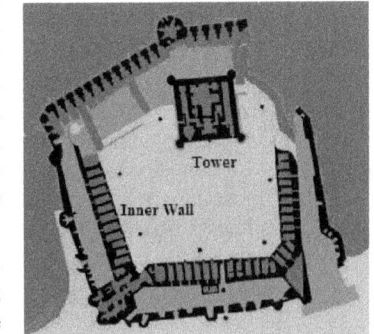

Approaching the main entrance, I was reminded of a military decree that apparently sat on a marble slate fixed to the door leading the

main court. It said that any one who leaves the tower with anything will be hanged at the gate of the tower, and deserve the curse of God. Almost as if to reinforce the decree, or possibly to prevent me from entering the Citadel, a small group of police emerged from the station and headed towards me, some circling around the fortress anticlockwise to cut of my escape; I was surrounded, no, I was screwed!

I looked around, clowns to the left of me, jokers to the right, there I was, stuck in the middle with a shopping bag containing possibly the most controversial and incriminating documents in the world, the only escape being a narrow spit of land that headed north, out into the Mediterranean; unless I could swim all the way to Greece, I was done and dusted. It seemed pointless, but, almost instinctively, I headed down the spit anyway.

As I reached the dead-end, I turned to see a squadron of over a half-a-dozen cops slowly zeroing in on the entrance to the spit; they were in no rush, the gig was up!

'Indy! Quickly!'

I spun around. It was Saeed; he must have motored away from the shore in the speedboat, then circled back behind the Citadel, thinking he could pick me up there. The boat was edging in towards the spit, but it was clear it wasn't going to be able to dock; I'd have to swim for it. The question was, what to do with the shopping bag. There was no time to hold a royal commission as the police started running towards me.

The minute I entered the water and started wading out towards the boat, the bullets started flying.

'Sheeiiiit!'

'Throw it! Indy, throw the bag!'

There was no way I was going to throw the bag and risk it falling short and into the sea, not after everything I'd gone through. That meant that by the time I reached the side of the boat the water was chest deep. I handed the bag to Saeed, who placed it on the decking at the rear of the boat before helping me to quickly scramble aboard, where I subsequently collapsed on the deck, more from relief than fatigue.

'Imshi, Imshi!'

At Saeed's insistence, the driver gunned the throttle, causing the boat to rear up and, amid a final flurry of bullets, speed off into the night. The problem was, that with all the rain, not only was the shopping bag wet, but, so was the rear deck of the boat, and, in a blink, with the boat's sudden forward momentum, and the sloping surface of the rear deck, the bag silently slipped off the back off the boat and into the Mediterranean.

By the time Saeed and I realized what had happened, and looked back, it was too late, the bag had slipped beneath the surface and disappeared from sight.

'Saeed, we have to go back.'

'No, Indy, it is too dangerous. Beside, you would never find it in the night, especially not at bottom of the sea.'

I pictured the ink on the papers running and fading to nothingness, the pages of truth carried away and dispersed amid the ruins of Cleopatra's palace and the Pharos by the ocean currents, disintegrating as they went, much as the palace and lighthouse had done due to the tsunamis. I was devastated.

The stories from the wars tell the tale that you never hear the bullet that hits you. That's how it was with me. All I felt was the sudden pain to the chest and then I collapsed to the deck.

'Indy!'

Saeed knelt over me as I clutched my chest in agony. Then I slowly pulled my hands back expecting to see the gush of crimson essence exuding, pulsing, from my body. Nothing! There was no blood, not a drop. But I could see the bullet hole, right through the pocket of my shirt.

'The metal discs, they stopped the bullet.'

I took them from my pocket and examined them closely.

'Not a scratch, not even a dint!'

I went to sit up, to get to my feet.

'No, Indy, stay down. Let the vulture think it you are dead.'

I relaxed back to the deck, my mind turning back to Kareem's papers.

'I can't believe that after everything I've gone through, the train trips, the chases, the staircase, being shot at, that the papers just fell off the boat right as we were on the brink of freedom, that the whole trip was pointless.'

'Indy, the meaning of life it does not rest in the word on paper.'

'Tell that to those who believe in the "Koran", *The Bible",* and the other religious texts.'

'The meaning of life it is not found in the word that you read, the meaning of your life it is made from the thing that you do. It is what you do that give your life the meaning, and the meaning to your life'

'Actions speak louder than words, hey.'

'Indeed. Perhaps it is not the paper that are important but what it is you have learned from the journey of carrying them?'

I thought about where my journey had taken me since I'd arrived. It seemed to fall into two parts, the felucca trip, which was a sort of awakening, and the time from when I was given the papers, from Luxor and Karnak to Dendera and Abydos, then on to Amarna, Hawarra, Dahshur, Abu Raoush, Zawiyet el-Aryan, Saqarra, Abusir and Abu Ghurab, and everything above and especially below the Giza Plateau.

And the second part, which wouldn't have made sense without the first, in fact, without it I probably wouldn't have been ready to even look at Kareem's papers. And what if I'd not taken them, what then? The rest of the trip would probably have been a typical tourist trip; I would never have gone to Hawarra, or Abu Raoush, or Zawiyet el-Aryan, or Abusir and Abu Ghurab, and I definitely wouldn't have finished up in a network of ancient tunnels and chambers over a hundred metres below the Giza Plateau. I knew things no one else on the planet knew.

That was fine for me, but did someone have to die for me to have such an extraordinary journey, especially since the papers were now at the bottom of the ocean?

'But, Saeed, what about your uncle; Kareem's death will have been for nothing.'

'Perhaps, but his *life,* it has not been for nothing.'

He was right; death happens to all of us, it's what we do *during* our life that matters, not when we die, or even how we die. I had faced death, or rather it had confronted me, and I had been spared, for a purpose, although right then that purpose seemed to have sunk to the bottom of the Mediterranean.

I'd learned so much on the trip, or rather "re-membered" so much, but it still appeared I was a work in progress. Saeed, on the other hand, never seemed to be fazed by anything.

'I can't believe you're so calm about this, so accepting.'

'Indy, it cannot be changed; this it is the will of Allah...'

He tossed the backpack into my lap.

'…We must be grateful for what we are having, not be ungrateful for what we do *not* have.'

Once again he was right. I'd lost my iphone, *and* all the footage, I'd lost my computer, but, I had my life. And, as I took it out of the backpack and held it in my hand, I also still had the crystal ball, as well as the Blue Lotus essence, and the discs. But, most of all, I was alive and finally leaving Egypt; I couldn't be more grateful than that.

Don't look back

Thankfully the rain was easing and the surface of the water was reasonably calm which meant we were making good progress. However, as I watched the lights of Alexandria slowly disappear in the distance, I was still concerned. An Adventure? Yeah, you could say that.

'Do you think they'll follow us?'

'Yes, this is most probable, the crocodile he does not so easy give up it's dinner, but we will have maybe ten to fifteen minute head start, and this very fast boat. We can only be hope there is not other crocodile already in the area.'

'A patrol boat?'

'Yes.'

'How long until we reach Bill?'

Saeed grinned.

'Egyptian time or western time?'

Despite the situation, it seemed Saeed still had his sense of humour.

'Western time.'

'Maybe one hour: it depend on weather and the sea, and where is Mister Bill, maybe he is wait in it International water, maybe he come closer. What does it say it your crystal ball?'

'I don't know, and I don't know if I want to know.'

I put it carefully back in the backpack, the discs back in my pocket, and lay back on the deck of the boat, the rain lightly caressing my face; what a hell of a trip.

Over the next forty-five minutes or so I had virtually the whole thing run through my mind, from my first encounter with Crystal at Philae, the whole felucca trip, Kom Ombo, Edfu, Esna, El-Kab and Wadi Hillal, my experiences at Luxor and Karnak, and on the West Bank, particularly with Kareem, then the 'chase', Amarna, Frank and Mark at Hawarra and Dahshur, right through reconnecting with Crystal and Bill in the Serapeum, at Abu Ghurab, and my experiences at, in, and under the monuments at Giza, especially the Hall of Records, Thoth, and my ascent through the dank confines of the secret staircase.

At the end of it all I pictured myself, as I was now, lying exhausted on the boat, which led to images of Charlie Sheen in 'Platoon', that part at the end of the movie where he's being evacuated in the helicopter, with him totally wrecked, totally shell-shocked and transformed by his time in Vietnam, when they flashed back to how he looked when he first arrived, fresh-faced and innocent. I cried when I saw that, and was so upset, moved and affected I couldn't speak for over an hour after the movie. Now, I felt like I was experiencing it all over again, only this time it was first hand.

I'd changed, my eyes had been opened, my heart had been opened, my mind had been opened, and I would never look at the world the same way again, never feel about the world the same way again, never think about the world the same way again. But, was that a good or bad thing? Would I, like so many shell-shocked soldiers, suffer for years from Post Traumatic Stress, and mistrust the governments who had lied to us about so many things for so many centuries? Only time would tell.

The truth was out there, like a sleeping volcano, lurking just beneath the surface, and it was deep, travelling to the very core of everything, it just needed the Arne Saknussemms and Otto Lidenbrocks of the world to blaze a path beneath the surface to finally trigger its eruption.

'Indy, wake up. We are here, Mister Bill's boat.'

The rain had stopped and, as I sat up and looked ahead in the darkness, I saw the lights of a small boat. Well, I thought it was a small boat; it turned out we were still some distance away and, as we drew closer, the 'boat' morphed into what was a massive 'yacht' about a hundred feet long, the "Aurora"; it seemed the Minnow had undergone a facelift. As we pulled up alongside, our very own Thurston Howell III, Bill, was waiting on deck.

'Alex, good to see you; a day late, but better late than never.'

'It's a long story…'

I picked up the backpack and climbed aboard.

'…Permission to come aboard, Captain?'

'Permission granted.'

'This is some "small boat".'

'Just one of my little luxuries.'

'Don't tell me, you have your own private jet as well?'

'No, that would be pretentious, but I do have a helicopter back in Oz, although I don't use it that much anymore since I sold the gold mine.'

Safely aboard and the welcoming embraces out of the way, I turned to see Saeed was waiting back on the speed boat.'

'What are *you* doing?'

'I am going home.'

'Home, are you crazy, the Secret Police will skin you alive.'

'I do not have it much choice.'

Ever on the ball, Bill rose to the occasion.

'Of course you do, you can stay on board the Aurora; I need an Arabic interpreter I can trust, and I could always use an extra hand on deck, at least for a month or so until things quiet down a bit… '

Bill indicated for one of the members of the crew to get the first aid kit.

'...Besides, it seems you need a little medical attention.'

'This it is very kind, but what about it my felucca?'

I ganged up on him.

'I'm sure Gomar and Mohammed can handle things fine without you for a month. Saeed, you're *not* going back, not while the vultures are still circling, not while the crocodiles are still so hungry.'

'Then it's settled.'

Bill didn't even wait for Saeed to answer, he simply hauled Saeed aboard, and, handing the boat driver a huge wad of cash, sent him on his way. As the boat sped off back into the balmy Egyptian night, forgetfully I wrapped my arm around Saeed's shoulder.

'Ow!!

'Oops! Sorry. Anyway, Ahoya, we made it! And I couldn't have done it without you.'

'Indy, it would not be so if it had not been for you.'

We gave each other a huge hug, relieved that it was all over. Meanwhile Bill had given the order and within minutes we were underway and heading for Greece.

'Right then, have you eaten?'

'I had something for lunch, but if it's not too much trouble...'

'No trouble at all, I'll get the cook right onto it.'

'You have a cook?'

'Sure. You up for a cold beer as well?'

'Now you're talking!'

At that moment, a member of the crew returned from the cabin with the first aid to tend to Saeed, followed by Pernille, who looked like a million dollars.

'Well, look what the cat dragged in.'

'Pernille!'

'Alex, it's so good to see you.'

I gave her a big hug, then backed off.

'I've got something for you.'

Extracting the crystal ball from the backpack, I offered it to her.

'Here, this is for you.'

'Are you sure?'

'Yes.'

She cradled it in the palms of her hands like a newly hatched duckling, marvelling at its beauty.

'Where did you find it?'

'In a granite chamber deep beneath the Giza Plateau; it's pretty much all I've got to show for my adventures there, but I don't know what use I'd have for it any more.'

She gladly received it as if it were a cherished treasure...

'Thank you so much.'

...then disappeared back into the cabin.

Bill was right onto it

'What did you mean, "In a chamber deep beneath the Giza Plateau"?'

'After we left you at the Sphinx, Saeed and I eventually found ourselves in a series of tunnels beneath the plateau.'

'Yeah, Saeed told us that, he said the last he saw you was when a massive granite wall opened up at the end of a corridor.'

'That's right. Beyond the door, it led to a whole network of tunnels and corridors, to an underground lake and city, a spaceship, the Hall of Records, the Tomb of Thoth. I found the crystal ball on a red granite altar in one of the early chambers.'

'Hang on, a UFO, an underground city? And you found the Hall of Records?'

'Yep, but I didn't just find it, I explored it; it's amazing what's down there, millions of gold disks, anti-gravity machines, time machines, a giant robot.'

I took the discs out of my pocket and handed them to him.

'What do you make of these?'

'Whoa, freaky!...'

As he closely scrutinized and examined the discs he kept probing for more information.

'...Did you take any photos?'

I slumped into a nearby seat.

'That's just it, I had it all recorded as video on my iphone, but then the battery died, and when the secret door open, in the dark, and in a hurry to escape, I left it behind on the staircase inside the Great Pyramid.'

'No way?'

'I'm afraid so.'

'Oh, well. Still, I can't wait to hear all about it, but what did you mean by "that's pretty much all you've got to show for your efforts"? What about the documents, where are they?'

I briefly looked at Saeed, who, as the crew member bandaged his shoulder, just screwed up his face and shrugged, then back to Bill.

'They fell off the back of the speed boat when we took off, and they sank to the bottom of Alexandria harbour; they're gone.'

'You're joking, right?'

'No, after everything I went through to get them out of Egypt, they literally slipped through my fingers.'

Bill slowly walked up to me and put a hand on my shoulder

'Not all is lost.'

Slightly confused, I looked up.

'What do you mean?'

'I've got a pleasant surprise for you.'

'What?'

'I had a phone call from Dwight today; he'd been trying to call you for the past two days but there was no answer.'

'I guess the reception wasn't so great a hundred metres underground, and then my mummy answering service was on the blink when my battery died. How is he?'

'Dwight has Kareem's papers.'

'What? What do mean he has Kareem's papers, I saw them sink to the bottom of Alexandria harbour?'

'Well, he doesn't have the actual original papers, he has copies.'

'Copies?'

'Yes. While you were at Karnak he apparently started reading them, then decided there was too much to get through and he went downstairs and scanned them onto a USB stick. Just as he was finishing, the Secret Police turned up. Then Randy and he took off for the airport, but, before they left, Dwight hid the papers back under the sand on the roof for you to find.'

I almost leapt to my feet and hugged him.

'Are you serious, he's got copies of all of them as jpegs?'

'All of them, every single one, jpegs, pdfs, so though the originals may be gone, Dwight still has all the information, and he's been working systematically through them all since he got back to Cairo. He says they're dynamite.'

I collapsed back into the seat, this time with relief, and started laughing; all was not lost after all.

'What's so funny?'

It was Pernille's voice; she was returning from the cabin.

'I just told Alex about Dwight and the papers, which is just as well because the actual papers are at the bottom of the sea.'

'A lot of good they will do there.'

I knew that voice. It caused me to once again leap to my feet. Behind Pernille, following her out of the cabin, was Crystal, looking absolutely stunning.

'Now, there's a sight for sore eyes. I thought you were going back to Germany.'

'That was before events unfolded on the trip. Pernille and I now have things to do at the temples in Greece, and, since Bill was planning to sail there, he kindly offered me a berth on his yacht, which I gratefully accepted.'

Knowing Pernille would have showed her the crystal ball, I knew what I had to do to stay sweet.

'I have a little something for you.'

I reached into the backpack, took out my last remaining souvenir, and handed it to her.

'It's a bottle of Blue Lotus Essence from the resting place of Thoth. I'm sure the High Priests mixed it with wine to access altered states of consciousness and the Higher Realms.'

She opened it and sensuously took a smell, handing it to Pernille to do the same.

'It's exquisite, perfect! Now, let's get you out of these wet clothes, we don't want you catching cold before we get to Greece, there's a lot more work to do.'

Somehow, as she took my hand and led me towards the cabin, I understood that my life was about to change dramatically, that this was not the end of my adventure, merely the beginning.